PSYCHIC UNDERCOVER (WITH THE UNDEAD)

AN SDF PARANORMAL MYSTERY
BOOK ONE

AMIE GIBBONS

Printed in the United States of America

First Printing, 2017
Gremlin Publishing
Nashville, TN.

https://authoramiegibbons.wordpress.com/

ISBN-10: 1542774446

ISBN-13: 978- 1542774444

For my first reader
Because he was the first one to tell me
an early version of this book was good
And he inspires me every day
from hundreds of miles away

ACKNOWLEDGMENTS

It's never easy to thank everyone who helped with a book, and I'm sure I'll inevitably leave people out; it's not on purpose, I swear.

First up, of course, thank you to my family, but my parents and siblings in particular. Mom, you taught me to love reading. Dad, you were right, never should've taught me how to read, look what happens.

To my first reader, my twin six years removed, and the inspiration behind the plot twist at the end of this book. Probably shouldn't have subjected you to some of those terrible first tries, but look how well it turned out, baby brother.

And then to all the people who cheered me on during writing, then beta read and edited this book: Tiffany, one fantastic editor. And my many wonderful beta readers who helped smooth out the rough spots.

CHAPTER ONE

"**Y**OU CAN'T SHAKE A KITTEN in Nashville without hittin' a musician, Mama," I said, switching the phone to my other hand as I walked into the coffee shop.

"Hey, Special Agent Ryder," Will half shouted from behind the counter.

I waved and shook my head with a grin.

I've been telling him for nearly a year to call me Ariana. He doesn't listen. Honestly, I think it's just cuz he likes the idea of having an FBI agent as a customer. He thinks it's cool or something.

"I'm just sayin', you have the voice for it, you're already in Nashville, and you know your daddy and I have the connections. I don't understand why you waste your time playin' cop," Mama said.

I pointed at the phone and held up five fingers at Will.

"The usual?" he asked.

I nodded and he got to work as I turned to talk to the wall.

"I'm not playin' cop, Mama. I'm an FBI agent. I solve crimes. I help people."

"You're a civil servant in a job that pays you a tenth… a hundredth of what you're worth with your gift."

I rolled my eyes again. We'd been havin' this conversation for a year and we'd probably keep it up till I caved and became a famous singer songwriter or a TV psychic… or some kinda mix.

"Mama, do you object to me being a civil servant, or a low paid one?"

"I object to you being undervalued. You could do anything. Go to law school, become a performer, start your own business, but you're working for idiots and bureaucrats."

Why was she tryin' to get my dander up today?

"Mama, my boss isn't either and don't you go sayin' he is."

She snorted. "I was talking about the higher-ups. I would never insult

1

your Grant."

"Don't you start with that again, Mama."

"Of course not. Of course there's nothing going on there."

"Mama, just because you can't write one book without a romance doesn't mean-"

"I know, I know. I take it back."

My call waiting beeped and I checked the phone. Kat. "Mama, it's work. I gotta go."

"Love you, peaches."

"Love you too." I switched over. "Hey, Kat."

"Hey, Ariana," Kat said in her best girlfriend's tone.

"You want a triple shot, don't you?"

"Pretty please with a cherry on top?"

"This junk's gonna fry your system."

I know lecturing her won't do any good. She's been on coffee forever. I think she had a caffeine IV ran through her umbilical cord as a fetus.

"Yeah, like you're one to talk," she said. "You didn't get that short by drinking milk your entire life."

I'm really not that short. I'm five-foot-two. Okay, I really am that short. Mama always jokes my siblings took the height, and since I'm the youngest, I got stuck with what's left.

My brother, Mark, calls me the runt of the litter.

"Triple shot for the junkie, please," I said to Will as I clicked off.

He poured the extra shot into her mocha without me needing to tell him which.

I checked my reflection in the mirror next to the counter. I looked pretty good, considering it was pourin' cats, dogs, turtles, ponies, and dragons outside. My dark grey suit complimented my curves and the green silk top brought out my eyes.

"Two coffees, one mocha three shots, one frappuccino, one macchiato, and a latte," Will said my usual order as he rang it up.

We have an account with Alfonzo's. Grant set it up five years ago when the SDF, the Special Division Force, first started in Nashville and night cases became par for the course.

Grant's really good at cuttin' through red tape and bureaucratic bull, which is why he was named team leader in the first place.

Our division gets a lot of leeway cuz of the cases we deal with. Most of the time the main Bureau looks the other way when we bend rules or take shortcuts.

What are they gonna do, write us up for not waiting on a warrant to raid someone's home to stop a vengeful ghost from killing them in their sleep?

I actually wasn't there for that one; it was about two years ago, but I read the report.

Jet said the people tried suing them, claimin' there were no ghosts and they never called for help in the first place.

Pretty crappy move considering false claims like that undermine everyone who has a real complaint against cops who actually break the law.

But that's people for ya. They don't want to believe in the supernatural, so they don't. They make up stories to explain away the unexplainable. It's the only way they can cope.

Believe me, I know.

Not that I blame them really.

How do you sleep at night if you know the lock on your door won't do much good, and thresholds only keep vampires out?

The only reason I sleep is cuz I have charms against ghosts and supernatural doodads that act as a general ward that'll deter most of your basic beasties.

I also have my magic carpet, Pyro, who's better than a Rottweiler when he's home.

Will handed me the two trays of drinks and my phone rang again. Boy, was I popular this morning. He put them on the counter as I grabbed my cell.

"Hello?"

"Don't go to the office," my boss, Westley Mercutio Grant said.

And believe you me, if any man in this world can pull off that name, it's him.

"Dead body in an alley. Come straight here."

He hung up before I could even say good morning. He does that. It's annoying.

The text with the address popped up a moment later. West End at the bottom of Vanderbilt, just across from Centennial Park.

#   #   #

When I got to the scene, Metro officers were questioning the jogger who found the body and windin' crime scene tape around the wide alley between two restaurants.

"Hi, General!" I handed him his large coffee, with two creams already in, just the way he likes.

"How many times do I have to tell you not to call me that, Ryder?"

I call him General cuz General Grant.

He sounds like a crab, but really doesn't mind the nickname. He has some semblance of a sense of humor, which took me about six months to figure out cuz he never sounds like he's jokin' when he is and rarely smiles.

When he does smile, it's a sight. He has the best wide grin and full cupid's bow lips. His eyes are the color of iced over spring grass and they light up when he smiles. He's over six feet and all muscle. He played football in college.

Grant's only thirty-seven but his brown hair's goin' grey at the temples. He says it's because he has to babysit a ton of kids, i.e. the three of us on his team, and it's makin' him old.

He's always clean shaven, with wavy brown hair, and his clothes are always neatly pressed slacks and muted button-ups. I don't think the man owns one piece of clothing with actual color. He has tan skin that's a little wrinkled around the eyes, which I think makes him look as wise as he is.

From the way I describe him, you'd think I'm in love with him. I'm not. Mama thinks I am, but I'm not.

Really.

Okay, he's strong and commanding and his eyes really are just that pretty...

Anyway.

"About a million, General," I said, bouncing over to Jet.

I put the trays down because I knew what was coming next. Jet swooped me up into his arms.

He does it every morning. He's six-foot-four and I'm tiny me so it's funny.

"Hey, girl."

Jet's voice can only be described as warm chocolate. It's okay when he calls me girl.

"Hey, Jolly Roger." I hugged him back.

I call Jet that because he's a pirate. Okay, not really, but he does look like one.

He's lanky, has black brillo brush hair, a neat goatee, and an earring in his left ear. He's very pretty. Some mix of Asian, Hawaiian, black and white with slanted eyes, puffy lips and mocha skin, and boy, can he wear a color. Not many men can pull off pink.

He's decided I remind him of his little sister and has basically adopted me. He calls at night to make sure I got home safe, and goes shopping with me and Kat.

"You done?" Grant's cold voice brought us back to reality.

"Yes, sir," I said.

Jet put me down and picked up his camera again to take pictures of the alleyway.

I crouched by the body, regretting the decision to wear heels. They were sensible, short heels, but still not easy to crouch in. The rain pounded the crime scene, washin' away evidence.

Which was probably why Grant looked like he wanted to spit a lemon at me for wastin' time.

My hair was already frizzing and bustin' outta my ponytail and I pushed it back, slicking it with the rain.

I hate rain, it hampers my abilities. I can't smell anything but the rain, and my powers are always amped up by smells.

The girl was blond, blue eyed and petite. Her legs sprawled unnaturally and her long, black skirt was pushed up so we could see she had no panties on. She was barefoot and there were a few bits of gravel clinging to her feet.

I wanted to pull her skirt down and close her dead eyes.

"Wait for Kat."

It was like Grant read my mind. He knew I wanted to touch the body, not only to allow the poor girl some dignity, but also to get my Impression.

Whenever I touch someone for the first time, I get the First Impression, no matter how bad it's raining or how tired I am.

Most of the time, it's something mundane, like them gettin' their first puppy, losing their virginity, or gettin' married. But sometimes they have something really big in their past, like being murdered.

I've seen a guy rape his girlfriend in a moment of stupid blind passion, a woman bash her abusive husband over the head and hide the body, and a guy shoot his brother.

I don't get the full story, usually just some pictures and words. But sometimes I get them in theater quality, crystal clear picture, surround sound and smell-o-vision.

I pulled my hands back. The rain smacked my long, black coat and head. I wanted to reach into the clouds and pinch them closed.

I settled for closing my eyes for a moment and takin' a deep breath. I've seen some horrible things since I got my powers almost two years ago, but this beautiful young girl bein' dumped in an alley like she was trash... there weren't words for something like this.

At least she wasn't crawling with maggots. One thing the rain's good for.

"Neck," Grant said.

I looked at the neck. Nothin'. I walked to the other side.

Two perfect little holes right on the jugular.

"Vampire?" I asked, shaking my head. "I'm thinkin' copycat, Grant."

"Don't. We don't think anything until the evidence tells us to."

We don't know much about vampires cuz they're so secretive. What we do know is whatever agents have managed to glean in the last few years from short run-ins with them.

They don't like it when people get a whiff of the supernatural cuz it can lead back to them and that's when you get people fixin' to be vampire hunters. They wouldn't leave the body out with the telltale teeth marks.

Right?

"It doesn't fit what we know about them, that's all I'm sayin', sir," I said.

Grant nodded.

I could practically see the wheels in his head turning.

"Help Bridges bag and tag," he said, taking the camera from Jet. "Find out who owns this building and what they do with it, Kowalski."

Jet nodded and took out his phone.

I went over to where Dan was swirling printing dust over the wall. It was dry due to the overhanging roof; the problem was there were too many fingerprints showing up, all of them overlapping and mixin' together.

I set Dan's coffee by him, and he grabbed it and started chugging without a thank you.

Yeah, he's always a jerk. For some reason him and Jet have been best friends since boot camp, and when Jet joined the SDF three years ago because his fiancé Gallina was murdered by a demon, Dan followed.

Okay, technically the SDF asked him to join cuz he's a computer genius who can hack pretty much anything. He's arrogant as all get out about it.

Dan's about five foot eight and burly. His square face, floppy brown hair, and blue eyes would be sweet looking if his personality didn't ruin it. His black glasses and collared, checkered shirts really complete his geek-chic look.

Kat and Jet like him fine. I don't see it. He's nice enough to everyone else, he's like a normal person who can joke and chat like anyone, but he's nasty as curdled milk to me.

"Hello, Dan," I said.

He bobbed his head back, smirking. He's from New York, and thinks anyone from the South is a country bumpkin.

He called me Daisy Duke for the first month we worked together. Didn't stop till Grant heard him and ordered him to cut it out.

I'm not a genius, but I'm not stupid. I went to Vanderbilt for college and got a double bachelor's in political science and music, scored in the ninety-fifth percentile on the LSAT, and finished my senior year by taking online classes while I went through the FBI academy.

That was the longest seventeen weeks of my life, but I got by, and not on my looks, thank you very much. I read a lot and I'm a fast learner. But I'm from Alabama, so to Dan that means I have an I.Q. of sixty and my mother and father were cousins.

I was in the middle of bagging yet another cigarette butt, I'd lost count of how many this made, when Dr. Katrina Lang finally pulled up in her white M.E.'s van.

Dan got up to help Kat out of the van. She hopped down into his arms and still tripped on her heels.

Why such a klutz insists on wearing stilettos is beyond me. He caught her and held her up while she found her feet. She gave him her sweet chipmunk smile before hurrying over to the body.

"Hey, Kat." I handed over her mocha, sadly stone cold by now. She still took it with a smile and chugged.

"Thanks." She finally came up for air. "I needed that."

She's Asian-American, a few inches taller than me, and skinny. She has almond shaped, golden eyes, and other than that, her cute round face always makes me think of a chipmunk.

I love her, she's my best-friend, but she can't dress for the twenty-first century to save her life.

She's always in cute skirts that go out at the knees, with matching heels and sweater sets, or long dresses with big belts that make her waist look like a toothpick. Her shoulder length silky black hair is always either behind a headband or in piggy-tails, and the weird thing is, she pulls it off.

I put the blanket I always carry in my pack on the ground so Kat could kneel by the body without getting today's ensemble, a bright blue dress under her yellow slicker, dirty. Her necklaces clattered together and one of the Metro detectives snorted, sneering.

I shot him a look. Nobody asked him his opinion on her clothes.

"Problem, Detec-tiv?" Grant asked, starin' the man down.

He shook his head and went back to takin' the photos for Metro.

Ohhhh, what had gone down before I got here?

"Rigor hasn't fully set in yet. Based on that and the temp..." Kat's eyes went up as she muttered calculations. "She's been dead about five to seven hours."

She pulled her liver probe out of the poor girl and I looked away.

I hate watchin' that. When you can stick a probe in and they don't twitch is when someone's really dead to me.

Jet helped me bag while I waited for Kat to finish her initial exam and he waited on hold.

He was gettin' the runaround from some business types. If they thought they could ignore him till he went away, they didn't know Jet Kowalski.

He's the best leg man in Nashville; relentless as a coon dog.

"She was drained," Kat said. "She had sex before she died, possibly rape, but I can't tell more until I get her on the table."

She stood, face as impassive as Grant's.

"Kat?" I asked.

She shook her head. "She's dolled up, but my rough calculations say she's barely legal."

"Calculations?" I asked. "Like the length of leg bones, size of ears and stuff to estimate age? You can do those in your head?"

"I can't measure exactly by sight, but close enough to estimate. And look at her face. She still has some baby fat there."

And Mama thinks I'm gifted?

Speaking of...

Grant motioned and Jet and Dan jumped to without more explanation needed, herding the Metro detectives out of the alley and behind the tape, far enough away that I could only hear the pissed off voices, not the actual words.

"Take it up with our boss," Jet said as he walked back.

I knelt on my blanket and pulled my incense out of my kit.

I always keep the kit in my car. It has the basics: fingerprint powder and the tape to lift it, bags, tags, collection tubes, and nitrile gloves, cuz I'm allergic to latex, and I added the blanket, a wooden bowl, and sandalwood incense.

Sandalwood seems to be the best to boost the psychic juices.

I don't know why. I don't know anything about my gift even though I've had it almost two years.

I wish I knew why I'm psychic, like if a grandma or something was then at least I could say it's genetic, but no one in my family (and it's not small) has any kind of powers. I was never bitten by a radioactive spider or had any strange medical procedures done. I didn't get hit by lightning, or die and come back.

I just woke up on a random day, fall of my senior year, and had a perfectly normal day going to school and meetin' a guy for dinner.

He took me to a nice restaurant in Printer's Alley. He wanted it to be a surprise.

It wasn't.

We were driving and I asked where we were going. A bright light flashed, and I saw the giant glowing Printer's Alley arch right over the parking sign.

I thought I was going insane until we pulled right into the alley. Then I didn't know what was going on. The next time it happened, I was less shocked, but it took a few times for me to realize the visions were here to stay.

I lit the stick, put it in the bowl, and took a deep breath.

It's always scary to touch someone the first time. It's worse when I know I'll probably see the person being murdered.

It'd already been hours and had rained. My visions are like forensic evidence in that if I get on the scene right away, there's a ton of psychic energy cuz something traumatic just happened. So I can get a ton of stuff.

But I only get flashes off the dead of recent events, like within half a day or so. The more time passes, the more the energy dissipates, and I can't get much. And if a body's cold, psychically speaking, I can't even get the First Impression off it.

I let myself shake for a minute and grinned like an idiot before palmin' her cheek.

Flash.

The girl was walking, six inch screw-me shoes clicking out a tune on the gravel.

"Why are we going into the park?"

The vision expanded. She was walking across the lane towards the trees in the park.

"I like making love under the stars," a male voice answered.

I couldn't see whose arm she hung on, but he was about six feet tall.

"We'll get caught!"

"I like the risk of getting caught."

"Since when? You neverel," she slurred, fear leaking through her. "Neverrrral... Whatttt... Diddd youugl...?"

She dropped and he caught her, swooping her up.

My vision went black. Was that it? Maybe she passed out and didn't see what happened next. For her sake, I hoped so.

Flash.

She was under a tree, lying on the ground. She couldn't move anything but her eyes.

The shadow above tore off her black panties, slipped on a condom, and ripped into her body.

She couldn't feel it. It was like it was happening on a TV show.

It took him only a minute to come and he moaned like an animal. He tucked the used condom in his pocket along with her torn panties.

He picked her up and walked across the street to the alley. No worries about witnesses or security cameras?

He lay her on the ground in the alley, arranging her legs out and pushing up her skirt. He took off her shoes and pulled gravel out of his other pocket. He rubbed that into her bare feet and leaned over her.

What was he doing?

When he pulled back, her neck was bleeding freely. He pulled something else out of his pocket, those things sure could hold a lot, and leaned over her again.

The rain picked up as darkness took her. She loved the rain.

I jerked and crumpled in on myself like a kicked bag. My brain boiled and I half expected steam to pour outta my ears.

Tears spilled down my cheeks and my nose started to run.

She'd been awake. Oh God, she'd lasted long enough to see him violating her and had been there just enough to know she was gonna die.

"It's okay." Grant kneeled behind me, handed me a tissue, and pulled me back against his chest.

I held onto him like a lifejacket.

"He pulled a Rifkin, General," I sobbed after explaining the rest. "Raped her and took her panties and shoes, like souvenirs."

Jet stayed on the phone, finally got somebody apparently, but him and Dan stared at me.

I'd crumpled to the ground when I got my First Impression off Dan too.

Later that day, I was briefed by the director and told her about the First Impressions. Dan was there and once he knew what I could see, he knew why I collapsed.

He never asked how much I knew. I never asked why he did what he did. I think he hates me because I know his deep dark secret, but I won't ever tell anyone, no matter how big a jerk he is.

"She knew him," Grant said when I was done. It wasn't a question. "And he wanted us to think she walked barefoot from somewhere?"

I nodded, wantin' to turn around and bury my face in his clean-smelling neck.

I didn't. See, I have some sense of professionalism.

"Comb the park, find me that gravel and that crime scene," Grant said to the guys.

They hopped to like the good soldiers they are, Jet's ear still attached to his cell.

"I'm okay now," I said after another minute of letting Grant hold me.

"Liar," he said.

"Yes, sir."

He climbed to his feet and helped me to mine. I wanted him to wrap his arms around me again.

His arms help take the bite from the visions, help them drift away into the realm of bad dreams faster, but we had a job to do.

"I forgot to ask, what did the EMF reader say?" I said.

"No spikes."

Meaning no ghosts.

Kat gave me a hug, then her and Grant bagged the body. Jet and Dan got back soon after.

I didn't move the whole time.

I couldn't.

"The park's parking lot is made of gravel," Jet said, ear still on the phone.

"And I found where I think the attack happened," Dan said. "It looks like the ground's been disturbed."

Grant nodded his strong nod, which in Grant language means, "Show me."

Dan left, Jet and Grant following.

I stayed.

Grant turned at the mouth of the alley. "Ryder, move your ass."

"Yes, sir."

I ran as he turned, and caught up to him at the streetlight.

"I'm never gonna wear heels to work again," I said under my breath as the light turned and I had to fast walk to keep up with the guys.

Dan led us just past the parking lot to a line of trees.

"Ryder?" Grant asked.

"This is it, General." I pointed to the smudges in the hard packed dirt. "That's where he raped her."

We photographed everything and checked the scene for evidence. I

10

found a few stray black fibers, but other than that, nothing, not even a footprint.

"Why? Why relocate her? Why take the shoes? Is it part of whatever story he's trying to concoct for us, or is it some kind of fetish?" Grant asked.

We knew better than to answer. Grant doesn't want guesses when he asks questions like that, he wants us to find the answers.

I just wished I had them.

CHAPTER TWO

O NCE WE GOT BACK to the office, I went down to autopsy with Kat.
We christened the girl Teri Doe. We don't use Jane or John Doe,
too impersonal.

Grant says that's the point of not namin' them, but everyone should
have a name. So we run through the letters for each new one. When we hit
Z, we'll start over again with different names.

Grant went up to see Irish in the lab. Jet went over the crime scene
photos while Dan got on his computer to figure out who owned the
building. Whoever it was had some really high priced lawyers who were
obviously workaholics.

Kat and I cleaned Teri, then I took her fingerprints and some blood. We
chatted about Kat's night with a nice guy named Jerry.

Dr. Snow is the other M.E. She didn't have a case so she helped Kat
start the autopsy while I ran the prints, blood, and clothing up to Irish.

We have four teams in our division, two M.E.s and two forensic
technicians. The tech for the first two teams was Dr. Finn O'Connell, aka,
Irish.

Irish defined workaholic. He never left before seven and he was always
already at work when I got there in the morning.

"Hey, Irish."

I hugged him after putting the box of evidence down, arms barely
making it around his portly belly. His red Billy Graham beard tickled the
top of my head as I pulled back.

"Where should the box go?" I asked, looking around the lab.

It's large and defines state of the art. There's lots of doodads that
analyze things in ways I don't understand.

"Counter." He pointed to the counter along the back wall where there
was at least some empty space.

I had to scooch over a few doodads and Irish's laid out dancing costume to make the box fit.

"When's the next competition?" I asked as I pulled out the blood samples.

His eyes lit up as he took them.

"Two Saturday's from now." He put one of the samples into the machine to test it. (I really needed to start learning the names of these things.) "I need to practice the Venetian Waltz when you're not busy."

"She is," Grant said as he marched in. "And so are you."

He pointed to the blood vials. "Test the blood. She was drugged. I want to know with what. Run her prints and try facial recognition software to compare her picture to driver's licenses. Run the fibers from the scene. Go over her clothes. Check for fluids, prints, or anything else he might have left on her."

We both nodded along. Of course Irish had already thought of all this; Grant was saying it for my benefit.

"Ryder, you're assisting," Grant said.

He breezed out of the lab with the parting shot of, "And if I come back here and you two are dancing, you'll be doing your performance on the street while you look for new jobs."

Irish ran a blood sample through his mass spec machine (at least I remembered the name of that one) then started on the fingerprints while I went over every inch of her clothing.

"I think this may have been transferred from the perp." I picked up a black fiber with my tweezers after I photographed it. "We found some like it in the park."

He took the sample to a microscope and I pulled out another bag and labeled it.

We may get away with a lot, since most of the time our cases can't go to a real judge and jury anyway, but maintaining the integrity of evidence is sacrosanct.

It took hours for us to process everything. Irish confirmed she was drugged with GHB, big surprise, and it was long past lunch by the time I left the lab and got back to my desk.

Our division's a room the size of a football field, separated into four sections that each have four desks arranged in semicircles. The boss's desk is always the biggest.

I made a quick lunch of the leftover Chinese from the breakroom fridge and checked my email as I ate.

I honestly didn't know what to do after that, and none of the guys were at their desks, so I called Jet.

"Where are you guys?" I asked.

"At the club," he said.

"What club?"

"Oh right. You were in the lab. The building Teri Doe was found by is a private, *very* private, club, not a restaurant. Grant's talking to the manager now. He's very polite and answers all the questions, and we know he's lying through his ass. Dan and I are fingerprinting the place now. And Mr. Kurt, the manager, said we can have it all night because they're closing tonight out of respect."

"That's convenient."

"That's what I thought. I'm thinking we're going to pop in Thursday night with a warrant and talk to the members."

"But a warrant just means we get in, not that they have to talk to us," I said.

"Legally true, but *Grant*. They'll answer questions."

"Good point."

"So I…" He paused and I heard Grant in the background. "Grant's holding the manager and wants you down here ASAP."

Yay!

"I'm there."

I bounced up as I clicked off, slipped my gun into my belt holster, clipped my phone on, grabbed my purse, and ran to the elevator.

# # #

It took a bit longer to get there cuz I took a wrong turn onto Division and got stuck in the construction around Vandy.

Oops.

Grant was waiting in the parking lot and didn't look happy when I finally pulled up.

"Get lost, Ryder?" Grant said as I climbed out.

"Wrong turn. Sorry, sir."

"We have the manager in the back."

He turned on a heel and marched inside, leavin' me to grab my purse and scramble after him.

The inside of the club was brightly lit by fluorescents, but I could see different types of lighting on the ceiling. Small tables on a rich red carpet circled a hardwood dance floor, forming a half moon shape. Booths lined the west wall, a long bar ran along the opposite, and a stage was up front. The entire place was spotless and the only thing it reeked of was class and cleaner.

"I won't be able to get anything from here," I said, tappin' my nose. "It's been sterilized."

"I know," Grant said.

I must've looked surprised because he said, "I may not be psychic, but I do have a nose."

I smiled. "Right, sorry. Back room, you said?"

I rushed to the open door tucked between the stage and the wall.

It was a back hall as opposed to a room, and I had to wait for Grant to march in after me to tell me which of the six doors the manager waited behind.

He opened the second door on the right for me, like the gentleman he is.

It was probably the manager's office. The little desk was covered with files piled up neatly, the carpet was just as cushy as the one in the club, but blue, and the walls were covered with beautiful impressionist paintings.

The manager rose to meet us. He was a beefy man around thirty with a fantastic grey pinstripe suit, ruddy complexion, large nose, wide mouth, brown eyes, and thick black hair.

He reminded me of a German Shepard for some reason, floppy and friendly.

"Hello, Mr. Kurt. I'm Special Agent Ryder."

I stepped forward to shake his hand, grinning so hard I was surprised it didn't hurt.

Please don't let me see anything as bad as this mornin'.

Flash.

Mr. Kurt was flinching as a smaller hand squeezed his.

The vision widened to show the rest of the hospital room. The pretty plump woman on the bed screamed and her shriek was joined by the newborn's as he slid out.

He looked like a giant root covered in goo.

And was the most beautiful thing in the world.

The nurse wrapped the screaming baby and Mr. Kurt kissed his wife. The nurse passed over the tiny package and tears flowed down his face as he kissed the gooey baby on its forehead.

"Congratulations, he's beautiful," the midwife said.

"I'm a daddy," Kurt said, sobbing as he kissed the tiny face again.

I gave Mr. Kurt a completely genuine smile as I dropped his hand.

My First Impression of Grant was of him when his daughter was born. It's the only time I've ever seen Grant cry. I think it says something about a man when his most significant moment is when he becomes a father.

"Do you have more questions?" Kurt asked.

"One moment." I hurried out of the room.

Grant followed, closing the door behind him. "Well?"

"He just had his first kid, maybe a few months ago. A baby boy."

Our eyes met for a moment and I had that urge to lean forward to take in his sharp, clean scent.

I blinked and cleared my throat. "What did he say about the girl?"

"She was a singer here. Her name's Jo. He doesn't know her last name, age, where she lives, and she was always paid in cash."

I snorted. "So he's confessing to tax fraud… tax evasion? Is it tax f-"

"Ryder."

"Sorry, sir. So he's committed some tax crime by keeping her off the books and he confessed that to a bunch of feds? I don't think so."

"Exactly."

Grant handed me a picture of the girl in a group of five other teenagers and twenty-somethin's, arms around each other and smiling at what I guessed was a New Year's Eve party based on the hats and balloons.

"He had this on the wall in his office. You have ten minutes. Use one of the booths."

I nodded and sat down even though I have a hard time gettin' things from photos cuz they have to mean something to the people who took them.

Luckily most photos don't. Otherwise I'd drown in visions whenever I got on Facebook, and Instagram would be outta the question.

I put my bowl on the table and lit my incense, focusing on the picture, on everything from the party hats to the beaming smiles to Jo's sparkling eyes.

Flash.

I saw Teri, er... Jo, through a thick dream fog as she sang on the stage. She had a big, booming voice as she belted it. She was dressed in usual Nashville spring attire, a sundress and cowgirl boots, and the crowd was a mix of people, from the usual Nashville urban cowboys to punks to suits.

Genres like that don't mix at clubs. They're usually more theme specific.

I pulled out of the vision.

Well put sugar on a swine, that wasn't very helpful.

Flash.

It was the present. I could feel it. I heard voices but saw nothing but a blank slate of navy.

"I think they'll come back tomorrow." Mr. Kurt's voice? Maybe?

"Then we won't open," another guy said. "Ask them if they want to come to talk to our patrons. If they say yes, we'll move to the backup. Try to convince them it wasn't any of us. I don't want to move again."

"But we'll probably have to," Kurt said. "This Grant guy isn't going to let us slide by before digging up everything. He already has a man working on the subpoena for our taxes and business records."

"Either way, we'll need a new singer. I'll stop by Lonnie's and WannaB's tonight to find one."

"Are you sure I should stay away for a few days while you work this out?" Kurt asked.

"Yes. Jo wasn't one of us, but she was ours. And them leaving her like that... she was a message."

"Sir?" Kurt asked after a moment.

"You know, life goes on. I have to find a replacement and keep my business running,

but that girl's dead because of us. And now I have to find another one and... what? Hope the same thing doesn't happen to her? Where I come from, you don't use women like that. You don't drag women into a war."

The vision ended abruptly and I didn't hear more than a whisper of Kurt's response.

"Shoot." I shoved my stuff back into my bag.

I hate present time visions because they happen in the same time as in the vision, which makes me basically comatose for however long the vision holds me.

I looked around until my eyes landed on Grant. He was kneeling down next to the bar, photographing something near the bottom.

His face was set in hard lines as he pulled the camera away to look at the picture he just took. He stared at it, then at the spot he just photographed.

Focused Grant.

I watched him until he lowered the camera.

"Spit it out, Ryder," Grant said.

"How do you do that?" I asked. "I'm supposed to be the psychic."

"Today, Ryder."

"Yes, sir," I said, relaying what I saw and then heard.

"We will tell him we will come by on the weekend," Grant said. "Ryder, go over the floors and booths and bag everything down to a single spare string in this place. Kowalski!"

Jet jumped up from where he was helping Dan fingerprint the bottles and glasses behind the bar.

"Finish the photos." Grant tossed the camera to Jet before disappearing through the door and Jet caught it one-handed.

We finished processing the scene and Grant reappeared soon after.

The second we got back to the office, Grant said, "Ryder, you're assisting Irish," before marching upstairs to talk to the director.

I rolled my eyes and ran to the lab.

I never get to do anything on my own. Welcome to the life of the probie.

Irish had found Jo online. Her full name was Joanna Cass. Jet and Dan were already on the way to her house.

I scanned the mess of fingerprints from the walls.

If you want to know the definition of tedium, it's looking over about a hundred scans of overlapping swirls and trying to decide where one ends and another begins.

Irish was busy running DNA on one computer and comparing the threads I found to samples on another. It looked like all the threads came from the same black wool coat.

My phone rang and I looked up from my puzzle of dips and whirls. Oh man, I'd been at it almost two hours.

"Hello?"

"Director's office, now," Grant said.

"Yes, General," I said.

He'd already hung up.

"Bye, Irish." I gave him a peck on the cheek and darted out of the lab.

The SDF Nashville director, Tina Foster, is a nearly six foot tall statue of a woman, somewhere between forties and sixties, who has been in the FBI since law school, and rumors abound that she got the director job because of who her daddy is.

I straightened my skirt before walking into the director's front office, basically her waiting room. Her assistant's desk is in front of the door to her office and beige chairs line the opposite wall.

I always feel like a child going to the principal's office when I'm sittin' in that room.

"I… ugh, Grant told me to come up here," I said to the director's office gargoyle.

"She's expecting you," Mr. Crookshanks said in his scratchy old voice without looking at me.

I stared at the closed door. "Do I knock first or…?"

"Just go in, Agent Ryder."

If he were this side of the Crypt Keeper, he would've rolled his eyes.

I opened the door, hand shaking. Why? What was I afraid was gonna happen?

That I'd get fired?

Yeah, that was up there on the fears list.

No idea why.

Director Foster rose as I walked in. She was in one of her typical pantsuits, white today, and it set off her tan skin and dark hair. Grant was already standin' and based on the fading pressure prints on the desk, he'd been leanin' over to get in Foster's face.

"Close the door, Agent Ryder," the director said.

I did with a nod.

Her office reminds me of Mama's. Plush furnishings and carpet, lots of gold and royal blue, giant mahogany desk with every spec of paper lined up neatly.

Grant always says the director's office is like her, too dressed up and only serves the purpose of looking important.

He's said it to her face, too.

Of course Grant would never be so cowardly as to talk behind someone's back.

I shook her hand before sittin' in front of the desk next to Grant.

"Hi, Director Foster. What's up?"

Oh idiot! What's up? I'm not twelve.

She smiled. "Based on your vision, we believe it would be a good idea to get someone into that club tomorrow."

I nodded along. Well yeah, if they were that secretive, it wasn't cuz they were holdin' spelling bees and knit-a-thons.

"The club's finances are simple, well kept, and tell us if the owners want to leave, they can do so without leaving much of a trail."

Wow, this was more than they'd normally tell a rookie. Mostly for us it's, 'Tag along, pay attention, and grab the coffee.'

Grant doesn't go out of his way to spell things out.

So why was Director Foster?

I looked over at Grant. His face was set in hard lines.

Whatever was going on, he didn't like it.

"We think we should put someone in at the karaoke bar tonight," Foster said. "That someone will ask around to see if anyone's offering a job, and then see if she can't attract some attention, get in as the singer."

I looked back at Grant and he stared straight at the director while she looked at me.

What the hell happened in here before they called me in?

I almost missed Foster's next sentence and at first I thought I'd heard her wrong.

"I think that someone should be you."

"Huh?"

It took a moment for me to collect my jaw.

Undercover work? Me?

"No," Grant said, sounding like, well, like granite. "This is my case, Foster. I don't know why you're getting involved."

"It's my department, Westley."

She's the only one who calls him that.

She's the only one who dares.

His face didn't twitch, but whoa doggy, it's scary when he's mad. He doesn't yell when he's really mad, only when he's trying to scare a suspect in interrogation, or when we're annoying him.

When he's really mad, he sounds very cold... quiet... When he whispers, you're already dead meat.

"She's not ready for undercover work," Grant said. "She's a horrible liar and she has the most expressive face of anyone I've ever met. Find someone else."

Okay, ow!

I flushed and Grant looked at me, hard.

Oh great, I'd just proved his point.

"Agent Ryder," Foster said, "how many singing competitions have you won?"

"Um... as an adult or over my lifetime? Cuz I'd have to call Mama to be sure of the count."

"Point," Foster said to Grant. "Ryder, you will go tonight and you will get the singing position in the club. Now, you karaoke more than I do. Which is better, Lonnie's or WannaB's?"

I looked between her and Grant.

"Ariana, wait outside," Grant said, so quiet I'm surprised the director heard him.

"Oh no, Westley." Foster shook a finger. "If you have something to say, spit it out."

I don't think I want to hear this.

"She's green," Grant said, standing and looming over the desk. "She's never gone undercover. We can't risk it on a murder case. And if this bastard went after Jo, who's to say he won't go after Ariana if she does get in?"

I... *crumpled*. That's what he thought of me? Couldn't risk it on a murder case? As in, I'd screw it up.

"That's why she'll be bugged, Westley."

Foster looked at me and I forced myself to meet her eyes.

"Ryder," Foster said, "you're the only one who can sing well enough to be a professional. All you have to do is sing, get the job, and look around. You don't have to ask questions, or have an elaborate background story. We're using your background, just without this past year. You're a senior in college looking for a few extra bucks to help pay for law school. You will have a body cam on you the entire time with backup right outside. Can you handle this assignment?"

Well what was I supposed to say to that? "Um no, I'm scared it'll piss Grant off, and I'm scared he's right and I will screw it up?"

Not an option.

"Yes, ma'am," I said as strongly as I could.

"Fantastic." She walked to the door and opened it. "Which karaoke bar do you think is best to start with?"

"Um, I'd say Lonnie's, ma'am. Little less commercial. Also, WannaB's is posted. I don't remember if Lonnie's is but..."

"You're a federal agent. Just keep your sidearm concealed."

Little hard if I was going to dress to fit into the downtown crowd.

"Be there at nine. We'll have surveillance in place," she said as me and Grant walked out.

Foster shut the door behind us, and Grant cocked his finger at me.

I followed him down the stairs and into the bathroom on our floor.

It's where Grant likes to talk when he doesn't want an audience.

Whenever we say, 'Take it to the bathroom,' it means keeping something a secret cuz that's where our team discusses things, especially secrets.

"I can do this," I said, flinching as Grant looked down at me. "I've worked here for almost a year. I know I'm the junior agent. I'm the rookie. I get the coffee and I help everyone else cuz I can't do things on my own, but I can do this."

"You done?" he asked.

I nodded.

Sometimes I hate him. He won't argue like a normal person. He tells you what's what and lets you rant until you're out of breath and then expects you to do things his way anyway.

"You will have an earbud and camera on you, and we will be in the van just outside the entire time. You get yourself hurt and I will fire you on the spot."

He opened the door.

Discussion over.

"Grant, I can do this?" I said as we walked out.

It wasn't supposed to come out like a question.

"I know, Ariana," Grant said. "I know."

CHAPTER THREE

I GOT HOME IN PRETTY GOOD time, a minor miracle around six in Nashville.

I live in a new townhouse gated community in Germantown. The houses live in lines of grey and pink, each with its own little backyard and high fence. The inside isn't nearly as neat as the outside.

Grant says my place is a perfect representation of what's inside my head: cluttered, overstuffed, and half the time things aren't where I left them.

I dropped my purse next to the door and went straight for the bathroom.

I washed my hair and put it up in curlers. I wasn't going to be attractin' any attention with hair that decided to play a rat's nest for the day. I blew it dry and left it to set while I scarfed down some chicken and pasta leftover from the BBQ at Grant's last Sunday. I was making good time, at least until I paused at my clothes.

"What to wear? What to wear?"

The basic uniform of Nashville coeds is a sundress with cowgirl boots, and maybe a cowgirl hat. If I wanted to fit in, I'd have to do something similar.

But carrying on body with a sundress is a bitch. I've yet to find a thigh holster that stays put without cuttin' off circulation, the under bra holsters make me uncomfortable because they have your gun pointed up at you and unless your top is loose, the bottom of the gun prints on those anyway, and boot holsters only work without rubbin' your ankle raw if the boot's really wide.

I settled on a belly band made to be worn against skin, and my pink and turquoise sundress that was tight under the boobs and then flowed. It was super cute, but made me look pregnant with the way it billowed out, so I didn't wear it often.

I got dressed and was redoing my makeup when a rustlin' and movement in the mirror told me the sun had gone down.

I jumped to the side and Pyro shot past me, smacking into the mirror. He pulled back and shook out his top third like it was a head and glared (don't ask me how a flying carpet can glare, he just does) at me.

I giggled and Pyro flapped open and pulled me into a tight hug.

"Well good morning, baby," I said as he let me go. "Hungry?"

He nodded and flew into the living room.

When I first got Pyro, I lived in a state of perpetual terror. I found him through one of my first visions and after I rescued (stole) him, I always feared someone in my area would notice him, maybe see him flying around at night, or he'd go flying and never come back.

But he loves me. He doesn't remember his life before his last few owners so I'm the first person he's had who has loved him without expecting anything out of him or abusin' him.

By the time I got out to the living room, he'd already pulled out his cloth bag and was noshing away on a spool of red silk.

"Pyro!" I propped my hands on my hips. "You know better. Eat your cotton. You can have silk after you get some real food in you."

He dropped the silk, staring at me as I put it away and pulled out the blue cotton.

"Don't give me that look," I said as I cut off a chunk of cloth. "You know veggies before dessert, and yes I'm channelin' my mama right now."

I tore up some felt and sprinkled it over the cotton and Pyro shrugged before diving in.

I ran my fingers over his back as he ate, smoothing and scratching off loose threads as I told him about the dead girl and me goin' undercover.

He paused and grabbed his phone, typing out, "You sure you're ready for that?"

I shrugged. "I kinda have to be. I'm the only one who can sing that well."

"Want me there?"

"No! No, absolutely not. We can't risk anyone seein' you. I mean, I love the guys, but if they see a flying carpet, I'm kinda afraid they'll shoot you down."

"I don't like this."

"I know you don't, baby, but it's my job. Now settle down, I have to finish combin' you. Don't want your threads loose in the city. Remember what happened last time?"

"Yeah, yeah." He put his phone down and shook his tassels at me but settled down on my lap.

I was almost done when Grant called.

"Are you going to be on time for once?"

"Yes, General," I said, looking at the clock. Okay, maybe not. "I'm leavin' in a minute. I just have to take my curlers out."

"You should have already left," he said, voice practically a whisper.

I flinched. He really wasn't happy about this plan.

"Yes, sir. I'll be out in a minute."

He hung up.

"Duty calls, baby," I said, rubbin' my hand over him one more time. "And duty's in a pissy mood."

I put the threads in a spelled wooden box and Pyro peered at them over my shoulder.

"You sure this won't hurt them?" I asked.

He nodded and typed on his phone then passed it to me. "The box just keeps the magic from getting out. They're fine."

"I've got to ask. I've been keepin' these for over a year. What do I do with them? Are they like shed skin or more like sperm? Cuz you refer to them as *them*."

Pyro took back his phone, typin' fast as a teenager. "Yeah, it's sperm. Go find me a lady carpet. I don't have genitals, but I need some loving."

"Sassafras," I said.

"Hey, I imprint on my owners. This is your fault."

"I was never that sassy to my mama."

He looked at me.

"Well, I'm not anymore."

He crossed his tassels over his front.

"Fine!"

He uncrossed and typed, "They have magic, could be useful. They aren't really me anymore, but if you can find someone to teach you some spells, you could do something with them."

"I haven't really met other magic users, except that evil girl on Valentine's Day."

I pulled out my curlers and put on my boots. Pyro gave me a quick squeeze before shootin' out the open window.

"Be back by five thirty," I yelled after him. "It's getting light earlier now."

He'd only fallen asleep once outside when daylight savings time caught him off guard but cleaning him that night was so not fun.

He's about as cool as a cat when it comes to water, and after I bathed him, he didn't come out from under the couch for a day.

# # #

I made good time to downtown and parked behind the van in an alley we'd had sectioned off with construction signs.

"Thanks for joining us," Grant said as I climbed in the back of the van.

I grinned, wide and painful. Mama says I get the whole grinnin' when nervous thing from Daddy.

"Camera." Grant held up a gold necklace with a red gem and I moved my curls out of the way.

He stepped behind me and clasped the necklace on, fingers grazing my neck.

Heat rushed through my face and my skin rose like the general just called it to attention.

He walked back around and tapped the fake gem resting in the hollow of my throat.

"Testing." He glanced over and my eyes followed his to the monitor.

The picture of Grant was a wall of blue button-up, but perfectly clear, and I could hear both the real Grant and the electronic echo a fourth of a second later.

He handed me an earbud and I fiddled it into my right ear.

Grant told me all the general rules I'd heard a million times before, whenever one of the others went undercover, but I listened raptly cuz this time it was me.

"You ready?" Grant asked when he was finished.

I took a deep breath and my stomach wriggled.

What were the odds I wouldn't screw this up?

"Of course, sir. Hey, what do you think of my outfit? I think it'd work better with a cowgirl hat, and I can't believe I don't have one. I mean, I've lived in Nashville for how many years now? But I was-"

"It's fine," Grant said, holding up a hand.

I grinned. "Should I try not to babble like that in there?"

"No, you can babble. It's part of your cover."

"Really?"

"Yeah, ditzy college girl."

"Hey!"

Grant actually smiled. It was just a flash, but it stayed in his eyes.

"Where are Jet and Dan, sir?"

"Bridges is up front. Kowalski is already in the club. He's your first back up." Grant tapped his ear. "Kowalski!"

"Yes, sir?" came crystal clear a second later and I jumped.

"Club noise interfering at all?"

"Some, sir, but I can hear you fine."

Grant nodded at me.

"What?" I asked. "Oh! Test it, right. Jet, can you hear me?"

"Loud and clear, baby girl. I got your back."

"Okay," Grant said, opening the door.

I walked through Printer's Alley, smilin' at the few people around me. If the noise in the distance was any indication, Broadway was a lot more hopping.

Awesome thing about Nashville? It's always Friday night somewhere.

I walked into Lonnie's with no problems, no one at the door to card people on a weekday night, and it was pretty sparse, but that was a good thing. Less crowds in case anything happened and the guys had to get to me.

And even better, less wait to sing.

I inched by a group of older ladies smoking near the door and coughed as the cloud of stale cigarette air stung my lungs.

Oh yeah, this was why I hadn't been to Lonnie's in a while. Kind of hard to sing well when your lungs are gettin' coated with smoke.

I signed up to sing, grabbed a glass of wine and asked the bartender if she knew of anyone hiring singers. She said she'd let anyone who came in know I was lookin'.

I perched on a stool at the narrow bench running along the raised back of the bar, giving me a good view of the dance floor and stage.

I finished my drink, watching the performances, alcohol tangoin' with my stomach when my name flashed up on the board.

I walked up to the stage, hands shaking so bad I was sure everyone could see them.

I grinned as I climbed the stairs to the stage. Somehow the small amount of people made it worse, like maybe if it was crowded, they'd pay less attention to me.

The music started and the tension flowed out of my shoulders and my smile relaxed.

Oh yeah, I wanted them to pay attention.

And I was good at this.

I sang my heart out with the bouncy country song and took a deep bow at the end, grinnin' for real at the applause.

I climbed off the stage and into the still clapping crowd, blushing at the shouted compliments as I walked back to the bar.

I signed up again, putting on a sadder country song so I could get my wail on.

What if I sing all night and the guy doesn't even show?

Then I'll sing all night. Oh damn.

When I got to the bar, there was a guy servin' now.

"Hey," I said when he got to me, putting on my brightest smile and laying my accent on thick. "I'm actually here hopin' to get a singin' position a few nights a week. I know people hire from here. You know anybody lookin'?"

"Actually, yeah. One sec." He smiled and walked to the other end of the bar. He said something to a guy there and pointed at me.

The guy turned.

He was cute in a cowboy kind of way. Shaggy brown hair, rugged face with just a bit of scruff, light blue eyes, broad shoulders, a little short for a guy.

He wore jeans and a big belt so shiny you knew he'd never been closer to horses than a pony ride at a kid's birthday party.

"Hello, darling," he drawled in a Texan accent I was sure was fake (so the darling sounded like dahhlinn).

If you took that away, I was pretty sure it was the same voice I'd heard in my vision talking to Mr. Kurt.

"Hi!" I said. "Are you the guy hirin'?"

I looked at the bartender and he nodded then wandered off.

"I am. Len Lovell." He smiled with perfect teeth, but didn't offer his hand.

So I stuck out mine. "Ariana Finn."

He didn't move and I waved the hand in front of him.

"Are you germ-a-phobic or something?"

"Yeah. Sorry, darling. I'm sure you're not carrying nothing, but better safe than sorry," he said, sweet as chocolate puddin'. "I hope you're not offended."

"If you're offering me a job, I'm not offended." I put down my hand.

"Slow down, darling." He laughed. "I run a very private club. We're real particular about who works for us. You have to swear not to tell anyone anything about the club. Not the people in there or anything you see."

"You're not some kind of Manson family, or a sex club, or anything, are you?" I asked with wide eyes.

He laughed. "No. We have a lot of important people in our club, it's more a secret society than anything else. If you do get the job, you'll have to sign a confidentiality agreement. But the pay's good, and my clients are wonderful tippers."

"Okay. And you swear you're completely legit, like you just want a singer? No special favors on the side? Cuz I don't do that."

He laughed again. "And I don't do women, not that you aren't pretty."

My jaw dropped. I'd never met a gay guy before. I mean, I probably had, but not one I knew was gay.

"Close your fly trap, darling, it's not that uncommon."

I laughed and it was completely genuine. "My mama says close the fly trap too. Well, that'll be a nice change of pace."

His forehead drew together.

"I had a few problems with my last boss," I said.

Yeah, I wished I had that problem with my boss.

"So do I audition or somethin'?" I asked.

"How about you do a few more numbers here, just to make sure you're not a one hit wonder woman? And then, after I do a background check to make sure you're not a psycho, I'll tell you where you can come for a live audition."

"You can do a background check at night?" I asked, as though I didn't already know that was a duh.

"Yep, by the time you get one or two more songs done, darling, I'll know everything there is to know about ya."

"That's really scary when you think about it."

But I smiled back. Dan took care of all my background stuff. He basically took everything on record about me, bumped it all up a year and changed the last name.

I did three more songs, getting a good mix of pop and country.

Len was on his phone the next time I saw him and I waved as I headed for the bathroom.

"Having fun, Ryder?" Grant whispered in my ear soon as I was in the bathroom.

"Gah!" I jumped and someone laughed.

Probably Dan.

"Sorry, sir, kinda forgot you were there. What, the singing? Aren't I supposed to be doing that?"

Oops, that was a little sassier coming out than's safe when talkin' to a moody Grant.

"I wasn't reprimanding you," he said. "I was actually asking."

"Oh, well it's kinda hard to tell sometimes. Yes, I love to sing. We're gonna have to come back here. Is Len checking me out?"

"Not him, he's having someone from a different location doing the actual check," Dan said. "We're tracing it now."

"General?"

"Get back out there, but keep your distance. Let him come to you," Grant said.

"Got it, but one sec."

I turned them off so I could go to the bathroom, then went back out.

Len flagged me down from the bar. "Hey, pretty lady."

"Did I pass?" I asked.

"You are not a psycho."

"I actually knew that. I meant, do I get the live audition?"

I bounced on the balls of my feet. It wasn't part of the act, I actually do bounce when I'm excited. It bugs the crap outta Grant.

"Yes. You have a lovely voice." He gave me a card with an address and a weird, old looking symbol on it.

"Be there tomorrow night at six, just come in the employee entrance. Does that work for you?"

"Yeah, perfect. But... um... how late does the job go? I have class in the, well not early morning, but morning."

"Just until ten on week nights. Weekends start at eight and go till at least midnight. Most performers stay as long as the tipping holds out."

"Okay. Um, Mr. Lovell, what should I wear?"

"Anything you're comfortable in, just tasteful. I run a classy place."

"So no jeans?"

"No, nice jeans are fine, just nothing... sluty."

"Oh," I giggled. "I wasn't planning on going racy, Mr. Lovell. I mean, this is a job."

"Fantastic, I will see you tomorrow, and please call me Len."

I nodded with a big grin and he waved before leaving.

"Stay for a bit just in case anyone's watching," Grant said.

I looked around the club and still didn't see Jet. "Where's Jet, sir?"

"We switched out. He's following Lovell."

"So you're here?" I turned and Grant cleared his throat.

"Stop that, Ryder. You look like you're having a fit."

"Sorry, sir."

"It's okay, just go sit down."

I did as he said, sipping on my drink.

"Good job tonight, Ryder."

My heart swelled and I smiled.

Grant was proud of me. Me?

"Thank you, sir."

# # #

"I need a latte," I said to Jet and Kat as we headed to the office after breakfast the next morning. We'd talked over the case and drifted onto how Grant was not taking it with his usual cool-headed logic.

Kat checked her phone. "I think we have enough time to stop at Alfonzo's."

"And not be late?" Jet asked.

"Eh, so we're a few minutes late. It's not like-"

Jet's phone ringing cut her off and he lifted it to show us Grant's name flashing across the screen.

"We said his name one too many times," I said. "We summoned him."

"I've seen and read this in so many fantasy things," Kat said.

Jet shushed us and answered. "Yes, sir?"

He paled and stopped walking.

"Uh-oh," I said as his face twitched and his eyes darted back and forth.

"Five minutes, sir," Jet said, snappin' the phone shut.

"What?" I asked.

"We've got to get our stuff and meet Grant at Percy Priest. We have another dead girl."

# # #

Dan texted us the address and Kat let me and Jet tag along in her van.

The crime scene was on the west side of the lake, down south in some no man's land between Antioch and the lake where small bunches of suburbia kissed the woods.

In one of the hidden patches of civilization was a tiny shopping center with motels, a grocery store and a Chinese restaurant.

The girl was found in the industrial dumpster behind the restaurant when a worker took out the trash during opening for the morning.

The cops had already pulled her out, layin' her straight in the parking lot, and Kat made a face as we walked up. Grant and Dan had already gotten rid of the local cops somehow, but I could tell getting something off her after all those hands on her would be difficult.

She was an average height brunette with brown eyes, dressed in a knee length black party dress, again with no shoes, and I'd bet my badge, no panties too.

Kat did her thing even though from her face I could tell she wasn't going to get much of an initial impression either. Too many cops stompin' around, too much moving of the body.

"She was drained. TOD's one to three this morning," Kat said. "That assumes the temperature inside the can would be a bit warmer than the air outside. Other than that."

She waved me over, muttering under her breath about ham-fisted, clueless cops ruining her crime scene.

I kneeled next to the girl on my blanket, lit my incense, and hoped the scene wasn't too far gone.

I grabbed her face.

Nothing.

I shook my hands out and tried again. Nope. She was cold all the way through.

"Sorry, General." I shook my head.

"Nothing?"

Man, I hated that tone in his voice. Disappointment. The anger's scarier, but the disappointment hurts more.

"You're with Kat. You are going to help with the autopsy, and you are going to soak yourself in that sandalwood, do a vision dance, I don't give a damn. Just get a vision."

Wow! He was worse than normal crabby Grant.

I guess serial killers have that effect on him.

The boys finished the scene while I left with Kat.

"Where does he leave their purses or wallets?" I asked once we were on the road. "Jo didn't have one, but maybe that's cuz she was going back inside the club. Her stuff could've been there and someone just moved it later. But this girl wasn't dressed for the woods or gettin' fast food; she was out on the town. Why dump her there? And what's the thing with the shoes?"

Kat shrugged. "Could have lived near there in one of the suburbs, could have gotten off a little boat anywhere along the shoreline. And the Four Corners Marina is just down the road."

"Oh yeah. Yacht party?"

"Possibly."

We got to the office and unloaded Unla Doe. Yes, Unla. Hey, you try coming up with names that start with U.

I helped clean the body while we shot out theories. Each crazier than the last. We switched to analyzing what we already knew when we went off on a tangent and started talkin' killer clowns.

After cleaning, she gloved up and I braced myself.

Kat cut the chest and inserted the device that looks like big hedge clippers to crack it open.

I hate that sound. There's nothing more disturbing than seeing, or hearin', someone break a rib cage open. But you get used to it, supposedly.

Crack. "What else," *Crack,* "do we know?" she asked, voice even, like she wasn't prying someone's chest open so she could dive in. *Crack.*

"I'm not sure." *Crack.* "The rapes and taking trophies suggest serial killer, but he drained the bodies." *Crack.*

"He could be draining the bodies as part of his ritual."

"Maybe, but I don't think so. It seemed almost... like I could feel he didn't care about that part."

Kat put the chest clippers away and I froze.

"What?" she asked.

"Maybe he was hired!"

She flinched and I covered my mouth.

"Sorry."

"About what, Ryder?" Grant swooshed in through the sliding doors.

"I kinda yelled. Sir, what if the killer was hired?"

"What if, Ryder?"

"Well, I mean, that'd... um."

"We don't know more than we did before. If he was hired, fine, who hired him? Why?"

"It's about that club, sir."

"Well yeah, Ryder. What else ya got?" He turned to Kat. "Fingerprints and blood?"

"Over here." I led him to the plastic tray we put the evidence on.

He signed for it (like I said, chain of evidence is sacrosanct) and grabbed it to take it to the lab upstairs. "Vision?"

"No." I took my place by Kat again.

"Try harder." And he was gone.

"Rerr," I hissed. After the doors closed, of course. "Have you ever

31

worked a case like this with him? Cuz he seems to be takin' it pretty personal."

"We had one serial killer about three months after I started. After the third body was found, I almost quit, Grant got so bad. The guy killed and mutilated teenage girls and Grant did not take it well."

Mutilated?

I wrapped my arms around my stomach. "Enough said, thanks."

I lit incense and ran my hands up and down the body, but nothing. She was completely dead, not even a ghost of a psychic vibration.

# # #

"Hey." I met Jet at his desk. "Know who she is yet?"

"Miranda Parks." He looked up from his computer. "She was twenty-one, a junior at Belmont, and pre-law. Her prints were in the system from a background check she did for an internship at the legislature last summer. Dan and Grant left to talk to the father."

"She live around the lake?"

"Nope, lives with dad up in Hendersonville."

"Any connections to Jo?"

"Not that we could tell. Those guys are going to talk to her family and friends."

"She has to be connected to the club," I said. "Len said this was an attack on them. Whoever they are."

"I'm with ya, girl, but I can't find anything linking her to it."

"Kat finished the autopsy. Miranda was drained alive. I couldn't get a vision. But why there? A lot near Vandy and then a Chinese restaurant clear out by the lake? I don't get it. But based on her clothes, she was out partying."

"Wait, the Chinese place is open until two. Where does everyone go after a night drinking?" he asked.

"Denny's," I said.

Not that I'd been clubbin' for a while. Too many people in too tight of spaces meant death by visions for my head.

"Right. You go to places open in the middle of the night. Maybe she went clubbing, maybe to the mystery club, maybe on a yacht, or maybe a friend lived around there and she got Chinese on the way to their home."

"Okay, but no one ever goes partying alone, do they?"

"A young woman by herself? I hope not. But if she was heading home, or to somebody's place?"

"Then where was her car?"

"Taxi?"

"But why go there? Anything to connect her to someone who lived around there?"

"I'm looking up people she's Facebook friends with, but it's going slow and she doesn't have a lot set on public. I'm hoping Dan can get me into her account when he gets back."

"Maybe he did grab her from a club and just drove her out there and dumped her."

"Then why the production on the first one? He left her out in the open, obvious, and with staged bites. Why try to hide this one?"

"To drive us nuts?"

Jet shrugged. "Good a theory as any."

"So what should I do? Normally Grant tells me to assist someone."

"The rest of us do paperwork when we have downtime."

I wrinkled my nose. "I hate paperwork."

"Help me run down her Facebook friends?"

"Okay. Have you checked other social media?"

He gave me a blank look.

"Like Instagram, Twitter, Snapchat? Facebook's not exactly the hot new thing anymore. Lots of people are on it, but use the other ones more."

"Okay, you look into those."

My phone rang as I stood.

"I swear he's psychic," I said, hitting talk. "Yes, sir?"

"Get on tracking down her friends."

"Yes, sir, but Jet's-"

"Tell him to answer his damn phone. I want him interviewing the restaurant employees."

He hung up.

"Wow," I said. "Ugh, Jet, I think you left your phone on silent again."

He turned and grabbed it. "Shit! Four missed calls."

"He said go interview the restaurant employees. I'm supposed to take over for you."

He nodded at his computer, indicating I should use it so I could pick up where he left off, and ran to the elevator.

I sat down and copied the name Jet had highlighted.

"Too bad I can't get visions on these people through the computer," I said. "Please, please let me find something."

# # #

Three hours and about two hundred names later when the guys got back, I had pain shooting up my neck and nothing to show for it.

That I knew of.

Until we knew who was connected to that club, we couldn't say if Miranda's friends had any connections to them or not. All I found was none of the friends on Facebook lived around that part of the lake or had a yacht, at least not one registered in their name.

We settled around Grant's desk for an info swap.

"Friends confirm she didn't have a job, had a ton of friends but no one with a yacht, and no mention of a private club, but was seeing someone for a while now," Dan said. "The dad hadn't met him yet, but thought his daughter was spending too much time out because her grades slipped this past semester. One of her friends had met the guy at a party. He introduced himself as Carlos, no last name."

"Description?" Grant asked.

"Not much of one. Tall, Latino, curly black hair. The girl said she was drunk when she met him so that's all she remembers."

I said what I hadn't found, then Jet summed up the interviews. Nothing we didn't already know. A worker found the girl and called the cops and no one saw her there last night, alive or dead.

Grant gave us Miranda's family background. Fairly typical middle class upbringing, and her mom died from cancer two years ago. And he'd checked old cases to see if there were any vamp-looking attacks before the SDF was formed, none in Nashville. At least, none recorded.

"Ariana, go home and get ready," Grant said. "Be. On. Time. Tonight."

"Yes, sir."

"Kowalski, you're checking cold case files. Bridges, get into her computer. Emails, social media, snapchat, whatever. I want to know who she was seeing."

And we were off.

I got home, left food out for Pyro and opened the window so he could get out, scarfed some leftovers from my favorite Italian place, pulled my hair up in a clip, and changed into a red wrap dress and my camera necklace and earbud.

I sped to the club, stomach twistin' with bats.

The point of undercover is to find information you normally wouldn't be able to get cuz you need the information, but goin' in knowing so little… well, it wasn't the brightest move on our part.

The front parking lot was pretty empty. I drove around back and parked in the dirt alley area. The employee entrance and a low to the ground, shaded window were the only breaks in the brick wall.

I walked to the door and paused. Len had told me I could walk right in but shouldn't there have been some kind of guard for such an exclusive place?

I opened the door and a big guy looked up from a tiny table next to the door.

"Name?" he grunted.

He wore jeans and a tight black tee that showed off biceps as big as my head and tattoo sleeves. He was shaved bald with a squishy face and squinty eyes.

He looked like he was rented from Guards R Us.

"Um, hi." It wasn't too hard to act nervous. "I'm the singer… Ariana?"

I held out my hand for him to shake. He didn't.

"This way, miss."

He locked the door behind me with a flick of the wrist and led me down the back hallway I'd been in yesterday. He knocked on the door of the office and Len answered.

"Thanks, John. I've got her from here." Len smiled as he watched John walk away and I suppressed a giggle.

"Hey, Len!" I said and he jerked back a smidge. "Sorry. Volume. I'm a little nervous."

"That's alright, darling," he said in a general American accent. Apparently the affected Texan accent had left the building.

"What happened to your drawl?"

"I just felt like being Texan for a night."

I fought a smile. He still looked like a cowboy tonight with a gold shirt and a ten gallon hat.

"Okay, so how does this work? Do you give me songs to sing or..?"

"I've got a list of songs, separated by mood. I tell you what to go for and you choose a song you can do from the list. Our band can play anything in there."

He handed me a thick binder. I reached in a little too far to take it and grazed his hand.

Flash.

Len was shaking like a lamb as another blond guy leaned over him.

They were both naked and obviously happy to be that way. I couldn't see much of anything past them, the world was fuzzy white. Len felt happy, but terrified.

That was wrong. You didn't feel both at once. There was... something.

My stomach twisted. I didn't like this. Death hung on the air.

"You'll wake up and be like me," the second one whispered, running his hand up Len's arm.

His thick, shoulder length hair fell over his face as he angled into Len's neck. There was a flash of thin, almost needle-like fangs before they vanished into Len's neck.

Len jerked.

"...start, you do one romantic song, introduce yourself, wail it out, and then do about a half an hour of numbers from the country dance section, and we'll go from there," Len was saying. "What's wrong, darling?"

Could he hear my heartbeat increase, my uneven breaths? Did he notice me glaze over?

Did he know I knew?

"I'm trying not to freak out, actually," I said. "I mean, all I've ever done is karaoke; this is like a real job."

He smiled like he understood.

I placed a hand on my stomach as it lurched.

"Is it okay if I run to the bathroom and then come out and get going?

Stomach needs to be told it's gonna be okay."

"Of course."

Len showed me to the ladies room and went back to the office without glancing back.

Trusting or confident?

So that's why he didn't he want me touchin' him? Was he afraid I'd notice the cool skin? The lack of a pulse?

I ran the water in the sink just in case their hearing was a good as myths said.

"Houston, we have a problem," I said very quietly.

"What?" Grant asked.

"Len's a vamp." I couldn't stop my hands shaking. "I think it's a vampire club."

CHAPTER FOUR

"A RE YOU FUCKING KIDDING ME!" Grant yelled, making me flinch.
"Ow, little loud, sir," I said.

"Sorry."

I think that's the first time Grant's ever apologized for anything. Like in his whole life.

"Did you get a vision?" Jet asked.

"Yeah. I saw Len getting bit. And his hand was cold... not dead cold, just cool, like poor circulation."

"So you don't know if it's the whole club?" Grant asked.

"No, and I know, don't assume anything, but I can't help it. It's a feeling. Len talkin' about them like they're a group, I..." I took a deep breath. "I'm freaking out, General. What do I do?"

Mutters filled the background. Grant must've taken his mic off.

"Stick to the plan," Foster said after a pause as fat as a prize pig.

Where the crap did she come from?

More noise, definitely Grant's voice, and maybe one other.

"Ariana, get out of there," Grant said.

"No, stay there," Foster said. "You're in. We are not squandering this opportunity."

"Listen to me, you bitch-"

Buzzzzzzzzzz.

Holy crap and kittens on crackers, she cut Grant off.

"Stick to the plan, Agent Ryder," Foster said. "That's a direct order. And if Agent Grant wants to keep his job, he's going to remember the proper response to a direct order."

"Ummmmm."

"Your orders are to sing and touch people when you can to get visions. There's no reason to think you're in any more danger than before. I want to

37

know what they know."

"You fucking politician," Grant yelled, makin' me jump. "You're an irresponsible hack. What are you going to say when my agent's the next girl dead? You don't get to shove your bullshit orders down my throat when we all know you're angling for a promotion and my agent's life is on the line."

My jaw dropped.

Can she actually fire Grant? Because after that, she may fire him.

"General," I said, "if you keep doing that, I'm going to be distracted, and I can't afford that. Please, let me try."

"You don't ask him, Ryder," Foster said.

"Excuse me, ma'am, but he's my lead and he's saved my life more than once. If he thinks it's too dangerous for me, I'm trustin' his judgement. And so should you."

I clapped a hand over my mouth to keep from laughing.

I can't believe I just said that!

"The second anything goes sideways, get out of there," Grant said. "We'll be there in under a minute if you give the signal, but…"

"A lot can happen in a minute. I remember, sir."

"If you get yourself hurt, you're fired."

I actually laughed then. "Yes, sir."

I headed back to Len's office, stomach and head high on my bravery. I stood up to the director!

"Sorry that took so long," I said to Len once I got back to his office.

"You okay?"

"Just nervous." I grabbed the binder. "Pretty sure I know what I want to sing though."

We ran down my choices and Len okayed them, checkin' his watch. "You ready?"

Nope.

"Yup."

I followed him out into the club and had to pinch myself as the wall of noise hit me.

The place was packed! The parking lot was virtually empty maybe fifteen minutes ago. Where did they all come from?

Gulp!

Len took the stage and the generic eighties overhead cut off.

"Ladies and Gentlemen, this is Ariana Finn. She has graciously agreed to sing for us tonight. She's a senior at Vandy and is saving up for law school, but I figure we can forgive her for being a future bloodsucker."

The crowd tittered and my heartrate shot right through the roof.

Was that some kind of prediction?

"She's going to sing, you're going to enjoy it. Everyone, have a great evening at The Kickback."

So that was the name of the club.

He handed the mike to me. "Knock 'em dead, darling."

Gee, shouldn't be too difficult.

I took a sip of water as the music started, pretendin' Grant was telling my nerves to shut the hell up in his calm voice. I pictured his face in front of me as I started singing and the belly snakes calmed down.

The clubbers went back to their dancing, drinks and conversations, clapping for me between songs.

Me and the band did an eight song set then went on break.

They turned the sound system back on, and I moseyed over to the bar where Len sat.

"Sooooo?" I asked.

"So how do Mondays and Thursdays and alternating weekends sound?" he said.

"Wahoo!" I squealed, lunging and wrapping him in a hug.

Flash.

No picture, the world was bright red.

"Thanks, Quil," Len said. *"Miranda's Carlos's girl, that plus Jo…"*

"It's an attack against our nest. Even if the queen didn't order me, I would help," the other guy, Quil apparently, said in a beautiful purr of a voice. *"Let me talk to them one at a time tonight. Someone got away with Jo from here somehow without anyone noticing. Someone had to let him in. Are you sure Jo didn't?"*

"She wouldn't have," Len said.

"Then I'll question them tonight."

"What if it was one of us?"

"Why would any of us do that?"

"You're the investigator," Len said. *"You tell me."*

I blinked, nausea like too much candy sweepin' my stomach.

"Thanks, Len. I won't let you down," I said.

I excused myself and rushed to the bathroom to fill the guys in on what I'd heard.

"Nest?" Dan asked. "They actually fucking nest?"

I shrugged at the mirror. "I think it's safe to say they don't know much more about the case than us at the moment, and they're investigating too. Do I just keep doing what I'm doing?"

"Yes," Grant said. "We're running the faces you got with the camera through the system and we've gotten two hits off driver's licenses."

"Great, so that means-"

"Both are dead."

"Never mind. So we found a nest. And I'm in it. Oh yay me."

"Be careful," Grant said before I walked back out.

"Excuse me, Ariana, is it?"

My jaw turned to jelly and my knees weren't far behind.

The man in front of me was about six feet of pure, lean muscled goodness. He had short, soft blond curls that begged to be touched, chiseled features, and the prettiest eyes. Large and expressive, they were an impossible mix of green and blue.

I wanted to bathe in those eyes.

And that purr of a voice was most definitely the guy I'd heard in my vision. The voice slid over my skin like satin and I wanted to stroke his throat just to get closer to it.

The jeans and green button-up were obviously tailored and showed off his long, lean body.

Yum.

I grinned. "Ariana, yeah, that's me."

He smiled back, flashin' dimples and little boy charm.

Why was the song 'Black Velvet' suddenly playin' in my head?

"I'm a private investigator and I need to ask you a few questions, Ariana."

He opened the door next to the men's room and gestured for me to go in.

"Ummmmmm." I looked around.

Shouldn't Grant be sayin' go in or not?

But nothin'.

"I'm going back on soon," I said.

"Oh, I assure you, this will only take a moment."

"Well, okay."

I walked into a small office that didn't look like it got used often and he closed the door behind us.

"Please sit," he said, taking a chair in front of the desk and wavin' a hand at the other.

"Len already said he could spare you for a few extra minutes, and this won't take long."

With that voice, you can ask me anything you want.

I blushed and cleared my throat. "Okay. What about?"

"Just relax, please."

I frowned as he turned his chair to face mine.

Well that was a non-answer if I'd ever heard one.

He looked deep into my eyes and all thoughts but one shot straight out. My heart raced. Could he hear it?

"Name?"

"Ariana Finn," I said. "Didn't Len tell you that?"

He frowned.

Fear spiked my blood and my stomach lurched.

It's okay, the guys have my back.

Though, they were outside and would have to fight past a beefy guy who was probably a vamp to get in and save me.

Uh-oh.

"Are you a singer, Ariana?" he asked, forehead creasing.

"Yesssss."

My head ached from the inside out, like someone was pushin' too much inside my brain and it was trying to expand outta my ears.

I rubbed my temples. "What's going on?"

His eyes flashed and his frown deepened.

That's not a good look to get from a vamp holding you in a back room. I smiled. Apparently he wasn't getting whatever he wanted here.

He stared me in the eyes again and my breathing picked up.

With that same confused look, he grabbed my right wrist.

Flash.

I marched through the forest.

It was cold and my feet were starting to tingle even through the boots. The eyes (my eyes?) swept the sun tickled forest until I saw the boar.

My heart thundered and my vision sharpened. My arms pulled back a giant bow and let go, straight and silent, getting the animal between his eyes before he knew I was there.

I loaded him onto my sled with the rabbits, and started trekking home.

It was my first big kill. My father's spirit would be proud. My sisters would have food. I was no longer just the son of a dead carpenter.

I was a hunter.

I gasped, heart pounding.

I'd never had a vision where I saw through their eyes.

I couldn't breathe!

My brain sweated inside my skull, threatenin' to boil right over. I could still smell the boar's blood, practically taste its meat in my mouth.

I knew his oldest sister was named Helen; she took over the household when his mom and dad died and was a highly skilled seamstress and cook. She would make a stew with the rabbits and he'd sell the boar at market.

"What are you?" Quil asked, resting a cool hand on my forehead. "You're burning up."

He took a deep whiff and cupped my cheek with his other hand.

We stared at each other for nearly a minute, him breathing me in, and me cooling down.

Finally he asked again, "What are you?"

Have you ever had one of those moments where you ask yourself just a split-second later, "Why in the blazes did I do that?"

I opened my mouth, perfectly ready to lie and say I had an infection, when instead I said, "I'm a psychic."

He drew air through his teeth in some strange parody of a hiss. "You know what we are?"

I nodded.

"Why are you here?" he asked.

"I'm trying to find out who killed Jo," I said.

Why am I answering him!

I took a deep breath. What was it Grant always said? The best lies are mostly truth.

"I'm a fr... *was* a friend of hers. I figured out she worked here and I was hopin' to get in and... I don't know... look around. Find out what killed her."

"You mean a vampire?" he asked.

I gulped and nodded. "I saw her body. She had two holes in her neck."

He blinked quickly.

"You didn't know that?" I asked.

"Two holes in the neck?" he said.

I nodded again.

"What did you see when I touched you?" he asked.

Change of subject. Interesting.

"I saw you hunting," I said. "You took down this huge boar and you were really proud of yourself."

His eyes met mine again. "That explains it."

"Explains what?"

"Why I can't hypnotize you."

"Hypnotize?" I asked. "You guys can actually do that?"

He didn't answer.

"Hello! You're a vamp; unless that whole thing about your hearing being fantastic is a myth, you can hear me. Don't ignore me."

Okay, hollerin' at something that's about twice as strong as the average human is stupid.

He sneered and before I could blink, he was leanin' in front of me, face inches away.

My heart skyrocketed, hitting the moon, actually, it probably made it to Mars and planted potatoes.

"You would do well to mind your manners, little one."

"I will if you will."

Yes, I'm that stupid.

But he actually smiled. It was cold and made his eyes sparkle like snow.

His lips parted and slender fangs slid out, framing his two front teeth like pillars.

I gasped, breathin' so fast I'd need a paper bag if this kept up. His eyes looked almost red for a moment as he stared me down.

Then the color and the fangs were gone and I wasn't sure if I'd imagined them or not.

"Fair enough." He was across the room in a flash, reclining against the wall like he'd been there an hour. "I'm investigating her death as well."

I didn't say anything.

"You're not surprised?" he asked.

My eyes danced and his face turned cloudy. He was behind me in two seconds and I jumped in my seat.

How did they move that fast!

"I could make you tell me," he whispered in my ear, ticklin' the small hairs with his breath.

He took a deliberate sniff again. I tried to stand, but he put a hand on my shoulder soon as I twitched.

Where were the guys?

His cold fingers twiddled my ear and I froze solid as he took out the earbud and hung it in front of my face.

"Now tell me," he said, "where does a college girl get something like this?"

I gulped.

"I don't like being lied to, Ariana."

He closed his fist over the small electronic right in front of my face and it snapped, crackled, and finally popped.

"The back rooms are protected from bugs, but I hope that made my point."

So maybe the block made it fuzz out in the hall too and that's why Grant didn't say anything when the vamp took me back here?

He dropped the broken bug to the floor and walked around, sittin' in front of me again.

"The point being, we don't like spies in our midst." His voice was still so quiet.

Oh yeah, I got the point.

I wasn't leavin' this room alive.

CHAPTER FIVE

Y OU'RE GOING TO TELL ME who you really are and pray to God your answer makes me happy."

I didn't have time to wonder about the strangeness of the vampire sayin' pray to God.

"My name really is Ariana. I'm an FBI special agent. We're part of a semi-secret unit called the Special Division Force. We investigate the supernatural."

I honestly didn't know what I was supposed to say. I mean, when you're undercover you don't just spill your guts the second someone has you in a back room and is threatenin' to kill you.

At least the undercover agents who know what they're doing don't.

Quil looked at me a moment.

Then burst out laughing.

"I actually believe you," he finally said.

"So why are you laughin'?"

Did that mean he was gonna let me go or eat me?

I couldn't even try to stop him since he was so fast, and my gun wouldn't do much good.

"The audacity of the human race," he said. "This is not your world. I will let you go on your solemn oath to leave this to those of us who know what we're doing."

"That's not my call."

Oh stupid, stupid, stupid!

His green-blue eyes found mine again. "Oh?"

"I'm not the boss, in fact, I'm the probie. The most junior agent on the team. What to investigate or not isn't my call. And I can already tell you my boss won't back off, and the others were listenin' in, and will be in here any second since the bug's cut off. It's the same with you, Quil, you were ord..."

44

I froze.

Oops.

"How did you know that?" he asked, eyes fixed on mine. "And how did you know my name?"

"I had a vision. Len was on the phone with you and he said your name, and you said the queen ordered you to investigate."

Uh-oh. Wrong answer.

His eyes went stone cold and his nostrils flared.

Then his expression went thoughtful.

It wasn't much better than the pissed look.

"Ah." He grabbed my arm and pulled me up. "Come along."

"Ow! Where are we going?"

I dug my heels in, slidin' and stumblin' across the carpet.

He looked at me like no one had ever asked him such a question as he opened the office door. "I keep forgetting how brazen humans are getting."

"What, normally you just snap your fingers and they say, 'Yes master?'"

"Actually, yes." He made a face. "Well, normally when I need something, I hypnotize to get it and they say yes. I don't make them say master. Honestly, I respect humans. The leaps you've made in the last century have been very impressive. But I really do need you to be the human who jumps and says yes, because I need your help with something."

"I'm not one of those."

Unless it's Grant snapping the fingers.

"Apparently." Quil pulled me out the door and I had to go with him. If I hadn't, he would've just gone with the arm.

And I'm kinda attached to it.

"You want to investigate? Then investigate you shall."

He yanked me down the hall to the door in the very back and opened it, revealing a staircase down. Really far down.

"My team will come," I said, pullin' against his grip for God knows what reason. Not like I could make him let go.

I just prayed the necklace was working now that we were out of the blocked area.

Unless this area was blocked too.

He looked like he wanted to say, "Let them," but bit his tongue.

No, literally. He bit down, muttered something that most certainly wasn't English under his breath, and sighed.

"You will call them and tell them you're being borrowed, and if they want you to live, they will wait patiently for your return and agree to drop this case and any others pertaining to vampire affairs. At least for a little while."

"What's with you!" I said as he fished a cell out of his pocket. "Another girl was murdered last night, and she had some connection to you guys.

Y'all said so yourselves. Someone wants to send a message, and they're not killin' vamps, they're killin' humans. This is our jurisdiction."

His grip tightened.

My breath burned its way down my lungs and I swayed, vision darkening.

What the quack?

Flash.

She was the most gorgeous creature I'd ever seen. Long hair as black as ebony, and tinted skin. Her eyes were slanted like the people in the stories of Marco Polo.

Her name was Jade and she was a vampire. She lay on top of my naked body, bare as well save for her open robe, and bit into my neck.

It was barely a prick before pleasure swamped me. It wasn't merely pleasure of the flesh. It sang in my blood. I rose under her, letting her suckle me like a newborn babe as I rubbed against her stomach.

I was near fainting when she pulled me up so she was sitting in my lap and pressed my mouth to her bare chest, just above the breast. She pulled a tiny, delicate blade out of some secret fold in her robe and sliced above her heart.

I sucked and it was magic, pure and delicious moonlight. She leaned into me and, using my pathetic human teeth, I bit into her around the wound, sucking harder, the arousal rising higher. I knew I would come soon, even as blood flowed out of me.

I lunged out of the vision, goin' straight for Quil like a fat guy after a hotdog.

My teeth grazed his shirt and he pushed me back. I stumbled into the wall and put my hand on it to stay upright.

He leaned against the door, growlin'.

Blood thrummed through my body and I wanted to pull him back into the secret room with the sturdy lock.

I'd never felt such a ravenous need to jump someone I barely met.

"*Don't,*" he growled, "do that again."

"I didn't want to," I said, some spicy smell I was pretty sure was him swampin' me with each gasp. "Stay outta my head."

He glared. "What did you see?"

"You getting bit."

"Why did you try to bite me?"

The words took a moment to register and I didn't answer. That was two visions in maybe ten minutes, both where I was him.

My eyes felt like they were sweatin' and my face burned.

I turned and ran.

Quil didn't stop me.

I hit the back room and slammed on the boot brakes.

Grant and Jet held guns on the vamp bouncer and Dan was on the phone; dollars to donuts, he was callin' for backup.

"Oh thank God," Grant said, relief obvious even as he kept his gun on the bouncer.

My libido plummeted, and crash landed straight into guilt lake.

The guys were trying to save me while I was playin' with the vamp in the hallway.

Oh God, the hallway!

My hand flew to the camera necklace.

What were the odds they were too busy trying to save me to see our little moment in the hall?

"You're her people?" Quil appeared next to me and I jumped, dodging to the side.

"Who the hell are you?" Grant turned his gun on Quil.

"Guys?" I said. "Can you, um…"

"No," Grant said, staring Quil down.

The pressure skyrocketed, threatenin' to pop the room like a hot air balloon.

Two alpha males sharing air space! Mayday! Mayday!

"Fellas," Len said.

I jumped again. Where the blazes did he come from?

"Quil, if they could help?"

Len was asking something more than that.

The guys kept their guns trained and something told me the vamps could still take us all out before anyone could get a shot off.

"We should talk," Quil finally said. "We won't attack you, and you will get to hold onto the mistaken belief that you could actually shoot us before we could snap your necks… or that you shooting us would do any harm."

So that would be a no on the bullet thing.

Good to know… ish.

Grant lowered his weapon. "Talk."

Quil looked at the Hell's Angel bouncer. "Back to your post, John."

"Yes, sir." He closed the door and sat next to it again.

"Why don't we go chat in my office?" Len said, walkin' down the hall.

Quil followed him, and Jet and Dan looked at Grant.

Turning their backs on us. Was there any better way to say they thought we weren't a threat?

Grant nodded and the guys followed down the hall, Dan still on the phone, muttering, like that'd keep the vamps from hearing.

Grant jerked his chin at me and I went, him close behind.

"Maybe we should take them into the club," Quil said when we hit Len's office.

Him and Len locked eyes, little jerks and half syllables passing as an argument.

"Fine," Len said.

Quil turned to us. "If the others see us cooperating with you, they will be more likely to cooperate with you as well. If your science can help us see things we would normally miss, I think it would be worth having a few humans knowing some things about us."

"How do we know you won't kill us once we're surrounded by your friends?" Jet asked.

"Because I could kill all of you now, without you being surrounded by our friends."

"He has a point, sir," I said. "They move really fast. I mean, not Flash fast, but could definitely-"

"Please shut up!" Dan said, making me freeze.

What the quack was that?

"Watch it," Quil and Grant said as one.

I grinned.

Grant and Quil looked back at each other.

"I'm trusting you here," Grant said, tuckin' his gun away.

"And I'm trusting you," Quil said.

"Bridges, prop the door open and stay at it."

"Watch your backs. Got it, sir," Dan said.

Quil opened the door, spilling sound over us, and gestured gracefully towards the door. "Ladies first."

I looked around. "Huh, I just realized I'm the only girl here."

"Ryder, focus," Grant said.

"Right."

We marched into the club and more than a few eyes checked out the guys.

What made me think this didn't happen… like ever?

We walked around the club against the walls and Len took the lead, takin' the rope off a booth in the back with a reserved sign on it.

I turned and every pair of eyes I could see were on us.

I grinned at the closest pair.

The tension in the air coulda been scooped out with a spoon and served with hot fudge and a maraschino cherry.

I did the only thing I could think of, jumped back on stage and picked up the mike again.

Like it was planned, the overhead music died off.

"I'm sorry my break ran over, everyone." I smiled so big a bird could've flow in. "Let's get this place goin' again."

Len waved and yelled, "Yeah, get the party started. Y'all are acting dead."

That got a few chuckles. Quil nodded at the crowd and that seemed to clinch it. They went back to their conversations, but the dancin' was gone.

I'd have to fix that.

The guys piled into the booth.

Damn, wish I could hear the conversation.

My second set was over after about half an hour.

I hopped off the stage and headed for the booth.

My phone buzzed with a text.

It was from Grant. "Office. We'll meet you there."

Huh, so we were still tryin' to hold up my cover?

I rushed back and was the first one there. I grabbed my purse from Len's desk and pulled out my water bottle.

The door opened and I turned mid-swig.

And nearly spat out the gulp.

It wasn't Len.

"I never got an answer to my question." Quil shut the door behind him. "Why did you try to bite me?"

I pushed my lips together and put the water bottle down.

Oh boy, could he smile. His lips were thick and sexy, and those dimples... I wanted to lick those dimples.

"I have a rule about sex when I'm on a case. Women are a distraction I can ill afford, but if the seduction has the added benefit of getting your cooperation, I'm willing to break it."

Have you ever jumped out of a plane and felt that rush of adrenaline?

Well, it was shootin' through my body fast enough to get a speeding ticket on the autobahn.

"Gahhhhh," I said, licking my lips.

When did it get so hot in here?

Grant and Dan busted in, makin' me jump.

I honestly don't know what would've happened if they didn't.

"Anything you want to say to my agent can be said in our presence," Grant said.

"We were discussing your cooperation on our case," Quil said.

I stared at the ground, praying my face wasn't as red as it felt.

"We've listened to you for half an hour," Grant said. "So far all I've heard is bologna on how you want to collaborate, but you have not given us anything useful. Start talking."

"We have a hard time trusting humans," Quil said.

"We have a hard time trusting you."

"Throughout history, whenever things go amiss supernaturally, humans always blame vampires, and then the hunting starts."

Movement caught my eye and I focused on it. It was Dan. His fingers played over the handle of his gun like it was a security blanket.

"Always?" I asked. "Is there a lightbulb over my head?"

"You have a thought?" Quil asked.

I turned to Grant. "It's someone who wants us to go after these vamps. Not just playin' copycat to give us a red herring. It's someone who wants these vamps taken out. It's someone who knows they're here, knows we exist, and knows we're pretty much 'shoot first, ask questions later' types when it comes to perps. Someone's literally siccing us on this nest."

"They've taken two of our humans already," Quil said.

"Your humans?" Dan asked, hand still on the gun at his hip.

"Yes. They both had connections to the nest, and both knew we were vampires. Most humans here don't. Only ones dating vampires, or ones who are too observant for their own good, know what they're working for."

"He'll kill again," Grant said with an edge of finality. "He could be looking for another girl. Does your nest have any other places they like to gather?"

Quil shook his head. "No designated places, just their businesses, or other clubs, or their human's houses. This club is vampires only, except for the workers and significant others."

"So he's most likely here, General?" Dan asked.

"He won't grab anyone with feds breathing down his neck," I said.

"Hey, feds, we know when a human's in our midst," Len said. "The only humans here tonight are our workers and y'all."

"Not human then," Quil and I said as one.

He scowled.

"Or it's one of the workers," I said.

"Or it could be a vamp who didn't want to become one," Dan said.

Guess he wanted to have ideas too.

"No," Quil and I said together again.

"You two have a mind meld?" Grant's asked.

"Vamps are snobs," I said. "I've had a few visions tonight and there seems to be a theme with them. They think they're the best thing to walk the planet since Jesus and all humans want to be them. They don't change people unless the people are basically beggin' for it."

"So there's a traitor in my club?" Len asked, voice high and tight.

"We could try tracking his scent," Quil said.

"You're going to let us do our job, and that means questioning and fingerprinting all of you," Grant said.

"No," Quil said.

Grant's hand twitched to the gun on his belt.

"Try it, human."

"Put those things away," I said with a force that surprised me. "These are really expensive boots." I pointed at my shoes. "And if this pissing contest goes on any longer, they'll get ruined."

Len chuckled.

"Thanks, I think I'm funny." I turned to Grant. "This is no different than any other argument over jurisdictional turf, General. We do a joint investigation and use each other's resources."

"She wouldn't approve," Len said to Quil.

Who was she?

"She doesn't need to know," Quil said after a moment.

What did we just miss?

"We work together," he said to Grant.

"You follow our lead and if I say get out of the way, then move," Grant said.

"And if I say hide, be quiet, or run, you do that."

The two men nodded and I sighed.

"As for the questioning, I think they would be more receptive to chatting with a nice young lady than with a cop," Quil said. "Then she can get visions."

"Federal agents, technically," I said, then waved it off. "You're right, same diff."

"Are you up to it?" Grant asked.

"I can do it, sir."

I had no clue if I could do it.

"We'll be in the van; Jet's already there." Grant squeezed my shoulder. "And, Ariana, write everything down."

"Yes, General," I said with a half-hearted salute.

He gave a ghost of a smile and they left.

Jet came in a moment later with another earbud. I put it in with a pointed look at Quil. It was stayin' and he'd just have to deal.

# # #

After my set, Len took me around to meet everyone so I could get Impressions off them.

We did the other humans first. Quil had questioned them all and was certain none knew anything about the murders, but I had to be sure.

None of them even noticed Jo leaving, let alone who she was with.

"How could someone take her out without a room full of people and vamps noticing?" I asked Len as I crashed in a chair in his office after meeting the last waitress.

Oh yeah, I could get vision tired all right.

I was pretty sure if anyone opened my head to look at my brain, there'd be a sign saying, "Out to lunch, back in fifteen," imprinted on the grey matter.

"That's what we need to find out," Quil said from behind and I jumped and turned in the seat.

"Stop doin' that!" I said.

"Onto us, I suppose."

"Give me a second."

I caught a flash of fang from Quil before he turned and walked away.

"He's not usually so grrr, ya know?" Len said. "I think you got under his skin. What'd you do to the poor fellow?"

"Vision. I told him what I saw and it seemed to... um... ruffle him. Hey, he tried to drag me down those stairs in the back; what's down there?"

"Oh, darling, it's better you don't know. Humans that go down there don't come back up."

I gasped and he grinned.

"Most of 'em want to go when the time comes."

"I didn't."

He looked me up and down. "You sure about that?"

My mouth worked. "I don't know what to say to that."

"Can I be blunt, darling?"

"Sure."

"This is not meant as an insult, trust me. You are giving off a 'bite me and bite me hard' vibe."

I blushed. "Is that supposed to be dirty? Cuz that sounded really dirty."

"Sex and blood, it's all tied up for us. Every vamp worth his blood could tell the second you walked onto the stage that you're in heat."

My eyes flew wide.

"You... everything about you is screaming it's been a while, and that you like it on bottom."

"Gah!" I blushed, staring at the carpet. "I, ugh, this is not polite!"

He chuckled. "I'm telling you how it is. You like being dominated. Hey, so do I. But you're going out in the dog ring with a steak tied around your neck, because you have big flashing red lights telling everyone you're so hard up, you're ready to fuck the first man who shows an interest."

"Well, I never!"

I stormed out.

The guys could hear all that!

And Len never did answer my question about the door.

# # #

Turns out I could get more than vision tired.

I was at vision zombie after I touched about twenty vamps.

I glared at Len's office door before hitting the bathroom instead.

I flopped on my butt and leaned against the cool tile wall.

The door opened and I sighed.

"Yes, Quil?"

He sat next to me. "How did you know it was me?"

"Your smell."

"Sounds like something a vamp would say."

I turned my head towards him, eyes flickering open and shut. "I'm too tired for politeness so forgive my rudeness. Am I givin' off a 'do me, bite me, baby' vibe?"

He grinned. "Yes. You must know you project. Your face is expressive, your body language screams everything about you, you're an open book. It's not even magic that lets us know you want it, just predators who are apt at reading their prey."

"You consider yourselves predators?"

"We are predators. It's a fact. We eat other living things, including humans."

I met his eyes. "Do you want to bite me?"

"There's a lot of things I want to do to you. Most of them, you're too young to hear."

Heat flushed my body and I looked down.

Quil leaned over, breath light on my non-bugged ear. "I'll tell you about them when your team isn't eavesdropping."

He left and I took a deep breath, turning to rest my face on the wall tile.

"Ryder," Grant said, "do we need to get you out of there."

"I'm so tired, I'm not even embarrassed, sir. Soooo maybe? I think I can do a few more, but I'm pretty sure I'm runnin' a fever."

The door opened again and I shut up. Quil squatted in front of me, holding out an appletini.

"Perceptive guy," I said. "But that isn't gonna help."

"Actually, it will." He pressed the drink into my hand. "I've met a few psychics in my time." He sat next to me again. "Alcohol perked them up after a particularly trying day, and makes visions come easier. It will also lower the vision fever."

"This has a name?"

"Yeah. You're not the first psychic to walk this earth."

I took a long drink.

Yummm, sugar and vodka.

He clinked his drink against mine, sayin' something in another language, and we both drank.

"What's that?" I pointed to it.

"This is a margarita. Dave's special blend. We may turn him for his drink skills alone."

"Can I try a sip?"

He shrugged and handed it over.

My hand grazed his.

Flash.

"She doesn't smell right," Quil said.

The vision opened to picture and I saw him and Len at the bar, me on stage.

"That's called attraction, Quil," Len said. "I'm sure she's human."

"Oh, she's human, but she smells off. I'm going to question her."

"Come on, Quil, she's a nice girl."

"And me sitting her down for a few minutes won't hurt her."

"It might scare her off."

"I'll hypnotize her, she won't remember it."

"Quil," Len said.

"I have to question everyone, Len. And there's something off about her. I can smell it."

"That smell is human red bottom. Been at least a year for her. How about you two have a go instead of you questioning her?"

"Len."

"Been a while for you, too."

"I've been busy. And you are pushing it."

"What are friends for?"

Quil gave me a funny look as my eyes refocused.

"Is that warmth and blank look a vision?" Quil asked.

"Yeah, nothing pertaining to the case."

"I'll be the judge of that."

"Uh, no, ya won't."

He growled and I grinned.

"It bugs you, doesn't it? That you can't control what I see? That I could know so much about you just by a touch? Everything you've ever done, every embarrassing moment, and you can't stop me from seein' it."

His face was in front of mine before I could blink.

"I could kill you," he said, the words stirring the breath in my half open mouth.

"I thought you needed our help." I stuck my tongue out at him.

Not the smartest idea to be tauntin' him, probably; sometimes my tongue needs a freaking leash.

His eyes flashed and his hand flew up to my face.

I didn't even have time to think he was gonna hit me before the hand gently cupped my chin.

"Why did you try biting me?" he asked, eyes wide as he ran his thumb across my bottom lip, leaving a burn across it like I'd just sucked a stick of honey.

Why wouldn't he let this go?

"When I was in the vision, I was you. I saw through your eyes and I felt it. When you were bitin' her back was when I came to, and for a second, I was in both places at once."

He nodded once. "Your teeth are too sharp for a human's."

He swooped out of the bathroom before I could respond. I placed a hand on my lip.

What the quack did that mean?

"Ariana?" Grant's asked in my ear.

"Yes, General?" I dropped my hand and bit my lip.

"Do. I. Need. To. Pull. You?"

"Of course not, sir," I said. "I'll be back on my feet in a moment and I'll get the rest of the visions. So far it's mostly been them gettin' bit. Nothing about Jo, not even after I touched them a few times."

"Did you try to bite anyone else?" Grant's voice was inscrutable.

"No."

"Ryder, if this is getting personal..."

"It's not, General."

Oops. It's a bad idea to interrupt Grant.

"If this is getting personal," he said again in a harsher tone, "I need to know. This is an op, you're in danger, and we're working with unknowns. If your judgment's compromised, I need to know."

"It's not, sir. I can't help what I see, but I can swear I'm keeping this professional."

"We're watching."

#   #   #

I got back on the floor and had about fifteen more quick-snap visions of vamps dying, being reborn, whatever. Some vamps came and went from the club, but Len swore they were all vamps.

Didn't mean one didn't do it, but I didn't think so. Why would a vamp waste the blood by suckin' it out with a machine, right?

By four in the morning, when the crowds were thinned down to about five vamps hanging around, mostly talking about stocks of all things (I know!) I was dead on my feet.

No, not literally. That's a pretty stupid saying when you're in a vamp club, huh?

The guys got my spy cam and earbud and packed up the van while I slumped on a stool at the bar.

Quil sat next to me.

"Well, this was a waste of time," I growled.

The two appletinis did perk me up, but the exhaustion mixed with the resultin' headache did not do good things to my attitude.

"You thought this would be easy?" Quil asked. "How long have you been a fed?"

"Actually, a year next week."

The words were barely out of my mouth before the shooting started.

CHAPTER SIX

I SCREAMED, SHORT AND SHRILL AS the first bullet hit the bar behind me, followed by two more, sound suppressed by the roof but still shatterin' my hearing.

The bullets came in practically straight down. Had to be comin' from the roof.

Well, duh.

Quil shoved me behind the bar and I hit the floor hard on my knees.

Right, shooter.

Needed to do something.

I drew my gun as I looked around and up.

I shot and my ears exploded in pain. I'd forgotten how loud guns were without hearing protection. The world went fuzzy as I emptied my magazine into the roof.

The hail of bullets continued.

The other humans ran screaming for the back hall but the vampires were remarkably calm. About half ducked and half ran for the door. I guess ready to take out whoever had the audacity to shoot-up their club.

One blurrin' in their super-speed way to the door stopped short, an arrow sticking out of his chest. His eyes went wide as he pulled the arrow out, dropping it with twitchin' fingers.

On TV, they just turn into a puff of dust: clean and quick.

Not this guy.

He shriveled up like something was sucking moisture outta him with a wetvac.

His skin split, leaking blood and other fluids, peelin' back like burning bits of paper. His jeans and tank top sagged in as the muscles on his face and arms separated into smaller and smaller ropes, vanishing as they shrank and popped off, revealing yellow-ish bone.

His eyes grew and grew and it took me a moment to realize it was cuz his eyelids were withering away. The eyes popped out, hangin' by long, red strings of nerves.

With a *shhhhhrullllp*, his body fell in on itself, leaving a pile of stained clothing and wet dust on the dance floor.

It took maybe ten seconds.

It felt like a lifetime.

If I wasn't so shocked, I would've puked.

Actually, if I wasn't so shocked, I would've run too, so hey, let's hear it for shock.

The remainin' vamps blurred away. I caught flashes of wide eyes and fangs and then they were gone.

I was pinned down at the bar, couldn't get up without riskin' a bullet, though the lead storm seemed contained to the one area in the middle of the club.

The person wasn't even aiming. It didn't make sense.

Unless they just wanted chaos.

Quil stopped in front of my hiding spot. Before he could say anything, Grant busted in, gun ablaze and shreddin' the ceiling.

"There's another one with silver arrows!" I yelled just as another arrow appeared outta nowhere in the table next to Grant.

What was the archer using, jet fuel?

The lead storm stopped as suddenly as it'd started.

"The guys are on it. You go out back and get to the office," Grant yelled at me. He pointed at Quil. "You protect her."

What am I? Chopped liver?

Or maybe he saw me freeze and didn't think I could take care of myself?

Quil grabbed my arm and hauled me to my feet as my boss ran out, going into danger.

Without me.

"Do you have a car?" Quil asked.

"Out back. Where's Len?"

"Probably tracking whoever shot up his club."

We rushed for the backdoor, my boot heels echoin' in the silent space, the quiet almost perverted after the wicked chaos of the last two minutes.

I wonder if I'll have permanent hearing damage?

I hit the back hall and slowed, looking back at Quil. "Who co-"

Quil pushed me and I slammed into the hall wall hard enough to kick wind outta a bull.

"What the?" I gasped.

"Urglh," he said, crumplin' to the ground in the doorway, an arrow embedded in the doorjamb, right where my head had been three seconds ago.

"Quil!" I fell next to him.

His shirt had a slice across the chest and a bit of blood beaded up on the shallow wound.

"It's just a graze," I said, looking around.

No one.

So where did the shooter go?

I pulled on Quil's arm and he inched out of the doorway. "Close it."

I did; locked it too.

Like that'd do anything.

Quil shook, sweat beadin' along his curls.

I didn't know vamps could sweat.

"What's wrong with you?" I asked.

"Silver," he said.

"But it didn't get your heart."

"Doesn't have to, it travels through us." His voice thickened with his accent. "If it reaches my heart... arggg!"

"Wait, so your blood does pump?"

"Slowly." He closed his eyes and his body jerked straight. He said something harsh in what I was pretty sure was Italian.

"So it's poison?" I asked and he nodded. "Can I suck it out, like with snake venom?"

He nodded again. "Hurry."

"Um, pardon me." I tugged his shirt up and he hissed as it peeled off the wound. "Sorry!" I bunched it up under his arms, grunting as it slipped back towards the wound.

Good enough.

I leaned over him, bracin' myself on the floor.

"Will you know when it's all out?"

He nodded, mouth working.

I took a deep breath, staring down the scratch. Couldn't get squeamish with a life (ish) on the line.

I took another deep breath, put my mouth over the wound, and sucked.

He moaned as the blood rolled over my tongue.

It tasted... good?

His blood was thicker than old port and tasted more sweet than salty.

I sucked again, pullin' at the wound like it was something else, swallowing the blood like it was just another drink tonight.

I paused for breath and looked at Quil's face. His eyes were closed and his fangs were out.

I went back.

Almost eager.

Quil grabbed my hips as I sucked again, pulling me on top of him.

I straddled him, sucking again even as he pushed against me.

Like he'd pushed against his maker in my vision.

I stopped and he held me tighter.

"There's still some in there," he whispered. "Please, Ariana."

"But you're…"

"Sucking is arousing, even with pain." He grimaced. "There's still silver in there."

I leaned back over and sucked again, then again, and again.

I must've drawn out at least a pint of blood.

I knew the moment the silver left his system. He relaxed under me and another moan escaped him.

He wasn't hard, but somethin' told me that was more about his lack of blood than lack of interest.

"If I wasn't so scared that I can't feel anything right now, this would be really hot," I said.

He licked his lips.

"I'm scared and was being burned from the inside, and it's still hot. But you should get off me now so we can leave."

"Right!" I scrambled off him, twitching. "I, uh, have to get my purse."

I ran into Len's office and got it. He was still on the floor when I got back out.

"Can you walk?" I asked.

"I'll have to."

He rolled over and pushed up to his hands and knees. I leaned and slung his arm over me, pulling him up so easy I looked around for who was helpin'.

"Wow, this must be that adrenaline, you can pull cars off of people thing," I said as he leaned on me.

"No, it's our blood. It's magic, gives the drinker strength."

"Oh, okay. We need to get out of here," I said. "Do you hear anything?"

He shook his head. "No one's making noise out there."

We hobbled to the back door and I peeked through a crack with my gun up before going out, Quil half on me as we made our way to the car.

We hit the car and I leaned Quil against it as I pulled out the keys.

The back door exploded out, so loud it got through my shell shocked ears.

I screamed, droppin' the keys and bringing my gun up again, hands shakin' so bad I must've been scared.

Not that I could feel much of anything.

The guy stepped out and my jaw dropped.

Where was his face?

My mind couldn't make sense of the mess. There were boilin' red eyes smashed into a ball of orangey wax.

"Oh my God," I said.

Demon. It was a freakin' demon!

Quil was kneelin' in front of me by the time I got my gun up and grabbed the keys. He muttered something under his breath and crossed himself.

He crossed himself?

Soooo not the issue.

The demon was the issue. Right. Focus. I had to focus.

Quil unlocked the door and I pulled the trigger.

Nothin'.

I'd forgotten to reload.

Fuck!

Quil pushed my shoulder down and I slumped into the car. He zoomed to the other side and was inside and shovin' my keys at me in a blink.

"Go!" he yelled.

It all happened so fast, even the demon hadn't moved.

I jammed the keys in the ignition and turned and the car roared to life. The demon pointed the crossbow at us and shot.

I screamed as the arrow punched into the windshield between me and Quil, hangin' half in.

I threw the car into drive and slammed the gas, barreling towards the man thing.

He dove outta the way and ran inside where my big metal beast couldn't follow.

I put us in reverse, skiddin' over the gravel, then hit drive and shot out onto the street.

"Which way?" I asked.

Quil shook his head, eyes glued ahead. "Can't go back to the nest; they might follow."

"So thresholds really only do work on vamps?"

"Human ones work on demons fine. They don't for vampire lairs."

Good to know.

"And I can't risk a demon finding the entrance and getting down there. I won't endanger my people like that."

"Safe house?" I asked.

"Any humans I know, they might know, or follow."

"Can't have them finding more of your people," I said. "Right."

"I'm sorry... can't think... the speed with the blood loss..."

"I got it," I said. "I can't believe I'm doing this."

I took the next right.

Towards my place.

I beat it down the street like the hounds of hell were on my tail.

Which, who knew, maybe they were?

When we got to my apartment, I ran out and around even though the cold, quiet night said nothin' was out there.

Not like I'd hear it coming. After that, I probably had permanent hearing loss.

I got Quil out and he draped over my shoulder again.

I am way too short to have a six foot guy leaning on me.

We hobbled up the steps to my townhouse and I unlocked it, hands shaking so bad it took a few stabs.

I stepped in and froze as a force pushed against the weight on me.

"Invite," Quil said.

"Oh yeah. If I invite you in, can I kick you back out? Or is it like on Buffy where an invitation means you can always get in?"

"You can tell me you take away your invitation and I will literally be forced to leave. But considering that I saved your life and you saved mine, I think we can extend each other some trust."

"You can come in," I said.

We inched in and I kicked the door closed and pushed him onto the couch.

He stared up at me with wide, oh so innocent eyes as I paced through my living room.

I just wanted to grab Pyro and go for a flight until the sun rose.

I needed to think.

No, actually. I needed to call Grant.

"Hey, General," I said, breathin' a sigh when he picked up. "I'm at my place and I'll get to the office after I clean up. I just got back. The guy with the crossbow came at us as we were going for the car. Oh right, it's a demon, Grant."

He breathed hard and I knew he was struggling not to curse.

We'd dealt with demons only once before, and all we knew was they weren't from around here, were way too powerful, and could do some pretty funky things.

"Yeah, get here soon. If it's a demon, we're not going back until daylight."

"See ya guys soon."

He'd already hung up.

I turned to Quil. "What about you?"

He shrugged. "Is it too much to ask to stay here for the day?"

I shook my head. "Of course not. But don't you need a coffin, or metal shutters, or something?"

He laughed and it slid over my spine.

"I love pop-culture. No, just as long as I'm out of direct sunlight, I'm fine. I can even walk around during the day if it's overcast enough. The younger ones can't, they're asleep or walking zombies during the day. Us older ones can."

How old was he?

"Though we can get a bit groggy during the day, so it's usually not recommended to go for a stroll. I had a friend who forgot that, went out during a snowstorm, fell asleep, and woke up five hours later with his leg on fire. It took him nearly a week to heal the damage."

A week? Was that a long recovery time for a vamp?

"Okay." I nodded. He seemed so weak. "Are you gonna need to eat? Cuz you look like my oldest sister after a juice cleanse. Less bitchy and homicidal, which is funny since you're a vamp and…"

I took a deep breath.

"Are you hungry?" I asked.

"Ravenous," he said, the accent sliding in again.

"So you need blood?" I asked.

He licked his lips, nodding as he stared at my neck.

I took a step back. Yeah, like that'd help.

"I know we just did the life savin', bondin' thing, but I need my blood. And I… I'll kick ya out."

He scowled. "I don't take blood without permission."

"Really?"

He sighed. "We can take blood just for the sake of nourishment. And I mean we can take it, but that's… it's like rape. Tearing into someone who doesn't want it, making them feel things they didn't consent to feeling. Taking blood like that is a perversion. It takes a sick vampire to do that, just as it takes a sick human to rape."

He met my eyes. "Any vampire like that should be killed."

Whoa! Story there.

"So takin' blood's like sex?"

"Yes. It's an intimacy… you may not have felt it in that room, but I did."

I met his eyes. "I was, actually I am still, in shock. Kinda like after the first time I had sex, so hey, parallels."

His forehead pinched together. "Is there a man who needs to be killed?"

"Huh? Oh! Oh goodness no. It wasn't violence and blood… well, I mean I bled like a lot of virgins. I just mean I wasn't ready for that level of intimacy and went into shock for a while, and then, well, there's a story after that, but… how did we get to talkin' about this?"

He blinked at me.

"I… can you eat blood besides human?" I asked.

"Yes," he said with a small smile. "We don't take from live animals since that's close to bestiality for us, but drinking after killing them is not taboo, and blood from butchers warmed up works quite well. I like deer mixed with otter."

"So, surf 'n turf."

He laughed. "I like that. I'll have to start using that."

"How much do you guys eat?"

"A liter or so a day, depending on size and age. The younger ones need to eat more, and lose control more easily. But we mostly drink animal blood. We only feed on humans as dessert really."

I let the dessert comment slide, mostly cuz he was looking at me like I was a giant chocolate soufflé.

"Lose control?"

"Yes," he growled, eyes roving over me, leaving trails of prickling skin in their wake. "When we're starving, we can become like animals. Not unlike starving humans eating whatever they can, but that's why vampires have such a bad reputation among humans."

His eyes bore into mine, shifting red.

Whoa! Red?

Something told me that wasn't a good sign.

The air boiled and my heartbeat increased as he ran his tongue over his fangs.

Could he smell my fear?

"So I need to go get you food?" I said.

"Please," he said. "If I try to hurt you..."

"Where do I get blood for you?" I held up a finger. "Besides from me."

"Around here?" He paused. "Butcher in downtown supplies us. He's open all night." He gave me the address.

"Okay, so you stay here, and watch something very non-stimulatin' on TV."

I left, blood pounding in my ears.

Could he hear it through the closed door?

I locked it behind me and ran to the car.

For all I knew, the demon had followed us.

"Note to self, get silver bullets and garlic."

Just in case.

#   #   #

The butcher was very nice and polite, obviously knew what I was getting the blood for, and I was back in half an hour.

I opened the door and got a face full of carpet.

Pyro wrapped around me, bags of blood and all, and picked me up under my arms. He had me back out the door and next to the car in point three seconds.

"Put me down, Pyro," I said.

He did, but kept himself between me and my... uh... houseguest.

"It's okay." I patted my rug and brushed past him.

Quil was still on the couch and I tossed the first bag of blood to him.

He caught it one handed and bit into it, chuggin' down the entire pint in about ten seconds, Adam's apple bobbing up and down like a yo-yo.

He didn't spill a drop, which put him above most of the guys I knew in college.

"Do y'all ever have blood-bongs or chugging contests?" I asked.

"Yes." He stood and I barely took a step forward before Pyro was between us again. "I'm fully in control now, thank you."

"Down, Pyro." I stroked him and he moved, standin' just back and to the side like a bodyguard. "Why does he think you're a threat? What did you do?"

"Me?" Quil said. "I didn't do anything. He flew in and next thing I knew, he was trying to push me. I had to fight to stay in the house."

"Pyro!" I turned to him, propping my hands on my hips. "Bad baby."

Pyro flew to the computer, clicking buttons with his threads almost as fast as I could.

He flew up and pointed to the screen.

"You should have warned me! I get home and see a damn vamp on the couch. I thought he ate you."

"Then there'd be a body," I said. "I didn't know how to warn you we had a guest. And when did you start cursin'?"

Pyro crossed his tassels over his top, glarin' as only a carpet can. You know, without eyes.

"You could have warned me," Quil said.

"Nobody knows about him," I said. "I thought he'd see you here and sneak in and play dead like he normally does."

"Nobody?" Quil asked, turning to Pyro. "Don't you get lonely? I can already tell she's great company, but you don't have anyone else in your life?"

Pyro shrugged and hit the keyboard again.

"After my last owners, seemed like a good idea to keep a low profile for a while. I sometimes take drunk people on rides because they won't believe it the next day. I've stopped at least a dozen people from drunk driving."

"You what!" I said.

Quil laughed. "Where did you get him?"

"Sorry." I shook my head. "No one knows and no one's gonna."

"He said his last owners… Did you steal him?" Quil walked towards us.

"I rescued him." I held up a finger. "And that's quite close enough, thank you."

"I told you, I'm perfectly under control." Quil stuck his lip out in a childish pout.

Pyro shook his tassels at him and I nodded. "What he said."

He rolled his eyes. "You should get some garlic if you're going to stay in this profession."

"I already put it on my grocery list," I said. "Though I really don't like the idea of haulin' garlic around everywhere."

"Why not? From what I saw in that monstrosity you call a purse, you carry everything else around with you."

"It smells."

"Not if you keep it in the cloves and put those in a baggie. It would be a good idea. I really am going to have to insist."

"I can't believe a vamp is telling me to carry around something that's deadly to them."

"What? Garlic isn't deadly to us."

Whoa, really?

"Okay, explain." I walked past him and upstairs. "I need to change."

"I am perfectly fine with that."

He followed on my heels like a puppy dog.

"You stay here." I pointed to the floor outside my bedroom.

He pouted playfully again.

I grabbed clean underwear, black pants and a red top, and ducked into my bathroom.

"So explain," I shouted.

"Garlic doesn't hurt us. The smell curbs the bloodlust. If you have a hungry, out of control vamp, all you need to do is crush some garlic near us. The smell snaps us out of it."

"Why didn't you say that earlier when you were the hungry, bloodlusty vamp?" I asked, peeling off my clothes and wrinklin' my nose. Yikes, I smelled!

"Because I was in bloodlust. It was all I could do to stay on the couch. Can you tell your rug to settle somewhere? He keeps fluttering around me and dodging away every time I look at him."

"Then stop looking at him." I pulled the top over my head.

"Do you know how rare enchanted objects like this are? They have to be made on the Other Side"—the way he said it made it clear it was capitalized—"and then brought over here."

Pants on. "Other Side?"

"Where demons come from."

"Okaaaaaay. Why would a demon have something against you guys?"

I wasn't gonna even try to fix my hair. I pulled it back in a bun and clipped it.

"They could be mad because someone in the nest broke a deal. If someone summoned them and welshed, the demons could go after them and anyone around them, but this is more deliberate. Most likely it was someone else who summoned the demons and set them on us."

"Man, y'all's world is complicated."

"Yes," he said, voice wavering. "Seriously, call him off."

I peeked out of the bathroom.

Quil was bouncing on the balls of his feet fighter style in my room with Pyro flapping in front of him like a possessed matador's cape.

I bit my lip to keep from laughing.

"Pyro, honey, it's time for bed."

He settled on his bottom tassels, staring at me.

"You'll collapse as soon as the sun gets up anyway. You may as well be comfortable."

Pyro swept out of my room, leaving a pile of strings on the floor.

"You wouldn't think a carpet could have a snit," I said, kneelin' on the floor to brush up the threads.

I stayed there, holdin' the magic hairball in my hand.

"You okay?" Quil asked?

I shook my head. "I am so not okay."

"Why?"

"When something happens like that, a crisis out of the blue, I don't have fight or flight. I freeze. I was useless in there. Worse, I was a liability. You had to shove me under the bar. That man's dead because I didn't react quickly enough."

"No, he would have been dead either way. Grant reacted quickly and the demon still got Carter before it got scared off."

So that was his name.

"I was closer."

"Fine, it's all your fault. There, feel better? Didn't think so. You feel guilty? Good. Guilt is there to make sure you don't make the same mistake in the future. And crying about it now isn't going to do anything. Finding his killer will."

"You suck at this, you know that?"

"No, I suck at the sitting around feeling sorry for yourself and crying about it thing. I'm good at getting others to get up and get their asses in gear."

I pushed to my feet. "You sound like Grant."

He shrugged, lookin' around my room, far too interested.

There's nothing really special about it. There's a bed, closet, dresser, bookshelves stuffed with books and knickknacks just like the living room, and lots of pictures covering the generic off-white walls.

One of these days, I'd get around to painting the place.

"If I leave you alone all day, will I come back to find my stuff riffled through?" I asked.

I put the hairball in the upstairs box, went into the bathroom and grabbed my toothbrush and paste, shovin' the brush in and scrubbing a little too vigorously.

"Of course not. I'm too good to leave traces that I've searched anywhere."

I popped my head into my room again to roll my eyes at him and he smiled.

"Hey, how does your blood do this? I mean, I feel like I've had an entire night's sleep," I asked, putting the toothbrush in again.

He was at the doorway in a blink and I gagged on my toothpaste.

I spat into the sink and glared at him. "Don't do that."

"It bugs you, does it?" he asked, eyes heavy and far too focused.

"I will kick your butt outta here if you keep lookin' at me like that."

I rinsed out my mouth, keeping an eye on him in the mirror.

And yet another myth dispelled.

He sighed. "So we can't finish what we started?"

I glared at him in the mirror. "We didn't start anything."

He put his hands up. "That was a joke. I already told you, I have a rule."

I shook my head. "We'll cover the scene today. That's probably going to take all day. I'll see what Grant says about the joint investigation, and I'll tell you what I can, and you need to come up with some answers tonight."

He just smiled and backed away from the door. He kicked off his shoes and pushed down on my bed.

"Memory foam mattress, thick down comforter, but made out of synthetic materials." He pulled it back. "But Egyptian cotton sheets. Interesting. Based on this condo and your age, you come from money, but don't have all the fine things you could." He looked around. "So why?"

"What are you-?"

"Answer, you're allergic." He grabbed my allergy meds from my dresser. "And judging by the size of this container, you're very allergic."

"Are you done?" I wrinkled my nose at him.

"Not even close. But I can finish while you're gone."

He smiled and climbed into my bed, pullin' the covers up to his chin.

Was he actually going to sleep in my bed?

He blinked at me once he was all tucked in. How could someone so deadly look so darn cute?

I had the strongest urge to kiss his forehead and smooth the loose curls away from his face.

"Sure, make yourself at home. It's not like I have a guest room or anything," I said.

"The guest room wouldn't smell this much like you." He closed his eyes.

I tossed my hands up and walked out.

Pyro waited at the computer, a half page tirade facing me.

"I'm not readin' all that right now," I said. "But I caught the words pissed, stupid, and sex. It'll be okay, baby."

I reached out and he flew to the couch.

"Or not. Come on, Pyro. I gotta go to work. I know you want to protect me, but the big bad vamp isn't gonna touch me." I turned back to the stairs and yelled, "Are you?"

"Am I what, sweets?" Quil yelled back.

"Sweets?" I muttered as Pyro flew over and nuzzled me. "Geez, you save a guy's life and suddenly he pulls out the pet names."

Technically, I could kill Quil while he slept today, but he was sleepin' here.

He trusted me?

I wasn't sure how I felt about that.

CHAPTER SEVEN

THE SUN WAS JUST KISSING the sky when I reached work with our normal coffee orders and ran into Kat.

She looked me up and down like she could smell the blood. "Soooooo, what happened last night?"

"Yeah, okay." We hit the bathroom.

I summed it up for her... leavin' out a detail or two.

"And you took some vamp named Quil to a safe location." She smiled. "Where is that safe location, by the way?"

I took a deep breath. "He said he couldn't go home cuz the demon could get in. Vampire thresholds don't have the power to keep things out like human ones. And I couldn't just leave him there; he saved my life. So... I took him home."

"He didn't try to bite you?"

"He couldn't; he was too weak. And I brought him some blood. And..."

"What?" she asked.

"If I tell you something, do you promise on your mother's life you will not tell anyone, especially Grant?" I took a long gulp of my latte and she nodded. "Okay." I took another long drag. "I did something kind of stupid."

"Oh my God, you had sex with him!" She hit my arm, eyes stretchin' as wide as they could go.

Now why did she automatically jump to that?

Probably cuz my face was cherry red.

"No! Well, not exactly. Apparently silver hurts them even if it isn't in the heart. He said it's like poison. So when it grazed him, it got into his system. It moves slow cuz their blood moves, but like really slow. He said if it hit his heart, he'd die. So I did what you do when someone has a snake bite."

Her jaw dropped. "You sucked his blood?"

"I sucked out the poison."

Yeah, like there was a difference. She made a face and I knew she was thinkin' the same thing.

"I saved his life, which is only fair cuz that arrow would've went straight through my skull if he didn't push me out of the way in time. So I got it out, but apparently the whole blood sucking thing is very sexual for a vamp."

"No kidding."

"So he's at my house and actin' like… like we *did* something."

"You did do something."

"I know, but it was to save him. I didn't know it was so sexual for them until later."

"Was it sexual for you?"

"I was too scared to really be feelin' anything, but now? Kind of." I pointed at her. "This does not leave this room."

"Yeah."

"So how much do I tell the guys?"

"Oh crap!"

"Yeah! Do I tell him… them, the whole thing, or just leave out Quil gettin' shot?"

"Oh, you're putting this on me?" she asked.

I nodded.

"Okay, the guys will need to know about the silver being a poison, so tell it like it is, just leave out how hot it was. You sucked out the poison, that's it."

"Okay," I said and we left the bathroom. "This is going to be a bad day."

"Vision?"

"You know I can't see the future."

"But we can both see this will be a bad day. Good luck." She hit my cup with hers before heading to the elevator.

I walked into the bullpen and handed out the coffees, and the guys started chuggin' like there was no tomorrow.

"How are you so awake?" Jet asked me, eyes bloodshot and bleary as I grabbed my kit out of my desk.

I grinned.

I'm not answerin' that.

"Everybody move, we've got a crime scene that's already been waiting too long," Grant said.

"How do you know the demon's gone, sir?" Dan asked.

"Demons don't do daylight," Jet said, taking another long gulp. "They get yanked back at sunrise."

"Where?"

"Wherever the bastards come from. Hell, I don't know."

"The Other Side," I said. "That's what the vamps call it."

We loaded into our van and headed out.

"Who goes first?" Dan asked, looking at me.

Grant nodded from behind the wheel. "Ryder, you're up."

Gee, thanks, Dan.

"Oh dear," I said, then summed up the night.

"The next thing I knew, there was an arrow stickin' out of the wall and Quil seemed pretty hurt even though it was just a scratch. So I dragged him back and locked the door. He told me the silver was like poison. It travels through their blood to their heart, oh yeah, their blood does move, it's just slow, and then they die. I really don't get how that works. I mean..."

"Ryder." Grant gave me a look and I bit my lip.

"Right. Sorry, sir. So I did what anyone would do if someone was bit by a snake or something. I sucked it out."

My eyes were glued to my lap.

"You what!" Grant asked.

Jet crossed himself out of the corner of my eye.

Wonder what he'd think of the vamp he was crossing about crossing too.

"Ariana, did it occur to you their blood could do something to you?" Grant asked.

"Yes, General." Still couldn't look up. "He told me it does. It gives the drinker extra strength. I didn't know that until I was done, but it seemed like the best option."

I finished tellin' them about the demon and how I tried to run him down and he ran.

"Problem," Jet said. "If the demon doesn't have a face, then how did he get around the club, and talk to Jo, and take her without someone saying, 'Hey, man, where's your face?'"

"Maybe they can shift to make a face?" I said.

"Or copy someone else's," Grant said.

"Damnnnn." Dan whistled. "So that's how he did it. He made himself look like someone she knew and lured her out."

"But no one noticed her leaving," Jet said.

I smacked my forehead. "Dave! He was talking to her before she left. He went to the bathroom and then she was gone. If the demon was there, say dressed up as a vamp, then changed to look like Dave when he went to the bathroom, then he could've lured Jo out. They were hooking up, no one would notice them leavin' cuz it'd be normal. People don't usually take notice of things that are totally normal."

"Assumptions, but possible," Grant said, meeting my eyes in the rearview mirror. "Where did you take him?"

I wasn't stupid enough to play stupid and ask who.

"Okay," I said, "he said he couldn't go back to the nest, or another human's house cuz he'd put them in danger."

"Ryder!"

I flinched. "My place, sir."

He drew in a sharp breath.

"What!" Jet yelled. "You let a vamp into your home? Girl, do you know what he could do to you? General rule, if it has to ask to get inside, say no!"

"You should be glad that's not the rule, or your gender would never get any."

He glared at me.

"Jet, he saved my life. And he held himself back from attacking me when he was hungry."

I explained their bloodlust issues and the role garlic really played in the vampire life.

"So when you think about it," I said, "it was a good thing cuz now we know a lot more about them than we did before."

"Is there anything else you need to tell us, Ryder?" Grant asked.

I gulped. "No, General."

He eyed me in the mirror. "Kowalski, go."

Jet reported. After the shooting started, he found a ladder in a supply closet and hightailed it to the roof, and him shooting was what got the shooter to stop and run.

Grant nodded when Jet was done. "Bridges."

Dan went after the arrow guy, and lost him when the vamps ran after him.

"So they can outrun vamps?" I asked. "I don't think so, otherwise the guy would've gotten to us before we got to the car."

"Teleportation, maybe," Jet said. "Takes a minute to get the spell going, so couldn't just pop across the parking lot."

"Or they can turn into things other than humans and hide as trees," Grant said.

"Oh God, I didn't even think of that," I said.

That'd be truly terrifyin'. They could be anywhere.

# # #

"We're doing this by locations," Grant said when we got to the club. "Ryder, you're outside."

Of course I couldn't do inside the club, my being there could keep me from being objective with the evidence.

"Photograph and bag, get the roof and the dirt around the building, get impressions of footprints, and track them into the woods far as you can. Kowalski, main club. You know the drill. Bridges, offices and the bathrooms."

The guys hopped to.

"General?" I asked.

It's not a safe thing to second guess Grant, but I had to know.

"If you're taking the other rooms... I mean... those stairs down..." I cleared my throat. "We don't know what could be down there, sir."

"I know, Ryder. We'll see if we can get in there once we have backup."

I sighed.

"I'm not stupid, Ariana; we don't go into places like that without backup."

"Yes, sir." I nodded and rushed outside.

I snapped everything around the club three times over then climbed to the roof using the ladder Jet put up last night.

We still weren't sure how the demon got up there. He could've flown for all we knew. But then again, if they could fly, wouldn't they have flown away instead of runnin'?

Too many unanswered questions. And it wasn't like we could look for logical solutions.

Demons don't fit into the logical world and don't follow the rules of science as we know them.

When I finished and went into the club, the guys were just finishing up.

Jet had collected about a hundred bullets and a smattering of fingerprints, but we were already sure those wouldn't do much good.

It's not like AFIS has a demon database section.

Maybe we'd get something from tracing back the bullets?

After all the evidence was loaded up, the director was called and briefed, and Crowley's team joined us, we went down the back hallway.

Grant took out his gun and opened the door, gun up and ready.

The stairs were just as deep and dark as they looked the night before.

"Ryder, flashlight," Grant said.

I pulled my big utility flashlight out of my kit and shined it down.

"You behind me," Grant said, takin' the flashlight. "Then Bridges and Kowalski."

Crowley's team took the perimeter and he took up a guard position at the top.

We lined up and headed down.

The stairs were deeper than they first appeared. We just kept going down and down.

"Stop," Grant said after forever and a half.

"Sir?" Jet asked.

"How many stairs have we gone down?"

Jet shook his head.

"A hundred and two, sir," Dan said.

"That's my count too."

They were counting? Was I supposed to be counting?

"Ryder," Grant said, "you getting anything off the stairway?"

"I'm guessin' we're lookin' for magic here, sir?"

"Unless you know another way stairs could go five times longer than they appear. Look behind us."

I inched over and looked behind the guys up the stairs.

There was a long staircase behind us, but nothin' compared to over a hundred steps.

"The stairs are growing or something, sir," I said.

"Exactly. We're not going to make it to the bottom. We may not be able to go back up."

We were trapped! Oh hell no!

I turned and pushed on Jet to run past.

"Ryder." Grant caught my arms, pullin' me back against him. "Do. Not. Panic."

I thrashed against his hold, metal coatin' my tongue as my breaths came short and fast. "We're trapped, sir!"

He pulled me into a tight hug, holding my arms to my body like a straightjacket. "Ariana, stay calm. Panicking won't do anything to get us out of here. Take a breath."

I did.

"And another one. Go deep. Good girl. We will not be stuck here; I promise you. If I have to blow these stairs up, I will."

I took another deep breath. "Sir, wouldn't that kill us, too?"

"Yes, but at least we wouldn't be stuck."

I giggled. "But we don't have explosives on us."

"Yes, we do."

I smiled. Of course he did. "I'm okay now, sir."

He let me go but kept his hands on my shoulders. "Good."

"I'm sorry I panicked, sir. I just can't…"

"Never be ashamed of fear, Ryder. Be ashamed if you do something stupid because of fear."

I snorted. "You get that from a fortune cookie?"

"Don't be a smart ass, Ryder. Close your eyes, try to get a vision."

I nodded, resting a hand on the wall.

Nothin'.

"Sorry, sir. Um, I could call someone?"

"I don't want anyone else getting stuck down here, Ryder."

"No, I mean Q… one of the vamps. They might be able to tell us how to get out or something."

Grant took his own deep breath. "Shit. We try walking up first. If the stairs keep growing, we'll call him."

The him instead of them rang against the walls like an accusation.

Or maybe I was just projecting.

We walked up, all of us counting out loud.

The light spillin' outta the door up top got closer and closer and we hit the door in thirty steps.

I bust out and ran down the hall, gettin' out in the club before Grant could tell me not to, legs achin' more than they should've for such a short trip up. I whizzed by the person watching the door, couldn't even tell who it was besides one of the girls.

The guys joined me a moment later. Jet and Dan left to talk to Crowley's team and Grant sat at the bar.

He pat the stool next to him and I nodded, sitting down.

"I'm sorry, sir," I said. "I didn't mean to panic. I just can't…"

"You're claustrophobic."

"No, sir. It's not tight spaces, it's being trapped. I get the same reaction when I'm lost or stuck in traffic."

"Explains your driving."

I snorted.

"Ryder, do you remember the first thing you said to me when we met?"

Now why was he bringing that up?

"No, sir, I was panickin' then too."

"You said you were scared. You said it in about five time as many words, but you said it."

That made me smile.

"But you said you kept screaming, and singing, for help at the top of your lungs, because you knew someone would come. You had hope."

"Well yeah, I'd been missin' for two days, I knew my family would have every officer in the South lookin' for me."

"Next time we're in a situation like that, and you're trapped, sing. Quietly. To yourself. But sing before you run."

I remembered now. "You said that. And then added, unless someone's shooting, then find cover and shoot back."

He smiled. "Yeah, that sounds like me."

The guys came back.

"All clear, sir," Jet said.

"What now?" I asked.

"Office. We have evidence to go over," Grant said.

# # #

Once back at the office, I was put in a corner of the forensics lab with the evidence and told to get a vision or analyze every scrap of evidence until my brain fried.

Whichever came first.

"Nothing at the club?" Irish asked as I spread the evidence bags out around my corner.

"Giant staircase that doesn't let you get to the bottom," I said.

He shook his head. "Sounds like the stories my grandma used to tell me about our ancestors."

"Huh?"

"Little people, lass."

"Ohhhh, right, cuz you're a leprechaun. I forgot."

"Only a fourth."

"I still don't know if you're messin' with me when you say stuff like that."

"How often do you get visions off me?"

I rolled my eyes up, thinkin'. "I think just the first one."

He spread his hands as though to say, "See?" and I snorted, sittin' down as he went back to work.

I went over everything we'd found, from the photos to bullets to every spare scrap of thread to fluid samples.

Nothing, nothing, and yet more nothing.

"Ryder!" Grant yelled across the lab after I'd been there long enough to get a crick in my neck.

"Yes, General?" I popped up from the evidence nest.

"We're going to your place to have a chat with your friend."

Uh-oh.

"Okay." I got my purse and ran after him.

He had me take my own car.

It was still light when we got to my place so I figured Quil would still be asleep.

"Uh-oh," I said out loud when we hit my bedroom.

The bed was made and there was a note on my pillow, the handwriting large and loopy.

I picked it up and read out loud, "Grazie. See you soon."

Grant's face stayed blank as I met his eyes.

"How did he get out? It's still daylight," I said.

"Get Mr. Kurt on the phone. I want to know if he picked him up."

The manager answered after a few rings and he swore he didn't pick anyone up today.

"They could've had one of their humans do it, General," I said. "Quil had his phone on him. He could've called and they could've covered him with a blanket or something."

"That's a lot of could haves, Ryder. And a lot of questions for us."

"I know, sir. I'm sorry."

"About what?"

"I don't know. About not takin' his phone, about letting him into my place. I'm just sorry."

"What weren't you telling me earlier, Ariana?"

I sighed. "I like him, General. I wasn't keeping it professional. I mean, I was tryin', but I like him. And me takin' him back to my place was a huge risk. I trusted him."

"He saved your life. I don't blame you for that. But yes, taking him to your home, letting him in, that was a mistake. I expect you to learn from it."

"Yes, sir."

Grant told me stay home and get some sleep, and that he'd already told the guys to go home.

He said another team was covering the stakeout of the club tonight and that was all we could do until something turned up or until we could get the vamps to open up.

I ran errands, watched some TV, showered, and climbed into bed just after dark.

Pyro curled up in bed with me, strokin' my hair with a tassel.

"Good night, baby."

He tapped his good night on my shoulder and went back to petting me.

#   #   #

I woke up with the suddenness of falling.

What the quack?

My eyes searched the room with my heart pounding.

Thick blackout curtains cover my windows, leavin' me with little more than shadows created by light from the hall where Pyro'd left the light on.

One of the shadows shifted towards me.

Someone was in my room!

CHAPTER EIGHT

"AGHHH!" I SCREAMED MY BEST high pitched horror movie scream. A cold hand slapped over my mouth before I could get the volume up.

"It's me," Quil said.

I pushed at the hand and he took it away.

The light turned on and I moaned and closed my eyes against it for a moment.

"What!" I asked.

"I need your help." He walked into my closet without givin' me a second glance.

"No! Get out of there! What are you doing?"

"I need to find you something suitable. You need to be presentable, but not edible."

"What are you talkin' about?"

I pulled my sheet up, trying to slide outta bed and wrap it around me.

It wouldn't come off the bed.

"They always do this in the movies," I said.

"You notice your accent gets thicker when you're stressed?" he asked. "Can't wear a turtleneck, too much of a tease. Maybe this."

A dark green silk button-up flew out of the closet, landing on my bed and sliding off. A black suit skirt landed on the bed and he walked back out.

And froze, eyes popping. "You're naked."

"Yeah, that's how I sleep."

"Put these on, then I'll explain."

He rushed outta my room.

"You better," I said.

I got dressed fast and checked my phone. Four a.m.? Seriously?

A year and a half ago. I was out partyin' till four. What happened?

"Are you decent?" Quil called.

"No, and neither are you, otherwise you wouldn't have woken me up."

"Not a morning person, I see." Quil walked back in.

"It's not morning. See outside? Still dark. Not morning. What is this all about?"

He walked to my bookshelf and picked up my jewelry box.

"Stop pokin' through my things."

"I need to find you something for your neck."

"Why?"

"Ah, right." He turned back to the jewelry box and pulled out a few gold chains. "I don't see much silver in here."

"Gold matches my coloring." I crossed my arms. "Are you gonna tell me what's going on?"

"Yes." He continued pawing through my jewelry. "You should think about investing in some silver, just in case. You couldn't wear any today, of course. It's illegal."

"Quil, you're really startin' to annoy me," I said.

He met my eyes with a smile.

We were alone, in my bedroom, with danger far far away.

My heart rate picked up and he grinned wider.

Well, danger besides him was far far away at least.

"Here." He handed me the gold chains. "These will keep your neck covered enough not to be teasing."

"Teasing?"

"You need to pull your hair back, put on some makeup, and for the love of all that is walking, brush your teeth."

"Quil, I'm not doing anything until you explain."

"I will. I need to make a call first. While I do that, will you please get ready?"

"I can't believe you break into my home and have the audacity to comment on how I look or smell."

I stomped to the bathroom, pulled back my hair and strung the necklaces on.

Who was Quil talkin' to anyway?

Flash.

"I'm not sure I can do this." It was Quil's voice.

"I've been saying from the start this was too risky." Len? Probably.

"She's corrupt, power mad. That may be how they do things in Europe, but American vampires have been moving so far from that... I think we'll have support."

"You think Ariana can help?"

"If she can get in with our nest, maybe earn the trust of the queen, enough to get near her to touch her, we may learn her plans."

"You sure you're okay putting that little girl in danger like this?"

"I'm going to explain the danger. She can choose."

"Not what I meant."

"Don't go there, Len."

"You like her."

"Yes, I do. I will not let that affect my work."

"Bullshit."

"Lenard."

"Does Ariana know… what's going on?"

"No."

"You going to tell her?"

Quil sighed. "I don't know how much is safe. She's going to know too much after tonight already."

I snapped out of the vision. "What the?"

I brushed my teeth, mind whirlin'.

What's going on? Sounds like I'm meeting the queen? Why?

When I got out of the bathroom, he was back in my bedroom.

"Do you have any perfumes?" he asked.

I nodded.

"Where?" he asked, tone clipped and professional… and annoying.

"In here." I gestured at my bathroom.

"Bring them out here please."

"Why?"

"Because I need to find a suitable one and there needs to be a window to air the smell out." He tapped his nose. "Sensitive noses. We hate perfumes."

"Then why do you want me to wear one?"

"Because," he said through clenched teeth, "perfume will hide your scent. Any vampire who comes near you will just be able to smell it and not you. Would you want to eat an apple if it smelled like it'd been dipped in perfume?"

"Good point."

I grabbed the few tiny perfume samples I had and held them out to him.

"I don't wear perfume. My nose is pretty sensitive too. All I have are samples and little ones I got as presents over the years."

He looked over my hands and shifted one to the side, keepin' his hand carefully over mine.

"What? You don't want to touch me now?" I asked. "I don't bite."

Well, yeah I do, but only in bed.

"I do." He met my eyes and winked.

"Okay, I stepped into that one."

"Try this one." He pointed.

"Sassy Seduction." I sprayed a bit into the air.

He took a delicate whiff, frowned and stepped away. "That'll do."

I sprayed a bit on and put them away, rubbin' my nose. Too much perfume and I start sneezing.

"Time to explain. I've done everything you've asked," I said, clearing my throat, "*demanded*, and you haven't told me anything. Spill."

"Nests have rulers. Ours is a queen. She has abused her power and overthrown our previously democratic process and has become a tyrant. I want to overthrow her."

I nodded. So far so good, okay not good cuz that sounded pretty dangerous, but so far so truthful.

"How long has she been queen? Why overthrow her now?"

"She has been queen nearly fifty years. That is nothing for vampires. And she started imposing her will very, very slowly. I didn't even see what was really happening until recently."

"Wow, sounds like America."

"On a much smaller scale, and therefore easier to deal with."

"And that sounds like all small government arguments."

"Are you going to keep interrupting?" But he smiled.

I made a zippin' motion over my lips.

"The abuses didn't start out that way," he said. "First it was putting vampires in new positions, giving them power to make rulings outside our usual process for the sake of expediency, including me."

"You? Ohhhhh, so you're not just an investigator, you're like the Attorney General?"

"Something like that. Anyway, after that, one department enacted an anti-silver law, because it could be used to hurt other vampires. Then she enacted a ruling that vampire businesses must pay a percentage of their profits to her to pay for her administration. It went from there. Now, we are under her rule. What she says is law."

"And no one has noticed? Done anything? Voted her out?"

"Others have tried. Any vampire who has dissented in the past few years, in public or in private, has disappeared or had a sudden change of heart. The one who ran against her in the last race? She had me investigate him for telling humans about us. I found nothing, and then the evidence was suddenly there. He was executed for it last year."

"Yikes! That's when you turned on her?"

"I haven't officially. I would be the next killed. Which is why I have to be very careful. After that though, after I pushed back against her over what I found, she cut me out. I do my job, but I am no longer a confidant, and there are whispers she's planning something."

"Um, I just realized you said tellin' humans about you is a death penalty offense. What about us?"

"No one told you. You found out."

"So we're okay?"

"No. *I* am. Humans that find out about us are killed. At least officially."

I backed away, stomach lurching.

"No, no no," he said. "Not you. You're psychic, not considered human."

"Hey!"

"You are far too valuable to kill. But that's why we can't bring anyone on your team along. They would be killed before I could make my pitch to her to allow us to work with a few select humans."

"Why would she agree to that if she is killing humans who know about you?"

"I'll make the pitch to the nest tonight about having us work with you when our humans, which she has allowed to know about us, are being killed. And I'll explain how the FBI has so many more resources and a better understanding of science than us. She will have to call for a vote, if only to save face, and I can guarantee the vote will swing our way."

"You guys vote on issues like this?"

"We vote on all big issues, unless the queen gets her way and makes the decisions without telling any of us until it's too late. As I said, she's a tyrant. Tonight's like a town meeting. All vampires in Nashville and the surrounding areas are invited. Maybe two percent actually go to these, but that's enough."

"And how many will that be?"

"About two hundred."

"Ugrl," I choked, finally sputtering, "What! So there's like ten thousand of you just around here!"

"You sound surprised."

"I was thinkin' a few hundred of you across a state. How do what, *millions*? Like millions of you hide?"

"We don't. We're part of human society too, and just hide what we are. You're overestimating how difficult it is to be a vampire in modern America. We have vampire actors and politicians that humans just assume have good plastic surgeons after they don't age for thirty years. Then they retire or mysteriously die, and pop up somewhere else. The internet has made that more difficult, but if you change your look and someone matches you with your past picture, they just assume it's a distant relative."

My mouth worked and I couldn't even say when it'd dropped open.

"I can't... how big is the supernatural world?"

He smiled. "Compared to human numbers? Maybe a third of a percent of the population. But third a percent of seven billion? There's around twenty to thirty million of us *strange creatures* out there. Everything from vampires to fae to shifters." He smiled. "And people like you."

"Wow. How many psychics?"

"Not nearly as many as vampires. But we have no idea how many. For one, they pop up here and there without pattern or reason, so they have no community and usually hide what they are. You are the first in Nashville I've met. Which means nothing because I wouldn't know if I had met any others."

"Any ballpark figures?"

"Maybe a few thousand across the world, maybe more. I couldn't say."

"So I'm really valuable and you want to take me to the nest where they kill humans?"

"Well, yes, but-"

"Grant will never allow it."

"You can't tell him. I know what I'm asking from you, but the risk is worth the reward."

"Yeah, for *you.*"

"Not just for us, for you and your Bureau. You need to work with us to investigate this. And if we do not get at least the queen's fake permission, your people will start being picked off, one by one."

I paled and met his eyes.

"When you put it that way...," I said.

He nodded. "I thought that would get your attention. Our nest can not continue like this. I need to figure out what the queen is planning, and then..."

"Coup d'état?"

"Something like that. If I can get her off the throne by getting others to see what she has done as the tyrant taking over that it is, it will be easier."

"Vamps don't know?"

"They have been so conditioned in the last few decades, she controls so much of their education when they become vampires, they don't see it. If I kill her, I will be seen as a traitor."

I raised my eyebrows. "What if someone else kills her? You know, cut off the head of the snake?"

He shook his head. "Then her second in command takes over and it is much of the same. Her entire administration is in the same vein as her, and the people have bought it."

"How do you begin to undo that?"

"I'm still working on that. Assembling like-minded vampires and stopping the tyranny from becoming worse are my first steps."

I sat down on my bed. "You're askin' me to dive into vampire politics. I don't even like them in the human world."

He sat next to me. "I'm asking for your help. We need you."

"We or you?" I asked, flicking my eyes up to his.

He leaned in and my eyes slid closed as I licked my lips.

"You are quite literally flirting with danger, little girl," he whispered close enough for the air to brush my lips.

I opened my eyes and he stood up.

"I'm not a little girl."

He smirked. "Yes, you really are."

I stuck my tongue out at him.

"Case in point," he said, walkin' to the door. "Shall we?"

"What am I supposed to tell Grant?"

"On Monday, if all goes well, we'll meet to discuss how to work together. Don't tell him about coming with me tonight, or the queen, just about how I want us to work together permanently and how you would be the perfect liaison, because you are an agent but also supernatural."

If Grant ever found out I went off on my own, he'd kill me.

But this was huge.

A treasure trove of information. A chance to see how the vampire world really worked. A chance to help countless people, cuz we'd actually know what we were facin'.

"Ariana?"

"I'm thinkin'."

He nodded. "We need you. Lives depend on this."

Come on. Why did he have to say that?

"Fine. I'm in."

The gratitude in those big eyes was too much for me.

I shook a finger at him. "But if I get in trouble over this, I'll stake ya."

He laughed and it made my heart flutter like a butterfly on speed, makin' my lips throb along with it.

Oh man, I was in so much trouble.

"In the spirit of cooperation, I should tell you wood does nothing to us," he said.

My jaw dropped to somewhere around Tahiti.

"Again I have to say, I love pop-culture. If someone sticks wood through our hearts it hurts like hell, of course, but we live through it. Silver, fire, beheading, and the sun are the only things that kill us."

"Good to know."

"Can we go? The meeting's already started."

I hopped up and tucked my phone into its clip and put it on the side of my pants, pulled on my boots and slid my smallest gun into the boot holster.

"Ready?" Quil asked, lookin' at my boot like he thought I was being cute.

"Thanks for not lying to me."

"How do you know I'm not now?" he asked as we walked downstairs.

I didn't answer, just hit the kitchen, pulled some scraps of cotton outta their bag and lay them on the couch for Pyro for when he got home.

It must've shown on my face cuz it was his turn for the jaw trip to

Tahiti.

"You had a vision?"

"Yep. I heard you and Len."

"And you acted like you had no idea what was going on?" He opened the door.

"Yep." I grabbed my purse and locked the door behind us. "How did you get in?"

"You left the window open." He waved a hand like he was wavin' the subject off. "I can't believe you were faking all that in there. How much did you hear?"

"I just heard you talkin' about how you were taking a risk, but needed me so I could try to see what the queen was up to."

I got in my car and he climbed into the passenger side.

"Ummmm, where's your car?" I asked.

"When we get our speed up, we can run as fast as a car travels on side streets."

"Oh. So you ran here. That's convenient. Where to?"

He gave me the address and I punched it into the GPS.

One good thing about driving when all decent folk are asleep?

No traffic.

"You have garlic, right?" Quil asked outta the blue, staring straight ahead.

"In my purse."

"Good."

"Hey, what was with you skippin' out earlier?"

"I figured it was only a matter of time before you finished processing the scene."

It sounded like he got that phrase from a movie and was tickled pink about being able to use it.

"And you would go down the stairs," he continued, "find out you couldn't get down, and would come to me. So I took a nap to recuperate, then called a human to take me home."

"Which is where?"

"Behind that door."

"So you were gonna take me to meet the queen last night?"

"I was planning on setting the groundwork then, telling everyone we had a psychic who could help us, basically everything I plan to today. But this is better, this way a lot more of the nest will be there to see it and the queen won't be able to kill you right there if she sees you as too much of a threat."

I turned as the GPS instructed and the next one was onto West End.

"Are we going near the club?" I asked.

"Yes. Different entrance, but it's under that whole area."

"Whoa. How?"

"Underground rooms constructed over time and connected by tunnels. Mostly under Centennial Park for safety's sake. Heavy buildings would make it collapse."

"Literally underground. Got it. What's going to happen?"

"We'll go in. I'll introduce you directly to the queen. Do you have a middle name?"

"Kay."

"Ariana Kay Ryder." He nodded. "I will formally introduce you and explain how I want us to work with you, then call for a vote. Do not speak unless you are asked a direct question and the queen recognizes you. She is big on protocol and I don't want to give her a reason to hurt you. Can you do that?"

Not speakin', that's a pretty big one for me, but I nodded. "So, no questions?"

"No questions. Have your people found anything more on the case?"

I summed up the case for him and finished explaining just as we turned near the club.

"We have people sitting on the club," I said before thinkin' it might be better if Quil didn't know that.

"Thank you for telling me. I was afraid you weren't going to."

"Wait! You knew they were there?"

"Of course."

"And you wanted to see if I'd tell? Same as I did to you?"

"Yep," he said and I scowled.

We didn't say anything else as I pulled into the parking lot of a bunch of closed businesses near the park.

We got out of the car and I swallowed.

I was being really stupid, wasn't I?

"I don't know if I can do this," I said.

"You agreed," he said.

"I didn't sign anything or even shake on it." My voice went up and my hands quivered.

"Ariana." He stepped in front of me, takin' my hands. "I give you my word as a vampire that Len and I will protect you to our last."

"Len'll be there?"

"Of course. He's meeting us at the doorway."

We walked behind the line of businesses and Quil paused by a door.

"Remember what I said, do not speak out of turn," he said. "I beg you."

I nodded.

"Ariana, darling!"

I was wrapped in strong arms before I even put my head back into position.

"Hi, Len," I said as he let me go.

"Don't mind him." Quil shook his head. "He gets more flamboyant the more scared he is."

"Did Quil tell you the rules?" Len asked, tossing a frown at Quil.

I nodded, specifically *not* speakin'.

"Good!"

Quil pulled a large rock up from the ground and underneath was a set of carved out stairs. "I go first, then you, then Len."

The stairs were nearly as steep and long as the ones in the club. If it was all connected down there, the place had to be huge cuz the club was nearly a mile away.

We went down and hit a door just like the one at the bottom of the club, only this one we could reach.

I had to remember to ask Quil how to get around the spell on the stairs.

Quil did something complicated with his hands before pullin' on the door handle. It opened with a squeal.

Huh.

We entered a long, dim hallway with nothing but bare bulbs overhead.

Really, could there be any other kind of hallway with a vamp nest?

The hall opened into a large chamber. Paper lanterns hung off the ceiling like colorful bats, casting a warm glow over the dirt and stone. Columns made lines through the place, probably the only things keeping the domed ceiling up. Bleacher-like seats were carved out of three sides, going up at least twenty steps, probably enough seating for a thousand. There were maybe the two hundred vamps Quil had predicted, all whispering and glancing at us.

The vamps were dressed in everything from suits to ball gowns. One was in a wide skirt and powdered wig straight outta The Three Musketeers.

Against the fourth wall was a gold throne decked out with elaborate carvings and purple cushions. Vampires lazed on large dark red cushions around it, wearing silk robes and looking like pets more than anything else.

The woman on the throne wore a green and black kimono tied loosely at the waist.

As soon as I saw her, the light bent towards her, power suckin' oxygen outta the air.

Something in my brain prickled, almost like my psychic ability was bending, too.

Power.

The kind I had never felt before.

Quil had nothin' on her.

Holy crap on a cracker! What have I walked into?

She had black hair down to her butt that was straight as an ironed sheet, large eyes just as black, wide pouty lips that were a dark red I wasn't sure was due to lipstick, and creamy skin.

And she was without a doubt the vamp I saw in my vision with Quil, the one who made him.

He couldn't have mentioned that before?

CHAPTER NINE

"MAY I PRESENT TO THE court," Quil said with a bow to the queen, "Ariana Kay Ryder. A psychic with the FBI."

A gasp rose from the crowd and the mutters grew.

"A human?" The queen asked in a husky voice girls like me could only dream of.

The court fell silent.

"Aquila, what are you playing at?" she asked, smirking as she ran her eyes down and up me before focusin' back on him.

"Her team is investigating the murders of our humans and she has already given me more information than I could have possibly attained otherwise."

"What information would this be?"

Quil repeated everything I'd told him.

No! Crap on kittens, no! People weren't supposed to know details of an ongoing case. Quil was kinda like workin' with another police department, so we could share info, but this? Tellin' the queen and entire court?

Huge no no!

But I kept my mouth shut on account of not wantin' to be killed.

"Someone drugged them?" the queen asked as though she'd never heard of such a thing after Quil was done.

Quil nodded.

"How? Was it too much alcohol?"

"Um..," I said.

Quil slammed his hand over my mouth quick as a bullet.

"Will the court please recognize Ariana?" he asked.

The queen waved an imperious hand with a small, evil smile. "Let the human speak."

"Thank you, your majesty," I said in my best formal tone with a small bow. "Our M.E., that's the medical examiner, did the autopsies on Jo and Miranda. Our forensic tech confirmed both were drugged with GHB. The demon lured them outta wherever they were, wearin' someone else's face, and then raped and killed them. The demon left behind forensics we're runnin' now though."

I stared at the queen without really meaning to and her eyes sparkled as they held mine.

Her mind... tugged on mine.

I flinched and stared at her chin instead.

Note to self, do not look big, bad queen vamps in the eyes.

"So your human sciences can tell us things about demons we do not already know?" she asked.

"I don't know, your majesty, we're hopin'."

"If I may?" Quil asked.

The queen nodded at him.

"The science they have access to, the way of investigating is so different than ours, I propose we work with them."

Gasps filled the chamber and the buzzing of hundreds of lips movin' at once followed.

"Please!" Quil held up his hands and the whispers died down to a few mutters.

"I propose we bring in a few of Ariana's team. They are a specific division that investigates the supernatural." He took a deep breath and cold took my stomach.

What was he about to say that'd make him take a dramatic breath he didn't need?

"And they already know vampires exist through their work."

Screams shot off the edges of the dome, anger bullets ricocheting so hard I covered my ears as vamps jumped to their feet, yellin' and fixin' to do something to Quil... or us! I couldn't say what.

Quil pulled something out of his pocket and held it up to his lips.

A shrill whistle pierced through my hands and made me yelp as I hit the ground.

It obviously had the same effect on vamps cuz the yells died as they clamped hands over ears and a few collapsed too.

Quil offered me a hand, face unreadable as I took it and let him pull me up.

"She heard that?" the queen asked, staring at me.

"Apparently," Quil said.

I raised my eyebrows at him.

"It's like a dog whistle, frequency only vamps can hear... usually."

Weird.

He turned back to the crowd.

"Just listen!" he said, voice projectin' like before. "This branch of the government has known about us for years now. Known we exist. And they have not done anything to us. They have tried to understand the supernatural. That is all. This is a chance to pull select humans in, to form a partnership, for the good of us all."

He paused.

"I would like to put this to a vote tonight," Quil said. "We are facing demons, someone set them upon us, and we could use the help. Do I have a second for a vote?"

Everyone stared straight at us.

No, not us.

The queen.

I turned slowly and she was smirking, her pet vamps still loungin' on the pillows at her feet but... tense.

Like they knew something was about to happen.

"Collaboration with the humans, Quil?" the queen asked, raisin' a thin eyebrow. "My, my, that is bold. A joint investigation, where we let them see our world, our secrets. Now that's where I have the problem."

My heart raced and I fought the urge to look up into her eyes.

Quil put his hand on my shoulder and Len moved to stand at my other side.

Protectin' me?

"What if instead of bringing them in here, we put one of us in their group?" she asked. "That one would be a true liaison."

Quil tightened beside me.

What did he just figure out? What was happenin'?

"It's a brilliant plan, Quil," she said. "With one *little* adjustment. We'll turn her instead."

Uh-oh.

The queen's gaze fixed on my face and I met her eyes, oxygen rushin' right outta me.

She crashed into my brain; washed through it.

"You're so scared, little one. Don't you want to be safe? We can make you safe. You would have so much. A family to take care of you. You would be part of something."

Pictures popped in my head like bubbles. Quil biting me. Me welcomed into the nest. Being part of them.

Becoming one with them.

I have a family. And I don't want to get sucked into the Borg here.

The voice skipped away.

That wouldn't happen. I'd still be me. Just me with power.

I could save people with power.

I have power. I do save people. That's what I was tellin' Mama. And I don't answer to a tyrant.

"Who said I was a tyrant? I just want to protect my people."

There was that voice again.

She pressed in, reachin' for my memories.

For Quil's treason.

She'll kill him.

"Noooooooooo!" I screamed, jerkin' my gaze away.

I blinked and the world sharpened into reality. Vamps stared at me, mouths hangin' open.

Quil stared at me with wide eyes and crossed himself as I looked at him.

"What did I just do?" I whispered.

He shook his head, blinkin', eyes bouncin' around like he was tryin' to think… and think fast.

"Our queen was gracious enough to back off the little psychic when she saw her mental probe was upsetting the poor girl," Quil said. "Our queen is kind and of course would not want to turn her against her will."

"Of course not," the queen said, voice smooth, eyes flamin'. "We would want her to join us willingly."

Huh?

I kicked her o…

It hit me.

I wasn't *supposed* to be able to fight her off like that and Quil was coverin' for her.

Why?

Quil squeezed my shoulder. "As I was saying before, we should vote on whether to allow the humans and my investigative department to join forces to find and kill these demons and their summoner."

"I second the call for a vote," Len said.

The room held its breath.

"The court moves for a vote," the queen said with a note of formality. "All in favor of allowing Quil to work with a small number of humans in the FBI, say aye with a raise of hands."

Ayes came out slowly, like the vamps were wonderin' what the quack was goin' on here too. Hands went up until almost all of them were.

So they were waitin' to see what the queen wanted.

Yep, nothin' fishy goin' on here.

"Fantastic," Quil said. "We'll return her to her home and contact the FBI after they're up and in the office. Until then…"

Why was he babblin'? He sounded like me.

"Now, now, Quil," the queen said. "We can't be having her rush out. That would be rude. The meeting is basically over. She should stay and mingle."

She looked at me again and this time I damn well kept my eyes off hers.

"Let me get to know her," the queen said, tongue flickin' over her lip.

"I appreciate the hospitality," I said. "But I couldn't. I... um."

"I insist."

My breath snagged in my throat and I knew terror was playin' with my face cuz she smirked.

"We have to work on the case, my queen," Quil said. "She's vital to the investigation and we have to start tracking these demons. They may have already killed again tonight, or be about to. We're going to try to stop them before they can."

Good excuse.

I bowed and took a step back.

Quil grabbed my elbow, holdin' me there.

"May we be excused, my queen?" he asked. "We really must be out there trying to find them. The early hours are their time to strike."

The queen's smile stayed fixed and didn't reach her eyes.

"Go," she said with a wave of her hand.

Quil bowed and nearly took my arm off pullin' me outta there, Len close behind.

# # #

I don't think I took a full breath till we got down the hall, up the stairs, and out into the open air.

I hit my knees in the empty parking lot, arms shakin' as I wrapped them around my middle.

"What the fuck was that!" Len yelled as Quil moved the boulder back into place. "How did she do that?"

"I don't know," Quil said, runnin' his hand over his hair and holding it back as his eyes searched the night. "Ariana, do you know what you did?"

"I uh, fought her off?"

"There are vampires who can't do that."

"Sooooo?" I stared up at him, rubbin' my arms.

"So!" Len said. "I... I can't even. You have power. Power like a vampire."

"Okay? So psychics can-"

"No," Quil said, kneelin' in front of me. "Ariana, vampires, fae, gods, creatures that either were never human or are beyond them now can engage in mental battles; psychics are, at their core, human."

"I feel like I'm missin' something here."

He sighed and put his hands over mine on my arms.

"Ariana, humans can't kick a vampire out. They don't have the skills. It's like expecting a human to run as fast as a vampire. But you just did."

"So she's, what?" Len asked. "Part fae maybe? Descendant of a god?"

Quil shook his head. "You smell either of those on her?"

"I can't smell anything but her perfume right now."

"Take a whiff after she washes it off." Quil focused on me again.

"Ariana, can you do anything else? Do you have better than normal hearing or eyesight? Can you run faster than your peers? What about your sense of smell?"

"Oh, you've got to be kidding me, Quil!" Len said. "Not possible."

"What's not possible?" I asked.

"You being part vamp," Len said. "He wants to know if you have any other powers like us."

"Ummmm." I looked between them. "I thought vamps couldn't reproduce?"

"We can't," Len said. "And there's no such thing as Blade. There's no way any kind of mixing our blood, or biting mommy during birth, or whatever other bullshit Hollywood comes up with, makes a half breed."

"You do know that movie reference is like really old now, right?"

Quil sighed. "You're right, Len. Of course you're right."

"If it helps, I am a crappy runner," I said. "I have exercise induced asthma. My eyesight is good, I don't need glasses or anything, but nothin' special. My hearing is normal. My nose is pretty good, usually for sniffin' out food, but that's it."

"So, some natural power," Quil said, more to himself than either of us, it seemed. "Psychics can't be hypnotized like normal humans, maybe it's an extension of that. But still... after this."

He looked over my head at Len.

"The queen isn't going to let this stand. She'll kill her."

"What!" I said, jerkin' away and climbin' to my feet.

"Ariana, if you can fight a mind as powerful as the queen's, even if she was taking it easy on you, when you're just a human, imagine what you could do if turned?"

"Um." I looked between them. "Are you sayin' what I think you're sayin'?"

"Vampires have powers, levels of powers. You just showed tonight that you are already at a power level above most baby vamps. If you were turned, you would be well on your way to beating the queen."

"And that's why she dropped the whole turnin' me thing so licky skippy?"

"Um... probably. What is licky skippy?"

I grinned. "It's something my mama came up with. Kind of a mix between lickity split and pretty damn skippy."

"Well, yes," Quil said.

He looked down at me, takin' my hands, and the mirth leaked outta me as I met his eyes.

"Can you, ugh, do the mental whammy thing?" I asked.

"I can. It's what makes me such a good investigator." He licked his lips.

"Could you whammy me, if you wanted to?"

"I could try. Knowing the queen, she was going easy on you, since you're *just* a human. But I don't know. I don't know how much she was using on you. Maybe you could shake off a more aggressive attempt. Maybe not."

I licked my lips without thinkin' and he smiled.

"I never did tell you what I wanted to do to that tight little body of yours, did I?"

I shook my head. "Those things you said I was too young to hear? No."

"Feel like growing up a little bit? After that, I know I could use some fun."

My breath caught in my throat and I pulled my hands back, heart sinkin'.

Well there goes that.

"I'm a lady. You don't proposition a lady. You ask her out. You woo her. You're makin' it pretty clear you're only interested in one thing and men like that never last. I actually thought you liked me there for a minute."

Quil's forehead pinched up. "Are you saying you think I don't like you since I just made it clear I do?"

"Makes sense to me," Len said.

I jumped and half turned, makin' him laugh. "Forgot you were there."

"Yeah, I didn't want to interrupt, but sounds like an interpreter's needed here. I speak both genders fluently."

"Freeze!" someone yelled from behind.

We did.

"Turn around with your hands up."

Holy crap on a million crackers and cooked cats too!

I knew that voice.

I held my hands up and turned.

"Ariana?" Grant's asked, arms dropping so his gun was pointed down. "What the fuck are you doing here?"

I grinned so hard it was painful. "I was invited to a vamp meeting, General?"

He cocked a finger. "You both are coming with me."

Both?

I looked around.

Len was long gone.

So it looked like it was just me and Quil hangin' in the park.

"I actually need to be leaving," Quil said. "Sorry, Ariana. We'll be in touch."

And he blurred away.

Grant glared at me and his eyes, I sooooo was not meetin'.

"General, I-"

"Not. One. Word. Ryder," he said, swipin' his phone on. "Crowley, what's going on out there?"

Grant nodded along, and glanced at me. "No, hear him out."

He hung up and hit a few buttons. "Kowalski, stop trying to call Ryder in." Grant pursed his lips. "She's already here."

I checked my phone. Jet had called six times in the past half hour.

Oops, crap, and a pile of swear words all rolled into one steamin' pile.

"We'll be there soon," Grant said. "Process the scene."

Oh no.

Grant hung up and jerked his head at the van.

We walked over and I hopped in my side. Grant started us up and I opened my mouth to ask why they were over in this parking lot when he shook his head.

"Dead girl. No ID. Same MO. Why were you here?"

"Quil woke me up around four, General. He said he needed my help because... well, they have leaders in areas and the queen here is a real tyrant. She's abusing her people and is pulling a serious big gov move with them and-"

"The point?" Grant said.

"Okay, he said we had to get the queen to agree for us to work together and I had to go in to talk to them and couldn't bring you guys cuz you're just humans and she'd kill you and now we're going to work together and learn all this stuff about the supernatural. And the queen agreed to it. We're gonna set up a meeting to talk about this all and... and I think I'm done."

"That's it?"

Tellin' him about the whole queen mental whammy and me fighting her off was not gonna happen.

"Yes, sir."

"You didn't think to call in backup?"

Uh-oh, that was not a good tone. When I get mad, my voice heats up. Grant's the exact opposite. His drops to Arctic.

Judgin' by the fact that I suddenly wanted a sweater, I was in serious trouble.

"I did! Quil told me I couldn't, that he had to ease everyone into working with us and that meant just me. If we tried to go in with more than just one, they wouldn't have reacted well and we all could've died."

"You could have told us what you were doing."

"He told me not to."

"You don't answer to him, Ryder. Until I fire you, you answer to me."

"Until?"

We pulled into the next lot in the park and he parked and turned to me.

I stared down. Geez, still couldn't look him in the eyes.

I was able to look a-who-knows-how-old vampire queen in the eyes, but one minute with my boss glued my gaze to my lap.

"Why didn't you tell me, Ryder?"

"You would have told me not to go, sir."

"You're damn right I would have." He slammed his fist sideways into the dash, makin' me jump.

Grant grabbed my chin, yankin' it up. "You ever pull this shit again, I'll do worse than fire you. This stupidity and immaturity is unacceptable. You do not go off on your own. You do not make that call. You are green and fucking stupid. You got that?"

"I didn't-"

"Only words coming out of your mouth right now should be, 'Yes, sir.'"

"No!"

His eyes narrowed.

"No. I'm not a child. You want to yell at me, sure, but let me go. You wouldn't do this with anyone else."

He tightened his grip on my chin, pullin' my face close.

"If you were anyone else, Ryder," he whispered, "you would never have gotten this job. Even if you did, you would be fired right now. You have no sense, no judgment, and no respect, so if I want to grab your chin, I will. If I want to spank you like a child to get the lesson to stick, I will."

"Don't make promises you're not gonna keep, sir," I said.

What the frick has gotten into me! Did I really just say that to Grant?

Grant let me go, face locked up tighter than a chastity belt.

"We are going to get one thing straight right now, Ryder. You're a child and you act like it. You and I are never going to happen. It was cute at first, but get over it. I need an agent, not a groupie. Stop pouting, twirling your hair and batting your eyes. Grow the fuck up and do your job."

He got out of the van, grabbing his pack and slamming the door.

Just in time too.

I curled up on the seat, cryin' out shards of my heart as Grant marched past the trees into the park without lookin' back.

# # #

When I got to the crime scene just beyond the tree line, the place was already hoppin'. The guys had already bagged and tagged the scene and Kat and Grant were zipping up the body.

The woman was a tall brunette, pretty like the other two, dressed in a pair of undone grey pants and a blue silk top. And she had no panties or shoes. Par for the course by now.

Grant nodded at me stiff jawed and I knelt and touched the body without a word.

Flash.

She walked arm in arm with a large guy. I couldn't see his face.

"I love the ring, baby." She waved her hand in front of his face, a large diamond engagement ring shining from it.

She drifted to one side. "Whoa, I'm dizzy."

He wrapped an arm around her back.

"I really don't feellll wegrtlll..."

She slumped and he scooped her up and carried her past the trees.

It was the same as the first. He pulled down her pants, ripped off her underwear, slipped on a condom, and raped her unconscious body. He took her shoes and put them in his pocket, and leaned over her.

He shoved two small prongs into her neck and the blood flowed out into an attached vacuum. He tucked that into his pocket once he was done.

I jerked outta the vision, shakin' as I leaned back.

Into nothin'.

I looked up and Grant stared down at me.

Wow, he really was done.

I said what I saw, stood up, and dusted my knees off.

We wrapped up the processing pretty fast.

Jet asked where my car was. I told him, and Grant took my arm before Jet could say anything else.

"Right," Jet said. "Grant will take you to your car and I will see you later."

Grant pulled me back to the van and I didn't even try to fight it. We got in without a word.

"General?" I asked as he started it up.

"I am so mad at you right now, Ryder," Grant said, voice chipped ice. "I can't fire you. You know that. But you have to learn."

I looked up as the van started to move.

Was there an end to that statement?

Did I want to know?

"You have skated so long without consequences," Grant finally said after a freakin' long two minutes.

No, really, I counted.

"You're special, so you have been fast tracked, given preferential treatment, and haven't been punished for screw ups. That ends tonight."

My stomach lurched and my eyes filled with tears. "I thought I was doing what I could to get us a valuable ally."

"You're a junior agent. That wasn't your call. Give me your badge."

"Grant?" My voice broke.

"I don't want to hear it, Ryder. You are on probation."

I dug through my purse with shakin' hands, half blind with tears.

I handed it over and he took it without lookin' away from the road.

"You're on desk," Grant said, pullin' into the lot with my lonely car. "You will only go to scenes to get visions, and until this case is over, you will have nothing to do with any of the vampires in that nest. Go home. I want you in the office by nine."

"How long?" I croaked as I climbed out.

"Until I'm convinced you have learned your lesson and can be trusted."

He reached over, slammed the door and sped off, leaving me cryin' in the dark.

CHAPTER TEN

I DON'T REMEMBER DRIVIN' BACK TO my house, just strugglin' with the keys and bursting inside, then driftin' in and out on the couch until I had to get ready for work.

I was in the office just before nine with our usual coffee orders.

"Girl," Jet said as he took his cup.

He didn't hug me this time.

I opened my mouth, eyes stingin', and shook my head. Any words and I'd start to cry again.

I put Dan's coffee on his desk.

He nodded, givin' me a look I'd swear was sympathy if I didn't know better.

I put Grant's on his desk instead of handin' it to him, then sat at mine.

No one said anything for a minute.

Grant took a swig of his coffee. "Kowalski, the girl. Bridges, with Irish. Ryder," he said, gettin' up and droppin' a stack of papers the size of a Tolstoy novel on my desk, "you know where you are. Run the coffee down to Kat. Your ass better be back at this desk in five minutes."

He got on his computer and we all jumped to.

I ran the coffee to Kat, told her I couldn't talk, and she promised to find me once the autopsy was done. I was back within the five minutes, and got to work on the impossible stack.

Okay, here's the thing, when he said he'd do worse than fire me, he meant it.

Paperwork sucks!

I spent the morning buried in reports, spreadsheets, and financial records.

"Hey," Jet said around lunch time, droppin' a sandwich on my desk. My favorite, a BLT with cucumber, pickles and banana peppers thrown on.

100

"Wow, I must be in bigger trouble than I thought." I grabbed my baconey goodness. "What's this? Last meal time?"

He pulled his chair over and sat next to me. "You really stepped in it."

"I know."

"What were you thinking?"

"It seemed like a good idea at the time?" I shrugged. "Looking back, obviously I was an idiot, but I was tryin' to help."

"Ariana, please don't tell me you have a thing for that vamp?" He unwrapped his vegetarian sandwich.

Ya know what? If it doesn't have meat on it, it's not a sandwich.

"I can't."

"You're lucky Grant didn't fire you. You compromised a case, girl."

I didn't say anything.

"Ariana, you're the exception here. Everyone else had to be twenty-three and have experience. That's how it works. But you didn't. Every day, you have to learn on the job, in the field, and until yesterday, you weren't doing bad. But Grant vouched for you. When he invited you to join, he was sticking his neck out. And last night, you took an ax to it."

Tears stung my eyes.

"Girl, you scared us. When I couldn't get a hold of you, Grant's first words were, 'She always answers her phone.' He was scared. So was I."

"I'm sorry I scared you."

"Good. That's a start." He nodded. "I've got to go." He got up with his sandwich.

"What's her name?"

"Amber Chase. She was a manager of a clothing store in the West End mini-mall. I talked to her boyfriend. He was nowhere near the place last night. He was at their home down in Bellevue."

His lip trembled.

"And she never made it home. Jet, I'm so sorry."

I couldn't believe Grant put him on that, he really had no heart today.

"When did Kat put time of death?" I asked.

"Just after eleven, probably right after she closed for the night."

"That breaks his pattern though, why?"

Jet shrugged. "That's for me to find out. Bye, girl."

He walked away and I went back to the mountain of papers.

Grant sat down about an hour later, Jet and Dan close behind.

"Kowalski?" Grant said once they were settled.

"Name's Amber Chase," Jet said. "Twenty-six. Boyfriend identified the body. She was the manager of Dr. Blue's lingerie shop in that mini-mall. It's owned by a parent company that I traced back to a Todd Jacobson. Not much on him in the system. Still looking."

"Irish and I ran the fingerprints off the bodies," Dan said. "The prints on Jo were a match to the bartender, Dave Rattie. The ones on Miranda matched her father's. And the ones on Amber were, big surprise, the boyfriend's."

Miranda went off with who she thought was her father, and was raped by the demon in her father's form?

My stomach lurched and I gagged.

That was too sick.

"Miranda was at a yacht party the night she was murdered," Grant said. "The captain said he was talking to Miranda after and a man she said was her dad picked her up at the wharf."

"I don't think we're going to find these guys with the usual pound the pavement, General," Jet said.

Grant nodded. "Ryder, go up to Irish and go over the evidence."

I broke into a grin. "So I'm...?"

"No. You're still on desk. You just get to investigate right now because we need all hands and I need you to get a vision."

"Yes, sir." I ran up to Irish.

"You okay, lass?" he asked, starin' at me a little too hard, like he was fixin' to say something.

"You heard?"

"The entire building heard."

"Did you hear all of it?"

He eyed me over his microscope. "How would I know? I don't know what I don't know. Now do I?"

I rolled my eyes. "Grant got mean."

He raised bushy eyebrows at me. "You mean he got strict."

"What?" I crossed my arms.

"Let's just say the word millennial has been tossed around a lot lately."

My jaw dropped. "I am not being a typical millennial."

"I didn't say it. I think you're acting like you've been allowed to act because you're psychic. Most millennials think they're special. You actually are. Maybe try not to take advantage of it so much in the future."

"I don't even understand what I did, Irish." I walked over and leaned against the counter next to him. "I mean before last night, which was stupid of me. But Grant's actin' like this was the last straw and I don't know what the first ones were."

"That is part of the problem. You don't realize when you're getting special treatment or crossing the line."

"How am I supposed to know if no one tells me?"

"That's a good point. Like I said, you're acting like... you act, because everyone has let you."

I narrowed my eyes. "What were you going to say?"

"Ariana."

"Come on. How will I learn?"

"I was going to say… you act a little entitled."

I gasped.

"And spoiled," he said, holdin' up his hands. "I say this with love."

"How… how do I fix it then?"

"Accept the consequences of your actions and do it without complaining, don't come in late, don't ask for special little things no one else gets, don't run off on a case by yourself."

"I just said, I admit that was stupid."

"And stop acting like every personal thing is a crisis that the whole office has to hear about."

I wrinkled my nose. "Do I really do that?"

"This is the first time there has actually been talk about you that didn't get started by you telling half the office yourself."

He nailed me with his eyes.

"You are special, Ariana, and we are lucky to have you."

"Thanks."

But I still felt… deflated.

"I gotta get on the evidence," I said.

"Do you, my psychic princess. Do you."

I smiled and took the evidence to my nesting corner.

I took out Amber's top, runnin' my fingers over it. Irish had already run tests on the clothes and couldn't find anything out of the ordinary, but those were just for drugs or unusual substances.

I switched to the pants.

Flash.

The demon was over Amber's limp body. He took the condom off and tucked it into his pocket just like he did before. A drop of liquid flew off and landed on the pants.

"Oh my God!" I squealed.

Irish jumped off his stool, grabbing at his chest. "Don't do that, lass. My heart can't take it."

Right, Irish had heart problems. He'd had a heart attack when he was thirty-five.

"He screwed up!" I bounced to Irish with the pants and pointed to the spot. "Right here. I saw it. He took off the condom, put it in his pocket, but some of the fluid got flicked off."

"I ran it under the UV," Irish said, shaking his head. "How did I miss it?"

"It's kinda under the zipper," I said. "It's not your fault."

"Another thing about being an adult, Ariana, take responsibility when you screw up. I missed this and I shouldn't have."

"Okay then." I nodded. "Bad you."

"Let's run it."

He swabbed the spot while I grabbed the baggie for it and labeled it.

He scanned the sample into the computer.

It takes hours to run DNA through the computers to sequence it. Irish explained it to me once. Basically what they do is find sixteen alleles and look at them, and we can match it to DNA samples cuz the chances of two humans having all sixteen the same are astronomical.

I fondled the other pieces of evidence while he sequenced the first allele used to test.

"Oh dear," he said after a while. "Ariana!"

"Yeah."

He typed a few keys and pointed to the screen as a picture popped up.

"I don't get it," I said.

"That's the DNA."

"Um, I'm not an expert, but aren't there only supposed to be two of the swirly things?" I asked as Irish's fingers flew over the machine's attached computer.

"Yes. The double helix is one of the most stable structures in all of nature, that's why DNA evolved that way. This is…"

He ran his hands through his thin hair, mouth workin'.

"This is impossible," he finally said. "You know how DNA works, there's one strand and a complimenting one. These have one strand, and then these other two compliment it. And the bonds go between all three." He shook his head. "This can't be possible."

"Irish, we just proved the demons have DNA, and that it doesn't change when they change their looks!" I squealed again and hugged him.

"True, lass, but it's…"

I grinned and called Grant.

"Grant," he said.

"General, we got something huge. You have to get to the lab."

He hung up and blew into the lab not a minute later.

"Go," he said.

I looked at Irish and he rolled a hand in my direction.

"This was your discovery, lass; I just ran it through the computer."

"Okay. I was going over Amber's clothes, and when I touched the pants, wham! Vision close up, which was actually kinda gross, I mean, those things aren't pretty under normal circumstances and… not important, right. He took off the condom and put it in his pocket but some fluids flew off onto her pants. We have a DNA sample!"

"Ryder." Grant circled his hand, telling me to get to the point.

"Sorry. Focusing. We put it in the machine. And this is what we got."

I did my best Vanna White arm swirl at the screen.

"What the hell is that?"

"*That* is a triple helix." I bounced on the balls of my feet. "It's demon

DNA. Not only did he screw up by leaving DNA, we have proof that demons have DNA, and that they can't change it even when they change their looks, and it doesn't resemble anything around here."

"Ryder, calm down," Grant said. "This is fascinating, and I'm sure Irish will have fun breaking this down for a year, but it doesn't bring us any closer to catching them."

"Oh." My feet landed squarely on the floor. "Right."

"Go over the evidence, think about seeing where these demons are now."

I nodded and he left.

"This is still huge," I said.

"You don't need to convince me," Irish said, going back to his computers.

# # #

After another hour of playing with the evidence, I cracked my neck and sat back.

"What I need is a vision of the next victim before it happens," I said as I re-packaged the evidence. "Why can't I get those? Ya know, a nice painted out picture of who, where, and when. That would be helpful."

Irish shrugged, eyes glued to the DNA analysis.

"I'm outta here." I kissed his soft, cool cheek and left.

"Bye, lass."

"I told Len to have everyone connected to the girls make a list of possible enemies," Grant was saying to the guys as I walked up to our set of desks.

"That's gonna be one monster of a list to run down, General," I said.

"Yes, it is. We're meeting with them tonight. You're coming to get visions, Ryder, but you're on a short leash.

"Yes, sir," I said with a nod, goin' back to my desk and grabbin' the next piece of the stack of paperwork.

Grant met my eyes and gave a short, sharp nod.

I grinned.

CHAPTER ELEVEN

"WHAT DO YOU THINK IS gonna happen?" I asked after we sat at the otherwise empty café, practically wigglin' outta my seat.

Alfonzo's is usually open until nine, but when the FBI asks you to close early, you do it.

"The vampires think they may be able to follow the demon's scent off the clothing," Grant said. "They have been making suspect lists, and will tell us what they know of demons."

Quil opened the door and I sat up straighter.

Grant shot me a look and I smiled, mouthing, "Sorry."

He shook his head and rose as Quil, Len, and two women walked to our table.

"Good evening," Quil said.

He was dressed in black suit pants and a light purple button-up, and Len had shaved and was in jeans and a nice red top.

The two strangers looked to be in their twenties, human years obviously. The first had long blond hair, dark blue eyes, was about six inches taller than me, and had a lithe, athletic build under her jeans and silky blue top.

The second was a beautiful Latina with the prettiest cinnamon skin I've ever seen, nearly as tall as the first but with a curvy body in a red wrap dress, and large dark eyes.

"Hey, darling." Len wrapped his arm around my shoulders and I leaned into him.

"Hey."

The guys pulled out chairs for the women to sit, then grabbed their own. Gentlemen, my my.

Grant looked at Quil. "Hello again. Ladies, I'm Special Agent Grant. This is Kowalski, Bridges, and Ryder." He nodded to each of us in turn.

"Carla Dumount," Quil said, inclinin' his head towards the Latina, "and

Stephanie Interhiemer."

"Demons," Grant said. "Go."

"Everything you ever wanted to know about demons but were afraid to ask?" Len asked, grinning.

Oh, he was tryin' so hard to lighten the mood.

"Something like that," Grant said, staring at Quil.

"Demons come from what we call the Other Side. It's a parallel dimension," Quil said.

I nodded. We already knew that.

"They can't stay here during the day even if they want to. They have to be summoned to cross over," Quil said. "Which requires a massive amount of energy and usually an offering to get them to come. They then do jobs in exchange for payment they can take back to their dimension."

"As far as we can tell," Len said, "there are as many different types of demons as there are humans. Some are evil, some are not, they have lives, jobs, families over there. Many of the ones that come here are evil and or just like chaos."

"Other than that, we don't know much more general things," Quil said once it was clear Len was done. "We do know more specific things about certain types though."

"Types? Do you mean different species?" Jet asked.

Quil nodded. "We believe we're dealing with Sumnticors."

Of course, cuz you can't have demons with a boring, pronounceable name like Hulks or anything.

"They're ruthless, take trophies, and can copy human faces," Quil said. "They can block psychic powers, and are near impossible to kill. They're as strong as us and regenerate even faster. The only way to kill them is to dismember them completely and burn the pieces."

He smiled. "Actually, it used to be nearly impossible to kill them. They blow up just as well as anything else in this dimension, and no one can grow back from tiny pieces."

"You've done this before," Grant said. It wasn't a question.

Quil smiled. "Only on someone who deserved it."

"Are you confessing to a murder?"

"None in your jurisdiction."

"Who was it?"

"No," Quil said. "Now that your disapproval is noted, can we get back to the case?"

My lips formed into a little O of surprise. No one talks to Grant that way.

Grant leaned forward. "I don't trust you, and you're not giving me any reasons to."

"The feeling isn't mutual. I trust you."

Grant blinked.

Ohhhhh, point Quil.

"And you're trusting us because you need us," Quil said. "Science and human methods of investigation aren't going to help you stop these demons or find the summoner."

Grant didn't say anything, just kept starin'.

Quil sighed. "If you give us the victims' clothes, we might be able to track the demon."

Annnnnnd point Grant.

"Carla is the nest's best tracker," Quil said. "If there's anything of the demon on the clothes, she will be able to sort through the smells."

"And speaking of smells." Stephanie pinched her nose, shootin' me a snide glare.

Don't ask me how a glare can be snide, it just was.

"You're not exactly subtle, sweetheart," she said.

"Excuse me?" I asked.

"Hair back, high collar, perfume. I think you made your point to our Quil quite clear."

"I'm not tryin' to make a point," I said, clenching my fists. "I'm a federal agent and this is a case. I'm doing what I have to to make sure I'm not pushing any buttons."

I looked her in the eyes and reached for her hand.

She jerked it back faster than a surprised snake and I smirked.

"That was me proving a point," I said. "Something to hide?"

"I don't like bitches poking around my brain."

"Leave this personal shit out," Grant said.

I jerked and looked at him.

He was staring at Stephanie.

Ohhhh, so that was directed at her, not me.

She met his eyes then looked away.

"What does she contribute?" Grant asked Quil.

"I'm the demolitions expert," Stephanie said with a wide smile. "Once we track them, I can set up the explosives and we can blow them to hell. We just need to find them first."

Her big blue eyes landed on me.

"No!" Quil said. "I already told you that's not going to happen. We'll track them and use your grenades to kill them. We don't need to lay a trap, we're not going to, and that's final."

She crossed her arms.

"You want to use me as bait," I said. "It's not a bad idea."

"No," Grant and Quil said as one.

"Ohhhh, I love the smell of testosterone in the evening," Stephanie said.

"We shared, it's your turn," Quil said to Grant.

"Ryder, you're up." Grant waved at me.

"Oh, me, okay," I said. "Wow, really wish Irish would've come with us, but hey. Well, I found some semen on the clothes of the last victim, and we ran them... er, it, and it's most certainly not human. We, I mean every living thing on the planet, have the double helix; the DNA in the semen we found was a triple. Now, it's not much, and it's not like we have something to compare it to, but if you find the demon, we can tell you without a doubt if he's our guy."

"So you found it how?" Quil asked.

"Vision," I said. "Kind of a close up shot."

His eyes finally found mine and I saw pity behind the beautiful swirls of blue and green.

"How do you do it?" Carla asked and I jerked away from Quil's stare. "How do you see all that and not go insane?"

I flushed and shrugged. "I see, I tell, I forget the best I can."

"Wow. God bless you for bearing that burden."

I glanced at Jet. He stared at Carla, shock naked on his face.

I looked back at Carla and realized he was starin' at the cross hanging just above her neckline.

"You have the clothes here?" Quil asked.

"In the truck," Grant said.

"Then what are we waiting for?" Quil jumped up and the other vamps followed suit.

I stood with the guys and met Quil's eyes again.

He smiled, lickin' his lips, and my heart jumped up and caught in my throat.

He turned and walked out of the shop. I took a deep breath and followed.

Grant turned off the lights and locked up behind our group.

"Whoa!" Carla breathed when Grant pulled open the door of our big black van. "It's like CSI or something."

"Carla and I have a thing for cop shows," Quil said.

Grant pulled out the evidence bags that held the items of clothing and handed one over to Carla.

"They've been processed, you can touch them, but you have to use gloves." He handed her a pair of gloves and she tugged them on.

I'm the only one allowed to handle evidence without gloves, and even that's technically against the rules.

Carla pulled out the pants and took a deep breath. "Okay, I've got it. There's three separate smells. One's the girl, she was wearing perfume, second is some male, but the third's a trace of something definitely not human."

"Three?" I asked, then snapped my fingers. "Oh! Could the second be the guy he was impersonating?"

"Possibly," Carla said. "Do you have anything of his?"

"We ran the clothes he was wearing that night today." Grant pulled out the bags with the guy's clothes and handed them to her.

She took a sniff straight from the bag and nodded. "That's it."

"He said he hadn't seen her since the night before, and she'd changed since then," Jet said. "So unless he was lying, which, why would he, the demon's outside takes on the scent of the person he's copying."

"They also have their fingerprints," I said. "So outside changes but inside doesn't?"

"Okay." Carla nodded. "You get me within a mile of these guys and I will be able to track them."

"A mile!" I asked.

"They call me the shark." She grinned. "I can take one scent out of the wind and track it, like a shark with blood in the water."

"Damn, girl," Jet said. "Now that is impressive."

"Best tracker this side of the Atlantic," Quil said.

"They're probably looking for their next victim," I said. "Is the club open tonight?"

"It is," Len said. "I left it in Joseph's hands, he's my assistant manager. You don't think the demon would go back?"

"You guys are still keeping everyone close, like telling any humans that know about you to stay in, and not to leave with anyone, even their honeys, right?" I asked and he nodded. "Then the demons might go back because it's the only place to really find anyone outside their homes."

"To the club in the crime-mobile," Len said, pointin' to the van dramatically.

"And why are you here?" Grant asked.

Len pouted. "I'm the comedic relief."

"Obviously, but this is a real case, not a TV show. We don't need comedic relief."

"Special Agent Grant, *you*, of all people, definitely need comedic relief."

"He's staying," Quil said. "He's my backup."

"Meaning?" Grant asked.

"Meaning it's my job to keep him out of trouble," Len said, tossin' me a wink.

What the quack was that for?

Was it some kind of code meaning I was the trouble?

Oh wow, that came out soooo much dirtier than I meant.

"We'll go in our cars," Quil said, "and meet you there."

The vamps climbed into two cars on the street, Quil and Len in his convertible, and the two girls into a shiny black BMW.

Snazzy.

We got into our van and drove to the club, Jet and Dan makin' small talk I could barely hear in the front, Grant staring ahead, gripping the wheel so tight his knuckles were white.

"Sir?" I asked, keeping my voice low so the guys in back hopefully couldn't hear us.

"What, Ryder?"

"Why are you hurtin' the steering wheel?"

"Because my dad taught me to never hit a woman."

My stomach lurched.

"You mean me? Why do you want to hurt me?"

He took a deep breath. "Ever since you came to the Bureau, we have been turned upside down. The rules don't apply and there's this little pixy running around without a care in the world."

"I'm tryin' to act more professional, sir."

"I'm. Not. Done. You turned us on our ear, and you are my responsibility. When you're careless, it's on me. You could have died. And if you did, it would be on me."

"No, it wouldn't, you're-"

"I am the boss, Ryder. You're my rookie. If you die, if you get yourself killed being stupid, I will never forgive myself."

I flinched.

He was starin' ahead, but he looked… worried?

Maybe even scared.

"I'm sorry, sir. I'm so sorry I ran off on my own."

"It's not just that. It's where you ran to. These people are dangerous, Ariana. They could kill you, me, Kowalski, all before we could pull a weapon. I don't think you realize that."

"I do, sir."

"But?"

"I trust Quil. I don't know about the others. But I trust him."

"Yeah, so do I."

I grinned. Grant was never wrong.

"I don't like it though," he said.

"If you trust him, what don't you like?" I asked.

"You liking him, for one." His eyebrows went up. "Don't get any ideas. I'm worried he'll drag you into dangerous situations, I'm not jealous."

"Wow." I blushed, looking down. "We really are just airing this all out, huh?"

"Me ignoring it wasn't helping."

Grant pulled into the parking lot and parked next to the building in the loading zone, and turned to me.

"I have a teenage girl. And I've seen her through crushes that didn't pan out. I thought ignoring yours would help. It didn't. Direct seems best here."

"I'm not a thirteen year old girl, Grant."

"No, but you are a twenty-three year old one, and I see you as a child. One I have to protect. I don't like Quil because he is hundreds of years old, and hitting on a child I see as too young for me at thirty-eight."

He took my face in his hands and leaned forward and kissed my forehead.

"You are special, Ariana, and not just for your gifts."

He got out of the van and I took a breath.

I'm so confused.

I really wanted to call Mama right now.

I got out of the van and met the others in a circle near the backdoor.

Carla sniffed around. "They're not here."

"It's early," I said. "The first two weren't attacked till near dawn, and the last was around midnight."

"Maybe they spend the night stalking their victims, so they'll know how to lure them?" Jet said. "Which is why the first two were attacked in morning, and maybe he just got stuff off the third faster, so he killed her earlier."

"Makes sense. So then they'd be here stalking," I said.

"We split up," Grant said. "One team checks any places your people could be tonight, try to sniff out the demons, and one to stay with Ryder and see if she can get a vision."

Oh great, no pressure there.

I rolled my eyes.

Quil smiled at me and I wrinkled my nose, shaking it at him.

"Who's with me?" Carla asked, lookin' between Quil and Grant.

Ha, she wasn't sure who was in charge.

"Stephanie," Quil said. "So if you find them, she can be there as backup. And I'm assuming you want some of your humans on this?" he asked Grant.

"Yes, you three can take Jet and Dan and we'll take Len," Grant said.

"I believe," Quil said, "you mean the girls should take Jet and Dan, because I'm staying here."

"Why?" Grant asked.

"Because I've worked with a few psychics in my day and I can teach Ariana some tricks to open her mind's eye better. Also, I can track, so if she does get a vision and we go off after the demons before the girls can meet back up with us, you're going to need someone who can smell them coming."

"And Len can't do that?"

"Sorry." Len shrugged. "I've been an entertainer since I was alive. I've never really honed my sense of smell past tracking down my next boyfriend, and I know next to nothing about psychic tricks."

"But the demons don't smell like demons on the outside," I said. "Right? Wait, so how do we track them anyway?"

"They aren't always in a human guise," Carla said. "And there's a subtle smell of them under the human smell, I could tell on the girl's clothes. There was more than just the smell off that tiny dot."

Grant growled under his breath and whispered something harsh.

"Kowalski, Bridges, enjoy your dates for the evening," Grant said. "Stay in your group, no one goes anywhere alone, these things could be any of us." He paused. "How do we know it isn't? We've been around each other all day, and no one's gone off since sunset, but what about you four?"

"We've been together all day at the nest," Carla said. Quil nodded behind her.

Grant nodded once and waved them goodbye.

"Ladies, we would be honored to escort you," Dan said, eyein' Stephanie.

"Bridges," Grant said, "am I going to have a problem with you too?"

Too? Excuse me? Too! What was that supposed to mean?

Okay, I knew what that was supposed to mean.

"No, sir," he said.

They left in the BMW, earbuds and guns on so they'd hopefully be ready for anything.

"Okay," I said with a tight smile once it was just me, my boss, and the two vamps. "If we want me to get a vision, I have to wash this stuff off."

The perfume could block my powers, especially since I put on so much before we left.

"You don't go alone," Grant said.

"I've got her," Len said. "If anything attacks, I can zoom her out of there."

We all knew why it couldn't be Quil.

"I don't know if it's a good idea to leave those two alone," I said once we got into the club's bathroom.

"Oh they're just guys... yeah, we should probably hurry," Len said. "You know he likes you."

I snorted. "Yeah, with his penis."

"No, he's just... used to women of your generation being a little more responsive to the direct approach."

"You mean slutty."

"He wasn't trying to insult you... and anyway, I was expecting you to ask me which one."

He winked at me in the mirror.

"Oh, come on now." I grabbed some paper towels and wetted them, scrubbin' my neck. "Grant's made it clear that's not how he feels. And Quil... he has like four hundred years on me. And... if he's that easy, or thinks I am... I don't... I can't."

"He doesn't. He doesn't think you're easy. He likes you. He wants to see where it goes. What happened to you?"

I paused, lookin' at him in the mirror. "What do you mean?"

"Your reaction when Quil wanted to go home with you wasn't the reaction of a woman with a guy she likes. It was the reaction of one who has been hurt."

I tossed my towels and flapped a hand at him, grabbin' another bunch of towels to wet down. "It's nothin'... and so long ago."

"But someone did crush your heart."

I scrubbed off my neck one more time. "I was fifteen. Waaaaaay too young."

"You know in Quil's day, that was when they married off girls, right?"

I laughed and tossed the bunch of towels. "Yeah, I read Romeo and Juliet. But in my day, it's too young to be havin' sex. And I was so broken. I was depressed and... and I swore I'd learn from my mistakes. It's been almost eight years and I haven't made that mistake again."

"And that was?"

"Never sleep with a guy just cuz he says he likes you. Make him wait."

"Do you want to make him wait?"

I grinned. "No, I don't, but... I can't do that again. I can't."

"You wouldn't be. Learn to trust your instincts. Not all guys are looking to use and lose you."

"What's it like to be gay? Is it easier? Since you're the same gender, I mean?"

"Easier to communicate?"

"Yeah."

He shrugged. "Wouldn't know. You'll have to ask a bi person."

"Ha. Good point."

We headed back out and Grant and Quil were standin' across from each other, so stiff backed you could put tick marks on them and use 'em as rulers. Quil was double fisting it but both drinks were full.

Quil shut up mid-sentence as we walked up.

Why did I have the feeling they were talkin' about me?

"Um, so what do I do here?" I asked.

"I can help you try to get more helpful visions," Quil said. "What do you normally do?"

I knelt on my blanket in the spot Jo had been left in, spread her personal effects around me and lit my incense.

Quil took a deep whiff as he sat down next to me. "Sandalwood. Perfect. That was one thing I was going to suggest. The next is this."

He handed me one of the drinks and I smelled it.

"Whoa!" I jerked back. "That's strong. What is that?"

"It's a Cumberland River. Because you'll want to float down it after you drink one."

"Haha. What's in it?"

"Apple vodka, melon liqueur and champagne to top it off."

Grant made a noise in the back of his throat and Quil shook his head.

"Alcohol opens the mind and lowers inhibitions," Quil said. "More than a few drinks and they're useless because of too much input, but one or two good strong drinks should do her."

"I know," Grant said and I blushed.

The one time I'd gotten drunk with the guys was the day after my birthday.

We were in Atlantic city for the weekend and I'd had one too many.

Well, more like four too many.

All I remember is seeing a lot of things that weren't there, at least not physically, and passing out. Grant took me to my hotel room to sleep it off and stayed just in case I had any problems, which according to him I did. First I wanted to go back out to the casino to play with the unicorns, then there was a severe vomiting incident that I still don't remember.

"Bad experience," I said to Quil, takin' a long sip of the drink. "Ohhhh, sweet baby Jesus, that's delicious."

"Down it," Quil said. "I'll get you another."

I nodded and gulped it down.

"Whoo!" I slammed the glass down and Quil grabbed the top of it just in time to keep it from hitting the blacktop too hard.

"Maybe we'll give this a minute before I get you another," he said.

"Sorry."

"That's okay. Vamp reflexes here." He put the glass down. "Now, close your eyes. We're going to try something here. It will take a bit for the alcohol to work, but we can at least start."

I closed my eyes.

"The demon stalks his prey," Quil said. "He has one right now. Is watching her."

Cold fingers touched my temples and I hopped in place, taking a deep breath and clenching my hands as my heart sped.

Of course, he could probably hear it clear as a train.

"He is already planning on how to get her drugged and alone," Quil said. "Maybe there's a friend or family member he could reappear as."

I drifted away on that voice, sunk into it like a bath full of bubbles and port.

"They like pretty ones," he said. "They see her now. You can feel the rapist's lust. He changes to look like someone she knows, someone she trusts. Look back in your past, when you've felt safe and trusting. With a parent, a best friend, a lover. *Feel* that trust."

Flash.

"Yeah, don't worry, baby. I'm heading there right now."

She was nearly as short as me, had dyed red hair and dark skin, kind of a pug nose, but still pretty. She talked into the phone as she marched across the dark parking lot, the steps singing with the clickity clack alacrity of her impractical and hot heels, and a laptop bag swung with her.

"You said Quil told you they don't attack this early." She rolled her eyes at whatever the person on the other side said. "I can't believe how many rules you guys have. I will be there soon and you will see I am perfectly fine."

She unlocked the door of a blue sedan as she nodded.

"Yes, if any guy, even you, approaches me, I'll run the other direction."

Yeah, like she could run in those shoes.

"You too, bye."

She hung up and I caught a glimpse of the time before she snapped the cell shut. Just before ten.

"Hey!" a voice behind her called.

I couldn't see the face of the person, but it was a female voice, and it was wearing a long black coat way too big for the average height girl. "Sorry, Jen, but we need you back in there."

"Whyyyyyy? I'm supposed to meet my boyfriend."

"The computer just crapped out on us. We lost everything," the other girl said. "Unless we want an F on our project tomorrow, we have to load back up all the slides from everyone's computers and put them in order again."

"Shit!" Jen nodded. "I have to call my boyfriend back. He's not going to be happy."

"Does he own you?"

"He worries. It's sweet." She flipped on the phone and it blinked back off. "Oh come on! My battery died." She waved it at the other girl.

"You can borrow mine. It's inside."

"It's okay." Quil was behind me, holding me up as I gasped for air, his arms around me before I even remembered where I was.

I leaned into him and my breathing slowed.

"Ow!" he yelped, lettin' me go and getting on his feet before I could turn around.

Len stood over me with his arms crossed. "You told me to slap you."

"Yes, I did." Quil nodded, rubbing his head. "Good to know you're so quick to follow orders."

"What I'm here for." Len grinned.

Grant kneeled in front of me. "What did you see?"

I told them. "So do any of your guys have a college girlfriend named Jen? She's black… maybe Indian ethnicity, dyed red hair, great taste in designer shoes?"

"Shit, that's Ron's girl," Len said.

I twisted Grant's wrist to check his watch. "She hung up the phone at nine fifty, and it's nine forty. Holy crap on a cracker! I actually saw the future! Only a few minutes, but I've never seen the freaking future before!'"

"Celebrate later," Grant said. "Where does she go to school?"

"Vandy," Len said. "She's in the MBA program."

"Owen Business School is up on twenty-first, sir," I said. "Other side of the campus."

"I don't know her number, but I'll call him," Len said.

He walked a few feet away and we waited in silence. I grabbed my incense and blew it out, wrappin' it up in its plastic and putting it away.

I turned and reached for the bowl and my hand grazed another, making me jump.

I looked up to meet Quil's eyes.

"I wanted to help," he said.

I nodded. "O… okay. Thanks."

He put the bowl in my purse and inched to the side so I could get up and grab my cloth.

Len walked back to us. "It's the busy dial tone and he's not answering me. Quil?"

Quil nodded and pulled out his phone. "Yeah."

He walked away and I looked at Len.

"If Quil calls, he'll answer him," Len said. "You don't ignore the boss when he calls."

"He's Ron's boss too?"

"Not like you'd think of it, but Quil's third from the top in the hierarchy. He calls, you answer."

"Ah," I said.

Quil wandered back over a moment later as he hung up. "Ron's calling her right now, telling her to stay with the group. Let's go."

We hopped in our cars and sped up West End. Grant called the guys and told us to meet them there, and we pulled in front of the Business School after only a few minutes.

Almost dead on to when the demon was supposed to show up.

The guys pulled up with the lady vamps and Grant nodded at them and they ran inside.

"Ariana, if you can get a vision again, now's the time," Grant said.

I closed my eyes, tryin' to focus.

Nothing.

The others came back out with Jen and her boyfriend showed up a minute later. They got in the car after Carla smelled him for demon and they zoomed off.

Carla put her nose to the air and took a deep drag of the night. "He was here."

"You're sure?" Grant asked.

She gave him an 'oh please,' kind of look. "Sure as silk thongs, Special Agent Grant."

I didn't ask what that was supposed to mean, it seemed kind of obvious anyhow.

"And he went this way." She pointed beyond the building into the heart of campus.

The business school was right on the edge, so that left a lot of tree and brick dotted campus to cover.

"More trees, what a shock," Dan said. "What's with these guys and woods?"

"Trees help cover the scent," Carla said. "But he's close enough I think I got him." She set out with us following close behind like she was a bloodhound.

"Hold up," Grant said after a moment. "We do this in teams. Carla you're with Jet and Len up front. Dan, Stephanie, and Ariana next. Quil and I will bring up the rear."

"Stephanie should be in the back with you," Quil said. "If the demon drops in on us or those three, you two can bring out the explosives. If they get the drop on the middle group and it has Stephanie, she'll be messing with those instead of protecting the humans. She'll get the demons, but they could get these two first." He pointed to Dan and me.

Grant stepped up to him and it looked like another pissing contest was brewing.

"Actually we should do this in pairs," I said and everyone turned to look at me. "If we're running after the demons, it's a lot easier to keep track of one partner than two. Someone in one of the groups of three could end up the odd man out and the demons could take advantage of that. It should be Carla and Jet, then me and Len, you and Stephanie, and then Dan and Quil. The demons will probably think there'll be one or two groups, go after me and Len, who, let's face it, look the weakest, and you and Stephanie will be there to back us up. And then there'll be Dan and Quil behind you just in case."

"Okay. Good idea," Grant said.

I grinned. He said good idea.

"Weapons out," Grant said. "Quil, any sensitivity to specific weapons or metals?"

"Like us with silver?" Quil shook his head. "Unknown."

"Earbuds all in?" Grant asked, lookin' at me.

We all nodded.

"Stay in contact," Grant said. "Anyone's earbud goes out, Kowalski and I have GPS for them and we all haul ass to catch them. Stay in eyesight of the group in front of you and stay quiet."

We set out.

Carla took the front, sometimes zooming ahead with her vamp speed with Jet in tow, then she'd pause to get the scent again.

Len dragged me with the super-speed at those times and I hoped Stephanie and Quil were doing the same with the other guys.

Though I had a hard time imagining Grant being okay with being dragged around like a rag doll.

It's weird to be hauled like that, to see the trees fly past you while your toes skid over the leaf and pine-needle covered ground.

We must've circled through the campus at least three times before we heard it.

Whoosh.

CHAPTER TWELVE

L EN TACKLED ME TO THE ground before I even registered the sound and the arrow flew overhead.

What was it with this guy and freaking arrows? Wouldn't silver bullets make more sense? I mean, come on! Join the twenty-first century!

"Come on." Len jumped to his feet and pulled me up by my arm before zooming us back up the path towards the third pair.

"Who hired you!" Carla screamed.

We followed the sound to where she was spraying the demon in girl's clothing down with something from a canister. Mace?

It screamed and clawed at its face.

"Ewwwwwww," I said as the girl pulled off her skin in pieces. The orange wax showed underneath and I gagged.

"I'll second that."

I jumped in a half turn. Quil and Dan had just appeared behind us. I was so shocked, I couldn't even tell which one said that.

Quil walked to Carla and the demon and gave the thing a vicious kick.

It rolled over in the dirt, ripping off clothes and skin alike, large black coat already discarded next to it.

"Where's your partner?" Quil asked.

"No partner," it hissed through a hole in the face area since it'd already torn off its lips.

I looked at the pile of shredded bits and sure enough an almost intact pair of lips twitched on the ground.

Ewwww. So much ew.

"I was summoned alone," it said.

So the shooter the other night was the summoner?

"Then who hired you?" Quil asked.

"Sorry. I never got his card."

Demons can be sarcastic? Who knew?

Its empty eyes, still the dark brown ones of the girl it was impersonating, landed on Carla. "I've never fucked a vamp, but you're cute enough to make me reconsider my rule."

Carla launched herself at the demon and Len caught her, pullin' her back into him with soothing noises.

The demon jumped to its feet and lunged.

Quil caught it around the throat and sprayed its eyes with mace with the other hand.

The demon shriveled in on itself, strugglin' to get its hands up to its face as Quil sprayed them.

It screamed a long, shrill sound that made me and the vamps flinch.

Quil squeezed it so hard its cry cut off.

And its eyes popped out.

How many times could I think ewwwwww without it becoming redundant?

"What did the man who hired you look like?" Quil asked, calm as a cat on a sunny porch.

"Vampire, not man, and I never saw his face," the demon said, its voice high as a kid on helium now. "He said he needed to teach your nest a lesson. That you insulted him. When he summons me, I come out in a warehouse."

"Address?" Grant asked it.

"Human numbers mean little to me."

"You don't know?" Grant growled.

Quil looked at Grant out of the corner of his eye and the demon shoved Quil back, speedin' past fast as the vamps could move.

Stephanie pulled something out of her pocket and pressed on it.

BOOOOM.

The trees evaporated in front of us and the concussion knocked me and Jet on our butts.

My ears rang as I pushed to my feet. About twenty feet in front of us the trees were just gone, organic confetti with spots of waxy stuff for ten feet all around.

My eyes darted, taking in the damage in the dim light.

"There could have been people there!" Grant screamed, getting in Stephanie's face.

"Finals ended last week and the summer semester hasn't started," she said, starin' him in the eyes. "The place is deserted. Back off!"

Grant stared her down and her eyes widened.

"What are you?" she asked.

I opened my mouth on reflex and slammed it shut.

Oh crap! She meant Grant?

Quil and Len traded a look and Carla inched closer to Grant, taking an obvious deep breath.

"Interesting," Carla said.

Quil gave her a look and she mouthed something that looked like, "Later."

The silence boiled over as Stephanie stared at Grant... almost scared.

The silence made my skin itch and I asked, "Grant's not human?"

"Of course I'm human, Ryder," Grant said.

Carla made a small noise and he turned his glare on her.

Stephanie took a breath and backed away, hand near her pocket.

Like she was ready to pull out a weapon if she needed to.

"Holy crap on a cracker!" I said. "Grant, were you holding her eyes, like they do to humans? Like hypnotizing?"

Carla made another small noise and I growled.

"Carla, what? What is it?" I asked.

She looked at Quil and he nodded.

"He's human," she said. "But there's something else in there. I could pin it down more if I could have a taste."

"No," Grant said.

"Sir, did you know?" I asked.

"No," Grant said.

He didn't look surprised, but then again, it was Grant. Playin' poker with him was worse than playin' with Germans.

"Would you be able to smell it if he was strongly something, like a quarter?" I asked.

"Depends," Carla said. "Some things have magic that disguises them. Leprechauns, for example. You can't smell anything off about them. Like fucking chameleons. And even a powerful psychic like you wouldn't get a vision off them."

I giggled.

"What?" she asked.

"Oh." I flapped a hand. "Our forensic tech always tells us he's part Leprechaun, cuz he's Irish."

She raised her eyebrows. "He may not be joking."

I blinked. Huh.

Grant took a deep breath. "Focus people. Is the demon dead?"

"Yes," Stephanie said. "Since he was leading us in circles, I placed some charges around, figuring they may come in handy."

"How many more?"

"I placed a dozen, so eleven left."

"Gather them back up."

She zoomed off without so much as a smirk and my jaw dropped.

He'd scared her.

I looked down on the ground where the demon had been. The torn off skin was nothing more than liquid flowing into the dirt; the shredded clothes were still there.

"Wait," I said, "where's that big black coat?"

Everyone else looked around.

"Shit!" Quil said. "It returned to the summoner."

"And now we don't have anything to follow," Carla said.

"We have the information that it was a vampire who did this," Quil said. "And we know that coat is what the summoner used to connect himself to the demon."

"And we know that either the summoner was here Thursday ni... actually Friday morning," I said as a disturbing thought entered my mind. "Or they have a vampire in your nest working with them."

Quil's eyes met mine.

"Someone from our nest?" He pursed his lips. "I hate to think it, but it is possible, but... Well, at least that cuts it down considerably."

"It does?" Jet asked.

"Yes. Our queen has many enemies, of course," Quil said. "But if they're going after humans connected to us, and not her humans specifically, it means it's a grudge against the nest. Probably an unhappy business partner."

He paused. "I can think of five nests that could have the power and resources to summon a demon and control it who might have a problem with us. They're on the grudge list we made. I have it in my car and I can give you information on their businesses, and even on some of their humans."

"Do it," Grant said.

We hiked back to the cars and Quil pulled the grudge list out of his car. Len grabbed a laptop out of the back and showed Grant the info they had on the suspects and the nests they belonged to, as well as their financial dealings.

It was a ton of info. What, were they like the IRS for vamps in the entire South or something?

Len started to explain the different databases he was giving us and Quil took my arm.

I looked at him as he pulled me to the side. I opened my mouth and he lay a finger on my lips.

"I just wanted to say you did wonderfully tonight," he said. "We wouldn't even have this much if not for your vision."

I nodded and he walked back to Len and Grant.

Len finished his presentation and we got it downloaded.

"We'll need to meet up with your nest and question them," Grant said.

"I'll set up something casual, say it's a party to meet our new partners, and then Ariana can see if she can pick anything up," Quil said.

Grant nodded. "We'll run these down in the morning. You guys should stick together, but I think you'll be safe tonight."

"He has a connection with the demon. He'll know it's dead," Len said. "It takes a while to summon a new one so he won't get around to it till tomorrow night hopefully, but we'll take your advice."

"Do any of you live together?" Quil asked and we all shook our heads. "I just mean, if the summoner knows you're working the case, which he probably does, he could go after you. And you are not safe until you're inside." He looked at me. "None of you."

"He's only ever gone after women," Jet said, looking at me too.

"But that was just the demon's preference," Quil said. "The summoner could go after anyone associated with us. All of you have to be accompanied home."

"Oh man, that's a good one." Dan barked a laugh. "I'll have to remember that."

"This isn't a trick," Quil said. "If you want to go alone, it's no skin off my nose, but Ariana will have an escort to her door and that escort will have vampire strength. Len?"

"I got her." He took my hand and bowed over it. "My lady."

"Oh jeez." I sighed, but gave him a smile.

Carla tossed the keys to her car to Len and he caught them. "I was planning on hanging at the nest tonight anyway."

"I live near Ariana, if you want to get me home," Jet said to Len.

"Absolutely," Len said with a grin, letting his eyes rove over Jet, "tall, dark, and handsome."

"He's straight," I said.

Len's face fell, full on hammin' it up.

"And I'd be willing to escort either of these," Carla said, pointing to Dan and Grant. "Or both. I can catch a cab back to the nest."

Grant scowled, but swallowed it back. "We live close and thank you for the consideration. I have to drop the van off at the office first."

"And while we're in the van, maybe you could show me some of the computer stuff?" Carla asked.

Dan nodded, caught Grant's eye, and straightened his face to one of perfect professionalism.

We departed, stopped at the office to get our cars, and drove one after the other.

The boys walked me to my door and I called Jet fifteen minutes later to make sure he got home safe. He did. Grant called me before I could check on him to let me know he was safe and to stay in till morning.

Yeah, like I didn't already know that.

"What is wrong with Quil?" I asked Pyro, petting his soft back. He nuzzled my head and pointed at the window.

"Yeah, go ahead, I'll be fine."

He straightened out, wavin' for me to get on.

"Not tonight, baby. Got to stay in."

He nodded and flew out.

I grabbed my Kindle and pulled up the romance I was in the middle of.

"At least someone has a sex life," I said.

A knock on the door a few minutes later made me jump and I walked to it as quietly as I could.

What if the summoner decided to go after us himself?

I stood on tiptoe to see through the peep hole.

My stomach dropped out as I unlocked and opened the door.

"Hi."

CHAPTER THIRTEEN

"HI." QUIL SMILED, WAITING.

"If you're really you, then you don't need an invite cuz I already invited you. And if you're a demon, I'm not inviting you in," I said, and stood back.

"Good," Quil said, stepping over the threshold. "I should've thought of that. If you'd invited me in without thinking, I would have had to lecture you or something, and that would really ruin the mood."

He walked past me and I turned with him, closin' the door behind me and lockin' it.

I rested my back against the door. "What, did you go half the way home, change your mind, and turn around?" I asked, hating how weak my voice sounded.

"Actually, I went all the way home, turned around, came half way here, turned around, was almost home, then turned around and came here."

He reached forward, putting his hands on my hips slowly, like he was waitin' for me to say no or something.

"Carla called me after she dropped your teammates off and told me I was being an idiot, that I should take you while I have the chance. That anything could happen any day, not necessarily even murder or a hazard of your job, but just an accident, and that I should get as much of you as I can, and I realized I haven't even kissed you yet."

He was babbling as bad as me. He was nervous?

"No, you haven't."

It was all I could think to say as his hands inched under my top.

I rested mine on his arms, starin' up at him.

"I am a stupid, stupid man."

He lowered his head and my heart sped up.

I hadn't been kissed in months, hadn't had sex in years.

Our mouths met, soft at first, then he pressed me against the door, kissing harder.

Oh. My. God.

I wrapped my arms around his middle and pulled him as close against me as I could get with the height difference.

Were we really going to do this? In the middle of an investigation we were working together?

We kissed forever and I couldn't catch my breath.

"Mmmmmmmm," I said.

"Unhuh," he said.

He slid his hands down and lifted me up. My legs wrapped around his middle and I pressed into the kiss, the better leverage making it deeper.

He carried me up the stairs and into the bedroom and kicked the door closed behind us.

He dropped me on the bed and shrugged off his suit jacket, hanging it on the bed post and crawlin' on the bed with me.

We kissed until I was sufficiently breathless again.

He pulled and undid the first button on my shirt. "You were such a tease tonight. All I wanted to do was rip this off you."

"I don't like this shirt anyway," I said, voice breathy and high.

He grinned, meetin' my eyes as he grabbed either side of the buttons and pulled.

Pop, pop, pop.

The threads snapped and I laughed.

Quil pulled the top off my shoulders and tossed it aside. He pulled me against his chest and buried his face in my neck, suckin' on the sensitive hollow.

"And the braid," he said, grabbin' it and pulling my head back to look him in the eye. "I know you said you weren't trying to press any buttons, but the braid was begging for me to undo it."

He got on his knees and I turned. He undid my bra first. I swore next time I'd be wearing a prettier bra as I shook it off.

He undid the braid and my scalp tingled as he pushed his fingers in to shake the last vestiges of the braid at the top out.

"There, that's better." Quil ran his fingers around to my exposed middle and kissed my neck, breathin' deeply.

I gasped as every tiny brush of his lips sent sensation straight down my body. He drew back and settled in front of me again.

"Undress me," he said.

My fingers shook as I tried to get the first button and he chuckled.

"Calm down, sweets." He pulled me in to kiss me again and my fingers stopped shaking and moved over the buttons smoother and pushed the shirt off before tugging the undershirt over his head.

I lay back on the pillows and he grinned, grabbin' my skirt and panties and tuggin' them off in one motion.

And just like that, I was naked as the day I was born.

"What made you change your mind?" I asked as he stared at me. "I thought you had a rule?"

"I do. I'm breaking it."

He kicked off his shoes and undid his pants, pulling them off easier than I could have, leavin' him in black boxer briefs and socks. He took off the socks and covered my body with his, kissin' me as he rubbed against me, so hard I was surprised he was stayin' in his shorts.

I reached down and rubbed him through the cloth and he moaned, pullin' back to take the underwear off, movin' so fast I almost didn't see the motion.

He was ripe, rearing, and ready to go.

He trailed his hands up my legs and I parted my knees. He stayed on his and grabbed my breasts, massaging them and making me moan now.

He leaned over me and sucked on my breast, pulling in as much as he could. The sensation shot straight down to my groin and I humped up, body beggin' him to be inside.

He pulled back. "It's like you feel every tiny touch down to the bone."

He put his weight on me, but stayed too low for me, suckin' on my neck.

"Quil, I'm ready to go. Trust me. I want you inside me."

He kissed me and grabbed my thigh, pullin' my leg up and to the side and pressed against my opening.

He pushed and I whimpered as he forced the closeness more open.

"You sure you're not a virgin?" he whispered, pushin' a bit harder.

"Positive, just small… and it's been a while since anything besides a gyno's been down there."

Oh stupid Ariana, like that was something you said during sex!

He shoved in and I grabbed onto his hips as he moved on top of me.

I may as well have been a virgin for all the room my body had for him. But it felt so good, just havin' him in me, our bodies melded as close as two people could possibly be.

He went slow and my mouth found the cool, smooth skin of his chest, body knowin' what to do even as my brain went out for a coffee break.

I squeezed him and he barked something in another language, bendin' so he could kiss me.

He pulled back and I opened my eyes as he planted his hands on either side of me.

"You ready, sweets?"

I nodded.

"Grab your legs, pull them up."

I did and he rose higher, changing the angle.

I barely had a chance to catch my breath before he started poundin', moving fast and hard enough to make me cry out.

I squeezed, curlin' up to build the pressure below as I held my legs harder.

Pleases fell from my lips as it built.

I didn't even know what I was begging for.

The heat and pressure crested and I tossed my head back, holding on hard to ride the orgasm out.

I relaxed against the bed and he lay on me, moving slow again.

"Good start," he said. "I'm going to make you come more times than you ever dreamed in one night."

I chuckled. "Pretty big words. How do you know how many times I've dreamed of comin', because I can do like ten on a good night with a vibrator in real life."

He met my eyes but kept going even as the surprise made his rhythm change. "That is awesome! Do you know how many girls would kill for that?"

I grinned. "Most I've come with a guy is four. We'll see if you can beat that."

He went faster again and I bit his chest.

Quil grunted and I let him go.

"Do that again," he said, voice ragged.

I bit him harder, keeping my teeth dug in for a moment longer, only lettin' go so he could keep moving.

I licked and teased his nipples as he moved faster, nippin' him randomly.

He groaned from deep in his throat and thrust, losin' rhythm as he grabbed my bedpost.

The post splintered and the brass bed knob crashed to the floor as he convulsed inside me.

He moaned and collapsed on me.

He slid out and inched down to lay his face next to mine. He stroked my hair and cupped my face to kiss me. I felt warm inside as I kissed him back and slid my leg over his body.

"I can't go again that fast, sweets."

"Mmmmmm." I nuzzled his neck, nippin' at it.

"Well, if you insist." He eased open my legs and lowered his face in as I grabbed the bars on the headboard.

\#   \#   \#

"You are very loud," Quil said, lying next to me in the pillow, restin' his forehead against mine.

I giggled. "I hope there's no one wandering around outside."

"Shower?" I loved his eyebrows as they jumped over his beautiful eyes and made the question all the more wonderful.

"I don't think I can walk," I said.

He got up, swooped me up in his arms and carried me to the bathroom. I curled up into his chest like a contented kitten.

Huh, my bite marks were already gone.

"How do you not have a heart attack with this thing?" He set me down (I was a little shocked my legs held me) and tapped my chest.

"I don't know," I said as he stepped in and turned on the water. "Doctors have checked it, but as far as they know, I'm perfectly healthy. I don't even have high blood pressure. We have required physicals every year and I passed."

He started the shower and put me under the water, grabbing the loofah and rubbing it down with my lotion soap. He scrubbed me down. It was soothing and sweet. There is nothing like showering with someone you just had incredible sex with.

Nothing.

He bent down to scrub my legs and kissed my knees, making me giggle.

Quil stood and got behind me, scrubbed my back down, pausing to kiss my shoulders. He reached around with soaped up hands and massaged my breasts.

"I guess I know what your favorite body part is."

"What's your favorite?"

"Your voice," I said without havin' to think about it.

"That's not a body part."

I giggled. "Whatever. Still my favorite."

He picked up the loofah and handed it to me.

"Oh, so it's your turn now?" I asked.

"It's only fair." He kissed my hand.

I scrubbed him down, takin' my dear sweet time about it.

After he was completely clean, I pushed him down to his knees and grabbed the shampoo.

"Best part for last," he said.

"Huh?" I leaned over to look in his face, my wet hair swinging down like a thick whip.

"Your hair's another favorite of mine." He tugged on the end and I slapped his hand with a smile, straightening back up.

"I'll do you first. Then you can do me," I said.

"No complaints here."

I rubbed the shampoo into his soft, thick curls and he sighed.

After I was done with him, he stood and slid his wet body against mine as he moved behind me, and went to work on my hair, massaging like a pro stylist, and rinsed me off.

He kissed my neck and pulled my head to the side by the hair.

"May I?" he asked.

I didn't think. I didn't want to.

"Yes."

He clamped an arm around my waist and pulled me into him so tight I thought my skin would start crumbling in.

I reached behind me and grabbed him by the base, pumpin' him against my bottom.

He bit in.

Pain shot through me, dissolving into pleasure as he sucked.

Magic. Had to be.

He didn't make a noise, but I felt him come as he spilled against my skin.

My knees gave and he held me up, supporting my body like I weighed no more than a piece of cardboard.

He kept suckin' as he lowered a hand under me. He slid a finger inside and moved it, pressing forward. I gasped and pulsated on those fingers as he grabbed my breast, squeezing almost too hard. He stretched his hand up and flicked my front as his finger moved faster.

"Yes. Please." I closed my eyes and my mouth went slack.

My back arched and I bent my head back as intense pleasure took me and I rode harder into his hand as I gasped.

He withdrew his fingers and teeth, and licked the wound clean. He washed my juices off his hand and his own off my leg.

"How are you still standing?" I asked.

"Barely."

I turned off the water and found my legs enough to step out of the shower. I grabbed one of my big, fluffy red towels and rubbed him down with it. He did the same to me. After we were both as dry as we were gonna get, I grabbed his hand and led him back to my bed.

He snuggled up next to me, pulling me into his body with one strong arm. I rested my head on his chest.

"It smells like us now." He yawned.

"You're tired?" I asked.

"I was up all day planning, organizing, comforting, being strong..." He trailed off with another yawn. "You are comforting, your smell, your fast heartbeat."

"Sleep sweet." I shifted to kiss his chest, then settled down next to him.

# # #

A tickling on my face drew me from the depths of sleep and I was just conscious enough to bat it away before the heavy darkness took me again.

The soft thing slapped my face enough to get through the fog and I groaned, wavin' it away.

But I was awake enough to realize what it was.

131

"Pyro, baby, leave me alone."

He responded by smackin' me with a tassel again.

I felt Quil's heavy arm over my waist and his body pressed up next to mine.

I hadn't been so close to another person, breathing or not, for over two years, and I did not want to end it just cuz my magic carpet was feeling pissy.

I finally forced my eyes open to see Pyro over us. He crossed his tassels and landed next to me.

The door was open and evil, bright light streamed from the hall.

"Pyro, what the hell is your problem?"

He flew to the wall, bracin' himself under the light switch and flickin' it on.

"Ughhhh!" Quil said. "I'm going to kill your Pyro, sweets." He pulled the covers over his head.

"Not if I do first."

I dragged my butt outta bed and checked my phone. Before six a.m., I could've slept for another two hours before the alarm went off, but nooooo, my flying carpet wanted to scold.

"What?"

Pyro responded by rushing past me to the bed.

"Hey!" Quil yelped as my carpet tried to wrap around him.

He was quick, but Pyro can do up to sixty mph on a good night, and is pretty agile. He managed to roll up around one thick arm and lifted Quil from the bed.

"Call off your carpet or I'm going to hurt him."

Quil sounded more cranky than anything as Pyro flew-dragged him into the hall.

"Pyro, put him down, now!" I yelled.

I'd only ever yelled at my baby once.

Pyro froze, dropped Quil next to the stairs, and flew by me, diving under my bed.

"Oh dear." I sighed. "You want to sulk, you can, but you don't grab people and threaten to drop them down the stairs." I looked at Quil as he got up. "You okay?"

He laughed. "This wouldn't have been the first time I was kicked out of bed naked, sweets."

"Oh really? Well, I don't know about you, but I'm awake and I don't see me going back to sleep."

"I'll stay up with you, but the second you go to work, I'm going back to bed." He leaned down to kiss me and I flinched away.

He scowled and I chuckled.

"We had sex, your fluids are everywhere, we showered together, I think we are officially intimate enough for you to use my toothbrush."

"Are you saying my breath stinks?" He placed a hand dramatically on his bare chest.

"Yeah, and so does mine." Now *that* he didn't deny.

I brushed my teeth and handed the toothbrush to Quil after a quick rinse.

I watched him in the mirror and laughed.

"What?" he asked once he spat out into the sink.

I shook my head. "I just realized this is the first time a guy has ever used my toothbrush."

"Oh, so I should be honored." He grinned as he pulled me close.

"Yes," I said, pressin' into him.

Then jerked back as he hardened.

"I'm exhausted."

"But you're naked, and you smell good, and I have the strongest urge to screw you into the wall."

He grabbed my breasts and his thumbs (miracle of nature that opposable thumb) flicked over my nipples, making them harden despite my logic.

Tired or not, my body remembered last night.

"If we have sex, I'll fall asleep again and then I'll be late, and I'll really be dead," I said.

He lifted me up and my legs went around him like they belonged there.

"Take my blood," he said.

"What?"

"That would solve both problems. You'll be stronger, you'll need it for today, and I'll be… *satisfied.*"

I wrapped my arm around his neck and lowered my mouth on the other side. He held me on him with one arm and pressed my head in with the other as we started to sink up and down.

For a cold blooded creature, he sure did warm up fast.

I latched my lips on and sucked in as much of his sweet skin as I could without rippin' any of it off, nipping until he let out a deep throated moan. I locked my arms around his neck tighter and bit with all my strength.

Let me tell ya, human teeth aren't meant for tearin' into solid flesh like that. It took some serious work to break the skin.

When I did, the sweet, thick, cold blood inched into my mouth, and I fixed my lips around the wound to suck as hard as I could. It flowed down my throat like solidified magic, waking me up like a triple espresso.

Quil cried out under me, hands scramblin' over my back. He screamed, low and deep as he jerked inside me and his hands pressed down. I didn't even want to know how much control it took for him not to clamp down and risk breaking bones.

133

"'Bout time I made you scream," I murmured as I pulled back.

I still wasn't done, need throbbed within me, but he was spent again, and weaker from the blood loss. He peeled me off him and set me on the counter next to the sink.

"You can make me scream anytime you want, sweets."

He went down on me, slidin' a finger in.

I came so fast I probably would've gone without his help.

We lay on the bathroom floor, curled up I don't know how long.

"I have to go to work and I lost the ability to walk," I groused the best I could while still shinin' in the afterglow.

"No," he mumbled into my chest, snuggling in.

"But I have to work. I have to find a demon summoning vamp who's gunning for your nest, remember?"

He groaned and slipped off me.

"Oh crap on a cracker!" I said. "How am I gonna cover up the bite?"

"Cover up what?" he asked, runnin' a finger over my neck.

My hand flew up and I felt my perfectly smooth skin. "What happened? I know you just scratched me, but there should be a scab."

"Healing properties." He stuck out his tongue and tapped it. "There's different types; my saliva can heal minor flesh wounds quite well."

"So the saliva can heal us, the blood makes us stronger, and the bite induces pleasure instead of pain, is there a reason for all that?" I asked.

"Hell if I know, sweets."

He snuggled into my chest again and I massaged his head, the wet hair not as soft, but it still felt as good as it looked.

"My best guess," he said, "is all those are to make it so we can feed without weakening humans too much, or having to fight for it, or worrying about others seeing the marks and knowing what caused it."

His voice softened and I looked down, his eyes were closed.

"Quil, I do have to go to work."

"Five more minutes."

I gave him thirty.

CHAPTER FOURTEEN

I SLIPPED OUT FROM UNDER QUIL and left him snoozing on the floor while I got ready.

"Hey," I said, kneelin' next to him when I was ready. "You hanging around today?"

"Yeah," he said, cracking his eyes.

"Okay, we need to come up with some kind of plan to talk to the potential suspects. I have to talk to the team about it."

Really I meant I had to talk to Grant about it.

"But I'm thinkin' we're going to have to set up some kind of casual meeting with the leaders. Maybe at the club. They don't need to know we're feds, and we can try to question them and I'll get some visions. Can you set that up?"

He nodded and held out his hand. "Here, give me your phone."

I fished it out of my bag and handed it over. He pulled himself up onto his elbow and punched in a number.

"This way you have my direct number. Who are all these?" he asked, scrollin' down my contacts.

"Ashdina's my oldest sister." I sat on the floor next to him and grabbed the phone.

He held on with a playful grin and we played tug-a-war for a minute until he finally relinquished his hold.

"Thank you!" I said, stickin' my tongue out at him. "So anyway, she's the oldest, thirty-four, she's a doctor."

"Oldest? How many siblings do you have?"

"Four." I pointed to the phone. "The next is Ava Jolene, who's thirty-two, she's a journalist."

"And the next." I scrolled down to the Ms. "Is Mark. The guys got normal names. He's twenty-nine and a lawyer. And then there's Mikey. He's

135

only a year older than me. Mikey's what Mama calls a perpetual starving artist. He wants to be an actor so he's always auditioning, but..." I shrugged and shook my head.

"How does he support himself?"

"He lives with Ava, so that helps, and he works as a mechanic. He's like me. We're the babies. We were the ones who would spy on the other three. We would make up stories about how the older ones did something bad whenever they shoved us out of their rooms and told us we were brats. It was always a 'me and him against the world' kind of thing."

"What changed?"

"How do you know somethin' did?"

"Your voice."

My hand flew to my left arm.

The scars had faded over time so I didn't have to keep my arm covered, but sometimes I swore I could still see them.

"What?" he asked. "What happened?"

"That isn't who I am anymore," I said. "I can't... talkin' about it now sounds so stupid."

"You can trust me, sweets." He pulled me onto his lap and wrapped his arms around me. "You trust me to know this about you, to not tell anyone, to not judge you for it, and to not ever bring it up again if you don't want me to."

I nodded.

"When was it?"

"About eight years ago."

"I'm guessing by the wrist that you cut yourself?"

I nodded.

"Why?"

I shrugged. "I was depressed. Lookin' back, I know I didn't actually want to kill myself cuz I made the cuts side to side, and you cut straight up the arm if you want to die."

"I can't imagine you ever being depressed."

"I ummmm, had or have still, maybe... bipolar disorder. It's so mild now, I'm not sure if I just grew out of it, but I don't even need meds, so I'm okay now. But as a teenager, it was bad."

I couldn't even look at him.

"I ugh... my middle sister, Ava... when I was little, she was like a second mom, you know? She's nine years older than me and she was the one who took care of me and Mikey growin' up. She was the one who changed our diapers and made dinner when our parents had to work late."

"Sounds like my sister," Quil said. "Different century, but same idea."

"Yeah, well. I don't know when exactly, but some time around high school, my sister changed. She wouldn't babysit us anymore, wouldn't play with us, and when Mama asked her to cook or hang out with us after school, she'd throw a fit, say Mama was a bad mom and she should be with us instead of makin' Ava do it."

I took a deep breath. "A few years later, she was in college and I was takin' politics classes and tryin' to learn more about the world. I wanted to be a lawyer then, so I was pretty heavy into it. And my sister and I had some real different ideas about what was best goin' forward. She was a journalism major and... you know how journalists lean, so we disagreed."

I flicked my eyes up and Quil met them, obviously confused.

"She had her friends over for a dinner and her and Daddy got into it. I jumped in, and she... she got *mean*, fast. She started attackin' me, sayin' horrible things about how I was brainwashed by Daddy and his politics and couldn't think for myself. When I countered, sayin' she was brainwashed by her friends and she was just showin' off for them, well then she just got worse."

I shook my head. "At this point, I can't even say what was said, but I was upset and our parents were, the party was ruined, and I ran outta the house. I went to my boyfriend's place. He'd been tryin' to go further for a while, and that night, I just felt so betrayed and vulnerable, and I... let him."

Quil took a sharp breath.

"God, it hurt like hell, I soooo wasn't ready. And afterwards, I was a wreck. I went home and Daddy had been tryin' to call me. When I got in, he knew something happened. He was threatening to kill the guy. I started cryin' right there in the living room and Daddy hugged me and I told him I was just so upset at what Ava said.

"He was so pissed, he called up Ava, screamed at her over the phone. Ava came over the next day when they were at work and just tore into me. God, I didn't know how much she hated me until that day. I started cryin' and she laughed. She just... she enjoyed that she'd hurt me. She said people like me deserved it because we were so horrible to other people. She said I was the reason women were paid less than men, minorities were abused, and gay people got beat up."

"She what!" Quil yelled.

I jerked.

"Sorry, sweets. How could someone blame a kid for that?"

I shrugged. "Daddy explained it later. Said Ava had hatred in her heart. She was upset over some law or case or another that'd just happened, and she saw me as a safe target. It was that day I knew my sister didn't love me anymore.

"After she left, I called my boyfriend, annnnnd he didn't answer. And later, he didn't answer. I knew he loved me, he was so understandin' the night before, so I didn't get it. Took me a few more calls and texts over the day for him to finally text back that the night before did not go well and he didn't think we should see each other anymore."

Quil made a sharp noise and I shook my head, starin' at my hands.

"I *broke* that night. Something in me shattered. Mama and Daddy were downstairs and askin' me to come down for dinner. I hollered I'd be down in a minute and I went into the bathroom. I grabbed some scissors and cut my hair off. It was longer than it is now and I just slaughtered it. But it wasn't enough. So I grabbed the razor and just started slicin'. I watched the blood come out on the floor and I must've passed out cuz the next thing I knew, I was in the hospital."

Quil hugged me tighter and I licked my lips.

"My parents were so mad at Ava, told her she needed to come in and apologize. Now, I don't know what she said besides no, but she didn't come in, and based on stuff Mama let slip over the years, Ava said something along the lines of I should've killed myself and done the world a favor. Either way, Daddy cut her off that day, said she could come back to apologize but until then, she wasn't gettin' a penny."

I tapped my wrist. "Anyway, Mikey was sixteen and wanted to be an actor. Mama and Daddy were supportive, but wanted him to finish school, grow up a bit, and he wanted to go off on his own. After they cut Ava off, he figured a good way to get himself kicked out, aka *free*, was to go after me. So for weeks, he constantly attacked me, my boyfriend leavin' me, me bein' too stupid to know he was usin' me, me being stupid and couldn't think for myself… stuff like that. Daddy lost it and sent him to military school. He got kicked out and bounced around prep schools till he was eighteen. He dropped outta school the next day and went off with Ava to California."

"And you don't talk to either of them any more?"

"Mikey apologized like a year later. He explained he had nothin' against me, just wanted to go off and do his own thing and not answer to Mama and Daddy. Ava and I haven't spoken since. The stuff she writes though… she talks about her conservative family as though we're a bunch of ignorant backwoods bumpkins she feels sorry for because we just don't know enough to see the light."

"I'm so sorry, sweets. Do they know?"

I knew he meant my coworkers.

"Nope. Mama made damn sure the records weren't gonna get out. She was makin' it pretty big as an author by then, but she still had her law license, made sure they knew she'd sue their butts off if any of this stuff got out. So as far as anyone looking into my past is concerned, it never happened. They know I have a history of bipolar disorder, but that's it."

"Is that how you think of it? Never happened?"

"Most of the time," I said.

"Thank you for telling me."

"Just don't go usin' it against me. I have some trust issues."

"Yeah, don't blame you."

I nodded and slipped off his lap. "Now you know two things about me no one else does, well except my family, who knows about this." I waved my left arm.

"So I should feel privileged?"

"Very." I glanced at the clock. "I need to be goin'. I promised I'd stop bein' late."

"That's okay. I'll be fine here."

I gave him a quick peck and waved my finger at him when he tried to deepen it.

"Don't start that again cuz then I'll never get out of here." I paused. "Wait a second. We were all over each other, doing things I could barely even imagine, smellin' each other all over. How did I not have a vision that entire time?"

"Oh, right!" He walked over to his pants in the bedroom, pulled out a small leather bag and held it up.

I reached out for it and he jerked it away.

"Don't touch it! Don't even smell it. It's a gris-gris. Voodoo. If it's close to a psychic, within about fifteen feet or so, it helps slow the juices, but if you touch it, you'll have it on you all day and you won't be able to get anything at work. I brought it because I knew if we were close, you would start having visions and that would be distracting. I was going to tell you about it, assure you that it would be safe to get intimate, but you never gave me the chance."

"I almost feel like I should be mad at you. I don't think I am, but it seems a little... presumptuous? Anyway, where did you get it?"

"Voodoo priestess. I took some of your hair to make it. Is that okay? Please don't be mad at me."

"I'm not. I think it's kind of sweet actually. Kinda like a guy buying non-latex condoms. I'm allergic to latex. So it's kind of presumptuous, like you know you're going to get some, which the guy I'm talking about didn't, but... the point is, it was sweet. I'm okay with this."

#   #   #

I actually made it on time even after a line at the coffee shop.

Grant looked up when I put the cup on his desk and I grinned.

"Morning, General!"

"You're too awake," he growled.

It was just supposed to be a general comment, but my face, my stupid, God dammit expressive face, must've done something cuz Grant froze, eyes icin' over.

He *knew*.

He stood and cocked a finger at me to follow and I put the coffees on

139

Jet's desk.

"What did you do?" Jet asked and I just shook my head as I ran after Grant.

Grant closed the bathroom door behind us and held up a finger when I opened my mouth.

"I don't want to know. I don't want your excuses. I don't want to hear you tell me it's not any of my business. We are in the middle of a case. He is the head of a kind of collaborating agency that could very well be in on all this."

I opened my mouth again.

"No, you don't get to talk. You compromised the case, not to mention your own safety, yet again."

He breathed hard and paced around the small bathroom like a bull.

"I don't know what to do with you," he finally said in a soft, low tone. "I can't fire you because you are an asset, and I don't want to fire you. I already put you on desk and it didn't help." He shook his head. "Fine, I want to know. I want to know why you'd do this. I want to know why the fuck you would jeopardize, not only the case, but all that, over a guy. Especially a vampire."

"I don't believe I am," I said once it was clear he was finished. "I don't believe I am jeopardizing the case."

"That's it?" He scowled, meeting my eyes with his cold, hard stare. "That's your excuse? You don't even have a 'There's something about him,' or an 'It was love at first sight?' Or any of that bullshit? All you have is that a relationship isn't jeopardizing the case?"

I just looked at him. Couldn't let him get me on the defensive. Once you're on the defensive with Grant, you're as good as done.

"Then what about your life, Ariana? Because he is a vampire, and that is asking for trouble."

"No it isn't," I said.

Grant's eyes flashed and he was up in my face in a second.

"Oh really?" he asked in his dangerous, interrogator tone.

"He isn't going to hurt me. And a relationship with anybody is a risk. Trusting anybody is a risk, Grant. The fact that he's a vampire has absolutely nothing to do with it."

"Did he bite you too?" Grant asked.

My face burned so hot I coulda fried an egg on it.

"That!" He pointed at me. "Is why you're wrong. Because he is a vampire, there will always be the risk of something going too far, and he'll slip and take too much. Or that he'll decide that he loves you and wants to be with you forever and he'll turn you. There's that risk. And those aren't normal ones in a relationship, Ariana."

"He wouldn't do that." Damn my cracking voice.

"Not on purpose, maybe. Ariana, this is a dangerous path and I'm trying to help you. End it. Whatever it is, end it."

"Are you saying that as my boss?" I asked, finally looking up into his eyes again.

"I'm saying it as your boss and as your friend," he said.

"Quil isn't going to hurt me, General. And if he does, it'll be my fault, not yours. You don't need to protect me. As for the case, I will not tell him anything except what we agree on here, but since we are supposed to be collaborating, that should be everything anyway. I'm not going to let my feelings for him affect me as I work the case. And after this case, I'll be like anyone else in this office with a..." I paused. A what? "A someone."

"You done?" Grant asked and I nodded. "Good. You don't run off with him in the middle of the night on anything pertaining to the case. I don't give a damn what he says, you call me."

I nodded again. "Yes, sir."

"And you're wrong. You're my responsibility. When I saved you last year, you became my responsibility. When I offered you a spot on this team, I made you that even more. You are mine to protect. So if anything happens to you, I will blame myself."

He looked me in the eye. "So don't let anything happen to you."

I nodded, feeling like my insides were about to burst.

I was his. Even if it was just him seein' me as a kid, he cared enough to be worried.

I grinned. "Anyone tell you, you're kind of a chauvinist?"

"The director." He smiled back and patted my shoulder. "Every damn day."

"Time out over?" Dan asked as we walked back to our desks.

I grabbed my latte. "Yup. I'm ready to act like an adult again."

Dan snorted. "When did you ever act like an adult before?"

"Yeah, like you're one to talk, man," Jet said. "Seriously, girl, everything okay?" He glanced at Grant.

"I'm good, as long as General doesn't eat my badge."

"No promises if you three don't shut your holes and get working," Grant said.

"Sir, yes, sir," I said with a wrong handed salute.

Dan and Jet flinched. They hate it when I do that.

"Run down every one of these," Grant said once we were all settled. "I want to know every piece of every pie these people have their hands in."

He stood and slammed folders on each of our desks. "Each nest has thousands of vampires. We treat this like a gang war. It could be a fight over something like territory, or more personal. We don't know. What we do know is they aren't attacking the gang members themselves, they're going after outsiders who know about them."

I raised my hand.

"Yes, Ryder, something to share with the class?" he asked.

"I had an idea. We could have Quil bring in the leaders of the suspect nests. We all go in, undercover of course, and I get visions until something tells me something."

"Why all at once?" Dan asked.

"Remember what Len told us last night?" Jet asked. "They have government just like us. The nests are like different countries, but in the human world, if one country attacks another, the rest in the UN go after them. I got the impression it's the same here."

"A vamp summit," I said.

Grant nodded. "Good idea. Ryder, set it up."

I pulled out my cell and clicked to Quil's number. I looked up as I hit it and they were all starin' at me.

"You wanted me to set it up now, right?" I asked and Grant nodded.

I stood as it started to ring.

"Where are you going?" Grant asked. I pointed to the hall leading to the bathroom. "No, any call with someone we're working with doesn't require privacy."

I plopped back down in my chair.

"You calling for a reason, sweets?" Quil's groggy voice asked and I had to hold back a smile.

"Yes. I talked to Grant, he wants you to set up the meeting with your nest. We'll be there, acting as waiters or something. And then also set up a meeting with the people in other nests who are suspects. I'll get in close and get visions, see if we can't get the guy."

"You sound very professional." He sounded more awake. "You're in front of the others, aren't you?"

"Yup."

"And they know?"

"Yup."

"And you're okay with that?"

"Yup."

"And they're okay with this?"

"Nope."

"Figures," he said. "Oh well."

"Yup."

"I can call the leaders of the other nests. It's going to take some doing to get them over here, but I think I can wrangle it pretty fast for an emergency. And it will take a day for the travel. I'll call them and tell you when I have it arranged, but it will take until night at least. Most of us are asleep."

"Okay, one second." I muted the phone. "He says he can call them up, and he's pretty sure he can get them here, but we can't expect an answer until tonight. Then it'll take till at least tomorrow night for the meeting cuz they have to travel."

Grant nodded one stiff nod.

I unmuted. "Okay, do it."

"Okay, I will," he said, almost soundin' amused. "I'll call if I get answers before you get home. And if it's not till tonight, I'll be here to tell you then."

So many things were implied in that sentence, I turned red before the guys.

"Bye," I said.

"Goodbye, sweets." We clicked off.

"Blush on your own time, Ryder," Grant said.

I nodded. "Of course, General."

"So we have until tomorrow night to learn everything we can about these other nests," Grant said. "Crowley's team's helping us out. But this is still going to be a marathon. Get on your computers and get going."

So we did.

I had the Charlotte nest. Jet worked on the Kansas one. Apparently their king got the whole state, who knew? Dan was on the Atlanta one. Charles Crowley had Miami. Amanda Stone, Haile Temang, and George Wallace, from Crowley's team, were on St. Louis, Orlando, and Indianapolis respectively.

The most likely suspects according to Grant after going through the info he got from Len were Atlanta, Miami, or Kansas, but the others had some red flags, so they were on our list too.

My phone buzzed with a text about two hours into our diggin'. Kat. I flicked it open and she was asking me to meet her in the bathroom. I got up and took a peek over Grant's shoulder on the way.

And stopped dead. He wasn't checking out another one of the possibly hostile nests. He was checking out the Nashville one.

"Problem, Ryder?" he asked without even turning around.

They were going to be our allies, so we needed to know about them. Also, there could be some kind of paper trail between one of them and another nest that would show who was the traitor, if there even was one.

"Of course not, sir." I shook my head and kept on to the bathroom.

Kat was already waiting in there. "Nope." She shook her head when I opened my mouth. "Give it a minute."

Sure enough, Jet joined us a moment later.

"Now you can explain," Kat said.

"You know if we're not back soon, Grant's gonna kill all of us, right? And I'm in enough trouble as it is."

"Then talk fast," Jet said, crossin' his arms.

"He came over. We had sex. We are, I think, in some kind of relationship now. Neither of us are going to let it affect the job. And Grant already lectured me on dating a vamp, so if you two want to, go ahead."

"He does know if he hurts you, there's an entire office who will gang up and silver-shoot him, right?" Jet asked after taking a minute.

"Not to mention your family," Kat said. "I wouldn't want to date you with your ex-Marine and now politician dad."

I shrugged. "I think Quil and Daddy will hit it off... I mean, when, if, I introduce them at some point. I mean, it's new... I'm not plannin' anything or, um, anything."

Kat snorted. "So, details. What's he like? Did he try to bite you? Did you let him?" She eyed my neck.

"Okay, I'm outta here." Jet held up his hands and left, closing the door a little too hard behind him.

Kat looked at me and I felt the fire on my face. I must have some kind of hormone problem that causes excess blushing cuz there's no way any normal human lights up like a Christmas tree at every little thing.

I gave her the fuzzy watercolor recap of events and she giggled with me.

"Oh man, I need to find me a man. I'm getting old over here," she said.

"Oh please, you're not even thirty and you look my age."

She placed a hand on her chest. "Thank you! And this is why I love you."

"You want a nice guy, go find one. Stop dating the crazies."

"I don't date crazies."

"You described your last three, count 'em, *three*, boyfriends as man-children."

She shrugged. "They were."

"So, go find an adult. Or hey, there'll be lots of nice vamps at the party, and we'll probably be in contact with them after this so..."

She was shakin' her head so hard I stopped talkin'.

"No vamps," she said. "That's a little too bad boy for me."

"Quil's not a bad boy. He's... he's a man."

"True. So, did he bite you?"

I nodded. "He bit, I bit. There were just a lot of fluids."

She made a face and I took a deep breath.

"Overshare, got it," I said.

"That's just a little too kinky for me."

I snorted. "After the things you told me, I can't believe you're sayin' that with a straight face."

She shook her head again, makin' the pigtails dance. "I see biting going beyond that, but hey, to each her own."

I shrugged and grabbed the door.

"Ariana?"

"Yeah?"

"I'm happy for you. No matter what the guys say, I think he'll be good for you."

I smiled and squashed her in a one armed hug.

That was one at least.

# # #

We dug through financial records, social media pages, business records, and contracts all day. It was like trying to untangle a huge ball of string, since everyone's dealings were mixed up with everyone else's, and we only had what Len had down on his computer.

How does Len have all this info?

"Oh, red flag!" I screamed sometime around dinner.

"Is she always this loud?" Amanda asked, flashin' me a smile to soften it.

"Yes," Jet and Dan said as one.

"The Charlotte king was supposed to have a meeting with Senator Charleston here last month, work out a deal between their nest and some Tennessee regulations that were affectin' a business in Knoxville. But the queen vetoed it. According to this, the Charlotte vamps are out millions of dollars."

"What was the deal?" Grant asked and I shrugged. "Find out."

Oh, like that would be easy.

"General?" I asked.

He looked up again.

"Could I just call him?"

"Who, Ryder?"

"The senator. Couldn't I just call and ask?"

"Ask about a secret deal he never really had with a bunch of creatures that don't exist?" Dan jumped in. "Yeah, good luck with that one."

"He's right, Ryder," Grant said. "If you call, you'll just be telling him how much we know."

"Right." I nodded. "Stupid idea."

"Call Quil," Grant said.

"General?" I asked.

If Quil knew then it would probably be in Len's info. Wouldn't it?

"Ask Quil to call the senator and ask what it was about," Grant said.

"Ohhhh." My eyes flew wide and I grabbed my phone. "Yes, sir."

"If the vamps know all this, why aren't they digging through the info?" Dan asked.

"Because, Bridges," Grant said. "They have the information, we have the resources to track the official records down and we're trained investigators. We know what to look for and how to spot patterns. And if you make me explain myself to you ever again you're going to have a boot so far up your ass you'll be licking leather."

Whoa! Someone was getting crabby.

Maybe it was the sittin' all day? Grant's more of a man of action than a research guy.

I dialed Quil and he answered on the first ring. "Hello."

"Hey." I told him about the deal and wanting him to call the Senator.

"Business again?" He sighed. "Well alright, sweets, but next time better be a call for phone sex."

I turned in my chair so the others wouldn't see the blush. "Focus."

He said he'd look into it but didn't think it was them and we hung up.

"Okay. That's one," Grant said with a nod. "A few hundred to go. Get back to work."

I did.

By the end of the day, and I do mean the end cuz we weren't out of there till past eight, my back, neck, wrists, and eyes hurt from being chained to a computer for hours. And we probably would've been in longer if Len hadn't called, invitin' us to a gathering at one of his human's houses to check out their nest.

"Do we have time to get home and change?" I asked.

"Just," Grant said. "We want to be there at the beginning."

"Yes, sir."

I ran out before he could change his mind.

# # #

I called Quil on the way home. He was already at the place, helpin' Len set up for the last minute party.

"So tonight is for us to check out your people, right?" I asked.

"Yes," Quil said.

"Is there anyone off the top of your head? I mean, they all aren't gonna come, sooooo, what if there is someone in your nest and he just doesn't come?"

"If there's a traitor in the nest, I think they'll be there tonight," Quil said. "It's a good opportunity."

I nearly missed the light in front of me was red and slammed on my breaks.

"Waitwaitwait," I said. "Is this party bait?"

I could almost see him shrug as he said, "Kind of."

"Oh dear. But the demon… If he summoned another one."

"Could show up as someone else, yes."

"And we'll be sittin' ducks."

"Carla will be smelling for demon."

"Oh, okay. And there'll be me to get visions off everyone. I'm lookin' at a long night, aren't I?"

"I'm afraid so."

"How many people?"

"Around five hundred."

"In one house!"

"It's more like in an old estate manor."

I whistled low. "That's a lot of visions for me. I'm not sure I'll be able to do it. This might be a waste of time."

"Possibly. I don't think so, but it's also to plan for the meeting with the other nests. We're looking at having them here as soon as tomorrow night."

"Wow! Fast," I said.

"This type of warfare where they go after civilians is unprecedented. No one wants an out and out war, and I made it sound like that's what would happen. Most of the leaders are coming themselves, which means they're taking this very seriously."

"How many we thinkin' tomorrow?"

"About two hundred, mostly higher ups."

I took a deep breath. "I'm gonna need a lot of alcohol for this."

CHAPTER FIFTEEN

I TOOK A QUICK SHOWER AND fixed myself up fast before headin' back out. It took a little more time than it should've, mostly cuz Pyro was arguing he wanted to go with me.

I told him absolutely not. We'd be busted so freakin' fast if he showed up at a vamp and fed party.

"Remember," Grant said as we pulled up to the front gate in the van, "we're there to gather information. Be subtle, chat, mingle. No one goes off on their own."

We put in our earbuds and Amanda said something to the gate guards to get us past them. I glanced at the monitors to make sure everything was workin' okay.

"Whoa," Amanda breathed over the earbuds.

"What?" Grant asked.

"Damn, you guys need to see this place."

"We're not here to sightsee, Stone. Is there a good place to let us off and park the van?"

"Probably behind the pool house, Grant," she said after a moment.

"Probably?"

"I will make sure it is or find another spot, sir."

The van stopped and we got out when Amanda gave the all clear.

The view was blocked by the, I'm assuming pool house. We did our checks on the tech and walked around the pool house.

Whoa so did not cover it.

The grounds sprawled around us, going on far enough to have the pool, its house, and a tennis court, and that was just on this side of the mansion.

And it was a mansion. It rose in front of us, all white columns, wraparound porch, and balconies on both upper levels, like somethin' outta an antebellum movie.

"Jaw up, Ryder," Grant said. "I'd think you saw houses like this back home."

"Oh, I mean, we have a nice house, but this... this is like a plantation. I was wonderin' how they'd get five hundred plus people into one party. Never mind, no fire marshal needed here."

"Ryder, breathe."

"Yes, sir."

"So you really think another demon will show?" Dan asked.

"I know it," Grant said.

"Sir?" I asked.

"Gut feeling, Ryder."

Huh, maybe his famous instincts were part of his magic?

# # #

"Hey!" Len greeted a little too brightly when he opened the door. He was in a grey suit with a purple top and matching hat. "No invites of course, but..." He stepped back, the meaning clear: 'Come in if you can.'

So we did.

"Won't that no invites thing keep out vamps?" I asked.

"If they haven't been invited before, yes," Len said. "But we chose this place because so many of us have been here for some party or another that I can guarantee everyone who wants to come will be able to."

The house was split in the foyer by large sweeping stairs, living room on one side and what was probably a dining room judgin' by the corner of a table I glimpsed on the other.

The large living room was a treat for the senses. The carpet was beige and plush. Thick, dark green velvet curtains covered the many windows, and the furniture was all squishy leather lined with velvet pillows. The walls were covered with soft, off-white wallpaper with gentle gold swirls, and all lined with modern art and shelves covered in leather bound books.

Classical music played in the background and I could tell it was live before I could even see the musicians.

"There's tons of people you need to meet," Len said, takin' my arm and leading me into the living room, the guys close behind.

"Is the queen going to be here?" I asked.

"Possibly. She sometimes comes to things like this, but if she does, well... we'll deal with that bridge if it comes up. So, we're all really excited. No nest in history has ever worked with human cops like this. This is the beginning of a new era."

"We'll see," Grant said.

"Oh, so serious." Len tossed a pout over his shoulder and Grant frowned. "Lighten up, Special Agent Grant. This is supposed to be fun."

"No. This is work."

"Can't it be both?" Carla walked up to us in a fantastic leopard print dress I could never pull off in a million years, from a group of other well-dressed partygoers congregating in the living room. There were maybe forty of them, suggestin' we really did get here early. I had no idea if there were any of the ones I met at the club Thursday night, they all blended together after a bit, and I plastered a smile on my face.

It was gonna be a long night.

"Over here." Len led us to the bar set up at the back of the room.

The man next to the bar turned and waved at us. He looked like an aged Calvin Klein model with his impeccable black suit, thick silver hair and classic, chiseled features.

"Guys, this is Tom. He's the owner of the property, and kind enough to let us take over his house at the last minute."

"Hey, I'm Ariana." I held out my hand.

"Hello, love," he said with a strong British accent as he took my hand.

Flash.

A young boy, maybe seven, cried as he held the hand of a young woman wearing black.

He was perfectly groomed and in a smart black suit. The vision focused in as he lay a white rose on the chest of a boy who looked exactly like him in a coffin.

"Mommy, why isn't Colin coming back?" he asked in a small voice.

The women fell to her knees and pulled him into a hug. "Because God wants him now, baby. It's okay. It'll be okay."

"But I'm going to miss him. Can't we ask God to give him back?"

The child's confusion washed over me and I knew it would be months before he truly grasped what death meant.

"Ryder?" Grant asked as my eyes refocused.

"What did you see?" Tom asked.

I guess Len told him about me.

"Um, you want me to say it out loud?" I asked.

He grinned. "Why not? We're all friends here."

"You at your twin brother Colin's funeral. You gave him a white rose."

"Oh." His face fell as he blinked and backed away. "You really are psychic."

"You thought I was lying, darling?" Len asked.

Tom nodded and gulped.

I looked from Tom to Grant. "I'm so sorry. I shouldn't have said anything."

"I asked." He took a deep breath and walked away.

"He can handle vampires, but not psychics?" I asked Len. He shrugged.

"Why did you tell him?" Grant asked.

"He's hosting," Len said. "I know he's not the traitor."

Grant got up in his face. "Not the point. You don't compromise an op. You don't tell people about her. You got that?"

"Look out, you're turning me on." Len's smile faltered and Grant's glare stayed right in place.

"You don't put her at risk. You. Got. That?"

Len gulped. "Yeah… got it."

Grant backed off and I sighed, rubbin' my chest bone.

"How many people did you tell?" Grant said.

"Tell what?" Len said.

Grant met his eyes again and Len grinned, but it didn't reach his eyes.

"I, ugh, told a few people," Len said. "Bigger draw, you know?"

"She's not a fucking sideshow. And you just blew this op."

"No! I only told people who were… I mean, only ones who could be trusted."

"If they know about her, then others do, and all we need is for it to get to that one person who's here tonight, who shouldn't know, because they'll be able to avoid her in a big crowd, and we'll never know it."

"The people I told can be trusted."

"To keep their mouths shut?"

"Yes."

"That's what Quil said about you."

Ouch.

Len's face fell and Grant walked off.

Something told me he'd be back soon.

"I swear, Ariana, I didn't tell anyone who'd ever do this, and most of them already knew from the nest meeting anyway."

I rubbed his arm. "Yeah, but Grant's got a point. You told people, they tell people, and then secret's out. And all it takes is the wrong person knowing to put everyone in jeopardy."

"There a story there?" Len asked as he grabbed one of the glasses of already poured wine and handed it to me.

"I, uh, told the wrong person I was psychic a bit after I got my powers. Kind of tried to keep it under wraps after that." I took a long sip, not even tasting anything past the metal coatin' my tongue.

Len stared at me.

"One of my friends had a big mouth, no clue who told the wrong person there, but I… um, was kidnapped."

His eyes flew wide.

"Yeah, by a group that wanted me to use my powers to help them. They were one of those groups of people who are hired to go around the country to riot and cause trouble, you know? They wanted me to help them keep the operation under wraps, tell them when the cops were onto them. I didn't know what I was doing and couldn't see the future, and they didn't believe me. They had me locked in a converted barn for over two days. And they…"

I took another long gulp. "Well, it wasn't fun. It could've been worse. Sooooo much worse. One of them... he wanted to try to break me, thought I was holdin' out on them. If the others weren't there, he would've... Anyway, Grant was leadin' the team of FBI agents assigned to my case. He busted in, gun up, scared one of the guys into peeing. The bad one, well, he tried to run and Grant knocked him out so fast. I'd never seen anything like it."

"He saved you," Len said, lookin' at something over my shoulder.

"Well, there was a whole team behind him, but yeah, Grant was the one up front and knockin' out teeth. Anyway, he untied me, made some joke about me singin' and they're all still in jail for kidnapping and conspiracy."

"I haven't heard this story."

I turned and smiled as Quil wrapped his arm around my waist. Grant stood next to him. So they were what Len had been lookin' at?

"Hey, sweets." Quil gave me a quick kiss.

"About time you got here."

My eyes drank him up. He looked good in his black suit and greenish blue top.

"You saved her?" Quil asked Grant.

"We did," Grant said.

"How did you know she wasn't some kind of demon?" Quil asked and I turned my head and glared. "I just mean those people could have had a demon trapped or something else with power, who just looked like an innocent girl, and these guys didn't know for sure before they saved you."

"She was reported missing by human parents," Grant said. "And I knew. We were looking for her over a day, and we found her because of the singing. A demon doesn't sing when it's trapped. It fights to get out."

"She's got great lungs," Quil said.

"Yes, she does," Grant said, lockin' eyes with Quil.

Was I missing something?

"Introduce us to others," Grant said after a moment. "Not sure it will do much good after you opened your mouth, but we can try."

Len's mouth worked and Quil said, "He's my man, this is on me, Grant. I'll take care of it."

"You better," Grant said. "Let's go."

"Of course," Len said.

"You ready?" Quil asked, takin' my hand.

I downed the rest of the glass, grabbed another and nodded.

"Good." Grant led the way and Len had to quick march to get to the first small group before him so he could properly introduce us.

"Hey, darling," Len said to the first vamp we came to, a short, baby-faced one with black hair and eyes so dark they were nearly black, and kissed him hello.

Grant held up a warnin' finger at Dan.

"This is Sampson DuMaj," Len said. "And Sam, these are the feds." Len indicate us dramatically. "Special Agents Grant." He paused. "What's your first name?" Grant shook his head and Len rolled his eyes. "Fine, and this is Jet Kowalski, Daniel Bridges, and Ariana Ryder."

The vamp shook everyone's hands and I got a quick film cut of him being turned on the ground with firing overhead.

Len decided the one on one meet and greet would take too long, so he jumped onto the bar and waved widely to get everyone's attention.

"Everyone, these are the federal agents of the FBI's Special Division Force." He introduced us all, said we'd be coming around, and told everyone to have fun and mingle.

Him and Quil led me around the room after my teammates peeled off.

It took a while for Grant to leave, but it was a crowded room and I was with two guys who so far had proved pretty trustworthy, as far as watching out for me, at least.

Dan was flirting with Stephanie when we found her. Quil made her shake my hand and all I got was her being bit two years ago. She was a bomb maker workin' for the DOD before she was turned.

I shook more hands than I could count and had a First Impression off of about half, I guess I met more at the club than I thought. But nothing tellin' me if any of them were traitors.

They all knew this time what I was, and every single one wanted to know what I saw when I touched them.

"Ohhhh, really?" Minnet, about the millionth person in, asked after I told her I saw her when she was on stage for the first time as the lead ballerina. I got a double-whammy off her and the second was of her being bit after a performance by a young man, or rather a young looking vamp, who loved her dancing. "You can get two off one touch?"

"I've gotten as much as three off one touch," I said. "Actually, I've gotten three coherent ones. I was drunk once, and only once, believe you me, and the entire world was a mix of visions. I saw about ten at once and just couldn't keep track, so everything was a ton of colors and voices that I could only get one or two words outta before I focused on another. That wasn't pretty. Grant had to take me up to the hotel room and lock me in there cuz I wanted to go out and play with the colors and unicorns. According to him anyway. I don't remember anything after my fourth drink." I frowned. "Or was it my fifth?"

"And you saw all that in that two seconds?" she asked. Even after two-hundred years touring around the world, she still had her melodious French accent.

"Yup."

I found out pretty fast vamps are touchy-feely. They hugged and stroked arms, and weren't shy about the public displays. They didn't do anything gross really, there was just a lot of kissing going on, and they hung all over each other.

I know the touchin' made Grant uncomfortable. Not them on each other, it was when they treated us like one of them that he started to get his lemon look.

My hair, arms, and even neck were stroked more times than a puppy in a pet store. I don't mind people touching me, I'm always runnin' my hands all over everything. I did even before I got my visions.

But Grant didn't like it. I saw his hand twitch to his gun more times than I could count. I was just waitin' for one to try to kiss him. Now that would have been funny. And potentially disastrous. But none tried to kiss any of our team. At least, not that I saw.

I made the rounds, Quil guiding me the entire time. He had no problems giving the other vamps quick kisses hello and I'm sure it should've seemed stranger to me than it did. Honestly, they all acted like it was so normal, it stopped bugging me the third or fourth time he kissed someone else.

Although, it may have been the alcohol makin' me so tolerant.

Len made sure to keep the drinks coming and I had four glasses in an hour to keep my visions going strong, way too much for me.

We met everyone there so far in the first hour or so. No traitors, which was a good thing, but it meant the vision marathon had been a waste of time.

I collapsed on one of the poufy chairs in the furthest corner I could find without wandering to one of the empty rooms. Quil sat with me, and lay my head on his cool, hard chest to stroke my hair.

"You did great." He kissed my burning forehead.

"My brain's on fire."

"I noticed. Do you need an aspirin?"

"Doesn't help. I tried in the past."

"Has it gotten hot enough for you to go to the hospital before?"

"Never life threatenin', but I seem to have a high boilin' point. It goes up to about one oh four or so and I'm fine."

"I think it's higher than that now. Let me know if you need blood, okay?"

"Oh okay." I closed my eyes and dozed on his chest.

People and vamps fluttered about me. Some stopped to talk to Quil, and I just lay against him. Even when they sat down with us and started petting me, I didn't move.

"How are you doing?" Grant's voice broke through some time later.

"I'm cookin', General," I said. "Nobody came up with… er, nobody's showin' up as a traitor."

"Why is she slurring?"

Was I?

"She's got a high fever and that's with alcohol helping her psychic powers," Quil said. "I'm getting worried."

"She needs food and water now," Grant said. "I'll be right back."

"Does food help the fever?" Quil asked.

Took me a second to realize he was talkin' to me. I shrugged.

"Is there food in the kitchen or somethin'?" I asked.

"Yes," Quil said.

I drifted off again and too soon something shook my shoulder.

"Come on, Ariana," Grant said, softer than I'd ever heard him speak to anyone. "We need to get some food in you."

Something smelled delicious and I cracked my eyes to see Grant holdin' a plate of roast, mashed potatoes and green beans, and a bottle of water.

My stomach rumbled and I nodded, takin' the plate, sitting up more, but keepin' half my weight on Quil and the couch.

Grant handed me the water and I chugged half of it before going for the food.

"Okay," I said after a few minutes and another bottle and a half of water, "I feel better. Little more sober. Little more with it."

"We've got more people coming in," Quil said. "Are you up for this?"

"She needs to rest," Grant said.

"No, it's okay. I can keep going. The alcohol is really helping with the vision exhaustion and the food and water got my fever down."

"Don't tell me you can if you can't."

"I can."

"Ryder."

"I *can*, sir. I know I can. Because letting you two down scares me more than anything I might see inside a killer's head or even makin' myself sick."

"I'm not that scary, Ryder."

"Disappointin' you is. Both of you. I'd face any fear not to disappoint you."

"Ryder, how much have you had to drink?"

"Ummmmmm. Not sure."

"That's what I thought. Take a few more minutes. Make sure you're okay. I'll get you another drink." He nodded at Quil. "Be careful, she talks when she's like this."

"She always talks," Quil said.

I snorted and Grant walked away.

"I've never been a jealous man, sweets," Quil said, makin' me freeze with a mouthful of mashed potatoes and look at him. "I have even shared women in the past. But I will ask you, do I need to be prepared for that here?"

I swallowed hard.

"No. I have feelings, he doesn't." I shrugged. "I'm moving on."

He stared into my eyes and I blushed.

"You're adorable, you know that?" he asked.

I grinned. "I've been told."

Grant was back a minute later with something that looked suspiciously like the Cumberland River drink.

"Ah, Dave's here," Quil said as Grant handed me the drink.

"Thanks, sir."

"Pace yourself, Ryder. You're no good to me sick."

"Yes, sir."

I sipped my drink as we went through the party rooms again, getting visions and chattin' with Quil.

He told me he was born in sixteen twenty-eight in a small town just north of Rome, his parents died when he was a teen, and he was twenty-six when he was made.

He'd been married, but his wife and baby died in childbirth. He was the oldest, had three little sisters, and he took care of them until they married. He was a hunter, and after winning a competition in archery, he was celebrating with friends when he saw Jade.

His wife had been dead over five years, and he hadn't touched another woman since. But she was exotic and exuded sexuality, like no woman he'd ever met. He was showing her how to shoot in the woods when she stripped. They'd had sex right there, and she turned him after. Which I already knew.

"So you loved her?" I asked.

"I did," he said. "For about fifty years. After that, we stopped seeing each other like that and I just worked with her, then for her when she established this nest. Don't worry, there haven't been feelings there for a long time." He leaned forward and slowly ran his hand past my knee to go under my skirt and up my thigh.

"Quil." I giggled and slapped the hand, but it didn't shirk back. "We've got people all around us."

"Oh, well that would be bad, someone could see." He slid his hand out and pulled me down the hall.

"Quil," I said with a warning finger as he opened one of the doors to reveal a bedroom. "We're working."

Quil sighed and leaned his head against my shoulder. "I'm going to run to the bathroom and get some cold water on me. I'll be back in a minute."

Then his weight was off me like it'd never been there and it was my turn to sigh.

I went into the kitchen, grabbed some fruit, and chatted with Tom and a few other guys. They said they were 'Len's boys.'

No, I didn't ask what that meant. I didn't want to know.

Quil was back in a few minutes, and the guys went to dance.

"So what happened to your sisters?" I asked, popping a grape in my mouth.

"They all married and had kids," he said.

"Well yeah, you said that, but you didn't keep track?"

"After I became a vampire? No. They thought I was dead. If I popped up again, it would cause confusion. Do you know how many vampires have been killed because people who knew they were dead saw them walking around town? I had to leave home. And I have no idea what happened after that. We didn't exactly have the internet and phones to stay in touch."

As though on cue, his phone rang.

"Speaking of," I said.

He pulled it out and made a face like someone just shoved a rotting skunk under his nose. "Now, what could he possibly want?"

He scowled at the phone, letting it ring as though debating whether to answer or not.

"Who?" I asked.

"King of Miami, pain in the ass if there ever was one. Oh no, he's not like the queen, in fact, he loves humans. He's one of the ones who have been pushing for vampires to come out for years. But he's old, powerful, and... imagine the god Pan, and you'll get a handle on Carvi. He wants to fuck everything that moves."

I laughed.

He pinched his nose for a moment before answering. "Yes?"

I got a hint of a pleasant sounding voice.

"No, we don't need you up here, honestly..." The voice cut him off and Quil rolled his eyes as it babbled on, I couldn't hear much of anything beyond a stolen syllable here or there.

Quil covered the mouthpiece. "Sorry, sweets, I apparently need to take this." He gave me a quick kiss, the guy was still jabberin' on, (man, he could talk like me, and that's saying something) and walked down the hall.

"Ooookay," I said, wanderin' onto the dance floor they'd made in the dining room by pushing the table to the side.

"That's a horrible way to treat a lady," Len said, grabbing my hand and spinning me around.

I laughed as we matched up in a waltz.

"What? Quil takin' a call?" I asked.

"And leaving his lovely date all alone."

"Ryder," Grant said over the earbud, makin' me jump, "stop dancing with Len, you need to get more of the new people."

"Right, sorry, sir."

"Earbud?" Len asked next to my ear.

I nodded as we broke off.

I looked around for people I hadn't met yet, but it was impossible to remember. I slipped down the hall to grab Quil.

No Quil. Huh. Maybe he went upstairs for some quiet?

Flash.

"What's wrong, sweets? Shouldn't you be out with your people?" Quil leaned over a small form that was obviously me in the living room.

"Grant's being a jerk. He said...he said...you know what, it doesn't matter. I just need to get away." I sounded really upset.

He wrapped his arms around me.

"Is there somewhere I can lay down for a minute?" I asked, voice cracking.

"Of course, sweets." Quil held me close and walked upstairs with me.

"Ariana, you okay?" Grant was leaning in front of me when the vision left.

How did he get over to me so quickly?

"You were really out of it," he said.

"I was?" I asked. "How long?"

"You were staring at the wall when I got here, maybe ten seconds ago."

"No." I shook my head. "That's not possible. The only time they take over a second or two is if it's a present time one."

"So this was a present time one," Grant said.

I shook my head again. "No, Quil was talking to me."

He'd been talking to me!

Our eyes met and I got the dizzies as ice slipped through my belly and I slammed my hand to my mouth.

"I just saw them go upstairs!" I said.

I took off, Grant close behind.

We pushed across the crowded living room, Grant barkin' at people to get outta the way.

I prayed we weren't too late.

158

CHAPTER SIXTEEN

IT TOOK TOO LONG TO get across the room and I kicked off my heels and sprinted up the stairs so fast even Grant couldn't keep up. I must've been breathin' hard, my lungs and legs had to be burnin'.

Couldn't feel anything through the fuzz though.

It's already had Quil alone over a minute.

Any cop'll tell you all it takes is a second. One second for the bad guy to take off with a kid, to kill you, to get you out of public to rape you.

One second.

I yanked open the first door. Bathroom.

"Grrrrr!"

Grant tapped my shoulder and put a finger to his lips, gun already out.

I drew mine and we hit the next room and the next. All empty. Guests were supposed to stay out of the upstairs.

I grabbed the next and twisted.

"Locked."

Grant jerked his chin and I scrambled outta the way. He kicked the door open and burst in, me close behind.

The demon with my face had my vamp by the throat with a silver whip. He bucked and struggled, but the silver dug into his skin, obviously close to cuttin' him as she pulled him across the carpet.

"Quil!" I yelled, running forward.

Whatush.

"Owwwww!" I fell to the ground as pain lanced through my arm and my vision went red.

Tears bleared my eyes as I lurched up, gun still in my other hand. I hadn't noticed the other whip. I should've.

She grinned my grin as she pulled the wicked object back for another strike and I scrambled back, lookin' down at my arm.

159

Couldn't help it.

A shallow slash trailed down my arm, at least six inches. Blood oozed outta the thin cut and dripped down to the ground from my elbow.

Grant brought his gun up and I followed suit.

"Don't do it, General," she said in my voice, holding up the whip. "One little cut with this will kill him."

"If you wanted to kill him, you wouldn't have been trying to drag him away."

She flinched. "Better dead than escaped."

"He's already dead," Grant said.

With a smirk she (it?) flicked her wrist, and I choked as the second whip twirled around my neck.

I gagged as she yanked and fell to my knees.

"Your little girl isn't, and I'll kill her before you can even squeeze."

Grant held stone still as I gasped and pulled at the evil, cold whip as she dragged me across the floor, the whip threatening to take off my head if I didn't wiggle to go with it.

My vision darkened and I met Quil's eyes before blacking out for a second.

I blinked back on.

I could breathe again!

I looked up just in time to see the demon pull back the whip and slash Quil across the leg. He must've gotten free while she was busy with me.

Grant double tapped her in the head, the shots shatterin' my hearing, and probably everyone else's too.

She screeched and clawed at the holes in her head, but orangey skin filled the holes as I pushed to my feet and lunged for my gun.

I grabbed it and shot her in the middle, flinchin' at the noise and hittin' her in the shoulder as Grant pulled a sawed-off shotgun out from under his jacket.

He pumped it and shot the demon straight in the face, blowing it away in a mass of noise and orange surprise.

My ears exploded, leaving only a ringin'.

And I thought our pistols were loud.

I risked a glance at Quil. His eyes were closed and he took breaths he didn't need as he leaned against the wall, tryin' to pull himself up.

"Stay down!" I yelled as Grant shot the demon in the middle, the noise so muffled the first shots had to have caused hearing damage.

Quil pushed against the wall and launched himself at the demon, taking her down and punchin' her in the ball of wax somewhere around where the face had been.

"Your invitation is revoked, demon!" Tom's voice yelled loud enough to clear my ears.

The demon screamed as she flew across the floor and through the window with a fantastic showering of glass shards.

Len and Tom ran in and fell next to Quil on the ground.

I ran to the window and raised my gun, ignorin' the fire in my arm as the wound crackled.

I shot, and shot again, and again. I emptied my magazine into her and the ground.

She laughed.

It wasn't any strange demon laugh, it was my laugh. The deep belly one I give when I hear or see something really funny.

Grant appeared next to me, with a... was that a grenade!

He pulled out the pin with his teeth and lobbed it at the demon. She shouted and zoomed away and the explosion took the tree outside.

I ran to Quil and fell next to his leg. The long gash wasn't clotting like I expected and the skin took on a sickly silver sheen no human skin ever saw.

"Ariana, can you suck it out again?" Len asked. "We would, but it's demon enchanted silver... even if we spit it out, it would burn us, and it would take too long. Even then, we'd try, but you'd be able to get it all out without problems."

"Yeah," I said as Len tore the rip in Quil's pants bigger to see around the cut.

It was about four inches long. Shallow, but it didn't matter.

"I can do it," I said. "But I can't with an audience."

I slipped off the camera necklace and tossed it to Grant and he caught it one handed as I took out the earbud.

"Once you're done, you know what will happen?" Len asked me.

I looked at Quil, who was watching me with pain filled eyes, sweat drippin' into them, and nodded.

"We can't help the reaction, and after how much you'll have to get out, he'll need blood too," Len said.

I nodded again and Len and Tom walked out, but Grant stayed by me, starin' with a complete poker face.

"Grant, if I don't do this, he'll die," I said.

"I get that. You don't need to be alone," he said with a voice to match his face.

"Bullshit!" I yelled.

He didn't even blink.

"You know why! Now leave or I swear I'll do this in front of you." My voice broke as tears slipped out.

Grant scowled and left, pullin' the door closed behind him.

Without another word, I lowered my face to Quil's leg and started sucking. I didn't bother spiting any of it out. We'd already wasted enough time.

And I'd need the strength for when he needed to take it back. As his blood filled me, I sucked harder, the process takin' longer this time since it wasn't just a scratch and the silver had already had time to travel.

I sucked forever, waitin' for Quil to tell me when it was all out.

Without warning, he pulled from my mouth with a moan and grabbed me, getting on top of me before I realized we got it all.

He kissed my bloody mouth hard, eyes red.

He growled and reached under me, tearing away my panties with one pull and bit down on my neck. It hurt! I could feel it as the fangs went straight into my jugular.

It hurt only a moment before pleasure rode through me and didn't stop.

I barely felt him slip into me and I hung onto him and let him do the movin' as he bent his body to take both of what he needed from me at once.

I held his head to my neck and whimpered as he moved. My toes curled and the world went dark as the pleasure of orgasm, teeth, and the certainty that we were both very much alive, okay, at least animated, took me.

Quil pulled his fangs out and licked my neck clean, but wasn't close to done with me. He grinned, staring down into my eyes with those beautiful swirls of sea, and moved slower, more deliberately. He stroked my arms as he lowered them to the ground and pinned them, supporting his weight by his hands over my wrists.

Excitement shot through my blood as I moved with him, strugglin' against his hold when I knew full well I couldn't break it.

I moaned as I felt myself tighten around him and he moved faster, going deeper as small sounds tore through his throat. He thumped in harder, to the point of near pain, and my world went dark as I pressed up against him for all I was worth, barely holding onto conscious thought enough to bite down on my lip and not scream.

I went limp with the release just in time to feel Quil clamp down on my wrists and come inside me.

He moaned into my neck and I trembled with the aftershocks as he pulled out.

The world was fuzzy again. How much did he take?

He stroked my hair and licked my neck again before going for my arm. I couldn't move as he did his pants up, pulled a clean towel from the walk-in closet, cleaned my wound the best he could without water, and wrapped the whip slash.

"You'll need to go to a hospital for this, I can't heal it because of the silver," he said in a husky whisper before lying next to me. "Thank you, sweets."

"For sucking your blood, or letting you take mine, or for not yelling at you for screwing me like that while an army, including my team, is right outside the door?" I asked.

How was I gonna live this down with the guys?

"All." He kissed me, his eyes alight with passion as he pulled back. "I don't care what your boss says. You saved me. And that was amazing."

"Oh no, it was, but... people are right out there."

He leaned back and ran his hands over my left arm.

"What are you doing?" I asked, exhausted and yet not at the same time as my body went out of whack due to his blood and my blood loss conducting a mini-war inside me.

"Making sure she didn't get you anywhere else," he said, checking that arm, then the injured one more gently, then down to my stomach, then each leg, brushing with feather-light fingertips the whole way.

"You're beautiful," he said once he was done.

I bit back a laugh. "Flattery will get you nowhere. I'm too sore to even think about more sex."

"Did I hurt you?" he asked.

"Just my neck. And that'll be okay. That's twice in one week I've had to suck silver out of you. How did you not die, I mean really die, before this?"

"Normally, people with silver aren't too dangerous because we move so much faster than humans, and I haven't had to deal with anyone sending a demon after me." He paused. "I've been bled with silver seven times now. The first five I either got to a doctor who was able to pump it out, or had someone on hand to suck it out."

"Why hasn't your leg healed?"

"The whips the demon had were enchanted. They can spell silver with their blood. It's the only thing that can hurt us and leave scars. I'll heal as slowly as a human, and I will have a scar forever." He made a face.

"I think scars make a guy sexier," I said, runnin' my fingers down the line of his jaw. He chuckled and I grinned right back. "Not that you need the help."

I glanced at the door. "I hope you know, I can't ever leave this room."

"I doubt anyone you're worried about would want to listen at the door."

"They'll know," I said. "We'll go back out there and everyone will know and I can't handle that. I'll go to work and no one will say anything, scratch that, Dan will say something, but the others will just know, and it'll be this big pink elephant in the room. I'm not the psychic or an agent anymore. I'm the agent who did a vamp at a work party after a demon attack while everyone waited outside."

"No," Quil said, staring into my eyes. "You're the agent who got silver out of me, yet again, and got pounced on, yet again, for your troubles. I didn't ask, sweets, I just rolled over and took you."

"Yeah, let's tell my boss that. Then I can try to pull him off you as he attacks you, probably with that silver whip the demon left, then watch as all the vamps jump on him, then as the other agents jump on them. Then have fun at their funerals because there will be a lot of dead people, and our alliance will go up in smoke. Just so I don't have to be embarrassed. I don't think so."

"Does your mouth just do that or do you actually have to concentrate to talk that much so quickly?"

"Don't tease me. What am I gonna do?"

"You're going to suck it up. You're going to get up, get your team to take you to the hospital. You're going to tell them to take their opinions and shove them in whatever hole you think is anatomically appropriate, and if your boss fires you, I will hire you as a consultant for the nest so you and your *many* talents don't go to waste. They loved you tonight. I saw you out there, talking and laughing. You fit here."

I pulled back and looked at him. "I'm not working for you. That would be too weird. And they won't fire me. The director won't let them."

I didn't know what to say about the rest of it.

"Even after this, unprofessional behavior," he said in a deep voice.

I giggled. He was doing a Grant impression.

"Yeah. She won't care. Hell, she'll probably say it'd be a good way to get intel from you."

"So you'll go back to work and just have to deal with everyone whispering behind your back?"

I nodded. "Pretty much. That plus the cold, disappointed shoulder from Grant, the snide comments from Dan, the worried looks from Jet. Kat will giggle with me over it, and Irish..." I paused. "I don't know what Irish would say."

A knock on the door cut off his laugh.

"What?" Quil yelled.

"Sorry," Len yelled through the door. "But Agent Grant's worried about Ariana. He said this shouldn't be taking so long, and he's worried you hurt her. He's, well, we'll have to subdue him in a second."

I heard cursing in the hall and flinched.

"Tell him I don't know how fast he is, but I'm not, and I like to snuggle after," Quil yelled.

Actually, we were done pretty quickly, but that wasn't the point.

"Don't you dare tell him that," I yelled, then said in a quieter voice to Quil, "Stop making trouble."

"But I'm so good at it." He pouted.

"Len, tell Grant I'm fine and I'm too embarrassed to come out yet," I yelled.

"Ariana?"

My heart sank at Grant's voice.

"I'm fine, General! I'm just resistin' the urge to dig myself a hole and stay there, that's all."

"Agent Ryder, if you're..." He paused. "*Done*, we need to check you out," he said in a completely un-telling tone. "Deal with your embarrassment on your own time."

"Why don't y-" Quil yelled, and I clamped my hand over his mouth.

"Just a minute, General!" I lowered my voice. "Seriously? You owe me. So you are not gonna say anything else to make this situation worse."

He nodded with big, innocent eyes. Then ruined it by licking my palm.

"You." I shook my head as I stood up.

I paused as I saw myself in the full length mirror on the door. My hair looked like a haystack in tornado season, my clothes were torn and bloody, my mascara was streaked from crying, and my face was as red as a radish.

"Oh yeah," I said. "I look great."

"You do," Quil said. I tossed him a look and shook out my hair, lookin' around. Where the blazes did my hair clip go?

"I look like someone who was just in a fight then had sex," I said, grabbing a tissue off the dresser. I dabbed it with spit and wiped under my eyes. "Or did both at the same time."

"Exactly," Quil said. "You look wonderful ravished like that."

"You are not helping."

"Wasn't trying to," he said. "I've got to go talk to my people. Let them see that I'm alive. Will you be okay for a minute?"

"Yes, I'll be fine. You go do your thing. It'll be easier for me to face Grant alone."

"You can wait in here until I'm back."

"No, I really can't. Got to face the boss eventually."

He nodded and opened the door, strollin' out with a cocky, "Agent Grant."

Grant came in and closed the door behind him.

He put my purse on the dresser, takin' me in with a long look.

"You dropped your purse downstairs," he said. "Still have your first aid kit in here?"

I nodded. "Box, probably near the bottom."

He riffled through my purse and came out with the little white box. He nodded at the bed and I sat on it.

He pulled the cloth off my arm and made a small hiss of sympathy as I whimpered. It hurt! He didn't say anything as he cleaned it off with the no pain antiseptic, then wrapped it with a real bandage.

"What was I supposed to do?" I asked once he was done.

"I don't know," he said. "I do know you're not looking at me. So you think you did something wrong."

I hardened my face and looked up into his eyes. He gave a ghost of a smile.

"That's a start," he said, then cleared his throat. "You should get out there. They're all pretty grateful. And they don't seem to have a problem with what you two did in here."

"Do you? Have a problem, sir?" I asked.

He kissed my forehead and stood up. "Yes. You ready?"

"Grant, are you okay?"

"If you hadn't wanted to…" He shook his head, holdin' out the camera necklace. I put it on and looked around for my earbud. "Would he have stopped if you didn't want to?"

"Yes," I said. "If I said no, he would have stopped. I wouldn't be with him if I wasn't positive of that."

"Okay." He grabbed my earbud off the ground and handed it to me.

I put it in.

He took a breath and looked at me.

"Sir?" I finally asked. "Is there something else?"

He walked out.

We went back downstairs and the party could not have been more dead if they were zombies and not vamps.

"I didn't get everyone, General," I said.

He shook his head. "The vamps let it spill you were psychic. In this crowd, if anyone didn't want to talk to you, they wouldn't have to. This is what happens when you work with amateurs. We can leave another team to keep an eye on the place, but I'm calling it."

"This has been one of the strangest nights of my life," I said.

"Stranger than when you were kidnaped?" Quil asked, walkin' up.

"No, that's why I said one of, cuz honestly while that was horrible, tonight was surreal on the level of Dali. And I'm-"

He grabbed my face in his hands and pulled me into a deep kiss. I smushed my body into his and stood on tip-toes to get closer.

That's one way to shut me up.

Grant cleared his throat and I pulled back.

"Right, and I have to stay." Quil rested his forehead on mine. "Can't go with the pretty girl, can't go with the pretty girl."

I giggled. "That's okay. Pretty girl needs a shower and can't have another night like last. I have to work tomorrow and I'm already about to pass out."

He nodded and backed away. "Make sure to get a lot of iron."

"I will. But what if the summoner is still here?"

"Then the rest of the nest will jump him if he reveals himself or tries anything." Quil turned to Grant. "Could you stay with her tonight? I know I took too much, and I don't want her to be alone, just in case."

Grant almost looked… surprised? Maybe. He nodded. "My thoughts exactly."

"See, there the big guy goes again, gettin' all protective and gettin' a guy to watch me," I said.

"Born four hundred years ago, sweets," Quil said with a grin. "Don't really care if I come off as sexist."

We kissed goodbye and Grant drove us back to my place.

We didn't say much in the van, and I didn't dare say anything about grabbing my car from the office when Grant dropped off the van, got his, and opened the door for me.

Yep, he wasn't leaving me alone for a second.

Considering the demon could've followed us, not a bad idea.

We got to my house and Grant went in after me.

Pyro barely had time to flop on the couch as Grant yanked off his boots at the door.

Grant looked up and around, squinting.

"Yeah General?" I asked as I walked into the kitchen and grabbed two bottles of water.

"Thought I saw something move," he said.

"Then why isn't your gun out?" I asked, grinnin' so he'd know I was teasing as I handed him the water.

"I was seeing things."

"Well, you are psychic or somethin' too, aren't you?"

"Nice try."

"Come on, sir. You had to have known. That there's something magic about you."

He shot me a look. "Sometimes, Ryder, I get the strongest urge to slap you upside the head."

"Haha. I'm gonna shower. You got clean clothes in your bag?"

"Always travel with a change of clothes, Ryder."

"I'll take that as a yes. Soooo, food and stuff, you know where it is. I'll clean up, then while you do, I can get the guest room made up."

I walked upstairs, pausing to look back as Grant sat on the couch next to Pyro. He stroked my rug, squintin' at him.

"Sir?" I asked.

"Why are you always moving this rug, Ryder? Every time I'm over here, it's in a different spot."

I grinned. "He moves himself, General. Likes the change in scenery."

He looked up at me. "Smart ass."

"Yes, sir."

I cleaned up pretty quick, didn't want either of us to be up too late.

We still had a demon to catch and were no closer to figurin' out who the summoner was.

"Sir?" I asked after he was cleaned up and his room was ready.

"Don't go there, Ryder."

"Huh? This is a question on the case, sir."

"Go ahead then."

What the blazes did he think I was gonna ask?

"How do we find the summoner? We've got demons who keep showin' up, but this person, there's no reason for them to come to any trap we set in person. And I don't know... I don't think the party tomorrow will do much good."

"I do."

"Really? Why?"

He met my eyes. "Because, tonight, the demon could have gone after anyone... easily. It didn't. It went after Quil. And it wasn't trying to kill him."

I drew a sharp breath. "You don't think it's an attack against the nest."

"Not per se. Tonight, whatever this is, Ryder, I saw it. It's personal."

"And if it's personal... then they're going to want to be there to see it go down?"

"More likely. Also narrows the grudge list down. I already called Crowley's team and they're getting an early start on the records tomorrow with the new focus."

"Looking for someone who'd want to hurt Quil?"

"Yes."

"Sir, I don't know... I mean, the dead girls."

"Ariana, whatever this plot is, they want to hurt the nest, yes, but if the demon just wanted to kill Quil, she would have. She was trying to kidnap him. It's personal."

"What happened to not assumin' anything, sir?"

He smiled. "It's not an assumption, Ryder. I can feel it."

"You always say that and you always end up being right, it's like you know..." I snapped and pointed at him. "You *did* know you were magic before!"

His smile didn't waver. "And now we know what we're looking for."

"What are you?"

"No idea."

"Sir!"

"Ryder, I don't know. Now, if Quil's the intended target, why kill the girls?"

I blew out a huff of air. "Fine. Well, Quil's the nest investigator. You kill girls to get him on the case and then... kidnap him when he's distracted because of it?"

"Possibly."

"Were we not even supposed to be on the case? I was thinkin' the bad guy was tryin' to sic us on the nest, but maybe they didn't even know about us."

"No, I think we were exactly where they wanted us, until tonight."

"Because the demon screwed up?"

"Yes."

"But who would want to kidnap Quil and why?"

"That's what we're for, Ryder." He pat my knee. "Get some sleep. We're starting over tomorrow." I couldn't even ask why before he said, "We've been looking at this wrong. We start over to see the evidence in new light. Quil's no longer another investigator. He's the intended victim. Perspective is everything."

CHAPTER SEVENTEEN

W HEN WE WALKED IN, EVERYONE in the office paused and looked at
us.

Correction, looked at me.

I went red faster than flippin' a switch on a neon sign.

That one second was all it took for me to feel like I was naked and walkin' into math class on finals day.

"Hey, Crowley," I said as Grant and I walked past him and he gave me a wave. "Good job on cleaning up the scene."

Team two had the job of staying up and processin' the crime scene last night and jumped on the research today. They probably didn't get a lick of sleep last night. I reached to pat his shoulder and he jerked away.

I know all kinds of emotions were swirlin' on my face.

"Thanks," he said, hightailing it to his desk.

He didn't even want me to touch him?

I was a leper.

"Ryder, come on, you're going to go through the evidence with Irish. Focus on Quil," Grant said.

"Yes, sir."

I put the coffees down on their owners' desks, and gave Kat's to her as she set up her laptop at Grant's desk.

"What you doin' up here?" I asked her.

"Forensic psychology," she said. "Trying to get a sense of the summoner from the attacks."

"Are you trained in that?"

"Only on the job, but it's not a real profile, more looking for patterns."

I nodded and went up to the lab with Grant and Sam from Team Three.

Sam walked back down with Grant.

What the quack? Did I need an escort or somethin'?

Irish looked up from a microscope and smiled at me.

At least one person was happy to see me.

"Hey, Irish!" I put our coffees down and hugged him.

"Hello, little darlin'," he said. "You okay?"

"You heard?"

"Oh, I heard."

I let him go and looked at him. "I'm so embarrassed."

"Eh, don't be. Two weeks from now, we'll be on another case and no one will remember this."

His cologne tickled my nose and I jerked away and turned to sneeze.

"Geez, Irish, what's with the cologne?"

He grinned. "Sorry lass, with the age goes the nose. Didn't realize it was so heavy."

I eyed him. "You're lyin'. Who is she?"

He blinked quickly. "How did you know!"

I giggled and slapped his arm. "You always do this when you have a date at night. So, what's her name?"

He grinned. "Mandy, and she is a lovely little thing. Bit younger than me. She wants to go dancing."

"That's if Grant lets any of us leave tonight. He may want you at the party."

Irish paled even more, not something I'd think was possible with his skin. "In the vampire nest? I'm not sure I can do that. And I'm a lab guy. I don't do field work."

I shrugged. "I was just sayin', it's possible. We might need you there to analyze stuff on the scene, to keep an eye on the evidence so I can have it with me, I don't know. I'm just talkin' here."

He nodded. "Yeah, but Grant wouldn't make me do that. I don't do field work."

Wow, he was scared.

"Are you scared of vampires, Irish?"

"Aye. A bit."

"Quil's a good guy, Irish. I swear he wouldn't hurt you."

"Yeah, but what about the thousands of others? And that queen, I don't want to meet her."

"Yeah. And she'll be there tonight." I shivered. "Geez, just got a chill. Well, I gotta get to work."

I got the evidence from the lockup and made a little nest in the corner again as Irish went back to analyzin' stuff I guessed was from last night.

I went over everything again, focusing on Quil, and got nothing for my troubles.

Grant came up to check after a couple of hours, Sam right behind him.

"Sorry, General. I have no clue why I can't get anything. Kinda figured I would cuz it's Quil, and last night I got that vision of him when I was just wonderin' where he wandered off to. But I'm getting nothing."

"That's okay. It was worth a try."

But he had his lemon look.

"What is it, General?"

He shook his head. "I can't figure out why you can't get any visions about him. Even if it has nothing to do with the case."

"Yeah," I said. "Even if the demons have something blockin' me seeing their plan, shouldn't I still see stuff about Quil?"

"Try someone else," he said, and held out his arm. "Try me."

I grabbed his arm with both hands and closed my eyes, breathin' him in, thinkin' about his strong jaw and sharp eyes, how his face crinkled up when he smiled, how he looked when he was mad.

I opened my eyes. "Nothing, sir."

He nodded. "Something is blocking you."

I looked around. "How? Maybe I'm just tired from last night?"

"Yeah, maybe." He still had that look though. "Or there could be something on the clothes blocking you."

"So we try this away from the evidence?" I asked.

"Good idea. Come on. Sapato, you're up here for the day."

"Yes, sir," Sam said.

I left my mess, promisin' Irish I'd be back to clean it up in a minute and we went to the bathroom.

"Try now," Grant said, holdin' his arm out again.

I grabbed it and focused on him.

"Still nothing, sir," I said, lettin' him go and turnin' my head so I could sneeze. "Sorry."

"I don't like this. Even after last night, you've never had this much trouble."

"Maybe I really just got cooked last night," I said. "But then why did I get that vision of Quil so easy?"

"That's what I want to know. Is there anything that could block your powers?"

"Just the gris-gris."

"The what?"

"Oh yeah! I forgot to tell you about that."

He glared down at me and stepped closer. "About. What?"

"Oh ummmm, Quil got one to block me, so we could be intimate without me gettin' flooded with visions."

"And it didn't occur to you to tell me this?"

"I forgot, but sir-"

He sliced his hand in front of me. "You knew about something that could block your powers, and you just forgot to tell your team about it?"

"Um, kinda, yeah." I flinched.

"Ryder." He took a deep breath. "How does it work?"

"If it's in the room with a psychic, it slows our powers, can't completely block us, but slows it."

"Has to be in the room?"

"Yeah, that's what Quil said. He also said not to touch or smell it, cuz that'd hurt my powers a while."

"How long does it work for?"

"If I don't touch it, no time after I'm outta that fifteen feet or so range. If I did, then he said something about me being out all day, soooo maybe twelve hours to a full day?"

"Shit. Ryder!"

"Sorry!"

"Did you have any visions after the one about Quil?"

I shook my head.

"Fuck! Someone there could have touched you with one in the crowd as we were leaving."

I pulled out my phone. "I'll ask Quil how long it could last if that's what happened."

Grant nodded and I called Quil. It went to voicemail so I left a message.

"Back on records," Grant said, holdin' up a finger. "After you clean up the mess in Irish's lab."

"Yes, sir."

# # #

Lookin' through Quil's finances, he had his hands in some pretty sticky stuff. Lots of real estate, a few politicians, but nothing so obviously out there it jumped out at me as a red flag.

And if it was this personal, I was willin' to bet it wasn't something to do with business.

Grant was looking into his personal stuff, figured I was too close to be doing that.

Quil called me back when he got up and confirmed the gris-gris only lasted about ten or so hours, maybe twelve if it was really strong, and couldn't do past fifteen feet as a maximum.

He also said he had a guy comin' by with our outfits for tonight.

Grant wasn't happy about it, but we had them checked for everything we could think of to make sure they weren't compromised on the way to us.

The whole day, everyone in the building had to do the buddy system, which was the real reason Kat was in the main office with us and why Grant had me and then Sam in Irish's lab.

None of us could even go to the bathroom alone.

It was daylight, the demon could not possibly be there. What did Grant think was gonna happen?

By the time we got dinner delivered, I was feeling pretty queasy about the whole situation tonight.

If it was personal, they weren't gonna stop, and I was willing to bet it was someone in Quil's nest.

"What about Jade?" I asked as we ate our Chinese. "They've got history and she knows he'd like to overthrow her."

"But she's the leader," Jet said. "These attacks make her look weak. Even if she doesn't care about humans, from what I've read, she'll care about that."

"And why would she try to kidnap Quil anyway," I said. "Yeahhhhh. I could see wanting to kill him for suspected treason, but not kidnap."

"We're missing something," Dan said.

If I'd said something obvious like that, he would've said something rude, like, "No shit, Captain Obvious," but I kept my mouth shut.

See, I can act like an adult sometimes.

After we ate, Grant gave us the outfits we were supposed to wear, and Jet, Dan, Crowley and Carl from Mender's team all made faces. They were in tight black pants and white collared shirts with purple vests. Mender and Sam were going in as party guests of Quil's, and I of course, was Quil's girl.

Mender and Sam were given dressy outfits that were miraculously the perfect sizes and looked fabulous on their body types. Len said he had an eye for that sort of thing, but come on, that's just spooky. They were both pretty pleased with them, a classy black dress for Mender, and a navy blue suit with a nice pink silk tie for Sam.

But my outfit took the cake.

It was a red party dress with a wide, ballerina-like tulle skirt that fell about my knees, and a tight corset bodice with gold tulle over it that tied at the base of my neck, leaving my arms and shoulders bare and the top of my chest pushed up and thinly veiled.

Two guesses who actually picked out the dress and what he was thinkin' with.

And mine came with accessories, soft red slippers that accentuated my tiny feet, wrap around gold bracelets for my wrists, ruby earrings, a gold hair clip, a pure silver push knife in its own holster with a clip, and a lace and velvet red garter belt.

He picked out stuff down to the undergarment. Was that sweet or weird?

The rest of Crowley's team was going to be on surveillance around the perimeter outside, armed with automatics loaded with silver bullets, mace, and grenades.

And they had no problems makin' fun of the guys who would be going in looking like waiters in Vegas.

I hit the bathroom at the end of the hall to get ready with Kat's help.

There was no physical way I was tying that top by myself.

"I get the shoes and the jewelry to go with the dress, but what's with this?" She held up the garter with a dirty grin that didn't belong on such a sweet looking face.

I grabbed it from her. "He likes my thighs." I slid it on quickly then loaded up the real accessories.

My gun went on the belt around my waist, with the silver knife and extra magazines on the other side, the wide skirt hidin' them perfectly.

"It's kind of like a little private joke," I said.

"Not very private anymore," Kat said. "I think it's more like him buying you underwear, and I hope Grant didn't see it."

She knew full well Grant and both lab techs went over the clothes and accessories before letting any of us put them on.

"What did he say?" she asked as I put on the camera necklace.

"He just handed them over, the garter on top of course, and gave me one of his looks." I frowned. "You know, the look?"

"I've only gotten that look once, and that's when I was flirting with the Metro PD's coroner at a crime scene. We'd already examined the body and loaded him up, but apparently it was still inappropriate."

"I don't see why. You guys were just hopin' to get lucky while you were staring at a dead body," I said with a completely straight face.

"This coming from the girl who actually got lucky with a dead body?" She kept her face straight too.

For about three seconds.

Then we burst out laughing.

"Okay," I said after calmin' down enough to talk, "I stepped into that one. But you have to admit, he's a really hot dead body."

"They're all hot. I think it's a rule."

I nodded. "They usually don't change people unless they're attracted to them, and also, once you're a vamp, there's a confidence and power... I don't know, aura about them, and that makes anyone look better."

She nodded and I pulled my long hair back into the clip, still wondering when last night I'd lost my original gold one.

"What are the chances tonight will go well, we'll kill the demon, catch the summoner, and set the vamp world right again, all without me ruinin' this outfit?"

"Slim to none."

I sighed, starin' at myself in the mirror. "Probably."

I looked fantastic, like a princess.

Which was maybe the point?

I put in the earrings, did up my makeup, the dress matched the red velvet lipstick I'd picked for tonight, and we went out to meet the guys.

And I burst out laughing all over again when I saw them.

They didn't look bad. Really the opposite. They looked fancy, spiffed up to the nines... okay, maybe a little gay, but that's just cuz everyone knows gay guys have the best taste.

"Tell your boyfriend I'm going to kill him," Dan growled as he marched past me back to his desk and strapped his gun to his belt before covering it with the loose vest, lookin' like he'd rather be shooting the vest instead of putting his gun under it.

The beads glinted under the harsh lights and I slammed my hands over my mouth to keep the laugh in this time.

Beads! How did I miss the multicolored beads on the vests!

I pulled my phone out of my purse and snapped a quick picture of Dan as he finished fiddlin' with the vest to make sure the gun wasn't printing.

"Actually, that outfit is all Len," I said as I tucked the phone away, not bothering to correct him.

Two nights does not a boyfriend make, but I didn't want to get into it.

"Well at least we look good," Jet said, giving me one of his beautiful smiles. The purple really did look good against his dark skin. "Len does know we're just supposed to be servers, not any of *his boys*, right?"

I shook my head and pulled out a case of mints from my purse.

"Here." I tossed the canister to him. "Just in case."

He laughed and swooped me into his arms. "I'm going to call you Fairy Princess from now on. You look beautiful."

I hugged him back. "Thanks."

"Done?" a cool voice asked from behind.

Jet set me down and I turned, the dress swishing around my knees. Grant was spiffed up to the nines too, and actually made the slightly gay outfit look like a masculine daring fashion statement.

His face softened as I met his eyes.

"You look great," he said after a moment.

My breath stalled in my pounding chest and I cleared my throat. "You too."

"Okay," he yelled at all of us, makin' me jump.

Wow, if I didn't know better, I'd think we'd just had a moment.

"Tonight we are going in to get information. You all know your roles. Don't ask questions. The demon's seen our faces, it knows us, and it will be there. It will tell its master who we are. It's your job to watch and figure out who that is. Don't worry about trying to listen in on phone calls, we've already got the forensics team set up to tap any cell phones in that area in case the demon calls. Other than that, we are all cover for Ryder to get visions until she finds out who's behind this."

So, no pressure or anything.

He was only resting the entire case on my bare shoulders.

He tapped on his headset to talk to the teams already at the club setting up. "Backup, you're our eyes in the sky. Count every single body, dead or alive, going in and out. No one goes off anywhere without two or more partners. If something goes off outside the perimeter, it's irrelevant or a planned distraction. Any questions?"

No one was stupid enough to have one.

"Good," he said.

You wouldn't think anyone could be commanding and threatening while dressed like a Chippendales waiter, but Grant pulled it off.

We went in cars, just in case anyone was watching the club. Kat and the two lab techs went in her car to join the van to plan backup.

Poor Irish wasn't gettin' his date tonight.

Sam, Mender and I went in Mender's car. The guys posing as servers went in Dan's old Crown Vic. Servers showin' up together like they drove from the caterer's office hopefully wouldn't be too suspicious. We knew the demon wasn't there since it was still daylight, but others could be watching.

I rubbed my stomach as we walked to the club's back door.

The shot up roof let light into the middle of the main part cuz it was still daylight for another half hour.

Even so, I swear I felt eyes on the back of my neck and I rubbed it as Mender opened the door.

We crossed into the dark back room and my eyes didn't even have a chance to adjust before strong hands wrapped around my waist.

"Ah!" I yelped, hand flyin' down to pull my gun before familiar lips found mine and the hands around me pulled me in.

I slid my hands up Quil's arms and kissed him back, enjoying his cool mouth mingling with my all too warm one, before pushing him back.

He pulled me into a hug that lifted my feet off the ground like Jet always does.

"Which thigh?" he asked into my neck.

"The right," I whispered. "But, Quil, now isn't the time."

No one said anything as we held onto each other, but I knew what they were thinking.

"Yes, it is," he said, words barely a brush of lips on my neck. "If either of us suspects the other is the demon, we'll ask 'which one?' and the other will know to say right."

"That's why?"

"That's the main reason. I, of course, have ulterior motives."

He kissed my neck and set me down.

"I will keep things appropriate for the night," he said. "But all of you playing our humans will have to act the part, and I don't want one word to Ariana about kissing me or anything just because we aren't going to be acting. Is that understood?"

Wow! He sounded like Grant for a second there.

"You don't need to tell us," Mendor said in her prim way. "We know our parts. As for Agent Ryder, what she does is her business and Grant's."

I flinched. Now why did she have to say that?

Quil nodded, his face cool and impassive. "Agent Grant already knows all this. He'll deal."

He'd have to.

Quil showed us to the office, where the others were settin' up.

Kat cleared her throat as we entered the room and mouthed, "You're smeared," when I looked at her.

I pulled out a mirror, tissue, and the lipstick from my purse, and wiped and reapplied.

I looked at Quil, and sure enough, his mouth was smeared with my lipstick.

It looked kinda like fresh blood in this lighting.

"Quil, that color looks wonderful on you, I approve," Len said when we were all squished into the office.

It was large, but Crowley's team, the two forensic techs and Kat were already in there, so we were packed in tighter than those clowns in the Volkswagen.

"Excuse me?" he asked Len.

"Your mouth." He pointed to Quil's face. "And Ariana," he stood up from the desk I was practically squashed into and pulled me into a hug over it.

He gave me a kiss on the mouth and I pulled back with a squeak of surprise.

"Sorry, darling, I know how testy humans can be about all this, but it's what we do." He gave me a smile. "Besides, you look ravishing and I couldn't help myself."

"When a gay guy says he can't help but kiss you, then you know you look good, so I'm going to take that as a compliment," I said. "And by the way, the shade looks good on you too."

He giggled with me and wiped himself off with a handkerchief.

"You aren't going to try kissing any of us, are you?" Sam asked.

He's a perfectly nice guy, not at all homophobic really, but I guess even the open minded ones have a problem with gay guys kissing them on the lips.

"No, although I would love to get my lips on you." Len gave him a dirty smile and poor Sam went as red as my dress, his complexion no more up to their jokes than mine.

"I'm joking, darling," Len said. "No. But the visiting leaders may kiss you hello when you're introduced, it's only polite. No one from our nest has been holding up the custom since you are all so touchy, and we don't need to in front of the visitors to keep up pretenses because we supposedly see you all the time. I just kissed Ariana because she's practically one of us."

I was?

"If you guys keep this up, I'm going to spend all night reapplyin'," I said as I checked myself in my cosmetic mirror again. My lips were fine since it was just a graze.

"Where are our servers for the evening?" Quil asked. "They need to be here soon to set up with the real caterers so none of them suspect anything."

"Won't the caterer servers know the guys don't work with them?" I asked.

"No, for big events like this, the place we use gets temps from a general party planner staffing agency. Most of the caterers in this area will bid, get the project, and staff out of these agencies for the night instead of keeping people on payroll when they don't know when they'll need them," Quil said.

"Oh."

"But the rest are already here and showing up late looks bad, so where are they?"

"Right here," a cold voice said from behind.

I didn't need to turn or see over people to know that was Grant in the doorway.

"Everyone, out in the hall," Grant said.

The FBI personnel shuffled out.

The vamps didn't.

"Remember what I said at the office, everyone has their cameras on at all times," Grant said. "That means you, Ryder."

Now why did he have to say that? My face could not possibly heat up more.

"I am going to enjoy being your boss for the evening, Special Agent Grant," Quil said over my head.

Oh dear.

"You're going to remember this is work, and you're going to behave with my agent. You may kiss her like all of you do, but there will be no groping, and especially no going off by yourselves," Grant said.

"Don't speak to me that way, Grant. This is not my first operation, or my hundredth. I am not a rookie, and if you will remember, I have a few centuries on you."

"You're right, you're not a rookie, but you are the intended victim. We're here to protect you as much as to support her. Protocols tonight are in place specifically for the safety of both of you."

I didn't turn to see Quil's face but I could feel the tension meltin' away.

"Thank you, Grant," Quil said. "I appreciate that, and I will try to keep that in mind. But I can't stop investigating."

"I wouldn't either. But neither of you goes anywhere without a third, just in case."

"I can live with that."

"That's the point."

I smiled at Grant but he didn't look at me, eyes fixed firmly behind me on Quil.

"The others will be here soon, and the visiting leaders soon after that," Quil said. "Which one did you say would be playing Cocktail for the night?"

"Dan."

"Does he know how to mix drinks?"

"Oh yeah," I said before Grant could.

He may be a jerk sometimes, but he paid for college by workin' as a bartender for a fancy speakeasy up in New York.

The man knew his mixed drinks.

"Fantastic," Quil said.

Grant handed out earbuds, even to Quil and Len, and we put them in.

The guys left for the kitchen and those of us playin' guests followed Quil and Len into the main part of the club.

The vamps stayed on the side since the sun was still lighting the sky and coming through the holes.

"We doing anything about that?" I asked, pointing to the roof.

Len shrugged. "They have plastic over it and will fix it in a few days. Soonest I could get it going."

"I'm sorry."

He shook his head. "It's just… this is my club, my baby, and to have her injured like this, it hurts."

"I hate to say this, Len, but I think she's gonna get a few more bruises tonight."

He rubbed my arm. "I'm afraid you're right, darling. Just hope it's not worse than that, but I got a bad feeling about tonight."

"How bad?"

"I may not be psychic like you, but vamps, we got a sixth sense all our own. I haven't felt this queasy since I was down in New Orleans."

"What happened?" I asked.

He gave me a look. "Hurricane Katrina."

CHAPTER EIGHTEEN

"**B**LANCHE!" LEN SAID TO THE queen of Charlotte so loud I jumped.
The party was in full swing and I greeted people at the door with
Quil and Len, getting handshakes and kisses, drinkin' in visions so fast my
brains were near boiled by ten.

"Lenny, it's been too long."

They gave each other a quick kiss as he led her by the hand to me and
Quil.

She was as short as me, and her long red hair was curled into perfect
ringlets that bounced around like they thought they were in a shampoo ad.
She had bright green eyes, a pert freckled nose, and looked like a model in
her stylish green wrap dress and matching strappy stilettos.

"Blanche, my dear, you get lovelier every time I see you," Quil said,
kissin' her hello.

She wrapped her long fingers around his arms and pulled him in, trying
to deepen it.

Ohhhhhhhh, no honey. Nobody pulls that with my man.

I clenched my hands into fists, grinned big and bright and stepped so
close to Quil's side I would've bumped her if she didn't back off in the last
second.

"And this is Ariana." Quil held out a hand for me.

I took it and the only thing keepin' me from meeting her eyes was some
semblance of sense that said she'd know something was off about me if I
did.

"She's yours?" Blanche asked with what could only be described as a
kittenish look as Quil kissed my knuckles.

"She is," Quil said.

"Ariana Finn." I held out my hand and she looked at it.

So far, the only ones who didn't shake my hands were the ones who went straight for a kiss.

If she refused to touch me at all, we'd have suspect number one.

"She's so cute!" Blanche said, leaning forward and plantin' a kiss on my lips.

I got a quick flash of her being made, so weak I couldn't even see the scene around it, and focused on her as the vision cut off and she pulled back.

"It's so nice to meet you," I said, taking her hand and shakin' it.

She blinked, obviously surprised, but just smiled as I stared at her.

Nothing.

Huh.

Some people were just harder to get stuff off of than others, and I was gettin' tired.

And drunk.

"My lady," Crowley said, appearin' next to me with another of the giant Cumberland Rivers Dan had mixed up with some help from Dave. Before things got going, Quil hypnotized the real servers so they'd stay in the kitchen and let our guys circulate the food and drinks until the party part of the night started.

Crowley had a tray of the signature drink and some champagne flutes and gave me a look as Blanche took a drink.

"Too many?" Crowley mouthed at me.

I shook my head, mouthin', "Third, but needed."

But then again, if it was helpin', why was my vision off of Blanche so weak?

"What are these?" Blanche asked.

"Cumberland Rivers," Quil said. "Special concoction by our bartender. He's helping out the caterers tonight."

"Make sure to keep these coming," she said to Crowley, slippin' him some cash. "Thank you."

My opinion of her went up about ten points.

You can tell a lot about someone by how they treat "the help."

Speaking of. Marie, one of the queens, and an iced one at that, came up. She kissed Blanche and Quil, gave me a sniff, and grabbed one of the drinks.

"Darling, how are you," Marie said, light accent makin' her sound even colder.

Blanche and Marie wandered off and I leaned into Quil. "That everyone?"

Blanche's crew came in first, a lot of the leaders did that, sort of like someone to announce them or something.

"All except Jade," Quil said.

"You think she's coming?"

"She has to. It will look weak if she doesn't."

We had maybe a hundred vamps in the club, really not that many, and a handful of humans who were dates of the few nest members invited.

"Do you think it's one of these guys, or someone in the nest?" I asked.

"If I had to bet on someone coming after me, it'd be Jade. But like this? By making it look like an attack against the nest?" Quil shook his head. "It hurts her too, makes her look weak."

"Why is that so bad?"

"In our world, if you look weak, another vampire might move in on your territory."

"Even if it's not your fault?" I asked. "I mean, everyone seems to be being pretty nice about this. Rushin' here and everything. Doesn't seem like they think y'all are weak."

"No, them rushing here shows exactly that. They want to see for themselves what's going on. They want to help, maybe, but they are vultures circling, seeing if they could replace the queen with a second who is strong enough, or enough of a threat to their power, for them to want another throne."

"It's like countries back in medieval Europe."

"Not a bad way to see it. We have rulers of cities or city-states, all trying to protect their power and expand their territory."

"If leaders sometimes overthrow another territory to put a powerful second in charge, has Jade tried doin' that with you?"

He shook his head. "No."

"But aren't you a threat to her?"

"Yes, but they put in threats when they're powerful enough to be restless, but can be controlled by family ties. Jade can't control me anymore, and she knows it."

"Control? Like influence or like magic?"

"Closer to the second. Your maker has power over you, until you are powerful enough to resist. Jade has not been able to compel me for a very long time. And there is no affection to keep me tied either. No, she most certainly does not want me in my own city. My beliefs are too different from hers. With my own city, I'd be more of a threat."

Quil put a few guards on the front door with instructions that no one but Nashville's queen was to get in without them grabbing Quil and me to check them out first, and he led me over to our table near the front.

"I want to talk to people about the attacks," Quil said as we sat, "but I can't start without Jade."

"Why not?" I asked.

"It would be an insult to her. This is a meeting between the leaders and this is her nest under attack. This is technically her party. I was just the one setting it up."

"And the one who had the idea and actually cares and, oh yeah, isn't a suspect."

He smiled but it didn't reach his eyes. "I don't think it's Jade. It doesn't make sense."

"Well, I want it to be her. She... bugs me."

He smiled for real this time. "Are you always this feisty when you drink?"

"Lil' bit." I kissed him and for a moment, just a moment, things were okay.

"Everyone here, Quil?"

I jerked away from Quil so fast I think I bit his lip.

Speak of the devil.

Jade stood next to us, the timin' so perfect she had to have planned it.

Quil stood, bendin' over her hand like a gentleman, and pulled out the chair next to his.

She was gonna sit with us?

I must've made a face cuz she smirked at me as she sat.

"Hey, Jade." I held out my hand for her.

She stared at it and I shrugged and pulled it back.

She couldn't avoid touchin' me all night.

Quil stayed standin' and held his hands up as Len handed him a microphone.

"Now that we're all here," Quil said, "we need to talk about these attacks. We've already had federal agents search our club and dig into our finances. The attacks are calling attention to our nest, and that means they're calling attention to all of us. Whoever is behind these attacks has summoned not one, but two demons. The first violated and murdered three of our humans, the second almost killed me. As I already told you over the phone, this meeting is meant as a trap for the demon. We are ready for it, and when it comes, we are going to capture it and interrogate it."

Wait, he told them about that part?

Grant was not gonna be happy.

"So we're just supposed to sit here and play bait?" Blanche asked. "When I said I would help, I thought it would include more action."

"Yes," Quil said. "With all of us here, we can take one demon. We just need to find it. It can look like anyone, but it has a distinctive smell our tracker will be able to spot. Since all of you came in packs, and all of us and our humans have been together since before nightfall, we know it's not any of us right now."

I wasn't too sure about that. Jade came in alone far as I could tell.

"But once we start the party and dancing," Quil said, "the demon can, and hopefully will, slip in. Our guards will tell us of anyone coming in, and we will check that person out. If it smells like the demon, we'll make it talk until it tells us who sent it."

"What do we do if it doesn't show?" one of the other vamp leaders whose name I couldn't remember if you paid me asked.

"Or if there's more than one?" another one asked.

"It takes immense power to control just one demon," Quil said. "More than one, and even a group wouldn't be able to control both. It is most likely just one. But we also expect the summoner to be here as backup."

No, we expected them to be here cuz it was personal. Was Quil holdin' back info for a specific plan or just to hold back info?

With that, the vamps got up and the party officially got started.

The music started and the place was hoppin' so fast, no one just showing up would ever suspect they were all plotting twenty seconds before.

Quil pulled me onto the floor and we danced a Venetian Waltz. Which of course made me think of Irish.

Hope he's okay in the back room.

The difference in our heights made the dance a bit more difficult than it was when I practiced with Irish, and I thought for half a second I should've worn heels.

Which was dumb. Have you ever tried to fight in heels? It's not like it is on TV. If you try to fight in heels, you're more likely to break one of your ankles than anyone's head.

The floor filled around us pretty skippy and soon we were surrounded by people, the crowd thick enough I couldn't see the door.

We have people at the doors, no one will get in without them knowing, which will seem perfectly normal since this is a private party so people have to be on the list.

So why was my stomach in knots?

The song ended and Quil bowed, makin' me giggle.

"May I cut in?" a voice asked behind us.

I turned to see a beautiful man with dark wavy hair, a dominant nose the only flaw on his face, somehow makin' him prettier. And he most certainly did not come in earlier. One of our guards stood close behind him.

"Sir, ma'am," the guard said. "May I present Milo of Miami."

"Milo," Quil said, voice so cheery I looked up at him to see if the eyes matched.

They didn't.

"No need to sound so put out, Quil," Milo said. "My brother did say I was coming, didn't he?"

"No, he didn't."

"Oh well, must've slipped his mind. You know how he is."

"Yes, I do."

Was I missin' something?

"Hi." I help my hand out. "I'm Ariana."

Milo bent over my hand and took it to lift to his lips.

Flash.

He was so small, too small to work yet.

They should have known that. He struggled to keep the water bucket up. It was his job to take it around to the other slaves.

He tripped, his feet not used to the rough sand yet, and he fell, spilling water over the parched earth.

Someone yelled at him and he scrambled to his feet.

The world was hazy except for the boy. The whip came out of the clouds and he dodged.

More yelling and a bigger boy popped into view, holding the whip around a man's neck, eyes fierce and muscles bulging as he squeezed the whip until the man stopped struggling. He let the man fall and took the boy's hand.

The small boy blinked. He didn't need to be older to know his big brother was going to be in big trouble for stopping the man from beating him.

I jerked out of the vision just long enough to see Milo give me the same blank look I was giving him. He licked his lips and grasped my hand tighter, then...

Flash.

The two boys, young men now, danced in the middle of an arena, decked out like gladiators.

They twirled and sliced as one, and the vision expanded to show teeth going at Milo's neck.

His brother leapt in and sliced at the tiger's face, slashing through its snout with a warrior's scream. Milo slammed his stout sword into the beast's neck. It still didn't fall.

His brother sliced at its legs and the two front paws went flying. The beast fell with a roar, and the brother slammed his sword into the already bleeding neck. The tiger thrashed on the ground and then lay very, very still.

Together, the brothers threw their arms in the air, and the crowds screamed with them in triumph.

Flash.

A woman, tall and regal with her dark brown hair, golden skin, and beautiful large brown eyes, grinned as she tossed one of the young men into a tree in the woods.

He fell to the ground with a moan, bleeding heavily from his head.

Milo. Had to be because the other brother was bigger, his features less delicate than his brother's.

The brother grabbed her around the waist and she broke his hold and threw him to the ground.

He said something harsh as she straddled him and Milo pushed to his feet, so woozy he almost went down again.

His brother stared the woman down, gold eyes hard and stubborn.

The woman bit his brother in the neck, fast as a snake.

Milo grabbed a branch and lunged forward, swinging at her. Didn't she know who they were?

She caught the branch without even looking and used it to pull Milo towards her. She jumped on him and bit into his neck.

Pleasure took him as he blacked out.

The vision darkened and then came back on.

It was night and all Milo knew as he woke up was he was starving.

He smelled blood and sat up as the woman pulled two freshly dead bodies. Sure enough, his brother was blinking awake next to him.

She was one of them. Their mother told them stories of the bloodsuckers. He never dreamed he'd become one.

The woman dropped the bodies between the brothers and together they went for them. They drank deep, and when they pulled away with bloody mouths after a few minutes, they looked at each other, then at her.

Milo asked her something and she answered with a small smile. He got up and gave her shy eyes as he leaned in to kiss her. She returned it, wrapping her arms around his neck.

And while she was busy, his brother grabbed his sword and sliced, going clean through her neck from behind. She disintegrated in a bloody dust pile and Milo frowned, said something to his brother, and they started laughing together.

I panted as I pulled out of the vision, my hands grasping his for all they were worth. His grip was urgent, and he was breathing pretty heavy too, even though he hadn't needed to for about two thousand years if I was right about those Gladiator costumes.

He licked his lips again and sighed. "You don't know."

It wasn't a question.

We stared into each other's eyes until I jerked mine away and looked around, hopin' none of the other vamps noticed our moment. They weren't supposed to know I was a psychic.

And apparently they weren't supposed to know Milo was one either.

"What did you see?" I asked Milo in a whisper, not letting go of his hands.

"What did you see?" he asked just as quietly, lookin' around too. "Not here."

He tugged on my hands and I looked at Quil.

"We can't go anywhere alone. We should just dance and talk really quietly," I said. "What don't I know?"

He shook his head and started laughing. "It's too hard to explain. I never even understood it. Neither did he. He's the one they talked to. I just got some of the story, and I just saw it now. I can't believe you don't know, but no one's left to tell, except him, and as I said, they didn't give him much. I didn't even know she came here."

"Who's him? Who's she? Tell me what?" I asked.

"Oh Quil," a voice I was really beginnin' to hate cut in, "looks like your little girl wants to play with someone else."

I looked up to sneer at Jade and she smiled, stayin' just out of reach.

"Milo." Jade sounded almost surprised as he turned. "We are honored by your presence. Is your brother here?"

"No, unfortunately he has business at our nest, but thought I would be a suitable substitute. And actually, I was just saying hello to the lovely young lady. I would love to take you for a spin."

She smiled and took his hand without a flinch.

So either she didn't know he was psychic too, or wasn't worried about him seeing into her head.

Something told me it was the first as they danced away.

"Did you know he was psychic?" I asked Quil as he took me in his arms again.

He shook his head with wide eyes. "Never. But it makes sense, him and Carvi always seem to know things they shouldn't. What did you see?"

I gave him the gist. "I need to know what he saw. What did he mean by I don't know?"

Quil shrugged. "How would I know?"

I shrugged back.

"Did you see anything about him to suggest he summoned the demon?" Quil asked.

I shook my head. "But he's sneaky, he kissed his maker while his brother killed her so they wouldn't be bound to her. And he's hiding what he saw in my head. I need to talk to him again."

My eyes tracked him and Jade swingin' around the dance floor, and he looked at me over her shoulder before turning with her again.

He was grinnin' like a jack-o-lantern.

He knew something.

I needed to know what.

I looked up at the bar and caught Grant staring at me.

"You catch all that, General?" I asked, keepin' my voice low.

"Yes."

"Any thoughts?"

"A few. None that add up."

"You think he's a suspect?"

"I think they're all suspects."

"Be a little less obvious, sweets," Quil said. "It doesn't look like you're talking to me when you look over like that."

"Right, sorry," I said, leanin' into his chest. "Quil, you think Milo's in on this?"

"I wouldn't put anything past him and Carvi, but they have nothing against me personally, all our business deals have been amicable and our ideology lines up pretty well. We all would like to see vampires and magic out."

"I don't like him smirkin' at me like that. Like he's a kid sayin' I know something you don't know. He's way too old for that."

"Do you know how old he is?" Quil asked.

"Based on the Gladiator scene I'm pretty sure was in the Colosseum, I'm guessing Ancient Roman age."

He drew a sharp breath.

"You didn't know that?" Grant asked.

"None of us know how old they are, but there have been rumors," Quil said. "Some say two thousand years. Some say older."

"Powerful?"

"Yeah. Easily the most powerful this side of the Atlantic, maybe even the world. You don't know how hard it was for vampires through the dark ages. Most of them died from starvation or being hunted. To have thousands of years, well, it is not a feat many can claim or even expect to."

"Who's the oldest vampire in the world?"

"Recorded?"

I shrugged. "I don't know, you tell me."

"Oldest recorded was an ancient Egyptian vampire. He was about three thousand years old when he was killed."

"What happened?"

"Milo and Carvi happened. They took him out back in the nineties."

"Why?"

"No idea. Better question was how. I'm guessing Milo being psychic had a lot to do with that."

"Hey, how good is y'all's hearing?"

"Better than the average human, nothing like what you see on TV. They can't hear us whispering with the music and the crowd as cover."

I nodded. "Oh, okay."

We walked over to the bar where Grant was loadin' up a tray of drinks Dan just made.

"Dan, you are doin' awesome!" I said, takin' a glass of champagne.

He grinned. He actually looked like he was havin' fun.

"You okay?" Grant asked.

"Tipsy. Why I'm switchin' to wine."

"Champagne," Dan said.

Grant shot him a look and he held up his hands, going back to pouring.

"Only one suspicious so far is Blanche," I said. "And, well, Jade. She won't let me touch her."

"But she let Milo," Grant said. "She doesn't know about him."

"I don't think any of them do."

"Man knows how to keep a secret."

Quil put his hand on the small of my back. "We need to wander off.

Grouping up like this looks suspicious."

Grant nodded once and we walked back into the crowd.

"Hey," I said as Blanche danced up.

"Hello, pretty little girl." She grinned and grabbed my hand, spinnin' me around.

I focused on her and a quick vision of her getting married flashed through my head in perfect clarity and sound.

Huh, maybe I just didn't get anything strong earlier cuz I was tired?

We danced, spinnin' each other and trying to keep our drinks from splashin' out of our glasses. When hers sloshed over, she stopped and giggled, saying something to Quil.

"Ryder," Grant's voice came over the earbuds, "If you saw anything from her, scratch your nose."

I did.

"Okay, if it wasn't about the case, scratch again."

I did.

"Good. Go talk to Milo. He's been watching you and he winked at me and Dan. I think he knows we're feds."

I excused myself and downed my champagne to give me an excuse to go back to the bar.

I grabbed another one, leanin' against the bar and smiling at Dan.

"So, good party, huh? You gettin' good tips?" I asked, loud enough for people around to hear.

"Subtle," Dan said quietly.

"Okay guys, all I got off Blanche was her gettin' married. Couldn't tell if she was alive or undead, but there's no bad vibes on her."

"Try Milo again," Grant said. "Then see what else you can get off the leaders through another pass."

I nodded, grabbed another glass, and dove back into the crowd.

Milo was dancin' with one of the vamp underlings who came with the Kentucky ones if I remembered correctly.

"May I cut in?" I asked.

"With me or him?" the woman winked at me.

Her dark skin and colorful multi-layered garment suggested she was from somewhere around India originally, though it must have been long ago since I couldn't pick up anything but the lightest flavor of a foreign accent.

"With him," I said. "But thank you." I held out my hand. "I think we met up at front when you first came in. What was your name again?"

"Peri," she said, shakin' her head, making the bobbles on her pink head scarf dance as she took my hand.

Another quick vision of her killing her maker flashed across my eyes. Oh yeah, I remembered her. From what I saw about how he made her the first time I touched her, the bastard needed killin'.

I shuttered as I pulled back and she gave me a look.

"Caught a chill," I said. "So, may I?"

"Of course." She left and I took Milo's hands.

He smiled as we started dancin' and met my eyes.

"What did you see, when you touched me?" I asked him.

He smiled wider. "You mean what did I see that I'm not telling you? Or the scenes of you?"

My mouth worked. "How about we start with what you won't tell me?"

"Nope." He leaned in. "That one will cost you."

"What?"

"Let me think."

I rolled my eyes. "What about... what did you call them? Scenes? You saw?"

"I saw you getting your first vision. Your fight with your sister. Still not talking to her, I guess. Losing the virginity. The suicide attempt. Let's see, what else. Oh, you being rescued by that large server we both know isn't a server, who is now your boss. How you feel about your boss. And your night with Quil. I paused on that one, it was hot."

My jaw dropped. "You can pause!"

"Shhhhhhh," he said, dippin' me and pulling me up to hold me tight. "I've kept this secret for longer than you can imagine. Don't go blowing it now."

"You can do that though? Can you teach me? I'm barely learnin' how to do anything with my visions besides just have them."

"Ohhhhhh, teach you. I like this. I'd love to."

"Really!"

"For a price," he said before I got the last syllable out.

"Okay, like what?"

"How about you come down to Miami for a month? My brother and I teach you during the day, and, then teach you different things at night."

I jerked back to look him in the eyes. "You mean like sleep with you? With both of you?"

"Not together. We do have some boundaries. That's pretty much the only one. No sex with family. It's just weird."

"Wait, both of you teach me. Is he psychic too?"

"No."

But something about the way he said it made my hackles rise.

"You've got that look again," I said. "The I know something you don't know look."

"I know a lot you don't. I can skim visions off you while we talk, look for specific things, do the same for others too."

"Can you help us tonight? Do you know about the investigation?"

"I do. What makes you think I'll help you?"

"I… I don't know. You're kinda annoying but you seem like a good sort."

"Seem being the operative word."

"What do you mean?"

He met my eyes. "Do you ever feel like just shooting the cars in front of you out of the way when you're stuck in traffic?"

My breath caught as the music fuzzed away and the crowd noises died down, like someone shuttin' a door.

I couldn't look away as I nodded. "I get so frustrated."

"Okay. Take that feeling. That stuck in traffic frustration, but you can roll over everyone in front of you. You with me?"

I nodded again.

"Add it to the need to have your lover right then," he said. "The desire to make them scream… Even put them in a little pain. Take that bound up potential and imagine it being satisfied with you sinking your teeth in."

I gulped as heat flashed straight from my face to my groin.

"That is what it feels like to be a vampire," he said, lettin' go of my hands. "Pressure, sex, pain and power all rolled into one. Don't make the mistake of thinking us human, girl. You won't live to regret it."

I looked around.

We stood in an empty hotel lobby and my heart raced as I ran for the door.

Milo caught me around my waist, pullin' me back into him so tight I could feel his arousal against my back.

"We're still on that dance floor, Ariana. We're staring at each other, and we're only here in your mind."

I licked my lips.

"No. It's so real."

The intricate gold and red carpet was soft and thick under my bare feet. I could smell the leather of the chairs in the nook off to the left with the big screen TV and hear the gurgle of the waterfall takin' up the back wall.

"This place is real. It's one of the hotels Carvi and I own. You're seeing it because I'm projecting it. This is hypnosis, but so much more. Most vampires can not do this, trap you in your own head, but perfectly aware."

He turned me around and took my hands, dancin' with me like we'd just been on the dance floor.

Or still were.

"I could leave you here."

Panic shot through me and I jerked, but he held me fast.

"I *could*," he said. "I won't. But you have to understand what we're capable of, or you'll never understand what you're facing."

I shook. "I get it. Please let me go."

He pulled me into a hug. "Lost little lamb. You have no idea the power you could wield. You're not hard enough to have that kind of power without breaking. Yet."

"If being hard is what it takes, I don't want it."

"You will. When your people are on the line, you will. I've seen you kill. The witch who summoned the demon last February. You killed her and didn't lose one night of sleep."

"Because I didn't do anything wrong. She was a rapist and would have killed me and Grant. It was self-defense."

"I know. I saw. That ability to kill though? Almost all humans have it. But in the modern age, in *civilized* countries, they've been trained to feel bad about it. You don't. And I know why."

He still wouldn't let me go and I sighed, huggin' him back. "Why?"

"Now, now, that would be telling. Come down here with me. Meet my brother, spend the month with us, and I'll tell you all you want to know, teach you what I can."

"I can't. I have a job. I have Quil."

"He could come. It would keep him safe from Jade."

I pulled away and he let me.

The club turned back on around us like switching the TV channel and I clapped my hands over my ears at the sudden noise.

Milo took my hand and pulled me off the floor and out into the back hall before I remembered no one was supposed to go off, even in pairs.

"Milo!" I yelped as he shut the door behind us.

"Don't worry," he said. "Three, two, one."

The door burst open and Grant rushed through, hand on gun under his vest. He came to a dead stop as he saw us waitin' for him and closed the door behind him.

"Sorry, General," I said. "He just grabbed me and pulled me off. And he had me in his eyes, like full on hallucination."

Milo shrugged. "I knew he'd follow. We need to talk. I'll help tonight, but I don't do anything for free."

"What do you want?" Grant asked.

"I want to take you for a spin."

I blushed as Grant blinked in surprise.

Milo burst out laughing. "That came out wrong. I want to see into your head. You let me touch you, I'll help tonight."

"Why?" Grant asked.

"Do we have a deal?"

"I can't let you have free rein in my head."

"I know, you're a federal agent. You have state secrets, blah blah. I got it. I'm not looking for work secrets. I'm looking for personal ones. You want my help or not?"

Grant held out his arm and Milo took it before I could protest.

They locked eyes and didn't move.

"Um sir?" I said after a moment.

He didn't answer.

The door opened and Quil came in, breathin' a sigh like he was relieved when he saw me. He shut the door and looked at the guys.

"What the hell are you doing now, Milo?" Quil asked.

No answer.

"Milo's got some interestin' tricks," I said. "He did this to me on the dance floor. It's like a mind meld. He's looking around. He said if Grant let him do this, then he'll help us tonight."

Quil stared at them, eyes disco dancing.

"What?" I asked.

"I can't begin to think how he's doing this," Quil said. "That kind of power. It's like nothing I've ever seen."

The guys broke apart and Grant had his gun up and out before I could blink.

Milo held up his hands, face showin'… something.

Milo said something in another language and grinned. "That was interesting. Grant, I must introduce you to my brother."

"Talking to him in there told me all I need to know about him. My agent is not going down there."

He talked to someone else in the mindmeld?

How was that even possible?

"You don't own her. But, one deal at a time. Speaking of, I did promise my help. Quil! So good of you to join us."

"Milo." Quil nodded.

"Do you know what he is?" Milo grinned, pointin' at Grant.

"I do not. Care to share?"

"No," Grant said. "That was part of our deal."

"When?" I asked.

Grant looked at me.

"Oh! While you were inside your heads? Wow. Did he tell you what you were? Because he's not answerin' any of my questions."

"No, he did not tell me what I am. And he would not talk about you either."

"Well, that's not completely true," Milo said, winkin' at me. "I wouldn't tell him what I saw in your head, but let's just say you came up."

"Zip it," Grant said. "Ryder, you and Milo will be working together. Find who's behind this."

"Yes, sir, but-"

He pulled the door open and the noise drowned me out as he walked into the crowd.

"So," Milo said, clapping his hands together and shuttin' the door, "all of us going out will look suspicious. I say we make it look like a romp was going on."

He ruffled my hair.

"You're messing up my hair!" I squealed, batting his hands away.

"That's the point," Milo said. "It'll look like we all had some fun in the hall."

"It would take longer than this," Quil said.

"And everyone knows I'm with Quil," I said. "They'll probably figure we're working the case."

"But we don't want people to know Milo is working with us," Quil said. "Or that you're even working this. It's already bad enough they had to know we were trying to set a trap for the demon. You're not supposed to be an investigator, you're supposed to be my date."

"You're okay with this?" I asked him. "People thinkin' Milo and I did something in here?"

"With me," Quil said.

"It won't be the first time either of us had a threesome," Milo said.

"Ummmmm, how much... er, I mean, do you, when there's a threesome?"

"Neither of us is bi," Milo said, chucklin'. "When I say threesome, I mean the two of one gender payin' attention to the one of the other. You know, if we really want to sell this-"

"No," Quil said with a smirk. "Nice try, but no."

"No what?" I asked.

"He was suggesting an actual threesome, just to make it believable."

I blushed.

"Not *just* for that reason," Milo said. "I would love to have sex with you, you're cute."

Quil rolled his eyes. "You're as bad as Carvi."

"No I'm not. Carvi would be hitting on both of you and a lot more aggressively."

Quil made a face. "Good point."

"His brother likes you?" I asked.

"He has a crush on me."

"Emphasis on the crush," Milo said. "I love my brother, but he has issues. Quil is a rare breed of vampire. He has an optimism and sweetness in him and my brother is attracted to that. I wish I could say it was because he wanted to be closer to that feeling, but more often than not, he has a great deal of fun destroying it."

"And you want me to go down there?" I asked. "He'd eat me alive."

"Why?"

"You just said he likes to destroy sweetness. If he wants to destroy Quil,

I can't imagine what he'd want to do to me."

Milo smirked. "Oh, you're under the impression you're a sweet little girl, aren't you?" He laughed. "Remember, I've seen inside your head. I've seen you kill without remorse. You may be able to fool yourself, but I know you, and you can't snow the snowman."

I paled and looked between him and Quil.

"You've killed someone?" Quil asked.

"It was in self-defense! She deserved it."

"That's very practical," Milo said. "It's not sweet."

"I'm a good person. You saw the situation. What was I supposed to do?"

Milo walked up to me and grabbed my arms, trappin' me against the wall. "I never said you weren't a good person, that I disapproved, or wouldn't have done the same."

Milo bent down, smelling my neck and pulling me close as he rubbed against me.

I expected Quil to step in.

He didn't.

"There, that should get some of our smell onto each other," Milo said, lettin' me go. "Don't look so shocked, Ariana, I'm not telling you anything you didn't already know."

"You certainly aren't saying anything useful," I said.

He met my eyes. "Let me tell you something you don't know then. In a long term war, I'd rather go up against Quil than you, because you can be vicious, and far crueler than him."

"No! No, I'm not a mean person."

"I said cruel, not mean. There's a difference. You have it in you. And you know it. After all, the female of the species is deadlier than the male."

Quil snorted. "I think this is enough time."

"Eh, for a quickie," Milo said. "Just got to mess up us and our clothes some." He mussed his hair and tugged his top out of his slacks, unbuttoning a few down then re-buttoning with one off.

He went back in without a word, closing the door and leaving me and Quil alone.

"What was that last thing he said?" I asked.

"Oh, it's a Kipling poem. Means when push comes to shove, women are more dangerous, probably because they have children they put a lot of resources into to protect."

"I don't like the things he was saying."

"I noticed."

"You don't believe him!"

"That you killed someone?"

"No, that… I'm not sweet."

He smiled and wrapped his arms around me. "What if you aren't? Why is that so bad?"

My mouth worked. "I… I don't know, but I'm not a bad person. I swear."

"I never thought you weren't a good person. I know you are." He pulled me into a kiss and I melted into it, lettin' the world fall away in an all too natural way.

We finally broke and he rested his forehead against mine. "Personally, I find it a little insulting whenever his brother says I'm sweet, it's almost like he's saying I'm weak and he could break me."

"I think it's a compliment. I don't think I want either of us around his brother."

"Yeah." Quil grabbed the handle. "Shall we?"

"Yeah."

He opened the door and we rejoined the party.

I hit the dance floor with Milo and no one gave us a second look.

Geez, maybe sharing humans was common for them or something.

"What else did you see about me?" I asked as we started to glide, he was short for a guy and only had about four inches on me, so we moved together nicely.

"I don't know." He sighed, looking down at me. "I don't remember."

"Bull," I said.

"What did you see?"

I told him, finishing with, "Killing her like that was despicable. Your turn."

"Oh, that's cold."

"You're really not one to talk."

"I'm really not."

"So spill, what do you know about me? What were you talking about when you said I didn't know? Know what? Who's him, and who's her?"

"Find out. Get into my head. Dig around like I dug around yours."

"I don't know how."

"And imagine if you could only learn that."

"Your price is too high."

"I'm open to haggling."

"What else would you want?"

"From you? Blood. But I think I could work out a trade with Quil if you're serious about learning without paying for it yourself."

"I'm fine with paying for myself. I'm not fine with paying *with* myself."

He shrugged. "We can sit down with Quil once this is all over. See if we can't figure out how much juice you have. Me training you will help Quil too, like in investigations such as this."

I smiled back and nodded.

Finally! I finally had someone who could help me try to figure all this out. I finally met someone like me.

"I think we can work somethin' out then," I said. "Can't you tell me what you saw that you're not tellin' me though?"

"You notice your accent gets thicker when you want something?"

"Yes, now come on."

He pulled back and I actually saw pity in his eyes. "I don't think I should. I think it would do more harm than good."

"That'll be my problem then. Tell me!"

"Did you ever see anything and tell someone what you saw, only to wish you hadn't later?"

I sighed, finally spitting out, "Yes."

He gave me a pointed look.

"I need to know though."

Did anyone ever think the cat died of curiosity, not cuz he went out of his way to satisfy it? Cuz that's how I always interpreted the story.

"Well, this is one of those times, and I've learned my lesson about telling people things that would only hurt them."

He said it with compassion, but there was something in his eyes that said he was really enjoying my curiosity.

"Bull. You just like me trying to pry it out of you."

"As funny as your little face is when you turn red like that, I really am not telling you for your own good."

"Then you shouldn't have brought it up. You didn't have to say anything, I never would've known, and I wouldn't be dying of curiosity right now."

"I didn't mean to bring it up," he said. "It slipped out before I could consider what I was saying. And I was going to tell you, but then we were interrupted, and it's a good thing too, because this is one of those things that I would look back and say, 'You idiot, why did you tell that beautiful young woman that? Now she'll be too upset to sleep with you.'"

I jerked back, but he wouldn't release my hand. "I am not sleeping with you," I said. "And why would you say something like that anyway? You know I'm with Quil."

"Oh right," he said. "You're with Quil, you're in love with your boss, so another man in your life would be complicated."

"I am not in love with him."

"You of all people know better than to lie to a psychic."

Duh! I'm psychic. He doesn't have to tell me anything.

I squeezed his hand tightly and focused on his dark eyes.

"Now that's more like it." He grinned that stupid wide grin again and pulled me in close to his body, meeting my gaze. "You're trying to get a vision, aren't you?"

I nodded.

"I can help you with that, but for tonight, it should be focused on the job."

Right.

How selfish was I that I wanted to figure out what he was hiding about me when we had a killer to find?

"Good point. How do I do this?"

"Close your eyes."

I did.

He leaned in and kissed me.

"Hey!" I jerked back.

"Now, now, Ariana. We supposedly just had a threesome, don't make such a scene now."

"You behave yourself and I won't have to. I thought you were going to help?"

He sighed. "Fine, but for tonight, it'll be faster if I do this on my own. You'll only slow me down. Doesn't mean you won't be able to get anything, just you don't have the experience. First lesson, *know* you can pull anything you want out of someone. There are no limits, there's no chance about it. You just have to focus and you can see whatever you want."

He let me go and Quil stepped in.

How long had he been standin' there?

"Let us know what you find?" Quil asked.

"Sure," Milo said.

"Now why don't I believe him?" I said as he disappeared into the crowd.

"Milo doesn't make deals he doesn't keep," Quil said. "He may twist them, but he won't break them."

"So what do we do now?"

"Keep mingling, you keep touching people, try to get a vision."

"This is gonna get old."

I grabbed another drink and we hovered near the door leading into the hall by the bar.

If anyone new tried sneaking in, it'd probably be through there.

Quil stopped one of the queens as she passed, the one from Atlanta maybe?

"Marie, we've hardly had a chance to chat," he said.

"Hi!" I said, puttin' on my best smile.

Marie looked down her long nose at me. Her hair was so pale blond it was near white and her eyes were the lightest, most transparent blue I've ever seen. She was more ice queen than a flesh and blood one.

"Quil, this plan is stupid," she said, accent light and nearly as cold as she was physically, maybe Scandinavian? "If the demon is here now, we'll never find it in this."

She waved a long hand at the crowded club.

"Don't worry, Marie," Quil said. "I have it under control."

Her eyes went wide. "You were lying. This party is a cover for some other way to find the demon, isn't it?"

Well, she wasn't stupid apparently.

She smiled. "Quil, you naughty boy, what do you have up your sleeve?"

"I will tell you if it works, but until then." He tapped a finger to his lips and she nodded, still smiling.

"Marie, I believe you met Ariana earlier." He took my hand and placed me between them like I was a prize winning pup up for show.

"Nice to meet you," she said, not even trying to lean in for any kind of hello.

"Actually we met," I said, resistin' the urge to role my eyes. She wasn't going to make this easy. "But yeah, still nice." I lifted my hand like I was going to shake hers.

She stared at it.

"Oh right." I dropped my hand. "You don't shake hands, I keep forgetting." I looked up at Quil. "Am I supposed to kiss her like everyone else?" I looked back at Marie. "Sorry, I'm new at this. All I know is all y'all keep kissin' me."

Quil nodded along, stepping off to the side to give us some space. "It's our custom, sweets."

She gave me a smile that didn't reach past her lips and leaned over, pecking me on the lips.

Okay, focus on her!

Flash.

"I don't care what she is."

I clearly saw Marie in a fancy, very plush bedchamber. She was talking on the phone while she reclined on a fur covered bed as large as my bathroom. I couldn't hear the voice on the other line.

"Get rid of her. I can't have a psychic running about."

More talking.

"No, I have to go. If I don't, Quil will be suspicious, and then the rest will. If I want this to work, they can't suspect me. Which is why I have you."

The voice on the other line continued.

"You got the hair, just use it to make the gris-gris today and she'll be useless until you can kill her."

She nodded along.

"Of course, but they won't be able to do anything about it, they won't know who's holding it. You just do your job."

The voice said something else and she growled.

"Don't forget who made you. She's a hell of a lot worse than me, and believe me, if

tonight implodes, she'll do worse than kill you." She nodded again. *"Good. We understand each other then. Ta."*

I jerked out of the vision and away from her, but it was too late. She knew.

CHAPTER NINETEEN

EVEN QUIL DIDN'T HAVE TIME to twitch before her hand flew to my neck and she pulled me back against her.

It was a light grasp, but I knew she could snap my neck in less than a butterfly's blink.

She knew it too.

"Move and I kill her," Marie said in a low, sweet tone.

We faced away from the general party, too far in the back for anyone to really see, and even if they did, all they would notice was her caressing my neck, which half of Quil's people had already done last night anyway.

"What did you see?" she asked.

I gulped. "Well, um, you on the phone this morning."

She made a rude noise.

"She had someone else do the summoning," I said quickly. "That person's here tonight. And she's work-"

She squeezed tighter and I shut up, suckin' in what little air I could. Call me a coward, but I'm attached to my neck and I wanted to keep it that way.

"Marie," Quil growled. "If you kill her, there's nothing to stop me from killing you."

"Hence the point of a hostage," she said, still sweet as Eskimo Pie.

"Why didn't your gris-gris work on me?" I asked as she lightened up again.

Saying anything was a risk, but she needed me alive. At least for the moment.

"And how did you get my hair?" My eyes flew wide and my stomach sank. "My hair clip. It came out when the demon attacked."

"Stop talking," she said, adding pressure to my neck again.

Flash.

It was outside the room at Tom's where Quil was attacked.

Grant went over to near the wall and picked up my hair clip, keeping his back to the group of vamps.

Groans came from the room and he growled under his breath, resisting the urge to punch the wall.

He cleaned the strands of my hair off the clip before pulling a few of his own out and putting them in and placing it back on the floor exactly where he'd found it, and glanced back over his shoulder.

The vamps were too busy watching the door and the stairs to worry about him.

Good. His hairs were darker, and shorter, but could've been the little ones that frame my face at a casual glance. He pulled out a small metal thing I recognized as a tracking device and pressed it onto the clip. It was metal too so kind of looked like it was just another decoration on the clip.

"What?" Marie asked as I pulled out of the vision.

I must've been grinnin' like an idiot, and surprisingly enough, it wasn't my nervous smile.

I have to say it, sometimes Grant is a genius.

"Who took my hair clip?" I asked. "It wasn't the demon, it was kicked out by then. So it had to be one of the people there last night, but how? I touched most of them, but probably missed someone."

She squeezed my neck so tight it cut off all but the smallest bit of airway.

I gagged, sucking in air as hard as I could and Quil took half a step forward.

"Don't do it," she said with a hiss.

I clawed at her hand and she lightened the death grip just enough so the stars stopped dancing in my eyes.

"What do you want?" Quil asked. "*This.* All this. Hiring the demons, calling attention to our nest, trying to have it kill me, why?"

"Why do we do anything, Quil?" she asked. "And it wasn't trying to kill you."

He nodded. He already knew that, of course. "No, it was trying to kidnap me. Why?"

"You know why. Who would benefit from having you distracted? Who wants you dead or gone? That was the deal. I help here, she gives me you. You'd be a great second with a little bit of... what do the humans say? Reprogramming?"

Quil paled and my heart went out to him even as I sucked air through a straw.

Huh, turned out I had a gut sense too, and it was right about Jade.

Not that it'd help me now.

Were those birdies really flyin' around or was I blacking out?

"No, it doesn't make sense," Quil said. "It makes her look weak too. She would never hurt her own nest."

"But the demon went after humans, and we all know how she feels about them."

"No, I don't believe you. You're trying to undermine us. You did this."

"Of course I did, but I just did it for power. She solidifies her power base by scaring her people into submission, finds the vampire responsible, and sends him off to live with another nest who can properly control him because she still cares for him too much to kill him."

Her and Jade were going to frame Quil?

"No one would believe that," Quil said.

"Oh, they will. Everything's already laid out."

"How could she?"

"Power," a voice said from behind us.

I didn't have to see to know it was Milo.

"Jade knows Carvi and I are planning a summit next year to discuss coming out into the open, telling humans about magic," Milo said. "This was just the first step to undermining that. She would get rid of you, and then start picking off humans in other nests, which would bring in human authorities, and the resulting tensions would scare vampires into wanting to stay hidden."

Marie loosened her grip and I took a deep breath, the world solidifying again. Blood pounded through my neck and skull, makin' them ache down through my spine.

"And you didn't tell me this before because?" Quil asked, his eyes still on me.

"I just got the vision now, give me a break."

Give me a break? He was really up on modern day English. Which I guess wasn't too surprising. He had a long time to learn to adjust to new languages. I mean, he was alive before English was even created.

Marie took a sharp breath. "You're psychic too?"

Milo chuckled. "I'd tell you to keep your mouth shut, but I think that's the least of our worries. Now Marie, you really do need to let this lovely young lady go."

"You're psychic?"

Wow, she was really thrown by that.

"Yes." I could practically see his smug grin in his voice. "And I know who you hired to summon the demon."

"One word and I'll kill her." She tightened her hand again and I squirmed, makin' her squeeze tighter.

"Gah!" I tried to say, the words stuck in my throat.

"Marie, you know she's a fed, and that there are others here," Milo said with an exaggerated sigh. "And they're pretty damn good at what they do."

Flash.

Grant crept up the back hallway, holding the silver whip. He inched the door open and Milo talking came through as an echo.

"So," Milo said, "*why don't you agree to let her go in exchange for us promising no retaliation?*"

Grant motioned to Quil over her head, pointing to me.

I blinked and the scene was exactly like I saw it, just outta my eyes and not floating above Grant's head.

Holy crap on a cracker, did I just force a real time vision?

"So," Milo said in the exact same tone he'd just had in my vision, "why don't you agree to let her go in exchange for us promising no retaliation?"

Nope, I'd just forced a future vision. It was in the future like three seconds, but it was still the future.

"You go back to your nest and call off your demon," Milo said. "You give us Jade, her plans, everything, the vampire you turned to make him summon the demon, and your word as a vampire that you will not attack anyone in our nests or anyone attached to them ever again. In exchange, we won't go after you, and we won't tell the other leaders what you did. You know this is a sweetheart deal. You won't get out of here any other way."

"You give me your word you won't come after me?" she asked.

I squirmed in her grip and she clamped down.

"Stop that," she said, cold as an icicle.

I nodded, heart racin' as fear twisted my stomach.

Grant was gonna hit any second. He had to. But I was supposed to be brave! I should've been fighting to get away.

And all I wanted was to wake up in bed with Quil, the case solved, Jade gone, and me about to go to work to do something boring like paperwork.

Stop it! This isn't a nightmare. And you can't always expect Grant to save your butt.

I wasn't going to wake up. This was real, but I wasn't dead yet.

And I was gonna keep it that way.

I just needed to get outta her grip

"You should stop being stupid and take the deal," I said.

She squeezed harder and I sucked air, strugglin'.

She wouldn't kill me. Not with the two older vamps who'd take her down the second she didn't have a hostage.

"You think I won't kill you because you're the only thing keeping them from killing me," Marie said, wrappin' an arm around my shoulders to pin me to her. "You're right, I can't. Milo, that is a wonderful deal, but I'm no fool. You can lower that whip, Agent Grant. We both know you won't use it while I literally hold your agent's life in my hands."

Oh crap on crackers and kittens!

So she did know he was behind her.

"I can smell human and silver. You honestly thought you could sneak up on me?" she asked. "And you can stop trying your earbuds, my man overrode them five minutes ago. I would be insulted by this trap, but I know how stupid humans are."

Hey. Rude.

She'd backed us up into the farthest dark corner, Grant probably still hovered in the doorway behind us, and Quil and Milo were on each side. To anyone giving our group a casual glance, we were just a few people talking and hanging on each other.

But couldn't they see the tension, smell the fear? How could they not even be paying attention? They were all dancing and chatting, even the guys at the bar didn't give us more than a few quick glances.

How could her guy get into our system?

And then I knew.

Grant always tells me not to assume, and I didn't have any proof, not even a vision to back up my suspicions, but I knew.

My heart froze.

I didn't touch everyone here tonight.

There was a certain group of people I never even considered tryin' to touch.

"The summoner's-" I started as fast as I could, but apparently not even my roadrunner voice box can beat vamp reflexes.

She squelched my words with a firmer grip and I gurgled as I struggled to suck in air again.

I felt Marie nod above my head as she held me tighter.

And all hell broke loose.

The room erupted in front of us. Vampires I assumed were with her leapt out of the crowd at our small group, takin' Quil and Milo down.

She whirled and held me between her and Grant. The long silver whip in his hand was probably the only reason she didn't just snap my neck and be done with it.

I wasn't complaining.

Actually, no matter what she did, I wouldn't be able to complain on account of no air.

The world darkened around the edges like it does sometimes when I get a vision, but this time I wouldn't be gettin' any pretty pictures when the world blinked off.

Quil grunted behind us and something, actually someone probably, hit the wall off to our side.

"Drop the whip and move out of my way, or she dies and I'll make you move," Marie hissed at Grant.

My eyes found his and the world narrowed down to us.

I couldn't feel the hand on my neck or the lack of oxygen.

I swam on a wave of green champagne and it willed me to hear it.

To understand.

To *run*.

I snapped back to the present and Grant's eyes held somethin' I'd never seen there before.

Fear.

"She's going to use Ariana to trade," Milo called as the fight noises behind us grew.

Something was keeping Quil from running to my rescue and I could only imagine that it was something pretty bad.

Marie closed the delicate steel hand and I saw stars as my airway was completely blocked. I clawed at the hand, tears leaking out of my eyes.

And then Grant did the unthinkable.

He dropped the whip and walked out of the hallway with his hands up.

What?

"I don't need to tell you what I'll do to you and your entire nest if she dies," Grant said in a tone fitting his name.

"I do not fear humans," she said, lettin' me go and pushing me into the back hall past him.

"Do you fear our explosives?" he asked, lookin' at me.

I ran fast as my little legs could take me before he even stopped talking and she grabbed me from behind.

I flew.

The small popping was all I heard before pain flared in my neck and darkness took me.

CHAPTER TWENTY

"A RIANA?"

Something shook me in the darkness and I knew there was no way I was pullin' out of it without some extreme pain.

I started sinking back down, then..."Agent Ryder!"

Something wet sprinkled on my face and the darkness started to retract.

No, no, no! It would hurt too much. Why couldn't he just leave me alone?

The pain inched in slowly. It started with a conga line of screwdrivers through my brain, then danced down my brain stem and settled in my neck and shoulders, running round and round until my muscles seized into one big ball of confused, tied up barbed wire.

"Hey," that same voice said.

A hand cupped my chin as I came back to consciousness and my eyes refused to open past slits flirtin' with the room.

Thank God the lights were dim.

"And until this is settled," a voice very far away was saying, "no one's leaving. She wasn't working alone. Someone here is the demon and someone else is the summoner."

Voices rose and I couldn't distinguish between them. I did know one thing, they weren't happy.

"I don't care if you don't like this plan," Quil said. "I don't care if you feel tricked because I did not tell you the actual plan before. It doesn't matter because we found the traitor, and lost two of our own in the process. The only reason we didn't lose more was because of the humans sneaking in those weapons. So you can whine about betrayal and trickery, but you are not leaving."

"And," Quil said in a harder tone, "your leaders have already agreed. So sit down, shut up, and we'll get to you as soon as we can. Once this is over, you can file all the complaints with your leaders that you wish, but until then, no one tries to leave. If they do, they will be maced first and questioned later. If you want to get out of here quickly, you'll cooperate."

That's a little jackbooted. What about Jade?

I floated on the sea of pain, still not openin' my eyes for over half a second at a time.

"Come on, Ariana, open your eyes. I need you to open your eyes." It almost sounded like Grant's voice, but he would never sound so desperate.

"Agent Ryder, open your damn eyes!"

That was definitely Grant.

My eyes fluttered open.

I whimpered as the pain roared into reality.

I wanted to rip off my skull and slough off my muscles because then at least they wouldn't be attached to hurt me.

Grant held my face in his huge meaty ones, and I clung to him.

"Wh...'appened?" I asked, throat sore enough to make me not want to talk again for a week.

Jet, Dan, Kat, and Milo surrounded me. Quil rushed through the doorway a moment later. We were still in the hallway and Kat was trying to check me out.

"Guys, you need to back up," she said, voice tense.

Quil dropped in between her and Jet and grabbed my hand.

Jet and Dan did as they were told, but the other three wouldn't budge.

Okay, I got Grant and Quil stayin' by my side, but Milo? Seriously, what was up with that? He just met me. And yet he was leaning over with the other two, concern in his eyes even as that same stupid smile graced his face.

"Fine." Kat sighed. "Someone can hold her hand, that should be okay, but I need the space so two of you need to move."

Grant took my other hand. I smiled and met his eyes, trying to lose my pain in their cool green depths.

"Great," Kat said. "You two, back up, this isn't a large hallway."

My other hand suddenly felt very cold.

Why would it feel cold cuz Quil let it go when his hands were room temp?

A small whimper escaped me. I didn't know if it was pain, or my suddenly very lonely hand, or some combination of the two. I turned my eyes to Quil as he backed up.

He offered a small smile, but then was blocked by Kat.

She shined a light in my eyes. What was that supposed to accomplish? Cuz all it did was make my headache worse. The conga line went up from a waltz to a jive.

Yeah, I know that's a lot of mixed dance metaphors; the point is, it hurt.

Apparently she liked what she saw cuz her face looked a little less pinched. "No concussion."

Oh right, that's why doctors did the light in the eyes thing.

Grant tilted my head back towards him. "She needs to examine your neck after what Marie did. Hold still. That's an order."

I couldn't nod, but I blinked once and kept my eyes on his.

Kat poked and prodded and I tried, and failed, not to whimper and cry. Grant held my hand tightly, murmuring over it.

"Oww!" I cried out one last time as Kat gently maneuvered my neck over again.

"She's got full range of motion, I think it's just a little strained, but the shoulder's dislocated," Kat said after a few minutes.

I wanted to black out again cuz I knew what was coming next.

When a shoulder's dislocated, they have to pop it back in. And, as Quil already said, none of us were going anywhere until the demon and summoner were caught, which meant they couldn't call an ambulance and take me to a nice ER with doctors and pretty, pretty painkillers.

The summoner!

"Grant." Man, did my throat hurt. "The summoner's..."

"Shhhh," he said, placing fingers over my lips. "I know."

My eyes popped. "How? Ohhhhh, trackin' device."

His head snapped back at me. I'd never envied the ability to move your head before now.

"How?" he asked.

"Vision," I said.

"Humph." He turned to the vamps. "You said you can heal her?"

Quil nodded. "It will take both Milo and myself since I'm not trained as he is."

"Trained?" Jet asked, voice cracking all over the place.

If I looked at him, I knew he'd be holding back tears. Jet doesn't cry easily, but when he wants to and when he's trying not to, ya know it.

"Massage therapist," Milo said with another of his stupid grins. "I went to school about twenty years ago, but I still got it." He cracked his knuckles and wiggled his fingers at me suggestively. "We can give her blood and work out the muscles with some saliva. Quil's only does cuts, but I can help loosen her up."

Double entendre much?

Why is it every word out of his mouth came with that dirty tone?

"I can give her blood," Quil said.

"We're not leaving you alone. This won't be like last night," Grant said, keeping his grip on my hand.

"So orgy instead of menage a trois," Milo said. "Sounds good to me. But I got rules. I go first and I don't do men."

Oh crap. Grant's gonna punch him.

"Oh dear," I couldn't help but moan, regrettin' it as it blazed up my bruised throat.

"Don't worry, Agent Grant," Quil said. "We'll fix her up. Sweets, can you deal with a little embarrassment here?"

I blinked once.

"That's a yes," Grant said.

He shrugged off his vest and motioned at Dan and Jet. They took theirs off too. Grant folded them into a nice little purple silk pillow.

"This is going to hurt, Ryder," Grant said.

I blinked at him and he nodded.

Together, a lot of large hands rolled me over and I bit down on a scream as my right shoulder tapped the ground. My vision blacked out for a moment and I really wished I could stay there as the fire went back down.

"What did she do? What happened?" I asked as small hands moved my head to the side so it was restin' on the pillow. I would've killed for some water.

Grant held onto my hand as one of the others undid the tie up top around my neck and unzipped my dress.

"This feels so wrong," Kat said as she stood.

My head was towards Grant so I couldn't see where she went, but I figured she was close.

I felt hands I knew were Quil's run down my bare back and I closed my eyes.

I wanted my co-workers to get the hell out. We couldn't do anything like this in front of them.

But they already made it clear they weren't leavin', especially Grant.

So I settled for the 'bury your head in the sand' approach and just closed my eyes.

A rough wet tongue ran slowly over my sore neck, leaving it sticky with the healing saliva. My entire body shuddered with it as my muscles relaxed.

Whoa! Bottle that and you could make a fortune in massage oils.

"When the flash grenade went off, she thought it was the real thing," Grant said.

Huh?

Ohhhhhh, he was sayin' what happened in the hall.

"I pulled out my weapons as soon as she walked you past and hit the charge."

The tongue moved down to my shoulder blades and I moaned as hands started kneading my neck.

It was a good thing my eyes were closed cuz I couldn't look at Grant right now.

"It looked like she was trying to shove you away while she twisted your neck, but you hit the wall, and I double tapped her as soon as you were out of the way," Grant said.

I couldn't even imagine how fast he would've had to move to do that considering her vamp reflexes.

"She's dead," Grant said.

Good.

Milo ran his tongue down my spine and grabbed a big handful of my bottom, just cuz he needed to rest it some place as he leaned over, I'm sure.

The hands on my neck froze. "Milo, if you do not remove your hand, I will remove it for you," Quil said.

He probably didn't mean he'd just take the hand off my bottom.

"Oh fine," Milo said, moving his head. "Now that she's all oiled up, I'll take over the massage, since I'm the one who knows what I'm doing after all."

Is it wrong that I'm enjoyin' this?

Ya know what, I was injured, could barely speak cuz someone had tried to strangle me then tossed me into a wall, I wasn't gonna worry about it.

Milo's hands replaced Quil's at my neck and I had to admit he was quite clever with them.

"Saved me?" I asked, still not opening my eyes.

"You're my agent," Grant said.

"We helped," Milo said.

"No you didn't, you were busy with other things," Jet snapped from somewhere behind me.

"What happened there?" I asked, still dyin' for some water. Just a bit to pour down my throat.

"Marie had a backup plan just in case the gris-gris didn't work. They were supposed to jump me at her command and take me out while she got away with you then used you to bargain with," Quil said. "But she didn't anticipate Milo being there, ready to fight just as I was, and she didn't know I let Grant in with silver bullets and that whip."

"Why didn't tell me?" I asked.

"I have to tell you everything now?" Grant asked.

"No, sir," I mumbled, driftin' on a sea of comfort as Milo worked his saliva into my back.

What else could their saliva do? And why didn't they use it in hospitals or something? Hell, maybe they did.

"My shoulder?" I asked.

"Don't think about that," Milo said, and for once didn't sound like he was undressing me with his voice. "You just tensed up."

"We're going to pop it back in," Quil said. "You're going to have to be brave, okay?"

"'Kay. Grant, summoner?"

Milo worked his hands harder and I suddenly found it very hard to think of anything but them.

"We can't take him out yet," Grant said. "If we kill him before killing or banishing the demon, the demon will be free for the night. We have to find it and take it out first. And the summoner can't know we know until it's time."

"Kill?" I asked.

I could almost see Grant frown. "I meant arrest him."

No, he didn't.

I drifted away and bobbed back in.

I saw what happened to those girls. It was his fault.

And the worst circle of Hell is reserved for those who betray.

"After what he did, he'll be getting off lucky," Grant said.

"Who is it?" Quil asked.

"No," Grant said. "The only way this works is if no one knows."

"You know."

"I can hide it."

There was a pause then Quil said, "All right, I'm trusting you here."

Milo chuckled and rubbed a bit harder.

I floated on his hands.

Was it me, or did everyone go really quiet all of a sudden?

Small hands touched my shoulder.

"She tensed again," Kat said, pulling her hands back. "Ariana, I'm sorry, if I told you it was coming..." She trailed off.

"I get it." My throat burned even more as I tried not to cry.

"I have an idea," Quil said and I felt more than heard movement around me. "You want me to help, you need to move."

He must've been talkin' to Grant cuz next thing I knew, my hand was dropped, then picked up by a colder one.

"Sweets, open your eyes," he said.

The first thing I saw were his blue-green eyes sparkling with worry, right next to my face. He stroked my cheek. "I'm going to bite you, just long enough for her to pop your shoulder back while you're relaxed."

Bite me? In front of everyone? No way!

I blinked twice.

"Without drugs, I'm not getting this arm in without a lot of pain and possibly more damage," Kat said.

"Ariana, please, I know this is embarrassing, but this will make you better," Quil said.

"Let me," Grant said. Quil moved away and Grant leaned over my head. "Ariana, listen to me."

I blinked once.

"We need you mobile, and we need it fast because every minute that passes, we risk that demon getting away. Whatever happens when he does this, none of us will think any less of you."

"Promise?" I asked.

"Ariana, if you can do this, if you can accept this will help, no matter what you feel or how embarrassed you are, if you can deal with that and move on, then all that will show me is you can do the job when necessary," Grant said. "If all that's holding you back is your embarrassment, then get over it, because you will not lose my respect."

I blinked once.

He nodded and backed away and Quil took his place.

Milo chuckled again. I swear that man never did anything but smirk and laugh and make suggestive comments, though in all fairness I'd only known him about an hour.

"Say it and I will silver-shoot you right here," Quil said.

"Say what?" Milo asked. "That all it took was Grant asking her to do it and she jumped? Say that you mean? Okay, I won't say it."

He was still massaging my shoulders, and it still felt good, but I lost all love for him in the moment and wanted to silver-shoot him myself.

"Shush, troublemaker," I said, throat burnin'.

Even when I'm not supposed to talk, I can't help it.

"After I heal you and we catch the demon and summoner, you can take me and that whip in back and tell me to do whatever you want," Milo whispered in my ear suggestively.

I blinked twice and looked at Quil.

Quil kissed my forehead. "I can ignore him, sweets."

I smiled.

How was he so calm?

Nothing fazed him. He wasn't being all jealous. He wasn't being petty.

He just wanted me better.

"Love you," I said, closin' my eyes.

Quil kissed me lightly. "I'll say it when I know we both mean it. Right now, you're a little high."

I was? Probably the vamp saliva.

His fangs scraped my neck and I tensed, makin' pain shoot down my spine.

He bit down and pleasure swamped me.

Small, desperate whimpers escaped my throat and I rubbed into the floor beneath me, wantin' him on top of me. He sucked harder and I moaned, throat not hurtin' now.

Or maybe I just couldn't feel it.

"Hold her down," Kat said. "I can't have her moving while I do this."

One hand held down my left shoulder. I knew its feel and tried to move back into Quil.

Two hands pressed down on my back, holding me in place and helpin' build the pressure underneath. They were big enough to stretch the length of my back at the waist and the calluses spoke of a man who worked his whole life.

I didn't need to be psychic to know they were Grant's hands.

"This is wrong in so many ways," Kat whispered.

On some level I knew what was coming, I just didn't care.

Pop!

The pleasure amplified as my mind went black with ice and fire feuding in my shoulder.

It should've hurt.

It didn't.

The hands holding me down did it to make me hot. The teeth in me was like something else inside, makin' me tighten.

The vamp bite makes pain pleasure, some voice inside said as the wave took me.

A ragged scream tore from my throat, only adding to my agony fueled pleasure and my body arched as I came.

Tears streaked down my cheeks and my body twitched with the memory of the pain my mind wasn't allowed to acknowledge.

I don't know when Quil pulled back. Sometime between the popping back in and when the glow wore off enough for me to think again.

Strong hands pulled me up and helped situate me in a large lap.

"It's okay, you did great," Grant whispered as he cradled me and stroked my bare back.

Huh?

Oh crap! He thought the moaning and everything was from pain?

Maybe I didn't need to correct him on that one.

My top was stiff so everything was still covered, but it was slidin'.

I opened my eyes and Quil sat in front of us.

Just watchin'.

Grant scooped my hair out of the way and retied the top and zipped me back up.

I'd need to adjust the ladies before it fit right, but I wasn't doin' that in front of the guys.

"Need help standing?" Quil asked once Grant was done.

I couldn't think so much to focus on the actual words, just the beautiful mouth sayin' them, so I shrugged.

Ouch! Bad idea!

The pain snapped me back to reality outside those eyes and I reached for Quil.

He held me by the waist as I climbed to my feet. Grant stood behind me and the others were still bunched in the hall with us.

My legs gave out and Quil and Grant caught me from each side.

Grant let go and Quil pulled me into his chest. I held onto his thick arms like life preservers as he turned and gently pushed me into an office chair someone must've brought into the hall.

"Sweets, you're very week and still injured. I think you could use some of my blood," Quil said, kneelin' in front of me.

I blushed and he grinned. "I know. This isn't an intimacy I like sharing with a crowd either, but your team's pretty adamant about not giving us privacy, so."

I opened my mouth and my seared throat made me close it again. I blinked once.

In for a penny, in for a pound.

"Oh, please, please let me help," Milo said.

I glared at him.

He held up his hands, blinkin' innocently. "I'm offering to help. You look like you could use an extra boost, and like you give good *sucking*."

My face burned and I stuck my tongue out at him.

Quil held up his arm and I looked at him.

He didn't expect me to bite him in front of all these people? Suckin' was bad enough.

He nodded like he understood and looked around. "Does anyone have a knife? Not silver?"

Grant pulled a Swiss Army knife out of his boot and handed it over.

I gave Grant a look.

I didn't know what I was asking of him until he got it and turned around, takin' a few steps so he could give us some room. The guys and Kat turned too.

Milo didn't.

They couldn't leave us in case anything happened, but they could turn their heads without too much worry about something getting us five feet away.

I looked at Milo and he winked at me.

I sighed, givin' Quil big eyes.

Quil kissed me, short but deep.

He pulled back and sliced his arm so fast I gasped.

"Ryder?" Grant asked.

"Cut," I said, throat burnin' so I couldn't get the volume up.

Grant turned around and Quil held up his bleeding arm. Grant nodded and turned back around.

"Decent of them to give us some privacy," Quil whispered.

"If I give her some of my blood, she'll have an easier time getting visions," Milo said.

Quil looked over his shoulder at him. "And have her bound to you?"

"We still have a summoner and a demon to catch. Can't let anything get in the way of that, now can we?"

"True?" I asked Quil, hopin' that was enough so I didn't have to say more.

"Yeah. We can transfer powers through blood if the person is already susceptible to it. Here, I believe him."

I blinked once and Quil shot a glare at Milo as he hit his knees in front of me way too fast.

Quil held his arm in front of me and I closed my eyes as Milo leaned in, taking a long sniff.

I sucked on his wound and a small sound escaped Quil.

He wrapped an arm around my waist and pulled me to my knees in front of him, pressing me straight against him so he could rub against me.

I took another long drag and let him go.

He stared down at me and kissed my bloody mouth, pullin' back too soon with a sigh.

"I'm going to need a cold shower before I go out there," he whispered, resting his forehead against mine.

Milo cleared his throat and I looked at him.

"Are we seriously going to do this?" I asked.

My voice was back!

The blood going down must've healed it too.

"You want a psychic boost? I'm the original Energizer Bunny, baby."

"You better be talkin' batteries. And I'm not your baby."

I took his arm and pushed him back by his other shoulder when he tried to press against me too.

Which was about as effective as pushing a wall.

"Don't even think about it," I said.

"Too late." He grinned. "I'll think about it all I want, but if you want to pretend you're not attracted to me and push me away, I'll settle for fantasy land." He brushed my lips with a finger. "For now."

"Milo," Quil said, "stop it."

"I'm just saying, a threesome with death outside the door would be hot. We even have a crowd to cheer us on."

I looked at Quil. "Is he serious?"

"The eternal question," he said, holding the knife out to Milo. "Milo, please hurry."

"I don't need that," Milo said, biting his wrist and holding it out to me.

Oh dear God, what the guys must be thinkin' listening to all this.

I took his hand in both of mine and kept my eyes on Quil as I bent down and sucked.

His blood had the same thick, sweet taste as Quil's, but seemed to have a crisper edge.

Quil licked his lips.

"Do I taste better?" Milo whispered against my ear, lips quivering.

I shook my head and pulled back. "Different, but you're both pretty much the same goody-wise."

Did I honestly just say that?

"Most humans can't tell the difference. That's impressive."

"Then put me in a vamp blood blind taste test I guess." It was supposed to be snide, but came out in a soft whisper to match his.

He scooted forward and pressed against me and God help me, I didn't have it in me to push him back. He brought the bleeding arm to my lips again and I ran them slowly over the wound before clamping on to suck.

Quil glanced over at the guys and inched closer to me.

"I'm shocked how arousing I find this."

I let go and shook my head at him. "Don't even suggest it."

He grinned. "Then I'll just watch."

Milo made a motion with his hands and something flashed in the hall between us.

"Shield," Milo said. "They won't see anything but you in the chair and us in front of you if they turn, and won't hear me."

"No!" I said.

"Not sex, I just don't want to be quiet as you do this."

Milo inched behind me and pulled me tight against him, putting his wrist to my mouth. Quil pressed against my front and arousal shot through me.

I shook my head and Quil nodded.

"Bad timing," he said, but stayed up against me.

Like a human sandwich.

I switched to his arm and sucked him hard, makin' his head toss back.

His mouth jumped and quivered from a smile to desperate O to a smile again as he moved against me.

I let him go. "No time."

"I'm going to need to put some cold water on me then. Milo, behave."

Quil got up and rushed down the hall and Milo rubbed against my back in a rhythm and I went to his wrist, pullin' on him.

He cried out and I bit him hard, makin' him groan.

Flash.

Milo flew across the room and smacked his head on the corner of a chair hard enough to crack the skin over his head open so I could see bone.

"Milo!" his brother shouted as he jumped on the back of an assailant whose face I couldn't see. He had a broad back and was at least seven feet tall, way bigger than even the built Carvi.

Carvi secured his arm around the attacker's neck and got tossed over its shoulder.

The vision rotated. The attacker had some sort of long snout of a nose and bright pink eyes.

Demon!

It slammed a giant foot down on the vampire's middle so hard he had to have caused damage.

Carvi jerked and rolled up on himself with a groan as the demon drew his foot back.

The glint of metal on the edge of the large boot told me he had spikes on them and the poor vamp screamed as it slammed into his face, digging a hole into the side of his head the size of a candle.

A small woman with streaming red locks jumped in, caught the foot, and rolled with it to use the demon's momentum to take it down. I knew even before she bounced back up and turned that it was Blanche.

The demon groaned as it climbed to its feet and charged her.

She jumped and vaulted over it with the ease of an Olympic gymnast.

Another man with a thick black beard came in off the side of my vision, bleeding from a gash in his arm.

Took me a moment to realize that yellowish thing was a shard of bone stickin' out.

He slammed the demon across the face with a steel beam.

The demon flashed forward and tore the beam out of his hand, and swung it like it was the ninth inning of the World Series and the bases were loaded.

The vamp's head separated clean from his shoulders and was still flying through the air when both parts disintegrated into dust.

"The job is done," the demon said in a deep voice that would put even Darth Vader to shame. "But since I'm here."

It stepped towards Blanche and I got a shot of fear from her as she bounced on the balls of her feet.

They'd never seen anything like this demon. The power he wielded, it wasn't anything that'd ever crossed the earth.

The demon paused and started to twitch as a hole opened up through thin air in the space behind him. He growled and strained against an invisible force as it pulled him backwards into what looked like a large forest.

The rip in the air sealed behind him and just like that, they were safe.

Blanche ran over to Milo and immediately started licking his head wound, which was already starting to heal on its own.

Milo groaned and blinked his eyes open. Carvi crawled over to them, clutching his side with one hand and the deep hole in his head with another.

"Thanks," Blanche said to someone in the corner. "How did you…"

"Don't ask."

The visions expanded. They were in some kind of giant empty warehouse or maybe a gutted restaurant.

The two guys in the corner came out of the shadows, one big and bulky, about my age, with movie star waves in his brown hair and square, strong features so striking he had to be an actor.

He had a wildness about him, something that made me think of flight and fire.

The other man was shorter, slighter build, but everything in me went cold looking at him.

Out of the two of them, I'd take the big guy any day.

"You are quite welcome," the cold one said in a clipped British voice. "However, this merely rid you of him temporarily."

"Can't just say we still have to kill his ass, can ya?" the bigger guy asked. "No, has to be all pretentious."

The man turned cold eyes to the young man. "Please do not give me an excuse to kill you. She would not like it."

"Bring it on, Brit-tard."

"Boys!" Blanche jumped in-between them so fast both looked surprised. "I get there's a lot of issues here and I'm sure there's a reason for it, but is that demon going to come back?"

"No," the cold one said. "We will find him on the Other Side and we will kill him."

"What did he do to you?" she asked.

The cold blue eyes went icier than Grant's when he was pissed. "He killed my friend, and took someone of mine. I must retrieve her."

Milo pushed to his feet. "This that chick you were telling Carvi about?"

"No," the man shook his head. "She is… a complication. I promised my friend I would protect her though. That being said…"

"You have to save your girl."

"I must."

"Can we help?" Blanche asked.

"The young lady… she can not stay where she is."

"What the douchebag means to say is, we're going to have to drop her here," the big guy said. "Can you look out for her? She's not going to know anyone and… she's just a kid. She's going to need someone looking out for her."

"Of course," Blanche said. "We owe you a debt. We will care for her as though she were our own. Where… or when should we meet her?"

"We will bring her here after we have rescued my… our missing friend," the cold man said.

"You know I could bang that stick out of your ass," Carvi said, holding his skull together with sheer willpower.

The cold man blinked, taking a step back, and the younger one burst out laughing.

"Oh my god, you should see your face," the big guy said. "Dude, you look shocked that a guy would want to fuck you. It's hilarious. I'm going to have to record this." He pulled out a phone.

The cold man smacked it out of his hand, staring him down even though he was at least four inches shorter than the big guy.

"Try it," the big guy said. "I'm dying for a reason to take you out. Because honestly, she'd be a lot better off without you."

"Even when I am your best hope for saving your friend? You would risk her life merely due to your dislike of me?"

"Guys!" Blanche said, making them turn. "Seriously, I don't know what you two

have going on, and I don't care. You're going after the demon before it comes back for us, yes?"

"Quite right," the cold man said, waving his hand.

A slit opened in the air and the man walked through.

"Bye, gorgeous," the big guy said, winking at Blanche before he walked through too.

The slit zipped up and the building was deader than a liquor store on Sunday.

"What the hell were those guys!" Blanche yelled.

"I'd explain if I could," Carvi said. "As it is, my head is killing me, this is going to take weeks to heal, and I didn't even get to fuck that little pixie before she was abducted, or her lover. Some days just aren't worth it."

"That… that thing just killed…" Milo said, cutting off with Carvi coughing up blood.

Blanche grabbed an old fashioned phone off the wall and called someone, telling him an address and running back to Milo.

"George will be in here in a minute. He'll get the silver out of your head." Blanche gave Carvi a quick kiss on the cheek and he smiled. "He owned a huge territory. That's a lot of enemies. How do we find out who sent the demon to kill him?"

The brothers looked at each other.

"We'll find out," they said together.

Carvi curled up, pressing his hands tight to his head.

"Stop that," Blanche said. "You're going to pop your head if you keep squeezing like that."

"It would hurt less. When will George get here?"

"A few minutes."

"He'll be here in time, right?" Milo asked.

"Oh yeah," Blanche said. "The silver's in his head, the worst it'll do in a few minutes is brain damage."

"The worst?"

She shrugged. "It's Carvi, not like there'd be a difference."

She ducked as a slab of wood sailed by and she shot Carvi a glare.

Harsh words tripped from his lips between coughs.

"Could you two try to play nice?" Milo asked.

"He started it."

"When! When did I start it?" Carvi asked.

"Before that demon got here. You were threatening to hold me down and-"

"You what?" Milo turned to his brother.

"It wasn't a threat. It was an offer. She was fighting with Seti and he upset her. I thought she could use some cheering up."

Blanche made a rude noise. "What about his lands?"

"You were his second, I think that means you get them," Milo said.

"I'm not sure I'm old enough," Blanche said.

"You're powerful though, and we'll back you up," Milo said.

She leaned in, kissing him. Not the usual peck vamps gave each other, a real kiss.

Milo kissed her back. If he had a heartbeat, it would be racing.

"If you two are going to fuck, at least take it to one of the back rooms," Carvi grumbled, making them pull apart.

Milo looked at his brother as he held his head tighter.

Something pinkish oozed out.

Oh God! Were those his brains?

"Fucking demons," Carvi said as Blanche took Milo's hand.

"Don't worry," she said. "George will be here soon. He'll fix you right up."

"Can't come soon enough. Fucking witches."

"Yeah, those people," Milo said. "What the hell is going on there?"

"Witches, dead witch, kidnapped witch, innocent girl sucked into it because she banged the dead witch."

"And that last one is the one they asked us to keep an eye on?" Blanche asked.

"Yeah."

"So they'll be back?"

A door creaked in the background and footsteps echoed as someone ran up.

"Over here, George!" Blanche yelled, and the footsteps got closer.

"This has been the strangest day," Carvi said.

I pulled out of the vision and Milo froze against me.

"What happened to the girl?" I asked.

"Did you just get a vision?" he said, letting me go.

"Yeah." I turned, ignoring the little problem he had going on in his pants. "You, your brother and Blanche were being attacked and these guys saved you, and they disappeared with magic or something, and your brother was kicked in the head and his brains were coming out. It was awful. And confusing. What happened with the guys? Did they get the demon?"

"We don't know. They never came back, and we never met the girl they were talking about. But the demon also never came back."

"What happened with you and Blanche?"

He stood up.

Huh.

I stood too, aches gone, shoulder fine, everything in me awake and ready to go.

"Do you know I can feel emotions in my visions sometimes? I'm guessing you do cuz you could feel mine in yours. Well, I felt how you did about Blanche, you're completely in love with her, and I think you were hitting on me tonight to get to her cuz something happened. I don't like being used, Milo, and tonight, we don't have time for this."

Milo waved a hand and the air flashed.

"We're done," Milo said.

The guys turned.

Grant frowned. "Where did Quil go?"

"Oh, to the bathroom. He got a little… er, excited, and wanted cold water," I said.

"Why didn't I hear him leave?"

"Oh! Yeah, Milo put up a shield. I think he wanted something to happen. It didn't."

Grant locked his jaw and turned his glare on Milo.

Milo grinned, shruggin'. "Can't blame a guy for trying."

"I can when we have a killer on the loose. We ready?" Grant asked.

Milo grinned wider, jutting his hands down at his groin. "Soon as Ariana helps me with this."

"Sure," I said.

Grant shot me a look and I handed Milo my water bottle.

"This is pretty cold, it should work." I kept my face straight for all of a second, then burst out laughing.

Milo joined me as he swiped the water bottle out of my hand.

"You're mean," he said as he undid his pants. I blushed and turned away and he chuckled again. "I'm sooooo going to enjoy screwing you."

"Not gonna happen," I said.

I met Grant's eyes and his lips quirked up in a little smile.

"So we still need to find the demon?" I asked and Grant nodded. "How much time has all this taken?"

"About ten minutes."

"That's not good."

"No."

"You can turn around now," Milo said.

"Are you done up?" I asked.

"Oh darn." He snapped his fingers. "I knew I forgot something."

"You two ready?" Grant asked in a flat voice.

"Yes, General," I said.

"I already said I'm not telling everyone I'm psychic," Milo said.

"Ryder, can you handle it?" Grant asked.

"Of course."

I looked at Milo, a very evil idea forming in my mind.

"I don't like that look," Milo said, actually sounding nervous.

"I'll make you a deal," I said. "After this is done, you tell me what I don't know or I'll tell everyone you're psychic."

His jaw dropped for half a second before his mouth split into a smile. "Oh, that's devious. I like that. I'll tell you then. After we find the demon."

"Deal."

"But we have to be alone."

"Why? Is it really bad?"

"I don't know about that," Milo said, "I just want to make sure I get a shot when you're all vulnerable.."

"Still not gonna happen."

I smiled though as I walked past him out of the hallway.

"Yes, it will."

He sounded so sure I almost believed him even though I had no intentions of saying yes.

Okay, I had maybe one intention of saying yes, but like ten more of saying no.

"So we have a deal?" He grabbed my arm and pulled me back into the doorway.

"Deal." I held out my hand to shake on it.

He leaned down. "How many times do we have to tell you we don't shake hands?"

He fastened his lips to mine and gave me a quick slip of the tongue before pulling back, leavin' me leaning against the door breathless.

"That's how I seal a deal." Milo backed away. "We'll finish later."

"No, you won't," Grant said.

Milo rolled his eyes and held out his arm like a gentleman. "Shall we, m'lady?" he asked in the worst parody of a British accent I've ever heard.

"No," I said, brushin' past him.

Everyone we'd gathered in the big office doing surveillance were now in the main club, lined up by the stage.

Quil nodded at me, lifting his hand in a parody of tipping something into his mouth.

Oh, good idea.

"Hey, General?" I turned to him.

"Yeah?"

"I think I'm gonna need a very big drink."

Grant surveyed the crowd.

Quil had all his vamps lining the walls, and more than a few on each door so no one could try to get out, but that still left sixty or so standing in the middle with the random human scattered here or there.

"I think you're right." Grant nodded. "Dan."

"One giant Cumberland River with extra vodka coming up." Dan gave me a small smile and walked to the bar.

That was actually friendly. Wow.

"Let's start on this end," Grant said.

Quil nodded and raised his hands. "Everyone, the psychic is going to touch all of you. We have to find the demon. If you have a problem with this, we can discuss it later. If you're not the demon, just hold still and you'll be out of here soon, so don't make trouble."

What were the odds this was going to go that smoothly?

"I'll go with you and just make chitchat while I get stuff," Milo whispered. "With both of us, we can make sure neither one misses anything."

I nodded. All the vamps that attacked earlier went past me. I touched all of them and got nothing.

It wouldn't happen again.

I looked at Grant, and he nodded.

Milo kissed my cheek, drawin' more than a few looks.

Quil walked up to us and kissed my other cheek and Milo shrugged, going towards the bar.

"Is that makin' sure they all know I'm with you?" I asked.

"Little bit," Quil said with a wink. "But it's more of a reminder that you are with me in the sense that if any of them try hurting you, they will deal with me."

I snapped my head around to look at him. "Is that gonna happen?"

"Possibly. We can't expect the demon to just wait for us to get to him."

I nodded, licking my lips as my heart rate picked up.

We had a demon to catch and a traitor to deal with.

Dan brought me my drink and I gave him a huge smile and downed like a fourth of it.

"Another satisfied customer," Dan said.

"Funny, that's what I always say," Milo said, suddenly behind me.

"Eep!" I jumped, sloshin' my drink over its glass.

"And I'll be saying that to you by the time the sun rises." Milo grinned, coverin' my hand with his and bringing my glass to his lips, taking a long sip as he stared me down.

Quil cleared his throat and Milo let go of my glass. I downed some more.

"How long till this kicks in?" I asked.

"For visions or lowered inhibitions?" Milo asked.

"Milo," Quil said.

"What? You can be there too," Milo said.

"Or you could stop hitting on me and go talk to Blanche," I said.

His smile didn't waver. "She can come too."

"What happened between you two?"

"It was so long ago, I don't remember."

"You guys live thousands of years, a few isn't that long ago."

"That attack was over twenty years ago."

"No, it wasn't."

"What are you talking about?" Quil asked.

"The demon attack when Blanche got Seti's territory," I said.

"Yeah, that was back in the nineties," Quil said.

"No. The guy had a smart phone. It wasn't twenty years ago."

Quil looked at Milo.

"Yeah, it was. I remember wondering what the hell it was," Milo said.

"I don't get it."

"Think harder," Milo said.

"Milo, stop being difficult," Quil said.

"You're assuming the people were from around there."

"Huh?" I asked.

"They were from the future. Finally figured that out when smart phones were invented and I remembered that's what I saw."

My jaw dropped and Milo burst out laughing.

Pop, pop, pop.

My mind didn't register the noise until after Milo grabbed me and whirled, pushing me to the ground behind the bar so hard my knees and palms smacked the ground before I could react.

My glass shattered under my hand, slicin' my palm open. Blood flowed out of it but it started to knit up before I even really felt the sting, leaving a long, aching scar in about five seconds.

What the?

"Ariana, are you okay?" Quil dove behind the bar with us and I nodded, brain movin' through mush as I looked up.

Milo met my eyes, mouth working as he shook on his knees.

The wound in his chest grew, the skin crumblin' into it like it was a sinkhole.

"Milo!" I pressed my hands to the wound, tears blurring my vision. "No, no, no. Please no."

"It's silver, sweets," Quil said, voice distant and weak.

"I didn't see that coming," Milo whispered as my hand fell through his chest into the goop. "Dying saving a lady. Good way to go. My brother... look after him."

"No! I can get it out. I've done this twice with Quil! You'll be fine!" I dug my hands in, pullin' out goop and pieces.

If I could just get the silver out.

"Ariana," Quil said, sounding very far away.

"No! He's really old so that means he has more powers. I read vampire books. The older ones can do things. They're stronger. One little silver bullet won't take him out."

"Sweets, it's silver," Quil said. "It went through his heart... No vampire can live through that. No matter how powerful. He's already dead."

"No!" I scooped out another handful of goo and tossed it aside.

Milo's chest collapsed in and the decay spread down his legs.

I met his eyes again as his skull crumbled in and they finally closed.

The goop on my hands turned to dust and I stared at them as the clothes caved in, leaving nothing but dust and a mound of cloth in a wet spot on the ground.

CHAPTER TWENTY-ONE

I PULLED OUT MY GUN AND silver knife.

Someone was going to die for this.

Chaos reigned through the club, vamps runnin' everywhere, trying to get out as the ones at the edges tried to keep them in.

Jade tossed one out of her way and opened the door. She turned in the doorway, tossin' me a wink.

I brought my gun up and aimed at her and she disappeared.

Screams and pounding echoed through the room and I pulled on Milo's power, taking a deep breath as I searched the club, imagining my magic zooming in on the culprit.

There!

At the back door were two piles of clothes saying someone went down.

"Quil!" I said, jerking my head at the door.

Quil took off, zoomin' so fast even if the guy knew he was coming, it wouldn't do any good.

Quil zoomed back, arms locked around the man.

"I believe this is yours," he said, shovin' Crowley down to his knees in front of me and Grant.

When did Grant come up to me?

Not important.

I couldn't believe it. I'd been right? It was just a hunch. And Grant's always telling me not to assume. Apparently when you assume, sometimes you are right.

But why? He was leader of the second team. He'd been with the SDF since its inception. Also, the demon said the summoner was a vamp, not just the person who hired the summoner.

But demons lie. But why would he lie on this?

"I thought he was." Grant leaned over Crowley. "Why?"

"She paid me," Crowley said.

Even though Crowley was stupid enough to betray the Bureau, he wasn't stupid enough to try lying to Grant.

Quil held the gun he took from Crowley up and looked around the club.

"Quil, don't point it around unless you want to kill them," I said, voice harsh and I didn't care.

He looked at me.

"Basic rule, don't point it at anyone you're not ready to kill," I said, aiming at Crowley.

"Ryder," Grant said.

"I'm not killin' him yet, sir. I know we have to find the demon first, but then, I get to kill him."

"You're not killing anyone without my say so," Grant said.

"No, sir." I kept my eyes on Crowley. "He was tryin' to kill me and killed my friend instead. He betrayed us."

Grant was probably givin' me the glare. I didn't even glance up.

"Three innocent girls are dead, even more innocent vampires, and you almost killed my agent," Grant said. Took me a second to realize he was talking to Crowley. "And you did that for money?"

"Look at what we put up with!" Crowley said. "We get paid ridiculous government salaries when we put our lives on the line every day, while these creatures are living it up."

"Charles Crowley, you are under arrest for conspiracy to commit murder, attempted murder, murder, conspiracy to commit rape, and treason." Grant got behind Crowley and snapped his wrists in handcuffs, haulin' him to his feet by his shoulder.

"I'm not a fool, Grant," Crowley said way too carefully. "I wouldn't attack if I didn't think I could get away."

Meaning the demon was here and ready to pounce?

"I know that," Grant said just as calmly. "We'll catch your demon."

"Yes, but will you catch her before she kills her?" Crowley looked pointedly at me. "The only way to save your little psychic is to either kill me, which will set the demon free, or to find her very quickly."

"Len, will you take responsibility for him until we find the demon?" Grant asked.

I looked around and Len had come up behind us at some point. He nodded.

"Ariana, hurry check him," Grant said.

I stepped forward and rubbed Len's face. His stubble was around Jason Statham and scratched my hand.

Nothing.

I nodded as I backed up.

Grant nodded. "Take him into the corner and watch him like a hawk.

Actually." Grant drew one meaty fist back and slammed Crowley straight across the jaw.

The man's head snapped back with an explosion of crimson, then slumped forward as he collapsed in Len's arms, nose gushin' like Old Faithful.

"Well that makes babysitting easier," Len said, hoisting Crowley's unconscious body over his shoulder. "But that's not nearly as interesting as demon hunting."

"I'd trade ya if I could," I said, lookin' over at the mass of vamps.

They looked so scared. Most of them were innocent, being kept in here against their will, because one of them could be the demon.

If she hadn't slipped out yet.

Something told me she hadn't. She had a job to do.

My eyes jumped down to Milo's ashes. It seemed so wrong that he should be dead.

That someone so alive and bouncy and ridiculous could be ripped from the world so quickly wasn't only wrong, it wasn't possible, and yet he was gone. Thousands of years of life over and reduced to a pile of ash.

Because he saved me.

What were we going to tell his brother? They were so close, even after so long, how was one supposed to go on without the other?

"You okay?" Quil asked me.

I shook my head. "He was just there. He died saving me. Didn't even think, just grabbed me and got in the way of the bullet as he shoved me down. I can't even remember exactly what happened. But he took the bullet meant for me."

"Meaning it's your fault he died?" Quil asked.

"No," I said. "It's Crowley's, and the bitch who hired him." I met Quil's eyes. "I will kill her too after this."

"We don't know it was Jade."

"I do."

Milo's blood boiled in me, the power the only thing left of him. "And I don't care if I have to wait years for my chance, I will kill her."

Quil kissed my hair. "I'm beginning to think Milo was right about you. You are downright scary right now."

I nodded. "Right now, I'm thinkin' he was payin' me a compliment."

I *knew* it was Jade because I knew exactly what she was feeling.

Betrayed.

Quil had become her enemy politically, and had been working against her. Centuries of him having her back made the sting of him working against her so much worse.

And that made it so much easier to set an evil plan in motion, even if there were casualties in her own nest.

I knew it as surely as I knew I'd be the one to kill her.

"Bring on the visions," I said. "I'm ready."

Quil, Grant, and Jet flanked me.

Jet handed me my wooden bowl with sandalwood incense burning.

Quil had the suppressed twenty-two loaded with silver and Grant had his nine mil.

Why the guns?

The silver wouldn't hurt the demon even if she was in vamp form.

I stepped to the first vamp in line, one of the ones who came from Kentucky as far as I could remember.

We didn't see doubles of anyone, so I figured whoever the demon was impersonating was somehow killed before, but we couldn't be sure, after all, it could just look like a vamp or human that wasn't in the club and everyone would figure she was with someone else.

I hit vamp after vamp, human after human, focusin' on their secrets.

I had way too many flashes of people getting bit or having sex.

It just made me think of Milo.

I'd only known him maybe an hour and in that time he'd hit on me so many times my head spun, but it was weird how I'd miss his stupid little remarks after only having heard them for such a short time.

Maybe it was cuz I knew he'd been makin' them for two thousand years and never would again.

Because he saved me.

I went down the line with betrayal and destruction on my mind, visions of the vamps' guilty acts coming out like a river. Milo hadn't been lying when he said his blood would help.

Every single person I touched could be my last. The second I got close enough, the demon could grab me before my bodyguards could do anything and take me down.

The thought didn't bother me.

If the demon struck, I was ready.

Flash.

A blond vampire getting it on with a human in the back of a van and biting her.

I drew back and shook my head. Maybe the next one was the demon, or the next.

Flash.

Her killing a female vamp, probably her maker. She wanted the territory.

The next was a human and I paused, blood hummin' with anticipation, viscera playin' a perverted game of Twister in my stomach.

I was halfway through and nothing so far. Where was it? Why didn't it just attack already? Why drag it out?

I touched the human.

Flash.

Him watching a surgery on TV and knowing that he wanted to be a doctor, then another of him getting the acceptance letter to Georgetown, already planning to leave even though his parents needed him at home.

I hit a few more.

"Do you think this is the demon's plan?" I asked. "To give me a heart attack waiting for it to get me?"

"Probably, considering the rate you're going," Quil said, leanin' in to talk softly in my ear. "Are you sure you've been checked and doctors said you were okay?"

"Yes, but I wasn't waiting for a demon attack then, so maybe we should have Kat do the blood pressure test after this."

We went over to the wall near the back to get Quil's vamps watching the exits. They could be copied just as easily as anyone else, which was why they were in groups of three.

Hit, hit, hit...flash after flash, and I had nothing.

We finally got over to our group of agents and lab techs. I gave Irish a small, weak smile.

"You look like you need some more alcohol, lass," he said softly, eyeing the vamps.

I nodded. "You look like you could use a drink too. You're pastier than usual."

"Yes, well, it's been a long night, and any moment now someone's going to jump out and attack again, I'm a little nervous."

"How do you think I feel?"

He licked his lips. "That bullet almost hit you."

"I know."

"How could Crowley do it?"

I shook my head. "I don't know, I mean he's one of us, but..." I shrugged.

"And he was the summoner?"

"Yup."

A small spasm shot across Irish's face. I knew exactly how he felt. He'd known Crowley for years, even before the SDF was formed. He'd been the forensics guy in the terrorist task force, and Crowley worked in that before they both came over when our division was formed. I mean, they weren't best buds, but they were the casual 'go grab a drink at a pub' type.

"You're stalling," Quil growled, takin' a deep whiff, and Irish stiffened. "And you smell weird. Why?"

"I di...didn't know you c...could smell that through the cologne," Irish stuttered. "I'm part leprechaun."

"That wasn't a joke?" I didn't know why I was surprised. Honestly, after everything I'd seen, especially in the past week, you'd think nothing would shock me.

"No, but I'm only a fourth." A nervous smile to rival mine went up on his face. "My grandma was full leprechaun."

"Yes, and you shouldn't have worn that horrible stuff tonight," Quil hissed. "Although, even those that are part fae still smell horrible without it, so it's not much difference."

None of the guys jumped in to tell Quil to chill, not even Grant.

"Sorry, Irish, I've got to get everyone," I said as I reached forward. I held onto his hand and rubbed his head a few times. "Nothing, you're you."

"Good to know, I was actually getting worried that I wasn't," Irish said, forcin' a smile. "I know we're stuck here, but I really need to go to the bathroom." He gave Grant a pleading look.

"Hold it." Grant shrugged, and our small tightly packed group moved over to Mender.

I got a vision of her and Crowley having sex.

When had that happened?

Then a flash of when he was dragged over by Quil. I could feel the intense betrayal she felt when he said he was the summoner.

She wouldn't look me in the eyes as I pulled out.

"Um, sorry?" I said.

She shook her head. "Just doing your job."

"Yeah."

They'd been in the office at night and must've gotten carried away. It was recent, like last few months, but I couldn't tell time besides that.

Something told me they'd been seeing each other since.

We finished with our people and went back to checking Quil's vamps around the wall.

Quil bounced on his heels behind me and I could practically feel him spoilin' for a fight, a walkin' puddle of rotten eggs.

I squeezed his hand and he kissed my knuckles.

"Hey, Carla."

She nodded back.

I stroked her arms and neck and got a few flashes of her over the years, nothin' bad. Apparently she didn't have a lot in her past to feel bad about.

"Hey, General," I said. "I think I need another drink. My visions are getting weaker." I picked up my sandalwood from the bowl and took a deep sniff. "And I need to go to the bathroom, can't concentrate with a full bladder."

I blamed Irish for saying he needed to go to the bathroom. Whenever anyone says that it makes me want to go.

Grant pressed his lips together. "This wasn't supposed to take so long, and it'd be the perfect time for the demon to get you."

I shrugged.

Maybe I wanted the demon to come after me.

This was takin' way too long.

"Fine," Grant said, "make it fast."

"Hey, as long as you're going?" Dan jogged over from the bar. "It's totally girly to be taking a leak together, but I've needed to for like half an hour now."

We walked to the back and Irish flagged us down.

Grant clenched his jaw. "Come on."

Quil left Len, Carla, and a few of his other trusted, and already checked, vamps, in charge for a minute.

"Make this quick," Grant said, leadin' us into the Men's bathroom.

There were little dots clearly visible on one of the urinals and I wrinkled my nose.

"Yes, General," I said, headin' for a stall.

"And while you're in here, you can wash that stuff off," Quil said to Irish.

I sat down, not even embarrassed they'd hear me pee. Dan and Irish were going out there in the urinals.

How in the world do guys do that?

"Is that necessary?" Irish asked.

"Yes," Quil said as I quickly peed. "I've heard rumors that leprechauns can wield their luck if they focus, like to block a psychic. That, plus that horrible smell, could be blocking Ariana. Besides, I don't trust anyone who insists on wearing cologne, and I especially don't trust anyone who is part fae."

"Grant, my boy, could you help me out?" Irish asked. "Vampires like supernatural things a little too much, which is why they're so fond of our Ariana." He gestured to me as I went over to wash my hands.

Gee, thanks Irish.

"And they really hate us, so I'd really rather keep my cologne on just so the rest of them don't know."

"We do hate fae," Quil said. "But I don't know who told you we like their taste. We can't stand it. If anyone's much more than about a fourth, we don't even want to eat them. It's not poison, but it's like drinking mud in your wine."

"Ariana?" Irish asked me. "Your Quil is making me nervous. Any kind of fae and vampires don't get along."

"Irish," I said, "Quil won't hurt you. If you don't trust him, at least trust me."

I turned off the water and walked over to them. Dan was just zipping up and went over to wash his hands, but Irish hadn't gone yet.

If he needed to go that badly, he might lose it before he could cuz he was looking pretty scared. But I didn't want to see him going. Apparently guys can handle that, but I can't, it's just weird.

Irish's eyes met mine and I couldn't decipher his look.

"Leave him alone," Grant said slowly, as though he'd just made up his mind about something. "I've known he was part leprechaun for a long time now, and I don't want any of your people becoming distracted."

"He could be the demon," Quil snapped.

"No, because Ariana would've sensed that because the demon wouldn't have the same powers to block her like that," Grant said, giving me a look.

"Touch him again, Ariana, just to make sure," Quil said.

"We need to get going," Grant said. "We don't have time for him to clean off. We've been in here too long already."

He gave me another look I couldn't interpret. What was going on here?

"Grant, it couldn't hurt," I said, but he shook his head.

"That's an order, Ryder," he said, not unkindly, or even really demandin'. It was mere fact.

"Yes, General."

Quil and Grant shared a look.

"That's it then?" Quil snapped, so harsh I jumped, a twinge breakin' through the cold in my chest.

"Every single time he says jump, you listen!"

"Why are you yelling at me?" I asked. "He's my boss, Quil. And if he says don't do it, he has his reasons. Now seriously, we shouldn't be back here any longer than we need to be."

"I tell you there is something wrong with this man, your boss says don't even have him wash to check because it might take a few more seconds, and you listen to him over me?"

Quil tossed his hands up and swept out of the bathroom. Rules about not going anywhere alone be damned.

"Quil!" I yelled as the door swung shut.

What the hell just happened?

"About damn time," Dan said.

"Don't start, Bridges," Grant said, laying a hand on my shoulder.

"Start what, General?" Dan sneered. "This?"

He pulled out a gun and aimed it at me as his face and body shrank and softened into mine.

Grant pushed me behind him, whippin' out his gun almost as fast as a vamp could move.

I pulled my gun and knife again.

"You just needed Quil to leave," I said. "How did you know he would?"

"I didn't," she said in my voice, shruggin' my shrug. "I thought I'd have to take you all. Still, won't waste an opportunity. Silly boys, getting so jealous."

Quil's soooo not the jealous type.

"After I kill you," she said, my own voice mocking me, "I'm going to take your little pet vampire back home and he's going to die very slowly."

Why wasn't she shooting at us already?

Not that I wanted her to, but it would make more sense than mindless chitchat.

"So start shooting," I said. "We'll see who's faster."

"Any kind of fight, even two against one, would cause a ruckus," Irish said.

So that's why she was waiting. She didn't want Quil to hear the gun.

Grant turned his gun on Irish.

Wait, what!

"Now, now, Grant," Irish said. "You can't kill me without setting her free," Irish said.

"What?" I gasped, stomach droppin' as metal coated my tongue. I couldn't feel my knees and wet streaked down my cheek.

Not Irish.

"I thought you said you knew who the summoner was, you had a vision?" Grant asked.

"I saw you swap the hairs, I just put it together that it was Crowley after he attacked! Why is he saying it's him?"

"Because it was," Irish said. "I didn't even know Crowley was also hired. Grant, I don't need to kill you, just her. You can go."

"Not going to happen," Grant said.

"Why?" I asked Irish.

He was my friend. We'd practicing dancing for nearly a year. We'd hung out at his house. How could he be a traitor?

No. It was some kind of trick, like there were two demons. I would've known if he was a traitor all this time.

"Sorry, Ariana, I can't defy a direct order. I have to kill you and Quil." Irish really did look sorry.

"Order?" I asked, mind swimmin'.

He eyed the guns warily as his fangs slid out.

Fangs!

"How?" I asked.

"The cologne and my magic kept it hidden from the other vampires. Being part fae's also what made it so I wasn't tired during the day. And you never noticed I didn't go out into the sun anymore," Irish said.

"When?" Grant asked, still so cool.

"Over a month ago," Irish said. "The queen was planning this for a while. She knew about our division and thought we would likely get involved. She knew about Ariana long before she ever went into the nest." He looked at me. "I really am sorry, Ariana, I don't have a choice."

He did a double take at Grant. "Swapped out the hairs? You knew?"

"Why do you think I was telling Quil no about checking you?" Grant asked, eyes glued to Irish.

"You wanted to get the demon first?" I asked, strugglin' to breathe as an endless round of nos danced through my skull.

This couldn't be happening.

Quil had been right. Grant was trying to avoid a showdown with Irish until after we got the demon.

But he had to know this was a trap, right? He just hadn't known the demon took Dan's form.

Oh my God! Dan! What happened to him?

Irish leaped at me and I screamed, rollin' under his arms with my gun tucked to my chest. I bounced to my feet and pointed my gun at him, vamp blood makin' me fast apparently.

Thank you, Milo and Quil.

Small hands closed around my neck. Oh right.

The demon.

She picked me up and tossed me at the wall. I turned and took the hit with my left shoulder, fallin' to the ground and not even feelin' it.

The door burst open and Quil and Jet jumped in. Jet held the silver whip and Quil had a thing of mace and a gun with a suppressor.

Quil tossed me a wink before cracking a shot off at Irish with the suppressed gun, the sound echoin' off the tile but not nearly as bad as if any of us were to shoot.

The demon bull-rushed me as Jet brought the whip up and snapped it at Irish.

He knew too?

Quil grabbed the demon and took her to the ground.

"Back pocket," he yelled.

I lunged forward, pulling a can of mace outta his pocket.

He rolled off the demon and I sprayed her in the face, scramblin' back so the cloud wouldn't get me too.

"Grant!" Quil threw the suppressed gun and Grant snatched it out of midair like catching a banana.

How the hell did they coordinate that?

Grant tucked his gun in his pocket and aimed the suppressed one at Irish, the little pop sayin' he shot.

That thing couldn't have too many bullets left. Then again, we could always use our guns and just deal with deafness.

My doppleganger ripped off her face and another grew over it like one of those old Chia pets. The mace hurt her, but didn't debilitate her like it had her mate.

Maybe females were more resistant, or it could've been a special talent of hers, or she could've just been too filled with anger to feel much of anything.

She gave me a cocky grin and came at me again.

That first round took maybe ten seconds and I was already breathin' hard. I sprayed her and she ran right into me, knockin' me into the wall.

I hit the ground, air burstin' outta my lungs.

Quil grabbed the demon by the shoulders and spun her, slammin' his fist into her face. They traded blows, almost too fast to track.

Jet and Grant stayed on Irish, flickin' the silver whip at him to keep him at bay, but eventually they wouldn't be able to hold him. He was just too fast.

I gasped, pushin' to my hands and knees.

Had to get up. Had to stop them. Couldn't just sit here.

Couldn't let anyone else die cuz of me.

I shoved myself up, taking a deep breath and pullin' out my mace.

I ran, jumpin' on the demon's back and taking her to the ground. We hit hard and I pushed her face into the tiles and scrambled off her to get back to my feet.

She grabbed my ankle and pulled.

I flopped to my belly, sending my mace sliding.

The demon released me and I rolled over, pain shootin' through my side.

Quil sprayed her in the face, keepin' it going as she screamed and ripped it away, layers of wax and flesh littering the floor almost as fast as the spray could hit her.

Quil jerked as I got back to my feet, holding my side as metal sliced right where Quil had been.

Nice reflexes.

I looked up and Irish jumped back, barely avoiding the whip as he brought his knife up, catchin' the whip around it. He yanked it right outta Jet's hands and grabbed the end, bringing it up to bear way too fast.

Jet had been being careful with it since he didn't want to get any of us.

Irish didn't have that problem.

He snapped the whip so fast at me I couldn't take a step before it came for me, just toss my hands up on reflex.

Pain shot through me like fire as I stumbled back.

A gash ran down my forearm, bleedin' so heavy there had to be serious damage.

I didn't care.

I pulled my gun out and shot at Irish.

The blast echoed through the room, the hard materials makin' the bathroom the absolute worst place for a shootout. My ears rang and the world came into sharp focus even as my ears were useless.

Irish fell to his knees and dropped the whip, blood spreadin' around the tiny hole in his shirt around the belly.

I'd been aiming for his heart, but this would kill him too.

Just slower.

The demon jumped up and lunged for Irish.

She scooped up the silver whip, swingin' it easily as she said something, lookin' at me.

I blinked. Maybe the shot didn't hurt her ears like ours?

She waved her hand and my ears popped, the fuzz clearin' out.

"You're all so *delicate*," she said, vitriol dripping from the word.

"Still going to kill you," I said. "But thanks for fixin' my ears."

She laughed. Oh boy, was that the most disturbing thing ever, to hear my laugh from my face, when it wasn't me.

"Have you ever seen the Wizard of Oz?" she asked.

Huh?

"Of course you have," she said. "Everyone has. The second he dies, I'm unbound. And, let's see if I can get this right." She cleared her throat and landed hot eyes on Quil. "I'll get you my pretty, and your little psychic too."

She laughed again as Quil growled. "You killed my mate, you're going to pay." She turned to me. "Since you're the psychic, I'm guessing it's mostly your fault, so, I'm going to drag you and your vamp back to my side of things, and you're going to watch as I rape him, then I'm handing you over to some friends of mine, and it'll be your turn."

My breath caught in my throat.

I rushed her, cold certainty and vamp blood pushing me and I tackled her. I barely glimpsed the shock on her face so like mine and I bit her hand hard as I could.

She screamed and dropped the whip, rearin' her arm back and backhanding me across the face.

I went sliding across the floor, not feeling much of anything as I pushed back up.

We kill her now, or she comes after us later.

I wouldn't live like that.

Quil jumped in, mace up as he scooped up the whip.

"What will kill her?" I yelled. "We've got till the silver gets Irish."

"Explosives," he said, snapping the whip at her.

"How do you suggest we do that without dying?" Jet asked.

Grant stepped forward and took the whip from Quil, waving at him. "You, Kowolski, Ryder, out!"

Jet backed out right away and Quil backed up and grabbed my non-injured arm, pulling me back towards the door. He yanked me out as Grant whipped at the demon, twining the silver around her too easily.

Almost like magic.

And pulled out a grenade.

"Grant!" I screamed, lunging for him.

"Run!" Grant screamed, running for us as he threw the grenade behind him and Quil tossed me over his shoulder and ran up the hall way faster than the guys.

The explosion rocked the hall and sent us flying.

Quil turned and dropped me so he slammed into the door and flopped to the floor while I just skinned my knees.

"Quil!"

He groaned and waved a hand to let me know he was okay.

Tears blurred my eyes as I looked down the hallway. The smoke didn't hide the debris in the hallway, the damage about ten feet from the door.

The guys weren't that far from the bathroom when it blew. No way they survived that.

"Grant!" I yelled, somehow still able to hear.

"Girl!" came back a moment later.

I clapped my hands to my mouth and tears came out so fast I could barely see as I coughed on the smoke.

Jet limped over, Grant hanging on his slim shoulder like a giant bag of potatoes with arms. Jet sagged and let Grant slump to the ground and I fell next to my boss.

"Sir?" I asked.

He coughed. "Don't try that at home, Ryder."

I sobbed and threw myself over him, huggin' him as tight as I dared.

"How?" Quil asked behind us.

I looked up and Quil offered me a hand. I took it and stood, head swimming.

"Milo showed me a few tricks in our little mind meld," Grant said. "Shields fucking hurt."

Well if that didn't confirm Grant was magic.

"You going to be okay, sir?"

He closed his eyes and rolled over.

"Sir, you shouldn't get up," Jet said.

"We need to know what happened to Bridges," Grant said, pushing up to his knees. "Kowalski, find him. Ryder, call an ambulance."

"Yes, sir," we said together.

CHAPTER TWENTY-TWO

I CALLED THE AMBULANCE, JUST SAID there were injuries and we were FBI and needed discretion. We pushed the door open and walked out.

Vamps and humans crowded around the door and Quil had to order more than one to move.

The pain still wasn't hittin' me but the blood loss from my arm was definitely making me woozy. I leaned on Quil and he gave my shoulder a squeeze.

"I'd lick it for you, but..." he said.

"Silver, I know," I said. "Kinda surprised it hasn't healed. The last cut did."

Irish, my *friend*, was a vamp who tried to kill me, and who summoned a demon that raped and murdered three girls. It was so ridiculous that I pinched myself to make sure I wasn't dreaming.

I barely felt it, but something told me that was due to the shock and not cuz this wasn't real.

"The danger's over. The demon and the summoner are dead," Quil said.

The crowd erupted into questions and I looked around, trying to see something though them as they surged forward, touching Quil's arms and face and my hair.

Grant took me by the shoulder and we inched through the vamp crowd.

They petted us as we went but moved, lettin' us through and closin' back up behind us like a zipper as they shot questions at Quil.

We had to find Dan.

Grant led me to the bar and it took a second for me to realize Jet was behind us.

We walked around the back and there was Dan, half stuffed under the bar, eyes closed and head to the side.

"No!" Jet yelled, droppin' next to Dan and draggin' him out.

"Oh God!" I gasped as Jet pressed fingers to his friend's neck.

Dan groaned.

"He's alive!" Jet bent his head over his buddy and muttered, "Thank you, God."

Kat finally plunged through the crowd and joined us. She pulled something out of her bag and handed it to Jet. He waved it under Dan's nose.

Dan's baby blues fluttered open and he batted at Jet's hands. "Dude, what the fuck!"

"Smelling salts," Kat said.

"What happened?" Dan asked, grasping his head as he sat up.

Kat hit the floor next to them and I leaned into Grant as he wrapped his arm around my shoulders.

Kat pulled stuff outta her bag and shined a light in Dan's eyes.

"Ow! Kat!"

"Sorry." Kat put the flashlight down and started examining his head with gentle fingers. "The demon smacked you a good one, is what happened. Probably didn't kill you because the vampires would be able to smell a dead body."

"Lucky me," Dan said, still holding his skull.

"Yeah, you have a concussion," she said.

Grant steered me away from them and over to where Len still had an
~~cious Crowley in the chair.

~~~ust enough time to think Grant was going to kill him before he
~~d and uncuffed him.

~~ with a grin.

~~ knocked out?

~~wley asked.

~~s Irish."

~~yes and looked away. "I would have bet

~~mp about a month ago, said he was

~~ rubbed his jaw. "Did you have

ch.

, he wasn't working with

"Nope." Crowley looked very proud of himself. "We knew it was someone who worked with us after the tracking device on your clip was taken out of the house and somehow showed back up in evidence. He probably thought we'd notice if it was gone permanently, but not if it was just borrowed for a bit."

"Why did you think it was Crowley?" Grant asked.

"Oh, um," I said. "Well, he didn't want to touch me at the office, and someone was blockin' the voice transmission earlier so it had to be one of ours on security, and it just seemed to fit."

"Ouch," Crowley said.

I shrugged. "I know, don't assume. Won't happen again, General. But I don't get it, Crowley shot Milo."

"No, I didn't," Crowley said. "I was supposed to be a decoy Grant was going to discover was in on it and we hoped that would flush the real summoner out since he'd assume we'd only be looking for the demon. It worked too, just not quite right."

"When the demon attacked and started shooting, it disappeared into the crowd," Grant said, "but Crowley, Mender and I had suppressed guns on us in case we needed them tonight. He ran because the demon disappeared and Len assumed it was him and grabbed him."

"Which I totally planned," Crowley said. "That wasn't me being a dumbass and trying to go after the demon at all."

"Uh-huh," Grant said.

"It worked, didn't it?"

"But how did you know it was Irish?" I asked.

Grant met my eyes. "You mentioned you almost never got visions of him, and he didn't want to come tonight. Call it a hunch."

"Isn't that assuming, General?" I asked.

"No." And he gave me his full beautiful smile, making my heart fl "When I'm doing that, it's following up on a lead. When you do assuming."

I rolled my eyes. "So you're not a traitor?"

Crowley snorted. "It'd take a hell of a lot more than money to turn my back on my people."

"Okay, duh. I mean, you're like Grant. You couldn't be you're like mister loyalty, and besides, Grant would've known would've known, but obviously that's not true cuz Irish w know. How could I not know? What good is being psych tell you when one of our own went to the dark side? I'm should be fired. No, worse, I should be chained to the cuz I'm pretty sure you're not letting me off desk reports. But you know what I mean. It was bad. should've known. None of this would've happened him more. I mean I could've saved Milo and the other vamps." Ice filled my stomach. "She turned him *a month ago*. I could've saved those poor girls. I sh-"

"Stop," Grant said, catching my shoulders in those big bear hands. "None of this is your fault. Don't even think it. That's an order."

"That's an order I can't follow, sir."

"Hey." Quil appeared at my elbow.

"Anyone else dead?" I asked.

He nodded. "Two of my people at the door when the demon ran."

So the two piles of clothes I saw. "Any more?"

"No, but Jade's gone."

"Yeah, I saw her slip out."

"Ariana, you can't kill her."

"What?"

"We don't have any proof it was her. Our witnesses are all dead and as far as I can tell, they did all the work."

"We don't need proof! This isn't a courtroom."

"Except it kind of is. If I try to kill her without cause." He held up a finger. "That we can prove, I'll be the traitor."

I searched his face. "No, you can't be serious."

"If it was the Governor of Tennessee and you had no proof, what would you do?"

"Holy crap on kittens. I'll kill her then."

"If it were that easy, I would have done it already."

"But she's out there, and she wants you dead... and *me* dead!"

"And now I know it so I can be ready for her, but this won't be solved by a well-aimed bullet, even a silver one."

I blew out a breath. "So now what?"

"If I tell people here, they won't believe me, because who would attack her own nest? But I may be able to get to my people, in time."

"And until then?"

"We watch our backs?" He shrugged.

Grant nodded next to him. "We'll help, if we can."

Quil took his hand. "Thank you. I have a feeling I will need it. She knows I know now."

I frowned. "Maybe not. None of the people working for her lived, right? And they were taken out in the heat of battle, pretty much, so how would she know any of them told us it was her?"

Quil's mouth dropped. "Good point."

"She doesn't know we know," I said. "It gives us the advantage."

"And maybe this was enough of a blow to the nest she won't try it again for a while," Grant said.

"I'll still have to watch my back," Quil said.

I smiled. "Yeah, but you don't have to do it alone."

He kissed me.

EPILOGUE

"OKAY, HERE IS THE PATIENT'S chocolate," I said, keepin' my voice low just in case any of the busybody nurses were wanderin' past Dan's room.

They were *strict* about their rule that he not get anything but the hospital designated food and he (and his sweet tooth) was going stir crazy after only two days in the hospital.

When the ambulance showed up after the whole disaster two nights ago, the vamps scattered, leaving us to try to explain the mess to the humans.

Grant told the EMTs there was a sting, it was classified, and we needed medical treatment.

They sent the cops to talk to us after gettin' us to the hospital and we stuck to the classified thing.

Hey, it *was*... sort of.

"Thanks," Dan said, actually sounding like he meant it as I handed him the chocolate bar.

"You didn't get this from me," I said.

"Get what?" He took a giant bite, practically takin' out half the bar at once.

He rolled a finger at me. "So catch me up."

"Well, Grant's doin' better. I think it took him a while to recharge after whatever he did there." I held up my arm, showing off my bright blue bandage. "My arm was cut pretty deep but they don't think there was any permanent damage. I just need some physical therapy after it heals up a bit. Jet and Kat are okay, the vamps are healing, should be okay."

He swallowed. "When are they interviewing for the lab tech position?"

"They already have a stack of applicants. The basic interviews to weed some out start tomorrow, then Grant'll take those to interview. He already asked me to help, but that won't be for another two weeks or so."

"Help?"

"You know, touch them, find out if any have any big bad secrets. Not that I was much help with the last one."

"No, cut it out. I'm not Jet, I'm not going to let you cry on my shoulder about how bad you feel. You want a pity parade, call him or Kat."

I made a face.

"Why are you the one bringing me chocolate?" he asked.

He'd just called up the office, begging for someone not in scrubs and obviously trying out for the part of Nurse Ratched to visit with him over lunch and bring him chocolate since the surgery to fix his leg wasn't till tonight and he was going nuts.

"Cuz I am, okay," I said.

"Thanks," he said.

I broke into a grin. "You're welcome."

"Don't get all girly on me. We're not going to braid each other's hair or anything. But ya know, if you want to come over for a game or something..."

"What? You like me now or something?"

He scowled at me. "This is what I get for trying to be nice. You did good the other night, and I figure it won't hurt to have you there to touch the TV now that you're getting a hang of this psychic thing, that's all."

"Ohhhhh," I said, eyes wide. "Like have the psychic touch the TV and see who's gonna win so I can call my bookie, right?"

He shrugged. "Something like that. You're not completely useless."

"Gee, thanks. I'll see what I can do. Oh right, this morning we went over to Irish's."

"And?" Dan asked, landing hard blue eyes on mine.

"We found the girls' missing purses, underwear, and shoes there. I got a vision of Irish telling the demon to take them so we'd think sex-murderer. The demon kept one shoe from each though, and took it with him each morning when he left."

"Sick."

I nodded and glanced at the clock on the wall. "I gotta go, paperwork."

"He still got you on that?"

"Of course, it's Grant. There's no such thing as a 'get out of jail free' card with him."

"Don't I know it. Did I ever tell you about the Belle Meade ghost?"

I shook my head.

"I will after I'm sprung. Grant was pissed. Jet and I were on desk for a month."

"I'm hooked," I said as I stood and waved goodbye.

Vandy hospital wasn't too far from the office, so I was back within my lunch hour even after stopping off to grab a sandwich on the way.

I plopped back at my desk and dove into another stack of papers.

Grant was at his, buried under his own stack as he did the official report and the longer one, like the ones I was working on, at the same time for the case we just closed.

I couldn't imagine the red tape nightmare all of that would be.

But of course Grant would do the paper on this one himself. This was no normal case. This was not only big cuz of the new treaty with the vamps, but also cuz one of our own was the killer, once removed, but still.

Jet was helping out in the lab, mostly schlepping cuz he doesn't know any more about the intricacies of the sciences than I do.

"Ryder?" I looked up, it was Mender.

Oh dear.

"Can I help you with something?" I asked with a huge smile.

"Can I talk to you?"

She did *not* sound like the calm collected Mender I knew.

I nodded and got up. Grant gave us a look and I met it with pleading puppy eyes.

He sighed and waved.

We hightailed it down the hall to the bathroom.

"Did you tell him?" she asked the second the door was closed.

I knew she meant Grant. He wasn't her boss, technically she only had to answer to Director Foster, but technically doesn't really mean anything.

"No." I shook my head.

"Has he asked?"

"No."

"And if he does?"

I paused. What would I do?

"I'll tell him what I saw had nothing to do with the case and it's a personal issue."

"Okay." She nodded.

"You guys okay?" I held up my hands. "Not that it's any of my business, but..." I shrugged.

"Yeah. I get why he lied."

"Do you know why Grant asked him to play the bad guy?"

She smirked and rolled her eyes. "I actually asked him that. He said Grant told him he was the next best liar Grant knew, and they'd have to be able to sell it."

"Who's the best liar?"

She raised her eyebrows. "Grant is."

"Oh!"

She opened the door. "Hey, good job last night."

"Thanks, Mender."

I rubbed my arms, gave myself a second, and went back to working on those stupid reports.

My phone rang around five and my heart sang as I swiped it on.

"Hey, Quil!" I tried to sound professional as I flipped my chair around for a bit of privacy.

"Hi, sweets," he said. "I'm sorry it took me so long to be able to call. Are you feeling okay?"

"Oh yeah, my ribs are bruised, but not broken. And my arm has been stitched up and I'll just need some physical therapy on it to make sure nothing goes wonky."

"Good."

"How about you?"

"I'm fine. The nest is still recovering. I've had Len keeping an eye on you so I knew you were okay, but I didn't have time to call and chat. Everyone's pretty shaken."

"Like stalking me?"

"No, just calling and giving me updates."

"Ohhhhh."

Len had called a few times, said it was for Quil, but I didn't quite get why Quil couldn't do it himself.

But I kinda had a guess.

"And Jade?" I asked.

"Acting like everyone else, like she's upset by all this and glad it wasn't worse. She's talking about putting one of her people on Marie's throne."

"Has she kept you from calling?"

"Let's just say, she was watching me very carefully the past two days. She's let up now. I think she thinks I don't know anything. I'm still making sure no one is listening or tapping my lines. I am calling for a formal reason as well though. It's about our treaty."

"Yeah?"

"We were thinking an official meeting to discuss specifics. I will call your director and I'm assuming she will have Grant head it. We will work out something more formal, and I will see if I can get the queen to sign it."

"Will she?"

"Depends how far she's willing to carry this charade to convince everyone of her innocence."

"If she doesn't suspect anyone knows though…"

"But she was allowing us to work with the FBI. Pulling back now would look strange. We'll see."

"I guess. I don't think she's done tryin' to take us out though."

"Me neither."

"Sooooo, will I get to see you soon?"

He chuckled. "I was thinking tonight, but if you meant professionally, I think next week would be a good time for some of us to come down to the office. We'll have to work it out with your bosses, but once we do, we'd love to learn more about how you work."

"We being?"

"Carla, me, even Stephanie seems to like you, and she doesn't like anybody."

Stephanie? Really? Hey, who was I to turn my nose up at new friends?

"Run it by Grant."

"Next week or what I want to do to you tonight? Because I'm understanding, but that's just weird."

I laughed.

"No, you can run… *that* by me."

"Nine work?"

"Sounds great."

We said our goodbyes and when I flipped my chair around, Grant was gone.

Geez, he's pretty sneaky for someone so large.

I finished up the report and filed it, hittin' the bathroom before looking for Grant to see if I could go.

When I got back, there was a large box in shiny green wrapping paper in the middle of the perpetual chaos that is my desk.

I picked up the card on the top and it said. "Special Agent Ariana Kay Ryder," in Grant's handwriting.

I tore it open, not sparing the paper, no matter how pretty it was.

I had to slice open the tightly taped box with a knife, and then dig through a pile of multicolored tissue paper before I got to the prize.

A bright red cowgirl hat.

The note pinned to the top said, "Congratulations on one year, Ariana."

I picked it up and my badge was sitting right under it.

I put the hat on and covered my nose with my hands as a tear leaked out.

With all the chaos and clean up the past few days, I hadn't even remembered this was my anniversary.

Not only did I make one year, while I'd thought I wouldn't make it one week when I first started, but Grant remembered the anniversary, and my joke about the hat, and got me one.

I let my mind run over the last few nights, tryin' to make sense of the chaos.

And I pulled out my phone to call my mama.

"Hey, sweetie," she said.

"Hey, Mama, it's my one year anniversary!"

"Congratulations."

"Mama, you don't sound like you really mean it."

"Of course I do."

"I know you think I'm just a low paid public servant, but I'm doin' good here, Mama."

"You could do more."

No, I couldn't.

"Mama," I said, "do you remember what you said when I asked you why you started writin' romance."

"I said it was the seventies."

"And times were hard. The economy was trashed, inflation and unemployment ran rampant, and people waited in lines for hours for gas. You said you started writin' because the world was dark and you wanted to brighten it up with stories of good versus evil, honor and love conquering all. You were hoping your messages of hope and decency buried in all that fluff would reach people. Change them."

"I passed on my penchant for the dramatic to you, didn't I?"

"Mama, come on. You said all that, and you meant it."

"Yes, yes, I did."

"Well, times are dark again. And I can do something about it as an agent. I can save lives, protect people. But I can also work my way up, and maybe change the country for the better when the time comes for it. And you know where I get that from?"

"Me 'n your daddy."

"Yeah. I'm gonna make a difference, Mama. I'm gonna make you proud."

"Sweetie, I have never not been proud of you. I'm a little bit more now that you finally figured out that's why you became an agent."

"You knew! How did you know when I barely put it together?"

Mama chuckled. "You got a lot of livin' to do, baby girl. A mother knows her children. You have always wanted to help people and make a difference. I just wanted you to realize you do this because you know you can get up to where you can do more good than even now."

I put my hand to my forehead.

Never underestimate Mama.

I told her what I could about the case, which wasn't much, and planned a trip down home soon as I could make sure I'd have a weekend off.

I still had a lot of work to do.

I had to learn about my powers. Had to get them down to make sure no one ever died on my watch again.

And what about Carvi?

From the visions I got they were pretty close, and Milo's literal dying wish was for us to look after his brother.

I wonder if anyone's told him about Milo yet. Someone had to have called him, right?

And what if he decided to do something to Quil or me for his brother dying?

He didn't strike me as the forgiving type.

I shook it off.

Couldn't worry about that now.

I had a guy to meet and we had an alliance to plan and a queen to take down.

I found Grant, got the okay to go home and even take the next day off since I finished my report, and headed home.

We'd get Jade. We'd make her pay for the deaths of those people. And I'd get Carvi's number from Quil and call him, open up some communications there and extend a hand of friendship. I couldn't let Milo's last wish just die with him.

It'd be okay. We'd make it all okay.

Fine, my life's a bit complicated, but I like it that way.

Keeps things interestin'.

Thanks for reading!

- If you would like to know when my next story is out, you can sign up for my mailing list at https://mailchi.mp/afc38083307c/amie-gibbons, *and get a free story not available anywhere else.*
Check out my blog https://authoramiegibbons.wordpress.com/.
Like my Facebook page https://www.facebook.com/AuthorAmieGibbons/, and friend my author profile on Facebook https://www.facebook.com/authoramie.gibbons.10

- Reviews help readers find books. I appreciate all reviews: good, bad and ugly. You can leave a review on Amazon for this book here: https://www.amazon.com/Psychic-Undercover-Undead-Paranormal-Mysteries-ebook/dp/B01N4OCJE5/.

- This story is the first in the SDF series. The prequel short stories, other 6 books in the series, and my other works are available on Amazon from my page at http://www.amazon.com/-/e/B01651YIZU.

ABOUT THE AUTHOR

Amie Gibbons was born and raised in the Salt Lake Valley. She started making up stories before she could read and would act them out with her dolls and stuffed animals. She started actually writing them down in college, just decided to do it one day and couldn't stop.

She took an unplanned hiatus from writing when she went to Vanderbilt Law School and all of her brain power got consumed by cases, statutes, exams, and partying like only grad students in Nashville can. She graduated and picked her writing back up as soon as her brain limped back in after the bar exam.

She loves urban fantasy and is obsessed with the theory of alternate realities. Whether or not she travels to them in the flesh or just in her mind is up for debate.

She spends her days living the law life and her nights writing when she's not hitting downtown Nashville to check out live music or inflict her singing on the crowds at karaoke bars. She lives with her familiar and babies, 3 beautiful black cats named Merlin, Klaus and Elijah, who keep her in this reality... most of the time.

To hear about new releases, sign up for her mailing list: https://mailchi.mp/afc38083307c/amie-gibbons, and get a free story not available anywhere else.

The Magical Adventures of Evie Jones Compilation
EVIE JONES AND THE CRAZY EXES
EVIE JONES AND THE GOOD LUCK FUNDRAISER
EVIE JONES AND THE MAGIC MELTDOWN
EVIE JONES AND THE SPIRIT STALKER
EVIE JONES AND THE SHADOW OF CHAOS
EVIE JONES AND THE ROCKY ROULETTE

The Laws of Magic Series
THE TREETOPS EXPERIMENTATION (A MILLIE LEHMAN SHORT STORY)
SHIFTING ICE (A TYLER CARMICHAEL NOVELLA)
THE GODS DEFENSE
THE GODS' APPEAL (Future Release)
THE GODS' COURT (Future Release)
PATENTING MAGIC (Future Release)

The Order of the Sphinx Series
SPHINX ORIGINS (A SPHINX SHORT)
PARATA'S SHADOWS (BOOK 1 Future Release)

ONE IN INFINITY (A REALITY CROSSING NOVELLA)
CHAOS CANDY (A REALITY CROSSING NOVELLA)

The SDF Series
PSYCHICS INVESTIGATE ZEBRAS (AN ARIANA RYDER SHORT)
PSYCHIC SEEKS (AN ARIANA RYDER NOVELLA)
PSYCHIC OVERBOARD (AN ARIANA RYDER NOVELLA)
PSYCHIC MASQUERADE (AN ARIANA RYDER SHORT)
PSYCHIC UNDERCOVER (WITH THE UNDEAD)
PSYCHO (AND PSYCHIC) GAMES
PSYCHIC FOR SALE (RENT TO OWN)
PSYCHIC WANTED (UN)DEAD OR ALIVE
PSYCHIC SPIRAL (OF DEATH)
PSYCHIC ECLIPSE (OF THE HEART)
PSYCHIC (WILD WILD) WEST

The Elemental Demons Series
SCORPIONS OF THE DEEP
SCORPIONS OF THE AIR
SCORPIONS OF THE EARTH

Made in the USA
Middletown, DE
19 June 2022